DEATH AROUND THE BEND

ALSO BY T E KINSEY

The Lady Hardcastle Mysteries

A Quiet Life in the Country

In the Market for Murder

DEATH AROUND THE BEND

A Lady Hardcastle Mystery

T E KINSEY

THOMAS & MERCER

Text copyright © 2017 T E Kinsey

Published by Thomas & Mercer, Seattle

www.apub.com

Amazon, the Amazon logo, and Thomas & Mercer are trademarks of Amazon.com, Inc., or its affiliates.

ISBN-13: 9781503940109
ISBN-10: 1503940101

Cover design by Lisa Horton

Printed in the United States of America

Chapter One

'What do you think, Flo: the red scarf or the green?'

Lady Hardcastle held up the two silk scarves for my inspection.

'Why not take both, my lady?' I suggested as I continued to pack the rest of her clothes.

'Well, yes, of course,' she said. 'I was just trying to avoid overpacking. We're only going for a week.'

'I don't think a single silk scarf is going to make a great amount of difference at this stage,' I said, indicating the already well-crammed trunk on the bedroom floor and the accompanying collection of cases and bags.

She looked around. 'I see what you mean. Honestly, Flo, do we really need all this paraphernalia?'

'This "paraphernalia", as you so testily describe it,' I said, 'constitutes the bare minimum required for a week at a country house, and you very well know it.'

She sighed. 'I know, I know. But. I mean. Really. How will we ever fit it all into the motor?'

It was my turn to sigh. 'I thought we'd settled this, my lady. Dr Fitzsimmons is lending us his trap, and his man, Newton, will take us to the station. We are not taking the Rover.'

Several hectic, summery weeks had passed since we had accepted an invitation to spend a week at Codrington Hall in Rutland, home of Lord Riddlethorpe, during which time we had discussed the matter of taking the new motor car with tedious regularity.

On the one hand, the long drive up to Riddlethorpe from our home in Gloucestershire had the potential to be really rather entertaining. Seeing the beautiful towns and villages of the heart of England as we swept through, the last of the harvest in the fields, the livestock munching in the meadows . . . We had quite the most romantic idea of England in late summer, and the long drive would let us enjoy it at its finest.

On the other hand, there seemed to be at least a hundredweight of 'paraphernalia' to be transported, as well as a widow and her maid. August had been blissfully warm and summery. All the signs were that the good weather would continue into the first week of September, but one can never be certain with the English weather. I decided to pack for warm weather, but also to include her raincoat, galoshes, and at least two tweed suits in case the Rutland mornings were a little chilly.

The thought of spending many hours crammed inside the tiny motor filled us both with unease. And that was if we could even work out a way of loading the trunk, cases, and bags in the first place. We had dithered between the alternatives for many days until we had finally decided, or so I had thought, that taking the motor was far from practical and that the train was a much more sensible choice.

'Well,' she said slowly, still fiddling with the scarves, 'I know we said that . . . but it would be rather handy to have a motor while we're there . . . You know, for exploring and suchlike . . .'

'I'm sure Lord Riddlethorpe will lend us one of his many motors,' I said. 'He and his pals will probably be glad to see us pootling off into the village so they can get on with whatever it is that chaps get up to when the ladies aren't around.'

The invitation to Rutland had come second hand from Lady Hardcastle's brother, Harry. He had known Lord Riddlethorpe ('Fishy' to his friends – the family name was Codrington) since they had been up at Cambridge together. He had written to his sister to ask if she (and I) would like to be his 'do feel free to bring a friend' at a small gathering that Lord Riddlethorpe was arranging to celebrate the launch of his new racing car company. There would be a party attended by local dignitaries, and a few days of racing for the chosen few on Lord Riddlethorpe's newly-built personal racing track. It all seemed terribly exciting, and Lady Hardcastle had accepted at once.

'Do you think Lord Riddlethorpe will let you race?' I asked, taking the scarves and folding them for packing.

'I should bally well hope so,' she said. 'I'll be disappointed if he doesn't invite you to have a go, too.'

'Is he a progressive sort, then?' I asked. 'He won't think such pursuits unsuitable for women?'

'From what I remember of him, he's not too bad. I don't suppose he's writing cheques for Mrs Pankhurst and her suffragettes, but I do recall him having a set-to with some of the insufferable oafs who tried to make life unpleasant for we women students at Girton. I think he has a refreshingly open attitude towards us.'

'You've known him since you were at Cambridge, then?'

'Only to say good day to. He was at King's with Harry, so our paths occasionally crossed. He's a likeable enough fellow. I remember him being rather an eager puppy sort of a chap in those days. Friendly, cheerful, desperate to please – you know the sort. And boundlessly enthusiastic about pretty much every new idea that came along. He might have grown up since then, mind you; that was twenty years ago.'

'Then we shall have to hope that he's still keen on the idea of women doing inappropriate things,' I said. 'I've acquired quite a taste for motoring since we got the Rover. I should love to try something a little more powerful.'

'Me too, Flo, me too.' She stood for a moment in thought, and then walked round the bed and towards the door, where she stopped and turned. 'Oh, I'll tell you what, though, I gather the grounds are rather pretty, too. Will there be room in the luggage for my watercolours?'

I sighed theatrically. 'I expect so, my lady, and if not we can put them in my bag. I don't mind going without clean clothes. I'm just a humble lady's maid.'

I dodged a flick aimed at my ear as she left.

It took me another half an hour to pack the rest of her things. I didn't close any of the bags, knowing from long experience that, despite her protestations about how we always took too much, there would still be one or two last-minute 'Oh, I really can't do without this' items to be packed before we were finally ready to leave the following morning.

I went downstairs. Miss Jones, the cook, and Edna, the house-maid, had already left for the day – for the week, in fact, since Lady Hardcastle had given them the time off – so I was intending to put the kettle on for a relaxing cup of tea. My progress was halted by an unfamiliar and insistent ringing. It wasn't the doorbell and, unless Lady Hardcastle had been tinkering again, I was sure it wasn't one of the room bells.

'Are you going to answer the telephone or not?' shouted Lady Hardcastle from her study.

The new telephone. Of course. It had finally been installed after weeks of delays and what Lady Hardcastle had impatiently referred to as 'a great deal of frankly unnecessary palaver'. I still wasn't entirely certain we needed such a thing, but I was unable to deny the convenience of not having to traipse to the post office to send a wire.

I went through to the hall and picked up the earpiece from the wooden box mounted on the wall. I was still unsure of the etiquette of using the thing, but we had agreed that if I were to treat callers in the same way I would treat unannounced visitors to the house, I couldn't go far wrong.

'Hello,' I said loudly and clearly. 'Chipping Bevington two-three.'

'Hello?' said a strident, female voice. 'Hello? Is that you, Emily? Hello?'

I recognized our caller as Lady Farley-Stroud, the wife of the local landowner. 'No, Lady Farley-Stroud, it's me, Armstrong.'

'Armstrong?' she said. 'Is that you?'

'Yes, my lady,' I said. 'Shall I fetch Lady Hardcastle?'

'I say, would you mind awfully fetching Lady Hardcastle for me? I'd like a word.'

I put the earpiece on the hall table and went to fetch Lady Hardcastle, but she was already on her way out of her study. 'Is that Gertie on the telephone? I swear she's getting a little deaf. Did she say what she wanted?'

I shook my head and left her to it.

◆ ◆ ◆

By the time Lady Hardcastle had finished on the telephone, the tea was brewed and I was sitting down in the morning room for what I felt was a well-deserved rest. I put down the newspaper and raised an eyebrow enquiringly as she joined me.

'Did Miss Jones plan anything for dinner?' she said, helping herself to a cup.

'Nothing special, my lady,' I said. 'She suggested we might finish off that ham pie with a bit of salad from the garden. She didn't want to cook anything new that might result in leftovers, what with you and me going away for a week and all.'

'She's a good girl, that one. In that case, how do you fancy dinner at The Grange?'

'Me, my lady? Not just you?'

'No, both of us. Gertie specifically requested your presence.'

'Gracious,' I said. 'I'm moving up in the world.'

'So it would seem. She's developed quite a fondness for you since the farm poisoning. And respect, too.'

'How very flattering,' I said with a smile. 'Did she offer any explanation for this sudden invitation?'

'Sir Hector has a problem for us to solve, apparently. Something "suitable for your unique talents, m'dear", or so she said.'

'Unique talents, eh?' I said.

'We *are* uniquely talented.'

'Hmm,' I said, and poured her a cup of tea.

'Oh, come on, Flo, we are. Fake suicides, murderous circus folk, bludgeoned trumpeters, poisoned farmers, haunted pubs, missing trophies . . . We've solved them all. Who else around here can say the same?'

'Well, when you put it like that . . .'

'Exactly,' she said, dunking a triumphant shortbread biscuit in her tea. 'And the next mystery we have to solve is what on earth's bothering Hector so much that he feels he has to enlist the help of the local weird widow and her maid.'

I chuckled into my teacup. 'The Case of the Disobedient Dog?' I suggested. 'The Missing Cufflink Affair?'

'I do agree – it's hard to imagine anything especially exciting happening in their lives. I adore them, but life for them does seem to be something that happens to other people.'

'Although they did have a dead trumpeter in their library after their daughter's engagement party.'

'And Gertie was at The Hayrick when old whatshisname snuffed it and fell face-first into his pie,' she added.

'So death is something that happens to other people when they're around, too.'

'I say,' she said, looking up suddenly. 'I do hope no one's died.'

'I should have thought she'd have been round here already if they had, my lady. It'll be local kids scrumping apples or a misplaced set of fish knives, more than likely.'

'I think you're probably right,' she said, and put down her cup. 'But dinner and company will be most welcome, and a splendid way to begin our break.'

'Your break, my lady,' I said.

'Oh, pish and fiddlesticks. You'll be taking a break, too, as well you know.'

'Sleeping in the attic in a shared room,' I mumbled. 'Eating in the servants' hall.'

'Oh, shush. You know you'll be able to tag along with me, and we've already spoken about trying to get you a ride in one of the racing cars. And you do so revel in the below-stairs gossip. You'll have a fine old time, and you know it.'

I smiled. 'Well, when you put it like that . . .'

'Quite so. Now we've a couple of hours before we need to dress for dinner, so I think a little piano practice would be in order.'

'Right you are, my lady,' I said breezily. 'Have fun.'

'No, dear, for you. You really do need to put some effort in if you're ever going to master the instrument. I shall read the newspaper.'

She had been trying to teach me the piano on and off for many years, and had become quite zealous in her attempts of late. If I'm properly honest, I should have to say that I really quite enjoyed it, and was secretly rather pleased with my progress. Unfortunately, there was something about the idea of having to 'practise' that turned the whole endeavour into a chore. I'm afraid I exhibited a childlike reluctance to knuckle down.

'But I've still got packing to do, my lady,' I said. 'I haven't even made a start on my own things yet.'

'Pish and fiddly fiddlesticks,' she said. 'There'll be plenty of time for that later. Go now. Play.'

'Righto, my lady.'

She picked up the newspaper and squinted at it. 'I say, would you be an absolute poppet and fetch my reading whatnot for me? I left it on my desk.'

She had recently abandoned her reading glasses and had taken to using an old-fashioned lorgnette, which she seemed to be unable to manage to keep with her. The lens frame folded and swivelled into the handle, forming a rather intriguing silver pendant, which, as was the designer's intention, could be worn around the neck on a chain. For reasons unknown, Lady Hardcastle eschewed such conveniences.

I tutted, sighed theatrically, and set off in search of the errant eyewear.

Having retrieved the lorgnette, I went obediently to the drawing room and sat at the piano. I played for the best part of a mostly plea-surable hour and only threatened to punch the instrument once. Herr Mozart, on the other hand, was lucky he was already dead, or I'd have been on the next boat train to Vienna to give him what for.

According to our strictly-observed rota, it was my turn to drive, and so we at least appeared to be mistress and servant when we arrived at The Grange. My attire, though, ruined the effect. Lady Hardcastle had arranged for her favourite dressmaker in Bristol to fashion me a gown as a birthday gift, and I had decided to wear it to dinner. It was of dark-green silk ('It would complement your colouring beautifully, miss') with a richly embroidered bodice. There was sheer green silk covering my shoulders and forming loose sleeves, and more sheer silk falling from the high waist ('High waists are all the rage this season, miss'), though this time decorated with beads and sequins. It was quite the most exquisite thing I had ever worn.

Most of my experiences of dressing for dinner had been while we were on Crown business, where I had been playing the part of a society lady while I kept an eye on Lady Hardcastle. That night, though, I had no role to play, no fictitious title to hide behind. I was just Florence Armstrong, a lady's maid in a smart frock, and I was feeling decidedly exposed.

The house was a pleasingly ramshackle mishmash of architectural styles from Tudor to Gothic Revival, with a bit of Georgian thrown in for good measure. It entirely suited the delightfully eccentric present owners, the Farley-Strouds.

At the time, I felt distinctly uncomfortable about entering The Grange as a 'guest'. I'd been to the house many times before. I'd even entered through the front door before. I'd had lunch with Lady Farley-Stroud. And I'd been in many situations over the years where I had played the part of everything from street girl to earl's daughter. But somehow, being invited for dinner seemed distinctly odd. I wondered if perhaps it was because the Farley-Strouds knew me first as Lady Hardcastle's maid before they had come to see me differently, but they were always so charming and friendly that I decided that couldn't really be what bothered me.

When Jenkins, the Farley-Strouds' butler, answered the door and, with a smile and a bow, bade us enter, I realized what it was. The servants. The household servants knew I was 'nothing more' than a lady's maid, and although I got on well enough with all of them (even the domineering cook, Mrs Brown), I knew there would be one or two (most especially Dora, the housemaid) who would think me to be getting altogether above myself.

It was a warm evening and we were without coats, so Jenkins led us straight through to the comfortable library, where Sir Hector and Lady Farley-Stroud were already sipping pre-prandial drinks. They had spent the early years of their marriage in India (though I never did quite find out what Sir Hector's line of business actually was), and gin and tonic was still their favourite sundowner. Sir Hector was helping himself to a glass as we entered, and immediately set about making two more.

'Good evening, m'dears,' he said warmly. 'Wonderful of you to come, what.'

'Entirely our pleasure, Hector, darling,' said Lady Hardcastle. 'Gertie, you look lovely. Is that a new frock?'

Lady Farley-Stroud beamed delightedly. 'How kind of you to say so, dear,' she said. 'I've been trying to get Hector to notice it for the past half an hour.'

'Noticed it, m'dear,' he said as he handed us our drinks. 'Just didn't want to say the wrong thing – I've been caught out like that before. "That's a lovely dress," I say. "Is it new?" Then I'm treated to a stern lecture lasting, I should say, at least ten minutes, on how I never pay attention, and that it's a shabby old dress that you've had for years, and that if I cared at all, I'd buy you a new one. Can't win, m'dear. Can't win.'

Lady Farley-Stroud tutted, but continued to beam. I'm not sure I've ever seen so devoted a couple in all my days, though the Hardcastles came close before Sir Roderick was murdered in China.

Lady Hardcastle was similarly touched and was smiling broadly as she accepted her G&T.

''Fraid we've no limes, m'dear,' said Sir Hector, oblivious to the effect his exchange with his wife had produced. 'Can do you a slice of lemon, if you fancy?'

'No, darling,' said Lady Hardcastle. 'This will do splendidly.'

I sipped tentatively at my drink, trying to remain as unobtrusive as possible.

'Don't look so nervous, dear,' said Lady Farley-Stroud kindly. 'I've said before that if Emily treats you as one of the family, then we should too. And we did invite you especially, after all.'

Sir Hector winked. 'She's a little afraid of you, too, m'dear. She's told everyone we know about the time you brought down that chap outside The Hayrick. "Wouldn't want to get on the wrong side of her," she always says.'

I laughed.

'Oh, Hector! Really!' she said.

I looked around the library, trying to work out why it always seemed so comfortable and welcoming, despite being ever-so-slightly shabby and past its prime. Perhaps that was it. Perhaps it was the loved-and-lived-in quality that made it feel so cosy. The chintz-covered chairs had been fashionable once, as had the mahogany sideboard, but their glory days were behind them.

'Life really has become much more exciting since you two moved to the village, you know,' said Lady Farley-Stroud. 'I'm sure the most interesting thing to have happened before you came was the occasional bit of late-night shenanigans behind the cricket pavilion during the mating season.' She winked theatrically.

'Steady on, old girl,' said Sir Hector. 'Don't get yourself flusticated.'

'There were fewer dead people, though, I shouldn't wonder,' said Lady Hardcastle.

'No, m'dear,' said Sir Hector. 'Always plenty of murders around these parts. Somethin' in the water, what?'

I remembered our friend Inspector Sunderland from the Bristol CID telling us that we'd moved to what he described as England's 'murder capital'. He had told us, as we helped unravel the mystery of a murder that had been committed in this very library, that there were 'more murders per head of population in this part of Gloucestershire than anywhere else in the country'. It was going to be a relief to get away to Rutland, where no one was likely to die in suspicious circumstances and we could get on with the serious business of enjoying ourselves.

'But that's by the by, Hector, dear,' said Lady Farley-Stroud, clearly keen to steer the subject away from dead bodies. 'My point is that village life has been a great deal more eventful since Emily moved in. And it's wonderful to have someone living in your house. We were afraid that it was going to remain empty when we heard that the chap who built it wouldn't be returning to England quite as soon as he'd hoped. It could have fallen derelict, or become a haven for vagabonds. Terribly irresponsible of him, whoever he is.'

'Jasper Laxton,' said Lady Hardcastle. 'We heard from him just the other day, actually. He's staying in India for the foreseeable future, it seems – his business is suddenly prospering and his wife is trying to set up a school. I'm very seriously considering making an offer to buy the place from him, as a matter of fact.'

Lady Farley-Stroud very nearly clapped her hands. 'Oh, I say, how wonderful. Oh, do please stay, Emily, dear. She should stay, shouldn't she, Hector?'

Sir Hector had been sidling back towards the drinks tray when he heard his name. 'What?' he said distractedly. 'Who should do what?'

'Oh, Hector, do pay attention when we have guests,' said his wife impatiently. 'And don't you dare refill that gin glass. You've had quite enough already.'

I rather suspected that Sir Hector might well have found a surreptitious way to defy his wife's injunction, but the decision was taken from both of them by the arrival of Jenkins, who announced, in solemn tones, that dinner was served.

◆ ◆ ◆

The dining room was as comfortingly shabby and unfashionable as the rest of the house. It was clean and mostly tidy, but the furniture and decoration had all seen better days. We were just four for dinner, and we sat together at one end of a large, highly-polished dining table that could seat at least sixteen, or twenty if they were all good chums.

Whatever one might say about Mrs Brown's personality and the way she ran her kitchen and treated her subordinates, she was a fine cook. She had clearly been instructed to push the boat out for this evening's meal, and Jenkins, with the help of Dewi, the footman, brought in course after course of some of the most delicious food I had tasted outside the restaurants of Paris. Well, perhaps that's a tiny bit of an exaggeration, but Mrs Brown certainly treated food with a great deal more respect than she treated her underlings.

The conversation, assisted by copious quantities of very passable wine, was convivial to the point of jollity, and the Farley-Strouds each made a great effort to include me and make me feel welcome. By the time the pudding (an extravagant construction of meringue, liqueur-soaked fruit, and whipped cream) had been demolished, and Jenkins had left us with the cheese and port, I felt thoroughly at ease.

'Now then, Hector,' said Lady Hardcastle, helping herself to a generous slice of Double Gloucester and an even more generous glug of port, 'just what exactly is this mysterious mystery you've brought us here to discuss? I do hope it's enough of a puzzle for us to be able to repay you for this wonderful meal.'

I had been slightly surprised by the apparent extravagance of the meal myself, knowing as I did that the local landowners weren't nearly so wealthy as the rest of the village believed. I shared Lady Hardcastle's desire to do something to repay them for their generosity.

Sir Hector chuckled. 'Don't worry about the meal, m'dear. Just sharin' me ill-gotten gains.'

Lady Hardcastle and I both looked enquiringly at Lady Farley-Stroud, hoping that she might elucidate.

She tutted and rolled her eyes. 'Hector has been gambling. He and his old pal Jimmy Amersham – lives in a lovely old place over near Woodworthy – he and Jimmy will wager on almost anything that can race: horses, homing pigeons, bicycles, motor cars, runners . . . On one particularly desperate occasion, even ants crawling across the verandah rail. They went to a race meeting at Cheltenham last week and Hector actually managed to make a profit for once. So I have a new frock and we all had a special meal.'

'No point in hangin' on to it, eh? Might as well spend it while you've got it, what?' said Sir Hector gleefully.

'Quite right, too,' said Lady Hardcastle.

'It's not like the progeny will put it to any better use once we've pegged out, eh?'

'Be that as it may,' persisted Lady Hardcastle, attempting to get the conversation back on course, 'we do need to repay your generosity in some way, and you did mention a mystery on the telephone.'

'Quite right, dear, I did,' said Lady Farley-Stroud. 'But bear in mind that this has nothing to do with me, and that I think it the very apogee of silliness.'

We turned to Sir Hector.

He looked slightly abashed, but after a few moments spent composing his thoughts, he began. 'Feelin' a bit foolish about it all, now that Gertie puts it like that. It's Jimmy, y'see. Gertie's right, we do love to wager; been doin' it since we were youngsters. He'd bet me he could run to the oak tree faster than I, then I'd bet him I could swim across the river faster than he. As we grew up, we'd bet on anything – horses, athletes, you name it. The favourite wagers were always the ones where we were doin' the racin'. Our runnin' and swimmin' days are far behind us now, though, so we have to find our pleasures where we may. A few years ago, we saw a few young lads racing in some little go-carts they'd made. They'd found some wheels from somewhere, put them on old boxes, steerin' the front wheels with a length of rope. They took 'em up to the top of a hill and raced each other to the bottom. And that got us thinkin', d'y'see?'

Lady Hardcastle laughed. 'Don't tell me, you and Jimmy started building go-carts,' she said. 'How absolutely wonderful.'

'Got it in one,' said Sir Hector. 'Build 'em and race 'em. Annual event. Invite some old pals down, make a weekend of it.'

'And what's the mystery?' asked Lady Hardcastle, still doggedly trying to get him to get to the point.

'Comin' to that, m'dear. Comin' to that. Old Jimmy, y'see, can't bear to be beaten. Hates it. Me, I can take m'losses, but Jimmy gets in an awful black mood if he doesn't win. Sometimes think he'd do anythin' to avoid it. Startin' to think he might be doing just that now, d'y'see? Doing anything to win. A couple of years ago, I had Bert help me with some special developments, some little enhancements to the cart, make it more streamlined, help it round the bends and whatnot. He's quite the mechanic, our Bert – he doesn't just drive the motor, knows it like his own child.

'Anyway, we made all these tweaks and changes, and knew for certain we were going to win by miles, but blow me if Jimmy didn't turn up on the day with almost exactly the same tweaks and changes to his cart. Last year, same thing: we tried some cunnin' new changes Bert had read about from the motor racing world, and when old Jimmy wheels his go-cart to the startin' line, there's everything we're trying, right there on his own wretched cart. Only one conclusion, isn't there? The blighter's spyin' on us.'

Sir Hector looked genuinely aggrieved at this terrible turn of events, and I could see that Lady Hardcastle was trying hard not to laugh. Lady Farley-Stroud, too, was looking down at her empty cheese plate in a bid not to catch anyone's eye, and I decided it was up to me to say something.

'Are you sure, Sir Hector?' I said. 'Perhaps he's just reading the same periodicals as Bert?'

'Thought of that, m'dear,' he said. 'But what are the odds he'd do exactly the same things? All sorts of wild whatnots goin' on in the motor racin' world, and he just happens to try the same ones as us. No, he must be spyin'.'

'Might he have an informer in your own household?' I suggested.

'Thought of that, too. Wouldn't put it past young Dewi, I must admit, but he doesn't know one end of a spanner from the other. He'd never be able to tell Jimmy anythin' useful.'

'Are you overlooked?' I ventured. 'Is there some way your work could be observed?'

'Thought of that, as well, m'dear,' he said despondently. 'But we work in the courtyard – walled in, d'y'see. Walled in. No way to get so much as a peep.'

'The mystery, then,' said Lady Hardcastle, 'is how does Mr Jimmy Amersham manage to find out what you're up to and neutralize your engineering advantage by copying it?'

'In a nutshell, m'dear, in the very nutshell.'

'Do you know what I find always helps at a time like this?' she said.

'No?' said Lady Farley-Stroud expectantly. 'Do tell.'

'Wait a moment,' said Sir Hector, 'I know. It's your whatchamacal-lit, your blackboard thingy.'

'My crime board? No.'

Sir Hector looked to his wife for assistance.

'Don't look at me, dear,' said Lady Farley-Stroud. 'I've no idea how she does it.'

'Come on then, m'dear,' said Sir Hector. 'We give up. You'll have to tell us.'

'Brandy,' said Lady Hardcastle.

The Farley-Strouds both laughed. 'Then we'd better withdraw to the drawin' room and see if we can't offer you a drop or two.'

And we did.

We played several hands of bridge, where Lady Hardcastle and I were roundly beaten thanks to some extremely skilful play and a certain amount of reckless bidding from the old couple, who, we learned, had been playing together for over forty years and were seldom defeated.

When we became too befogged for cards, we moved through to the ballroom where the Farley-Strouds kept their magnificent baby grand, and Lady Hardcastle treated us to some Chopin and a little Schubert before we launched into a selection of ribald music hall songs, to which – to my gleeful astonishment – Lady Farley-Stroud knew not only the words but also the actions.

We left at two in the morning and walked home down the hill, having been assured that Bert would drive the Rover back to the house by nine o'clock the next day.

◆ ◆ ◆

Dressing, breaking our fast, and finishing our packing were all accomplished at remarkable speed the next morning following far too little sleep and while still feeling the after-effects of our splendid evening with the Farley-Strouds.

I regretted Lady Hardcastle's decision to give Edna and Miss Jones the whole week off. Couldn't they start their holiday on Tuesday? I wondered as I cleared away the breakfast things and had one last tidy round.

Bert arrived with the Rover as the hall clock chimed nine and declared it a 'fine little vehicle', before politely declining my offer to drive him home in it and setting off on foot. He said that the walk would do him good, but I also suspected that an opportunity to wander into the village and then take his time getting back to The Grange was also quite appealing.

Not long afterwards, Newton arrived in Dr Fitzsimmons's trap, ready to take us to the station in nearby Chipping Bevington, the railway never having quite made it as far as Littleton Cotterell. He was a stolid, henpecked man, whose abrasive wife was Dr Fitzsimmons's housekeeper. I had met her during our first week in the village and hadn't been favourably impressed. A convenient consequence of her domineering nature, however, was that Newton didn't bat an eyelid when I told him that I would help him load our baggage on to the trap. He didn't even comment on my strength, something which I found more refreshing and relaxing than any amount of 'Here, let me do that for you, miss' could ever be.

Within no time, everything was loaded and we were off on our sedate and steady way to Chipping railway station. Newton made no effort to engage either of us in conversation, but we were still sufficiently groggy that we were happy to spend the long ride in companionable silence. The sun was out, the air was warm, and I drank in the sights and smells of England at its late-summery best. From the trap's high vantage point, we could see over hedgerows that occluded our view when we were in the little motor car, and I was able to get an early start on my study of the countryside with a good long look at some of the West Country's finest dairy herds – from a reassuringly safe distance. Cows, as anyone with any sense knows, are terrifying beasts and should not be approached, but it was safe to view them from the other side of a sturdy English hedgerow. As the journey progressed and we drew nearer to our destination, I also managed a glimpse or two of some rather entertaining-looking pigs (Gloucestershire Old Spots, I sincerely hoped, though in truth I had no idea) rooting about near their little wooden huts in a field beside the road.

As we drew up at the station, the porter, who seemed to recognize us from our previous trips, hurried towards the trap with his trolley. He began cheerfully unloading the luggage almost before we had stopped moving. By the time Lady Hardcastle and I had clambered down and she had pressed a few coins into Newton's hand for his trouble, the sturdy little porter had piled everything on to his sturdy little trolley and was already on his way towards the sturdy little ticket office.

He was waiting for us as we walked in.

'Mornin', m'lady,' he said. 'Nice to meet you again. Just you have a word with Young Roberts there for your tickets and I'll see you to your train.'

'Thank you, Mr . . . ?' said Lady Hardcastle.

'Roberts, m'lady,' he said, knuckling the peak of his railwayman's cap. '"Old Roberts", they calls me. Young Roberts over there behind the counter is me eldest, see. Railways is in our blood. There's been Robertses here at Chipping Bevington station near sixty years now, startin' with me grandfather, Mr Roberts.'

'I say,' said Lady Hardcastle with a smile as she approached the ticket counter. 'How wonderful to be so well looked after. It's like visiting an old family business.'

Roberts beamed proudly. His son looked faintly embarrassed, but gave a conspiratorial grin when Lady Hardcastle winked at him. 'Two returns to Riddlethorpe, please,' she said.

The young man reached under the counter and heaved up an enormous, well-thumbed volume. He spent some minutes flicking back and forth between the pages and making notes on a scrap of paper. 'I don't think I've ever sold a ticket to Riddlethorpe before, m'lady,' he said when he had finished his calculations. 'I shall have to note it in my book. I likes to keep track of all the places I sends people. It's interestin', I finds, seein' where people gets to.'

She smiled warmly at him.

'Your quickest route,' he carried on, consulting his notes, 'would be to get to Bristol Temple Meads, then get the express to Birmingham New Street. You can get a connection from there to Leicester, and then change on to the branch line to Riddlethorpe. Looks like you've arrived at exactly the right time, too. If you gets on the next train here, all your connections lines up nicely.'

The truth was that we knew this already, having spent almost an hour the previous weekend poring over *Bradshaw's Guide* trying to work out the best way to get to Codrington Hall. But the young ticket clerk's pleasure in having worked it all out for us was so evident that it would have been churlish to tell him.

Lady Hardcastle paid for our two First Class tickets, and 'Old' Roberts led the way to the 'down side' platform, where we sat in the waiting room and awaited the local train to Bristol.

'You know, Flo,' said Lady Hardcastle, looking out of the window at Roberts as he carefully wrote our details on to tags and tied them to our baggage, 'this journey would have been so much more straight-forward if we'd sent our traps on ahead. I know they're really rather organized, but I do worry that something will go missing with so many changes of train for them to deal with. If we'd sent them in advance, they'd have more time to find them and re-route them if they went astray, don't you think?'

I said nothing. I had made this very same point several days earlier, but my concerns had been pooh-poohed. With everything else I had to contend with, I had decided not to pursue it. Being proven right and finally getting Lady Hardcastle's agreement was a hollow victory, though, so I decided not to pursue that either.

Instead, I said, 'Oh, we'll be fine, my lady. Everything will be unloaded and waiting for us by the time we've put our books back in our pockets and stepped on to the platform. They deal with much more complicated consignments than this every day. And even if something does go astray, it's all properly labelled. We'll just get Lord Riddlethorpe to send a man to the station to pick it up when it finally arrives.'

'You're right, of course. Still, I should have listened to you when you suggested it.'

My mouth was still hanging open in surprise as the train pulled up and we stepped out to board it.

Chapter Two

The journey was a long one. A hundred years earlier it would have been longer still, of course, but we weren't travelling a hundred years ago. Viewed with the impatience and lack of perspective of the modern traveller, it took an absolute age. Our changes at Bristol Temple Meads (Brunel's Tudor-style railway castle), Birmingham New Street (with its immense roof), and Leicester London Road (still feeling almost new) went without even the slightest hitch. We transferred from train to train with a clockwork efficiency that must be the envy of the world. Our baggage, too, managed to follow us with nary a problem.

The problem, for there was bound to be one, was that, as I've already mentioned, the whole proceeding took an absolute age. There are only so many conversations two travellers can profitably have about whether cattle are frightened by the passing trains (and serve them right if they are – dreadful creatures), or about whether trains might one day be powered by electricity in the same way that trams are. Lady Hardcastle, who followed developments in the world of science and technology with great enthusiasm, insisted that they would. The gentleman who was sharing our compartment at the time snorted his derision, but was wise enough to say nothing.

We read the newspaper. We read our books. We played word games. We devised fantastical biographies of the people we saw standing on the platforms of the stations we passed through. The handsome young man in the luridly striped blazer whom we saw somewhere just outside Birmingham, for instance, was a solicitor's clerk called Raymond, who was on his way into the city to audition for a part in a musical. His sweetheart, a girl called Mildred, who had a squint, a wooden leg, and a heart of gold, had packed his lunch for him and sent him on his way with a loving kiss to pursue his dreams. The snorting gentleman left the compartment at this point and never found out what became of Raymond and Mildred.

It was a relief when we finally disembarked at Riddlethorpe station to find not only that our baggage was all present and correct, but that Lord Riddlethorpe's chauffeur was waiting for us with his lordship's Rolls-Royce. Having so carefully planned the details of our expedition, we had been able to telegram Codrington Hall well in advance with our anticipated arrival time.

Despite the length of the journey, I was in a cheerful mood as we alighted to be reunited with our baggage. Lady Hardcastle, too, was in ebullient form, and swished through the station, charming everyone as she went.

Codrington Hall was a few miles from the small town of Riddlethorpe, and the drive gave us ample time to get to know Morgan, Lord Riddlethorpe's young chauffeur.

'Have you visited the house before, my lady?' he said as we drove along the surprisingly flat road. There were slight bumps on the horizon, but nothing that would properly qualify as a hill, and with ditches lining the road instead of hedgerows, the effect was to make the sky seem far larger than I was used to.

'No, we haven't,' said Lady Hardcastle. 'Is it a fun place?'

He laughed. 'Fun enough,' he said. 'Especially if you're interested in motor cars. But presumably you know his lordship well enough to know that.'

'Actually, I've only met him a few times, and that was years ago when we were up at Cambridge. He's a friend of my brother's, Harry Featherstonhaugh.'

'Ah, I see. Well, Mr Featherstonhaugh arrived last night, and he and his lordship seem to be very good friends indeed. There was much merriment in the billiards room, by all accounts.'

'Good-o,' she said. 'Are there any other guests?'

'Not yet, my lady. But we're 'spectin' quite a few. His lordship's got two more comin', and Lady Lavinia will be arrivin' tomorrow with a couple of friends of her own.'

'Lady Lavinia? Lord Riddlethorpe's wife? His daughter?'

'Sister, my lady. Lord Riddlethorpe never married.'

'A sister? All these years and I never knew he had a sister. Well, it'll be a houseful, then.'

Morgan laughed again. 'It'll be busy, my lady, but I dare say they'd need a good many more guests to actually fill the house.'

Lady Hardcastle smiled. 'Have you worked there long?'

''Bout a year. His lordship saw me tinkering with a motor car at m'dad's forge, and offered me a job there and then. Dad's a blacksmith, see? He wanted me to follow him into it, and I've learned a lot, but I don't reckon there's much future in it. I reckon motor cars are the future, but he don't see it.'

'So you do more than just drive for Lord Riddlethorpe?'

'Oh-ah, my lady. I'm his mechanic. I look after his racin' cars. You know about his racin' team?'

'Not in detail, no. Harry said that's what the party was for, but nothing further. He said his lordship has a racing circuit at the house, which sounds like fun. But I confess I don't know quite what to expect.'

'Thought it was a rich man's fancy?'

She looked thoughtful, as though surprised by this perceptive young man. 'As a matter of fact, I did,' she said. 'Have you read Kenneth Grahame's book, *The Wind in the Willows*?'

'Can't say I have, my lady.'

'It's a children's book, but it really is rather splendid. There's a character in it called Mr Toad. But no matter.'

'I'll be sure to hunt it out,' he said. 'And what of you, miss? What did you expect of your week away?'

'Me?' I said. 'Oh, I don't know. A break from the drudgery of serving such a demanding mistress, perhaps?'

'Tough one, is she?' he said with a wink.

'The worst,' I said. 'But she hides it when we're in company, so no one knows how I suffer.'

He laughed as Lady Hardcastle huffed and rolled her eyes.

'If you ever need to escape,' said Morgan, 'just you come down to the coach house. I'm always there, and I'd be happy to make you a cup of tea.'

'Thank you,' I said. 'But won't you be busy with the racing?'

'Oh, don't you worry about that. I've always got time for the oppressed masses.'

'Oppressed, my hat,' said Lady Hardcastle. 'And she'll be too busy racing to be taking tea in the garage, I'm afraid. We both shall.'

'You'll be racin', my lady?' he said with evident surprise.

'I shall be most disappointed if we don't,' she replied. 'Can't come all this way to a house with a racing track and not have a go.'

'Well I never,' he said slowly.

'To be honest with you, dear boy,' she said, 'we never did, either. But I've just recently bought a motor car of my own, and I have to say I'm really rather taken with this driving lark.'

'A motor car of your own, eh?' he said, apparently delighted to be able to talk about his passion. 'What did you get?'

'On the advice of my friend's chauffeur, I bought a Rover 6.'

'The Rover, eh? Not a bad little motor, that. Nice little two-seater. Little bit underpowered for what we get up to up at the house, but a good place to start.'

She smiled. 'I'm pleased you approve.'

'And you drive it yourself?' he asked.

'We take it in turns. It's such fun that I can't leave it all to Armstrong.'

He looked at me for confirmation, and I smiled and nodded.

'Well I never,' he said again. 'Well I never did.'

He spent the rest of the journey enthusiastically detailing all the things we might do to improve the performance of the little Rover, and from the gleam in Lady Hardcastle's eye, I could tell that we'd be outfitting a workshop of our own as soon as we got home.

The lodge gate of Codrington Hall was on the other side of Riddlethorpe from the station and we seemed to reach it in mere moments.

◆ ◆ ◆

The drive from the lodge house at the gate to the vast expanse of gravel in front of the house, on the other hand, took an absolute age. We seemed to travel for miles along a winding, wooded drive, past sheep, one or two curious deer, and a long-horned, shaggy-coated Highland cow that looked very much as though it wished it were somewhere much less flat and altogether more Scottish.

There were occasional tantalizing glimpses of the roof and chimneys of the house in the distance, but the drive had clearly been designed to hide it from view for as long as possible, building the anticipation. When we rounded the final bend and the house was revealed in all its glory, it was every bit as impressive as its architect had planned. A dish brought to the table is just another dish of food if it can be seen as the footman carries it across the room. But when the dish is covered by a magnificent silver cloche and the footman sets it down, still covered, before whisking away the cover with a flourish and a billow of steam, even the most pedestrian of dishes can seem like a culinary masterpiece.

Not that Codrington Hall was in any way pedestrian. At some point in the early eighteenth century, the Earl of Riddlethorpe had clearly had a bob or two, and had spent a goodly portion of his fortune on tearing down his crumbling ancestral pile and replacing it with an enormous new home, a magnificent monument to his family's wealth and prestige. Though many thought it old-fashioned and still preferred the Victorian frippery and folderol of the neo-Gothic, I was always impressed by the elegant symmetry of Georgian architecture. Codrington Hall was a stunning example of the beautiful simplicity of that period. Its only adornment was an ostentatiously pillared portico, sheltering vast, black painted doors, from which a gangling man in overalls was apparently coming to greet us, accompanied by two boisterous, almost exactly matching Dalmatians.

'What ho!' he called loudly over the excited barking of the dogs. Lady Hardcastle waved in acknowledgement while she waited for Morgan to trot round and open the door for her.

'What ho,' said the man again as she stepped out. 'Wonderful to see you again, Emily, old girl.'

'Good afternoon, Edmond, darling,' she said, kissing his cheek.

'"Edmond",' he said. 'You know it was only ever you and Mater that called me that.'

'Yes, darling, but I never could bring myself to call you Fishy.'

He let out a short bark of a laugh, which caught the attention of the dogs, who gave up their wagging investigation of the cases and trunks that Morgan was unloading from the motor car and came over to resume their own chorus of barking. Lord Riddlethorpe ruffled their ears fondly and pointed towards the front door.

'Off you go, girls,' he said. 'Back to the house.'

To my astonishment, the two dogs immediately obeyed, bounding off towards the house with ears flapping and tails still wagging wildly.

Lord Riddlethorpe took Lady Hardcastle by the arm and steered her towards the house. 'I'm so delighted you've come,' he said. 'Harry was a bit reluctant to ask, I think, but I said, "Nonsense, Fanners, bring Little Sis along and we can relive the old days." It'll be like being back up at Cambridge, what?'

'Well, I'm glad he thought of me. It's just the sort of break we need, isn't it, Armstrong?'

. He stopped in his tracks and turned towards me. 'My word,' he said. 'So this is the famous Miss Armstrong. How do you do?'

'How do you do, my lord?' I said cautiously, not quite knowing whether being 'the famous Miss Armstrong' was a good thing or bad.

He beamed at me. 'Don't panic, old thing,' he said. 'Fanners has been singing your praises. He's frightfully proud of his little sister, but he speaks so highly of you that a chap might think Emily here were your assistant, instead of the other way round.'

'Gracious,' I blurted.

'Gracious, indeed,' he laughed. 'For my sins, I am Edmond Codrington, ninth Earl of Riddlethorpe. But you must call me Fishy – everyone does, you know.'

'Thank you, my lord,' I said.

He laughed again and turned to resume his walk to the house. 'Morgan will show you to the servants' hall, Miss Armstrong. We'll make sure they look after you.'

And with that, they were gone, leaving Morgan and me standing on the drive surrounded by luggage.

'Which one's yours, Miss Armstrong?' he said, gesturing to the pile of cases.

I pointed to my case, and he hauled it out and set off towards the right-hand side of the enormous house.

'We'll get you introduced,' he said, 'then one of the boys can carry your bag up to your room – I think they've put you in with Mrs Beddows's maid, but she's not here till tomorrow, so you should have the place to yourself tonight, at least.'

'Mrs Beddows?' I said.

'One of Lady Lavinia's friends. She's a bit quiet, but you'll like her, I'm sure.'

'Mrs Beddows?' I said, again.

He laughed. 'No, her maid. Mrs Beddows is a right cow.'

It was my turn to laugh.

He conducted me down the side of the house to a flight of stone steps that led down to the servants' entrance, where he let himself in, gesturing me to follow him. 'Labyrinthine' is a word much overused. Actually, it probably isn't overused, now I come to think of it, but it's certainly a word that has lost some of its power by being used to describe any vaguely twisty route, and now no longer seems adequate to describe the system of passages beneath Codrington Hall. I quickly gave up trying to remember landmarks and turns, and instead devoted all my attention to following my guide. Theseus would long since have run out of thread before we finally reached the servants' hall, and poor old Ariadne would have died an old maid, ravaged by regret that her lover was lost forever for want of a bigger ball of thread. A *much* bigger ball of thread.

Eventually, we reached the spacious servants' hall where the staff would congregate and eat. A footman sat at the long table with newspaper spread in front of him, polishing a large silver dish. He looked up as we walked in.

'How do, Evan?' said Morgan cheerfully.

The footman nodded.

'This is Miss Armstrong, Lady Hardcastle's maid. You couldn't do us a favour and run her case up to the spare room next to Lily and Rose's, could you? She's sharin' it with Mrs Beddows's maid when they get here.'

'I got this polishin' to do,' he said sullenly.

'Go on, it'll only take you a couple of minutes.'

'Why can't you do it?' said the footman in the same resentful tone.

'I've got to put the motor away, 'aven't I? Go on, you lazy beggar. You could have done it in the time it's taken you to sit there tellin' me how busy you are.'

'Mr Spinney won't like it if he finds out I've been galivantin' about the house while I'm s'posed to be doin' this.'

'Mr Spinney would be delighted that you'd helped a guest feel welcome and comfortable in his lordship's home,' persisted Morgan.

'Mr Spinney would indeed,' said a deep voice from the doorway to our right. 'Up off your backside and do as you're asked, Evan Gudger. This instant.'

A tall man with thinning dark hair entered the room and inclined his head towards me. 'How do you do, Miss Armstrong? My name is Spinney, his lordship's butler. I trust you had a pleasant journey.'

'How do you do, Mr Spinney? Yes, thank you, it was long, but comfortable.'

'Good, good,' said the butler. 'Welcome to Codrington Hall. One of the housemaids will show you to your mistress's room while Evan here takes your case up for you, and we can get you settled into your own room later. Dinner is at eight, and his lordship prefers to dress informally. You're welcome to dine with us, or we can have a tray sent up to your room, as you prefer.'

'Thank you, Mr Spinney,' I said with a smile. 'I'm sure I shall be all in by the time I've finished my day's work, so a tray would be most welcome. You're very kind.'

'Not at all,' he said warmly. 'I always feel that his lordship's guests have come to relax, so it's our duty to try to give their servants a break, too. Of course, should you desire some company, we're a friendly enough crowd, but I know I relish a few moments on my own once in a while. Now then, boys, off you go. Let's get our guests settled.'

I nodded my thanks, and followed the maid out of the hall, along more labyrinthine passages to the servants' stairs, and eventually to Lady Hardcastle's room.

Lady Hardcastle was sitting at a small desk by the window, writing in what appeared to be her journal, and while I made a start on the unpacking, she continued with her writing.

The room's furniture was the traditional country house hotchpotch of styles. The aristocracy didn't really go in for buying furniture; they inherited most of it, and bought only the individual items they felt they lacked. So the bed (a monumental construction of carved mahogany) didn't match the wardrobe (delicate and fussy with an inlaid flower motif), which didn't match the writing desk and chair (Louis XVI with fiddly gold bits). The tallboy looked newer, and the washstand might have been bought that year. Somehow, though, when it was all set against the wonderful green wallpaper, it didn't seem at all wrong. I got closer to the wallpaper to take a better look.

'William Morris,' said Lady Hardcastle, who had noticed my perusal.

'I thought it might be,' I said carelessly.

'Don't fib,' she said. 'It's called "Larkspur", and I'm surprised to see it here, to be honest. Someone in the Codrington line must have had artistic ambitions.'

'You've seen it before?' I said.

'A tutor at Cambridge had it in his drawing room. His wife was a rather gifted artist herself. She was very proud of her William Morris paper, but it's not the sort of thing earls buy.'

'Well, I'm glad someone did,' I said. 'I like it.'

'Me too.' She finally put down her pen. 'What's it like below stairs?'

'Huge and surprisingly quiet, but that might just be because I didn't see the busy parts. The butler seems friendly.'

'Spinney,' she said absently, as she looked out of the window.

'The very same. How did you . . . ?'

'Fishy – I suppose I ought to get used to calling him that; everyone else does – Fishy gave me all the gup on the staff.'

'The "gup", my lady?'

31

'The gup, the gossip, the tittle and, what's more, the tattle.'

'I've never heard the word before,' I said, folding a shawl into a drawer.

'Really? My father used it all the time.'

'Ah, that would explain it.'

'Old-fashioned, you think?'

'A tiny bit, my lady. Upon whom else were you vouchsafed "the gup"?'

'Goodness, Flo, I was pleased enough with myself for recalling the name of the butler. You expect me to remember everyone else as well?'

'Sorry, my lady. I sometimes forget that your poor old mind is ravaged by creeping senility.'

'Indeed it is, dear, indeed it is. There was something about the cook, who's an absolute poppet, apparently, but don't ask me her name. Young Morgan Coleman has made quite an impression with his chauffeuring and mechanic-ing, but I'd surmised as much for myself. He mentioned the housekeeper . . . Mrs . . . Mrs . . . Mrs McSomething, I think.'

'You've done well, my lady,' I said. 'And you've remembered many of their names into the bargain.'

'As fly as ever, me, dear. He did also say when dinner was, but I've quite forgotten.'

'Eight, my lady. Informal.'

'Oh,' she said forlornly.

'You don't like black tie, my lady?'

'Oh, I don't care what everyone wears,' she said. 'I was just dismayed that it's such a long way off – I'm starving.'

'Shall I see if I can get cook to knock up a sandwich for you?'

'It's tempting, but then I shan't want dinner. I shall have to endure.'

'You're a brave little trouper, my lady.'

'I bally well am, at that,' she said, finally deciding to pitch in and help with the unpacking. 'Shall you be eating in the servants' hall?'

'I've been offered supper in my room,' I said.

'Have you, by crikey? Will you avail yourself?'

'I rather think I shall, my lady. I quite like the idea of a peaceful evening in with a hearty meal and an edifying book.'

'What a splendid idea,' she said, making such a thorough pig's ear of hanging up a dress that I gently took it from her and gestured for her to resume her seat by the window.

Once everything was put away, it was time for Lady Hardcastle to ready herself for dinner. Having ensured that she was shipshape and fully Bristol fashion, I took my leave and vanished once more into the maze of servants' stairs and corridors.

After less than ten minutes' wandering, I managed to find my way back to the hall, which was by now a hive of activity. Mr Spinney saw me milling about, and took a break from instructing a junior footman on the best way to remove a spot from the sleeve of his jacket to come over to see me.

'Is everything to your mistress's satisfaction?' he asked kindly.

'It is, thank you,' I replied.

'Splendid. Is there anything else we can do for her?'

'No, I think everything is in hand,' I said. 'Perhaps you might send someone up later to put her trunks and cases into your luggage room?'

'Of course, of course. And how about you? Is there anything we can do for you?'

'You're most kind. Are you absolutely sure about your kind offer of supper in my room, though? Would the rest of the staff think me too rude? I shouldn't want anyone to think that I didn't want to eat with you, but the luxury of an evening entirely to myself seems too good to pass up.'

'Not at all, not at all,' he said with a smile. 'They're a welcoming lot, but dinner can get a bit boisterous, and I can perfectly understand that you might not want to have to deal with that after a long day's travelling. I'll have someone bring you a tray when we've finished serving upstairs. Have you been shown to your room?'

'Not yet,' I said. 'But I'm sure it can't be difficult to find. I'll just keep heading upwards until I find a room with my case in it.'

'That's the ticket. Now if you'll excuse me, I need to get back to young Billy and his grubby sleeve.'

I smiled my thanks, and set off back the way I'd come and up the stairs. This time, though, I passed by the first floor landing and carried on upwards towards what I presumed were the servants' quarters at the top of the house. I finally emerged into a plainly decorated, yet oddly cosy corridor, and walked towards the only open door, at the far end, on the left. Sure enough, there was my suitcase next to a sturdy iron bedstead by the window. Another bed stood nearer the door, and both had been made up with crisp fresh linen and warm-looking blankets.

I unpacked my things and settled into the armchair in the corner with my copy of H G Wells's *The Time Machine*, which I thought was well overdue to be reread.

Chapter Three

I slept like a countess. If a countess had fallen on hard times and had taken to working as a lady's maid, that is. My accommodations were at the more luxurious end of the servants' scale, though, so I had no cause to grumble or gripe – I had slept a great deal more comfortably than many.

I readied myself for the day, and set off down the secret stairway to see if I could scare up a pot of tea for Lady Hardcastle. The approved procedure in most country houses would be for me to make my way to the servants' hall and wait for her to ring for me, but Lady Hardcastle was unimpressed by such ostentatious displays of status, and preferred a cuppa and a chat while she gathered herself together.

The kitchen, once I found it, was alive with efficient industry, and I introduced myself at once to the cook.

'Good mornin' my dear,' said the cheerful, plump queen of the kitchen. 'I'm Mrs Ruddle. Welcome to Codrington. Did you sleep well?'

'I did, thank you, Mrs Ruddle. And thank you for the delicious supper you sent up. I don't know when I've been so well looked after. I hope no one thought me above my buttons for not joining you all down here.'

She laughed. 'Not at all, my dear. We'd all take the chance if it was offered, wouldn't we? So long as you're comfy, we don't mind at all. 'S not like you won't be pullin' your weight while you're here, is it? Might be a nice little holiday for your mistress, but your work won't stop, will it, eh?'

'You're very kind. And speaking of my work, I don't suppose there's any water on the boil for a pot of tea? I'd like to take a tray up to Lady Hardcastle, if I can.'

'Of course, my dear,' she said, bustling back to work. 'I'll get the girl to put it all together for you. Would your mistress like some toast? I bet she'd like a round of toast. I'll get Patience to put a round of buttered toast on the tray for you. And how about you? You must be ready for somethin'. Just you help yourself at the table in the hall, and Patience will bring the tray out when she's done.'

I sat at the table in the hall and helped myself, as instructed, to eggs, bacon, and toast. I was going to ask about the delicious tomato sauce I'd just tried when a woman of about forty, dressed in black, swept into the room. The housemaid I'd been going to interrogate suddenly remembered urgent business elsewhere and all but evaporated from the table. The woman sat down.

'Good morning,' she said, in an incongruously plummy voice. 'You must be Miss Armstrong. I'm Muriel McLelland, Lord Riddlethorpe's housekeeper.'

'How do you do?' I said. 'Florence Armstrong. People call me Flo.'

'Pleased to make your acquaintance,' she said, and sat at the table next to me.

By any objective standard, she was extremely attractive, with a fine-featured face topped with honey-blonde hair and set with eyes of such a dark shade of blue that they might have appeared black in some lights. It was obvious, too, that in a more flattering dress than that typically worn by a housekeeper, she would have a striking figure to match the beauty of her face. Her only adornment was a delicate brooch set with tiny pearls.

'It seems you have a hectic few days ahead,' I said. 'What with hosting a party this evening as well as houseguests for the week.'

'Oh, it's nothing we can't deal with,' she replied, helping herself to eggs and bacon from the recently replenished platter. 'I'd much sooner be busy than idle. Don't you agree?'

'Actually, I do. And speaking of which, there's Patience with Lady Hardcastle's tray. I'd best be off, if you'll excuse me.'

'Of course,' she said as I stood. 'If you fancy some company later, I take my break at around eleven. We could have a cup of coffee, perhaps?'

'If I can get away, I should like that very much. I can't promise, though – Lady Hardcastle might have other ideas.'

'I quite understand. I take coffee in my room – just ask one of the juniors, they'll point you in the right direction.'

I smiled my thanks, and took the tray from an already weary-looking Patience.

◆ ◆ ◆

'Good morning, my lady,' I said as I set down the tray on the writing desk and drew the curtains.

A croaky mumble issued forth from beneath the covers.

'I brought you some tea and toast,' I said breezily. 'They were just starting to take the breakfast things up to the dining room when I left the kitchen.'

There was another forlorn, slightly self-pitying groan, muffled by layers of sheet and blanket.

'Did we overdo it a little at dinner, my lady?' I said with a grin.

As she struggled out from her linen cave and sat up, I saw that she had, indeed, overdone things a little.

'It's my stupid brother's fault,' she croaked.

'Of course it is, my lady,' I said as I poured a cup of tea. 'A big boy did it and ran away. That's always the excuse I used.'

She harrumphed, but smiled gratefully as she clutched the saucer and lifted the cup for her first reviving sip. 'You've had dinner with Harry,' she insisted. 'You know what he's like. "Have another glass," he says. "Come on, sis, don't let a chap drink alone." And then, "I say, Fishy, this port's excellent. Isn't it excellent, Em? Here, let me pour you another." And then, "If there's one thing I've always loved about staying with you, Fishy, it's your excellent cognac. Where *do* you get it? Em loves a drop of brandy, don't you. Shall I top you up?" By the time I stumbled up here, the three of us had demolished half poor Fishy's cellar.'

'Politely declining never crossed your mind?'

'I should bally well say not,' she said, slowly recovering herself. 'If there's one thing Fishy's famous for, it's his cellar. It would be an absolute crime to pass up the chance to sample it.'

I rolled my eyes. 'I'm pleased you enjoyed yourself, my lady.'

'I really rather did,' she said. 'It's lovely to see Harry again, and Fishy turns out to be really rather splendid company.'

'Good-o,' I said. 'So the party this evening should be fun.'

She took a tentative bite of the toast. 'I think it might be,' she said. At least, I think she did. She said it with a mouthful of buttered toast, so she might have said 'I stink of night fleas', for all I know, but my interpretation made slightly more sense. She swallowed her mouthful. 'You were quite the topic of conversation, you know.'

'Me, my lady?' I said with some consternation. 'Why?'

'Talk mainly revolved around two subjects: motor cars and the competitive racing thereof, and the heroic exploits of one Florence Armstrong.'

I goggled.

'No, really,' she said. 'I'd have thought Harry would be a bit blasé about it all by now – he's known about mine and Roddy's exploits for donkey's years – you know how Foreign Office types like to gossip – but apparently, they are as nothing compared with a few punch-ups and some knife-throwing antics from a diminutive Welsh maid. His tales of your derring-do made quite an impression on Fishy, and he's determined to make your acquaintance.'

Lady Hardcastle's husband, Sir Roderick, had been in the diplomatic corps in the eighties and nineties, which meant that his wife was in a perfect position to indulge in a little discreet espionage on behalf of Her Britannic Majesty's government. She had been recruited before she had left Girton College, and her reputation in the upper echelons of the Foreign Office was well established by the time she employed me as her maid and eventually drew me into her world of snooping and skulduggery. In her position, I'd be a bit miffed at having my own contribution to national security downplayed in favour of a Johnny Newcome like me.

'I've not said anything to him, I promise,' I said. 'I really am most dreadfully sorry.'

To my immense relief, she laughed. 'You goose,' she said. 'I told him. I'm just delighted that someone else realizes what a tiny marvel you are.'

'Phew,' I said.

'You really are a ninny sometimes.'

'I just don't like people thinking I'm getting above myself, that's all,' I said defensively.

'No one thinks that,' she said. 'But expect to be cornered by his lordship at some point, and grilled at length.'

'I shan't crack, my lady. You can rely on me.'

'That's the spirit,' she said with a chuckle. 'But why not bask in the attention and glory for a while? You deserve a bit of recognition before you return to your life of drudgery.'

'And hardship, my lady.'

'Quite so. Just let Fishy chat to his new heroine and you can return to feeling like you're a member of the downtrodden masses.'

'I *am* a member of the downtrodden masses, my lady,' I said.

'You are, Flo, dear, you are. Now let's get me ready for breakfast, and I'll see what Fishy has in store for me today.'

◆ ◆ ◆

I left a vaguely presentable Lady Hardcastle to make her own way to the dining room, having helped her to dress in the first of the day's many outfits: an elegant grey linen day dress. I also supplied her with a couple of fortifying aspirin. Meanwhile, I disappeared into the servants' warren and returned the tea tray to the kitchen, where Patience took it from me and magicked it away to be cleaned.

Evan, the footman I'd met when we arrived, was sitting at the table in the hall, reading a newspaper.

'Good morning, Evan,' I said brightly.

He mumbled a greeting of sorts, but did not look up.

'Is everything in hand for the party this evening?' I continued, doing my best to be sociable.

'You'd-a known if you'd deigned to come down and sup with us last night,' he said, noisily turning a page in his (or, as was more likely, his master's) newspaper.

'I dare say I would at that,' I said. It clearly wasn't worth the bother.

Mr Spinney entered with a silver tray.

'What the devil do you think you're doing there, boy?' he barked.

Finally, Evan looked up from the newspaper. 'Readin',' he said insolently.

'Highly amusing,' said Spinney. 'I can see for myself that you're reading, and you know full well that I was asking why you're reading his lordship's newspaper rather than ironing it for him.'

'Already ironed,' said the young footman. 'Seems a shame to waste the opportunity to better meself, learn what's goin' on in the world.'

'Well, you can go and iron it again.'

'No point,' said Evan. 'Ink's already been dried. Be a waste of time.'

'I shall decide what's the best use of your time,' said the butler angrily. 'And I say that his lordship will receive his daily newspaper not only with dry ink, but with crisp, fresh pages, unread by the junior staff.'

'Can't unread the newspaper, Mr Spinney,' said the footman, standing up. 'All them posh words and dangerous new information's already up here.' He tapped his temple. 'Can't get it out now.'

Spinney sighed. 'Just iron the newspaper, boy. And be quick about it.'

Evan grinned as he took the newspaper and left the room.

Spinney sat wearily down and reached out to test the weight of a large teapot on the table.

'Feels like there's at least a couple of cups in here if you want one, Miss Armstrong,' he said.

I sat down opposite him. 'Thank you,' I said. 'Lady Hardcastle has just gone down to breakfast, so I have a few minutes.'

He poured two cups of tea and offered me one. 'I'm sorry you had to see us not at our best,' he said. 'I don't know what we can do about that lad.'

'Sack him?' I suggested.

He laughed. 'That would solve my problems,' he said. 'But not his. He's a troubled lad.'

'I should say he is. Why on earth do you keep him on?'

'We sort of took responsibility for him,' he said kindly. 'His father died at Spion Kop, mother drank herself to death a year later. She worked here as a housemaid, but there was nothing we could do to save her from herself. We took care of the lad as best we could, but he fell in with a bad lot. They led him astray. He was up before the beak last year for fighting in the town, but his lordship vouched for him and offered

41

him a job here to keep him out of the gaol. So we try our best, and in return he tries our patience.'

I was about to say something much less tolerant and understanding when the young man returned.

'His lordship's newspaper, Mr Spinney,' he said with a mocking bow.

'Put it on the tray,' said Spinney. 'And then get to your duties.'

'At once, Mr Spinney, sir,' said Evan with a click of his heels, and walked out, laughing.

'Trouble is,' said the butler, 'he's the only spare footman we've got, and I've had to give him the job of valet to the gentleman guests.'

'Crikey,' I said. 'I can see how one might be concerned.'

'Concerned doesn't begin to cover it, Miss Armstrong. Not even close.'

'I'll be about above stairs looking after Lady Hardcastle. I can keep my eyes and ears open, if you like.'

'It's a kind offer, but you'd have your work cut out. He's . . . ah . . . He's . . .'

'Taken against me?' I suggested. 'I rather thought he might have.'

'How's that?'

'He told me so in almost as many words.'

Spinney looked embarrassed. 'Please accept my apologies on behalf of Codrington Hall,' he said. 'We pride ourselves on our hospitality, even to visiting servants. *Especially* to visiting servants.'

'Please, Mr Spinney, think nothing of it. I anticipated that my decision to dine alone might cause some friction. It's my own fault.'

'It's not the opinion of us all, Miss Armstrong. We'd all welcome the chance to do the same, as I said to you before. He's got no place being rude to a guest.'

'I've had nastier people than he being more than rude to me in the past,' I said. 'You leave him to me, I'll keep a watchful eye on him and make sure he does you proud.'

'Well, I appreciate it, miss,' he said. 'But it really shouldn't be something a guest has to do.'

'Nonsense. It'll be no imposition at all.'

'I must say it would be a help. I can't be everywhere at once, especially not above stairs. I've already got Chanley looking out for him—'

'Chanley?' I asked.

'His lordship's own valet. He'll be showing him the ropes, but another pair of eyes can't hurt. We wondered if the extra responsibility might be the making of him, but with his attitude this morning, I'm beginning to have second thoughts.'

'Don't worry,' I said. 'I'll introduce myself to Mr Chanley, and we'll see what we can do.'

'Please don't feel you have to, Miss Armstrong, but every little helps.' He put down his half-finished tea. 'I'd better get the newspaper up to the dining room after making all that fuss about it.'

◆ ◆ ◆

As arranged, I waited for Lady Hardcastle in her room. As well as teaching me the piano, she had been trying to teach me to draw since just after Christmas, so I took a sheet of notepaper and a pencil from the desk and began to attempt to sketch the view from the window. I worked hard, trying to remember everything I had been taught, carefully judging perspective and shading, and before long I had produced quite the most childlike and disappointing scribble anyone had ever seen. I was about to screw it up and throw it in the wastepaper basket, when Lady Hardcastle returned.

'What ho, Flo,' she said as she entered. 'Hope you haven't been waiting too long.' She crossed the room to the desk. 'I say, have you been drawing? Let's have a look.'

I tried to cover the sketch, but she slid it out from beneath my hand and inspected it, frowning.

'The thing is, Flo, dear,' she said after a few moments' contemplation, 'I know that one is supposed to encourage one's students, to see the positive aspects of their work and offer praise for even the slightest hint of improvement . . .'

'But you see none?'

'Well, not "none", exactly . . .'

'But very little?'

'Have you ever considered photography?' she asked with a grin.

'You're a mean one, my lady,' I said, snatching the sketch back and throwing it in the wastepaper basket.

'Quite possibly.' She looked at my uniform and boots. 'Have you got any outdoor togs with you?'

'I have,' I said.

'Good-o. Run and pop on something a bit more practical. Fishy wants to show us round the estate. Nothing too warm, mind you. I've been told we can expect another glorious day.'

We chatted a little more while I laid out her own outdoor clothes, and then I raced off to prepare for our tour.

◆ ◆ ◆

We waited, as instructed, on the terrace at the rear of the house, overlooking the well-tended formal garden. Despite having long since learned the folly of her efforts, Lady Hardcastle was attempting to teach me the names and habits of the various birds that alighted on the low wall that formed the boundary of the terrace. Her doomed, but well-meaning lecture was cut short by the arrival of her brother, Harry.

'What ho, sis,' he said as he rounded the corner and saw us there, contemplating the lifestyle of the pied wagtail.

'Good morning, dear,' said Lady Hardcastle absently, still watching the little black-and-white bird. 'Did you sleep well?'

'Like a log, old thing,' he said. 'Woke up with a bit of a sore head, mind you.'

'You and me both,' she replied ruefully. 'I blame you, of course.'

'Of course,' he said. 'Wouldn't expect anything less. And good morning to you, young Strong Arm. I haven't seen you in aeons. How the devil are you?'

'Well enough, thank you, Mr Featherston-huff,' I said with a smile. I had known him for many years and always made a point of mispronouncing his surname. 'Though last winter is hardly an aeon ago.'

'Is that all it is? Well, well. One day I shall get you to say "Fanshaw", you know,' he said with a chuckle.

'You're more than welcome to try, sir,' I said. 'I enjoy a challenge.'

'So you do, so you do. I've been telling Fishy all about you and your love of challenges.'

'I gather you have.'

'You don't mind, do you?' he said. 'I shouldn't want to embarrass you, but you do lead such an exciting life. I thought he might enjoy hearing about it.'

'My life isn't exciting enough, then?' said Lady Hardcastle indignantly.

'Hardly, sis. You just swan about looking posh and gormless. It's Strong Arm here who does all the dangerous stuff.'

'I've been shot at.'

'In a drawing room in Dribblington St Nowhere, or wherever it is you live these days. It's hardly the same thing.'

'It was the dining room, and I nearly died. I should say I'm every bit as exciting as Flo.'

It was true, she had nearly died, and Harry and I had shared the anxious vigil at her bedside while we waited for her to recover.

'All right, all right,' he said, putting his hands up. 'My little sister leads just as exciting a life as her maid. I know when I'm beaten.'

'Beaten again, eh, Fanners?' said a jovial voice from behind us. Lord Riddlethorpe had emerged silently from the house through the large French windows and had joined us in admiring the view.

'What ho, Fishy,' said Harry.

'What ho, what ho,' said Lord Riddlethorpe. 'Good morning, Emily.'

'Morning, Fishy,' said Lady Hardcastle.

'And good morning to you, Miss Armstrong,' said Lord Riddlethorpe.

'Good morning, my lord,' I said with a smile and a hint of a curtsey.

He laughed. 'I'll get you to call me Fishy before the week's out, you see if I don't.'

'Best of luck, old chap,' said Harry knowingly.

Lord Riddlethorpe frowned in puzzlement, but pressed on enthusiastically. 'I expect you're wondering why I called you all here this morning,' he said.

'You're going to give us the tour, darling,' said Lady Hardcastle. 'You want to show off your new racing track.'

'I say. Am I that transparently vain?'

Lady Hardcastle sighed. 'We arranged it all last evening, dear. At dinner.'

He frowned again. 'I say, you're right you know, we did, didn't we. Quite a night, what? I've already had Spinney tutting at me over the amount we put away. No wonder some of the details are foggy.'

The other two reflexively clutched at their heads, while I hid my serves-you-right smile behind my hand.

'Come then, my fine friends,' said Lord Riddlethorpe, pointing, somewhat oddly, skywards and striding off purposefully across the terrace. 'Let us explore the new and exciting world of motor racing.'

We crossed the formal garden and cut through the kitchen garden to get to an arched doorway set into the boundary wall. On the other side was a flagstoned area that had clearly once been the stable yard. A coach house with large doors stood to one side. The doors were open, revealing not coaches, traps, or dog carts, but two gleaming, green single-seater motor cars. They had numbers painted on their sides. Motor Number 3 stood close to the wall to the right, while Number 2 stood in the middle. There was a space by the wall to the left. The old coach house clearly now served as his 'motor stable' and workshop.

A third sleek, strangely aggressive-looking machine stood in the yard. Number 1. Morgan had one side of the bonnet up and was tinkering with the engine. Another man stood beside him. He was of average height, with an incongruously chubby face atop a slender body, which gave him the look of a small boy in his father's overalls.

'Morning, Morgan,' said Lord Riddlethorpe jovially. 'You've all met Morgan Coleman, haven't you?'

We nodded and offered our own greetings.

'Morning, my lord,' said Morgan. 'Morning Lady Hardcastle, Mr Featherstonhaugh, Miss Armstrong.'

'And this cherubic chap is Ellis Dawkins, driver extraordinaire. He's the senior driver for Codrington Racing, and is a scoundrel, a cad, and quite the fastest chap on four wheels.'

We murmured our how-do-you-dos.

'Good morning,' said Dawkins. 'No one told me we was expecting such beautiful company.'

I raised an eyebrow in response to his leering smile. Unabashed, he leered again before returning his attention to Lord Riddlethorpe.

'What do you think?' said Lord Riddlethorpe proudly.

'Of the car, dear?' said Lady Hardcastle.

'Or of Morgan and Dawkins, if you prefer, but I was thinking of the car, yes.'

Dawkins turned towards me and winked. I pondered the potential consequences of flooring an earl's trusted employee with a sharp blow to the chin.

'Well, it's very long, isn't it? It's certainly bigger than our little Rover.'

'Faster, too,' said Lord Riddlethorpe, patting the motor car and making Morgan flinch as the precariously balanced bonnet wobbled a little, threatening to close on his hands.

'I'll bet. Is it difficult to drive?'

Lord Riddlethorpe smiled. 'No more difficult than any other motor. But to drive it quickly? That's another matter entirely. Fanners tells me you're quite the driver yourself.'

'Well, I . . .' said Lady Hardcastle, trying to affect an air of modesty.

'Come now, I'm told you bomb along the country lanes like you're in the Gordon Bennett Cup. You, too, Miss Armstrong.'

'Not I, my lord,' I said. 'I like to take my time and enjoy the view.'

He laughed. 'So it's just you, then, Emily, what?'

'I confess I have been known to put on a turn of speed when the mood is upon me, yes,' said Lady Hardcastle. 'Harry suggested there might be a chance to race this week.'

He laughed again. 'Did he, by George! You're awfully free with my motor cars, Fanners, what?'

'I thought we were all invited to drive,' said Harry, slightly defensively.

'Just teasing, Fanners. Of course you may drive, Emily, dear. Everyone can. Whole point of coming to stay.'

'You don't mind ladies driving?' she asked.

'Plenty of gels in the motor racing world, old thing. We're a truly egalitarian, twentieth-century sport.'

'Egalitarian, as long as one has sufficient oof to fund the running of a thoroughbred motor car.'

'Three thoroughbred motor cars,' said Lord Riddlethorpe, gesturing towards the old coach house.

'Crikey, Fishy,' said Harry. 'I didn't know you had three of the bally things. What do you need three for? Surely you can only drive one at a time.'

'Well, there's me and young Ellis, so that's one for each of us, and one for development.'

'Development?' said Lady Hardcastle.

'Trying to compete with the big boys,' said Lord Riddlethorpe. 'Missed our chance in the Grand Prix in France last year, but now we've got a circuit of our own at Brooklands, this sport is going to take off, and I mean to be champion.'

'Good for you,' she said. 'And that's why you have your own circuit?'

'Just a small one for testing, yes, but it does the job. We build 'em, test 'em, and before you know it, we'll be racing 'em against the likes of Mercedes, Panhard, Benz, and all that lot.'

'Aha. I'd heard about the new team, but I hadn't fully fathomed what that might entail.'

'All this and more,' he said, gesturing around the yard. 'And the official launch is tonight. I've invited a few Johnnies from the press, and I'm hoping to win over one of my rivals, see if we can't join forces to take on the Europeans.'

'This is all much more exciting than I was given to understand,' said Lady Hardcastle. 'Harry, you really are a duffer sometimes. Did you know about all this?'

'Sort of, sis,' said Harry. 'But it's all a bit over my head. All I really understood was the bit about Fishy getting a few friends together to lark about in motor cars.'

'There'll be larking with pals tomorrow,' said Lord Riddlethorpe. 'Jake's coming down with some chums of her own, and we can all have some fun. Come on, I'm dying to show you what we've built.'

He set off out of the yard towards what had once been magnificently landscaped parkland and was now a magnificently landscaped racing circuit. It took us nearly two hours to explore the twists and turns, the long straight, and the steep climb to the hairpin bend. It was probably the highest point in the unnaturally flat county, and when I asked about it, Lord Riddlethorpe explained that the original landscaper had used the soil dug from the ornamental lake to build an artificial hill, which he in turn had used to make his racing track more interesting.

By the time we had returned to the little hut at the starting line, I was beginning to feel hungry again. I was hoping we would soon be making our way back to the house so that I might slip down to the kitchen to see what Mrs Ruddle had prepared for lunch. To my dismay, Lord Riddlethorpe led us instead towards the centre of the land bordered by the racing circuit. I had seen glimpses of trees and a tall, Palladian rotunda inside the circuit as we walked round, but I had been too interested in Lord Riddlethorpe's enthusiastic descriptions of the track's features to pay too much attention to the gardens. It was, then, something of a pleasant surprise as we crested a small, grassy bank to discover that the racing circuit had been built around the lake. On the near bank stood the rotunda I had seen from the hill, which seemed to be some sort of summer house. As we came closer, I was further surprised to see that a picnic lunch had been laid out on the table inside. I was thoroughly delighted when it transpired that I was invited to eat with the rest of the guests.

◆ ◆ ◆

Lunchtime passed extremely pleasantly. At first, the conversation had been entirely about the new racing team and Lord Riddlethorpe's plans to dominate the motor racing world within five years. He seemed determined enough, and there was ample evidence in the form of the three exciting motor cars in his workshop that he was prepared to make an effort to fulfil his ambition. I wanted to learn more about it, to find out about the motors and the ins and outs of running a modern racing team. But I was acutely aware of my position as social interloper and didn't want to draw too much attention to myself by asking questions, lest Lord Riddlethorpe should suddenly remember that I was just a lady's maid and politely but firmly invite me to return to the kitchens to eat with the other servants.

I did manage to find out that Lord Riddlethorpe had been interested in motor racing since he had first seen it while on holiday in Ireland in 1903. The Gordon Bennett Cup had been held in County Kildare that year, and the sights and sounds had captured his imagination to such an extent that, on his return to England, he had set about learning everything he could about motor cars and their design and construction. Within four years, he had built and raced (and crashed) several motor cars before he met his current business partner, Montague Waterford. Between them, they designed the Waterford-Codrington 'Diocles' (which they named after a charioteer in Ancient Rome), and set about finding the engineers, coachbuilders, and other craftsmen needed to make their plans a reality. The resulting three vehicles, each with subtle differences in mechanical design that I had yet to fully understand, formed the basis of their new team, which they were to officially launch that evening.

From there, talk had turned to reminiscences. Lord Riddlethorpe and Harry talked about their time at Cambridge, rendering each other helpless with laughter as they recalled assorted undergraduate pranks and the disreputable antics of some of their friends, one of whom was now a cabinet minister.

Lady Hardcastle, it seemed, had been a bit of a terror, too. I knew that she had been an able scholar (she had read natural sciences), an excellent musician, and an active member of a number of political societies, but I had no idea she had also joined her brother in several pranks.

'I say, Emily, do you remember that business with the sheep?' said Lord Riddlethorpe between mouthfuls of boiled egg.

'Oh, my word, yes,' said Harry. 'You painted them in Girton colours and drove them across the Bridge of Sighs at St John's.'

'*I* painted them?' said Lady Hardcastle. '*We* painted them, brother dearest. *I* was the one who nearly got herself rusticated over it, though, I'll give you that.'

'Someone from one of the colleges stood up for you, though, eh?' said Lord Riddlethorpe. 'Old Dr Whatshisface with the glass eye.'

'Father wrote you a nice letter, too,' said Harry.

'They were both extremely helpful,' she said. 'You, on the other hand, kept schtum.'

'Well, it was the university that was ticked off, and Girton's not part of the university, anyway,' he said. 'Not properly. I didn't think they'd have much chance of getting you kicked out, but me . . . well . . .'

'I've always thought,' said Lord Riddlethorpe, clearly trying to fend off a family argument, 'that the university rather liked to see its undergraduates getting up to mischief. I think they make their regular stern threats of temporary expulsion just for the sake of appearances. I mean, look at Byron and his bear. Anyone else would have sent him down or had him thrown in gaol, but Trinity just shrugged and smiled and said, "Students, eh? What are we going to do with the rascals?" Gives them good stories to tell, what? Sets them apart.'

'I suppose you're right,' said Lady Hardcastle. 'And it made some of the boys take Girton a bit more seriously.'

'Boys?' said Lord Riddlethorpe with mock indignation. 'They were men.'

'They were silly little boys, for the most part,' she said.

The two men laughed.

Just as Lord Riddlethorpe had launched into another reminiscence about the Earl of Somewhere-or-Other and his dalliance with a barmaid at The Eagle, Spinney approached the summer house and coughed politely.

'Begging your pardon, my lord,' he said quietly, 'but you asked to be informed when your guests began to arrive.'

Lord Riddlethorpe fairly leapt out of his seat. 'Splendid!' he said. 'Come on, you lot, let's go and meet 'em.'

And with that, he was off, with first Harry, then Lady Hardcastle, then me trailing in his wake as one by one we struggled up from the table and followed him out and across the grass back towards the house.

I gave Spinney an embarrassed smile as I passed him, but he winked and leaned in to whisper, 'Just you enjoy it, my dear. Anyone who says you shouldn't is only jealous.'

I touched his arm in thanks, and hurried off to join the others.

By the time Lady Hardcastle and I rounded the corner of the house, Lord Riddlethorpe was already hugging someone of about Lady Hardcastle's age whom I presumed to be his sister. She was a small woman, with a warm smile and a ready laugh that had already burst forth twice before we reached them. Her eyes were quite the darkest I'd ever seen, but with a twinkle that hinted that her brother's sense of mischief and his enthusiasm for life might be a family trait. The long, straight nose was definitely a family trait, and might have made another woman plain and unattractive. But set in such a brightly animated face, it lent an air of elegant beauty.

Rounding the motor from the other side was a tall, slender lady who, by contrast, looked as though she would regard a smile as a bitter betrayal by her face. Her clothes were elegantly cut in the latest fashion, and her expression was one of studied contempt and boredom. Lord Riddlethorpe had said they would be fun, I thought.

Another lady had shuffled across the rear seat of the motor car and found herself at the opposite door to the one where the chauffeur was waiting to help her, so she struggled out unaided and stood behind the laughing woman, shyly waiting to be greeted. She was plump, with a pretty face but a frightened expression, and though she was taller than the laughing lady, and significantly heftier than the haughty one, she seemed somehow smaller than them both. Where her two friends looked poised and confident, she was much less sure of herself, and her timid manner and posture conspired to diminish her appearance.

Lord Riddlethorpe greeted the other two ladies warmly and turned to gesture Lady Hardcastle towards them. 'Emily,' he said, 'allow me to introduce my sister, Jake, and her friends Roz . . .' – the haughty lady nodded a greeting – ' . . . and Helen . . .' The timid lady smiled shyly. 'Lady Lavinia, Mrs Rosamund Beddows, and Miss Helen Titmus, allow me to present Emily, Lady Hardcastle.' There followed a round of hand-shaking and how-do-you-do-ing, which made it look as though Lady Hardcastle were passing along a receiving line. Lord Riddlethorpe was clearly impatient to be done with all the formalities, and as soon as Lady Hardcastle had shaken the last hand, he said, 'And Harry you all know.'

Harry waved and offered a cheery 'What ho', before Lord Riddlethorpe strode off, leading his guests to the house. Lady Hardcastle gave me a wave and a grin to let me know I was on my own again, and I turned back to the motor car, intending to tell the chauffeur how to find his way to the servants' entrance. I suspected that he already knew, but it never hurts to offer some friendly help. It was at this point that I noticed that there had been another passenger in the front seat of the motor.

'How do you do?' she said quietly. 'I'm Betty. Betty Buffrey. I'm Mrs Beddows's lady's maid.'

'The thin one?' I said, and she nodded. 'How do you do? I'm Florence Armstrong. I work for Lady Hardcastle. Call me Flo.'

'Righto, Flo,' she said.

'Did the other two not bring their maids?'

'Miss Perrin, her ladyship's lady's maid, travelled ahead by train. She should already be here. Miss Titmus doesn't have a maid. I gather she makes do with a cook, a housekeeper, and a maid-of-all-work.'

'Ah,' I said. 'I've not met Miss Perrin yet. All in good time, eh?'

'She's nice enough,' she said. 'And this is Finlay Duggan, Mrs Beddows's chauffeur.'

He touched his cap. 'Call me Fin, miss,' he said.

'I take it you both know your way around,' I said.

'Yes, thank you,' said Betty. 'We're regular visitors, aren't we, Fin?'

'Aye, that we are,' he said, lifting baggage from the boot of the motor car.

Evan Gudger was making his way across the drive with an exaggerated lack of haste.

'Hey, Evan!' called Fin. 'Get a move on, ya lazy wee beggar! I haven't got all day. I've got to get back to London.'

I smiled at Betty. 'Shall we leave the boys to it?' I asked. 'I'll help you upstairs with your bags. We're sharing a room.'

'Oh,' she said, smiling for the first time. 'That will be lovely, I'm sure.'

'Come on, then,' I said. 'Maybe we can cadge a cup of tea on the way.'

Chapter Four

I helped Betty settle into our room. I learned she usually had it to herself on visits to Codrington Hall, but she had assured me that it was going to be 'perfectly delightful' to have a companion for a change. She was certainly friendly, and gave every impression of being the sort of kind and generous person that one would be happy to have around. I decided that sharing accommodation with her would be 'perfectly delightful', too.

I had been extremely keen to find out more about her mistress, but I didn't want to put her in the position of having to be disloyal to her employer, given that I'd already made up my mind that Mrs Beddows was almost certainly not a nice person. Instead, I tried to find out more about our host's household, but Betty maintained an air of professional discretion and told me only that they were 'efficient', 'hardworking', and 'friendly . . . for the most part'. I was about to press her on the final caveat when I caught sight of the small clock on the mantel and realized that I ought to be helping Lady Hardcastle to get dressed.

I gave my apologies for rushing off, and hastened to Lady Hardcastle's bedroom, expecting to find her impatiently and inexpertly fiddling with her hair in an ill-advised attempt to 'try something new'.

Previous attempts had resulted in disasters of varying seriousness, and I felt it was always wise to be on hand to forestall any meddling.

I knocked and entered, and found, once again, that her room was deserted. I took the opportunity to lay out her evening clothes and to make sure everything was ready for the party. I found that her favourite blue evening dress was a little wrinkled and there was a slight mark on part of the embroidered decoration on the skirt. I wrote a note to let her know what I was up to, and took the dress downstairs to see what I could do about it.

There was much frantic activity in the servants' hall, and it took me a few moments to track down Mrs McLelland, the housekeeper. I thought she might be the best person to ask where, other than the kitchen, I might find a source of steam.

She was busy making notes on a list of some sort, but she looked up as I entered her room and greeted me politely. When I asked about steaming the dress, she waved towards the little stove in the corner of the room and said, 'Please help yourself. I've a kettle in here that I use.'

'Are you sure I shan't be in the way?' I said. 'You must have a mountain of things to do now that the guests are starting to arrive.'

Her expression darkened momentarily at the mention of the guests, and I saw an opportunity to test my impressions of Mrs Beddows.

'Does Lady Lavinia bring guests often?' I asked.

'She does, yes,' Mrs McLelland said, not looking up from her work.

'The same ones?' I asked. 'I mean, does she have a tight circle of close friends?'

'Yes, the same ones. Just Mrs Beddows and Miss Titmus. They were at school together.'

I waited patiently for the kettle to boil as I examined the dress to decide where best to begin my de-wrinkling. 'That must be nice,' I said.

'Nice?' she said, looking up. 'Well, I suppose it might be, but I'd not have chosen them as my friends.'

'Why not?' I asked.

The kettle, into which I had put only the smallest amount of water, had begun to boil, so I began work on the dress. With my attention on the silk, I couldn't see the expression on Mrs McLelland's face, but I could hear something odd in her voice as she said, 'I don't think it does to talk about the family and their choice of friends, do you?'

I politely agreed, and we returned to innocuous small talk as I finished bringing the wrinkled dress back to life. I offered my thanks and said my goodbyes, leaving her to her list-making.

On the way back towards the stairs, I bumped into Mr Spinney.

'Is everything to Lady Hardcastle's satisfaction?' he asked.

'It is, thank you,' I said. 'She seems to have everything she needs, and more besides.'

He beamed proudly. 'I'm delighted to hear it,' he said. 'Will you be joining us for supper this evening? Please don't feel obliged, mind you.'

'It's going to be a bit hectic down here, isn't it? What with the party and all. Are you sure you wouldn't be offended if I kept to myself again?'

'Most certainly not,' he said. 'You enjoy your leisure time while you can. Miss Buffrey usually takes supper on her own when she can, too. We'll send someone up with a tray for you both, and you can spend an evening gossiping together.'

'If you're sure that would be all right, then that would be lovely.'

'Are you partial to champagne?'

'As a matter of fact, Mr Spinney,' I said with a grin, 'I really rather am.'

He winked. 'I'm sure his lordship wouldn't notice if a bottle should find its way upstairs. I'll see what I can manage.'

'You're very kind. Thank you.'

'Think nothing of it,' he said. 'We all deserve a little treat once in a while. Now, if you'll excuse me, I have to brief one of the new footmen in the ways of Codrington Hall. We're not so very different from other houses, I shouldn't say, but it never hurts to make sure newcomers are familiar with the local customs.'

My mind boggled briefly at the thought of what strange customs the people of Rutland might feel the need to warn new staff about, but he took my amused smile as a sign of assent and went on his way.

◆ ◆ ◆

When I returned to Lady Hardcastle's room, I found her sitting at the dressing table.

'Ah, there you are, Flo,' she said, turning round. 'I wondered where you'd got to.'

'I was downstairs getting the creases out of your gown,' I said. 'I left you a note.'

'You did?' She looked around. 'Oh, so you did. Good thinking.'

I hung the dress up without comment.

She continued to examine herself in the glass. 'Not bad for forty-one, eh?'

'Not bad at all, my lady,' I said. 'You could easily pass for thirty-nine in a dimly lit room.'

'Cheeky wench. What about the barnet?' she said, prodding her hair. 'Do you think I should do something new with it?'

'I think you should leave your hair as it is, my lady.'

'What about the grey ones?'

'They make you look . . .'

'Old?' she suggested.

'I was actually going to say "distinguished", my lady, but you may have "old". How about "venerable"?'

'Anything but "distinguished". It's the sort of word one uses to make chaps feel better about being past their prime.'

I went into the adjoining bathroom to draw a bath for her. 'Were you ever in your prime, my lady?' I called.

'I can picture tomorrow's newspaper headline already,' she said, arriving suddenly in the doorway. '"Maid Mysteriously Drowns in Bath at Codrington Hall".'

I ducked out of her way and left her to bathe. She continued to chatter through the half-open door as she slipped into the warm water.

'Any gossip from below stairs?' she said.

'Not really. The junior footman is a bit of a handful and the house-keeper is rather . . . I was going to say "cold", but that's not quite right. A little formal, perhaps. Stiff. Proper. Nothing you could hold against her, but I didn't warm to her. Other than that, it seems like a very ordinary household.'

'Housekeepers are always odd. I think it's a requirement.'

'Possibly, my lady. What about the upstairs folk?'

'They're an unusual bunch, too,' she said. 'Fishy you've met, of course. Then, let's see . . . His sister seems nice enough.'

'Jake?' I said.

'Yes, "Jake". What an odd name to adopt voluntarily.'

'I've known more than one Jake in my time.'

'Yes, but they were all chaps, I'll warrant. This is because her name is Lavinia.'

'I'm not with you, my lady,' I said, puzzled.

'Evidently it was shortened to "Lav" at school, and it didn't take the wags long to get from "Lav" to "Lavatory", then to "Jakes", and finally to "Jake". The poor woman's named after a water closet.'

I chuckled. 'What about the others?'

'The closest of school chums, it seems. Rosamund Beddows is a difficult one to fathom. I can't quite work out whether her condescend-ing sneer is real or just an affectation to keep people at arm's length. Although from the way she talks to Helen Titmus, I suspect that it might be the genuine article and she might be an honest-to-goodness nasty piece of work.'

'And Miss Titmus?'

'"Titmouse", Roz calls her. Charming, but somewhat put upon by her more glamorous friends, I feel.'

'Lady Lavinia, too?' I said. 'It seems odd that Miss Titmus should choose to spend her time with people who bully her.'

'To be fair, no, not Jake. I think Helen and Jake are quite close, and she has to endure Roz's company as part of the bargain. They seem to come as a set.'

'Mrs Beddows does seem to like to be surrounded by the easily controlled. Her maid is terribly quiet and diffident.'

'Roz brought her maid?'

'Yes, my lady. She and I are sharing a room.'

'When did she get here?'

'She came in the car with the ladies,' I said. 'She didn't get out until you'd all gone inside.'

'Well I never,' she said. 'My vaunted powers of observation are obviously on the wane.'

'It's old age, my lady,' I said as she emerged from the bathroom wrapped in a silk dressing gown. 'You said yourself that you were getting on a bit.'

I got a 'harrumph' for my troubles, and we set about preparing her for the evening's festivities. Once she was finally brushed, polished, and ready to face the world, I slipped away to my shared room and supper with Betty Buffrey.

◆ ◆ ◆

I had lain for quite a while on my bed, reading *The Time Machine* and revelling in my unaccustomed leisure and sloth. Ordinarily, I loathe inactivity, but there's something about being away from home that seems to encourage indolence and turn it into a pleasure rather than a torment. Indeed, I was enjoying the solitude so much that I was very nearly disappointed when Betty finally came in.

Whereas others might bowl boldly into a room – especially one that had been temporarily designated as their own – with a 'here I am' flourish, Betty Buffrey entered quietly, almost apologetically, as though she felt that she might be intruding. It was true that she was unused to sharing the room when she was at Codrington Hall, but I very much imagined that she would have entered thusly even had she known the room to be empty.

'Evening, Betty,' I said cheerfully, trying to put her at her ease.

'Oh, hello, Miss Armstrong,' she said. 'I'm sorry if I'm interrupting. I can find somewhere else to sit, if you wish.'

'Don't be so silly,' I said. 'Come on in and join me. I'm the interloper, if anyone is – this is usually your room. To be truthful, I'd relish the company. I'd been enjoying being on my own, but the attraction soon pales. I rather fancy having someone to talk to.'

'Oh,' she said, sounding slightly surprised. 'Well, if you're sure, then I should like that very much. Will you be going down to supper in the servants' hall?'

I could see she didn't relish the idea. 'No,' I said. 'I'm afraid I took Mr Spinney up on his kind offer to send supper up here for us both.'

She relaxed. 'Thank goodness for that,' she said. 'I'd have come down with you, of course, but I really do prefer to be up here, away from the noise and the chaos.'

'Me too,' I half fibbed. I actually don't mind a bit of noise and chaos, and have been known to seek out boisterous company to liven things up a bit, but for this week I, too, was glad of the peace and quiet. 'Oh,' I added, 'and I also accepted his kind offer of a bottle of champagne. He said Lord Riddlethorpe wouldn't notice it missing, but from what I've seen of his lordship, it was probably his idea.'

'Gracious,' said Betty with a girlish giggle. 'How wonderful. I've never had champagne before.'

'You've never . . . ?' I said incredulously.

'Never been offered it before,' she said.

'Does Mrs Beddows not drink it?'

'She guzzles it down as if it's about to go out of fashion. But it would never occur to her to offer me any.'

'Well, we'll soon set that straight. I only hope you like it after all that anticipation.'

She sat on her bed and began unbuttoning her boots. She was still struggling with the second boot when there was a knock at the door, so I rose to answer it rather than simply call for whoever it was to come in.

I found Patience standing there, holding a very large, heavily laden tray. I couldn't see an easy way to take it from her so I stepped hastily aside. 'Come on in,' I said. 'Pop it on Miss Buffrey's bed and we'll sort it out from there. Are you all right?'

'Yes, thanks, miss,' she said, struggling towards the bed as Betty hopped out of the way.

'It's really very kind of you to bring us this,' I said. 'Thank you so very much.'

'My pleasure, miss,' said the young kitchen maid cheerfully. 'Gets me out of the kitchen for a bit, don't it?'

'It does, indeed. Would you care to linger? Join us in a sandwich, perhaps?'

'No, miss,' she said. 'Better not. Mrs Ruddle is lovely and all, but it don't do to take the mickey, eh?'

'No, Patience, I suppose it doesn't.'

'Patty, miss.'

'Righto, Patty,' I said. 'Well, thank you again for the supper. And thank Mrs Ruddle, too.'

'Will do, miss,' she said as she all but skipped out of the room.

Betty, now finally free of her other boot, had just come over to help me examine and unload the tray when there was another knock at the door.

'Come on in,' I called. 'The party's just beginning.'

The door opened, and in came Mr Spinney with his own tray, this time holding two bottles of champagne, glistening with condensation, and two glasses.

'Here you are, ladies,' he said, setting the tray down on the bed beside the food. 'A little treat for you both.'

'Gracious, Mr Spinney,' I said. 'Two bottles?'

'Well,' he said with a wink. 'No point in being stingy with it, is there?'

'It's jolly nice of you to bring it all the way up here yourself,' I said. 'Thank you.'

'My pleasure, miss,' he said. 'Adds a bit of mystery and tension if I go missing for a few moments on a busy evening. Keeps everybody on their toes. "Where's Mr Spinney got to?" they say. "Better make sure everything's perfect – the old codger could be anywhere. Don't want him to catch us shirking." Works wonders.'

Betty and I both laughed. 'You're welcome to linger,' I offered. 'Join us for a sip or two.'

'A kind offer,' he said. 'But I'd better be getting back. The trick only works if I really do appear out of nowhere once in a while. If I play the Charley-wag for too long, they get complacent.'

'Right you are, Mr Spinney. I hope everything goes smoothly this evening.'

'It's certain not to, Miss Armstrong,' he said. 'But the test of our mettle is how well we cope with the inevitable disasters, I always say.'

'Then I hope all your disasters are little ones.'

'Thank you,' he said. 'Have a pleasant evening, ladies.' He left, closing the door behind him.

'Well,' I said, indicating the two trays. 'It seems supper is served. What do you think: a picnic?'

'A what?' laughed Betty.

'A picnic. We'll set the tray on the rug, then we'll sit on the floor and eat as though we're on a riverbank somewhere, enjoying the sunshine.'

She laughed again. 'Mrs Beddows and her friends reminisce with tales of midnight feasts at their school, but this sounds much more fun.'

We cleared a space on the rug in the centre of the room, and set about laying out our feast. Morgan had said Betty was a quiet one, but it seemed she was happy enough to open up when she was safely away from the household staff.

'Ah, yes,' I said as I set out the plates and cutlery. 'I'd heard they were at school together.'

'Yes, one of the early girls' schools. Mrs Beddows, Miss Titmus, and Lady Lavinia—'

'Jake,' I said.

'Jake,' she said with a chuckle. 'What a horrid name. I think it was Mrs Beddows who came up with that one. But those three were "the best of chums", they say.'

'And remain so to this day, it seems.'

'Yes,' she said. 'Although between you and me, I've never quite been able to work out why. They don't seem to have very much in common apart from having all been to the same school.'

'Those are the experiences that bind us together,' I said, pleased with myself for this display of apparent sagacity.

'Like being in the army?' she said.

'Or prison. Actually, it's probably more like prison from everything I hear about these schools. Have you read *Tom Brown's Schooldays*?'

She shook her head.

'Well, it's no wonder the ruling classes are so peculiar, that's all I can say.'

She laughed. 'They do have access to nice things, though,' she said, holding up one of the chilled champagne bottles. 'How do you open these things?'

I took the chilled bottle from her, and removed the foil and cage. She ducked back and put her hand in front of her face.

'What are you doing?' I asked.

'One thing I do know about champagne is that the cork pops out and flies around the room.'

'Only if it's opened by an idiot,' I said. Gripping the cork firmly in my right hand and twisting the bottle with my left, I eased the cork out with a soft 'pop' and began to pour.

'I say,' she said delightedly. 'That's not at all how Mrs Beddows does it.'

'That must be because,' I said, topping off the glasses, 'Mrs Beddows . . .'

'. . . is an idiot,' she said gleefully. We clinked glasses.

◆ ◆ ◆

For the best part of an hour, we grazed our way through a selection of Mrs Ruddle's finest buffet food as we supped champagne and put the world to rights. As we neared the end of the first bottle, and I coached Betty in the arcane art of champagne opening, my previously quiet and slightly reserved companion became increasingly garrulous.

'Do you ever wish you could just jack it all in and go off somewhere on your own?' she said through a mouthful of smoked salmon.

I thought for a moment. 'Do you know,' I said, 'I really don't think I do.'

'What, never?' she said incredulously. 'A woman like you is happy to just be someone's servant for the rest of your life?'

'I'm not completely certain I know exactly what a woman like me is,' I said. 'But yes, I think I am. Lady Hardcastle and I have been through a lot together over the years, and I think we're more than just employer and servant by now – we're friends. And I'm more than happy to look after my friend.'

She sighed. And then hiccupped. 'That must be nice,' she said sadly. 'I can't imagine ever being friends with Mrs Beddows. Nor wanting to be, I must say.'

'It does make a difference,' I said. 'I can't say that many people approve, but I'd like to meet the people who could live the life that we have and still maintain the "proper" social walls between them.'

'The lives that you've lived?' she said. 'In Gloucestershire, or wherever it is? Are there stories to tell?'

And so for the rest of the evening I treated her to tales of our past. Over many retellings, I had honed versions of the stories that skirted around the delicate matter of our employment as agents of the Crown, but I told her as much as discretion would allow. I told her of my journey to Shanghai as Lady Hardcastle's maid when her husband was posted there by the Foreign Office. I told her of Sir Rodney's murder and our flight into the heart of China. I judged (correctly as it turned out) that she would be impressed by the story of my mastery of the Chinese fighting arts under the tutelage of a monk who had helped us to the Burmese border. And by the time we had sailed down the Irrawaddy in a rickety boat and then found our way on to a steamer bound for Calcutta, she was positively agog.

'Blimey,' she said when the story had finally brought us back to England. 'Well, no wonder you're close. What amazing women you are. I couldn't imagine doing half of what you managed, and Mrs Beddows would have been shot very early on for being vile. Probably by me.'

We both laughed. 'The more I hear of your mistress,' I said, 'the less I like the sound of her.'

'Oh, you just wait till you meet her,' she said, waving her glass at me and slopping champagne on to the rug. 'Then you can tell me whether you'd have shot her, too.'

'Oh, I'm a dreadful shot,' I said. 'Lady Hardcastle, on the other hand . . . Now, there's a lady who can shoot the sweat off a fat man's forehead at a hundred paces. I prefer more . . . personal methods of dispatch.'

She grinned. 'Perhaps you could take care of her for me.'

I laughed. 'She can't be that bad.'

'Oh, you don't know the half of it,' she said. 'Just you wait and see.'

I steered the conversation towards less homicidal topics, and we were soon trading stories of our childhoods. Once again, though, she confessed herself disappointed that her life in Norfolk hadn't been a patch on my life as one of the children of a circus knife-thrower and the wife he'd lured away from the Valleys. We were on safer, common ground, though, when my family returned to South Wales so that my mother could care for my frail grandmother. And when I entered service as a housemaid in Cardiff, our lives were parallel at last. Even if only briefly.

By now, the second bottle of champagne was empty and there was nought but crumbs on the tray, so we retired to our beds and left the mess until morning.

Chapter Five

Lady Hardcastle and I had agreed that the morning after the party would be a leisurely one, and that we should neither of us bother to rise early. It was something of a disappointment, then, when there was a soft but insistent knocking on the bedroom door at seven o'clock.

'Who is it?' I said, in what I hoped was a friendly tone, but which I feared might betray the irritation I felt at being denied my lie-in.

The door opened and Patty peered timidly round it.

'Sorry to disturb you, miss,' she said quietly. 'It's Mrs Beddows; she wants Miss Buffrey.'

'Not your fault, Patty,' I said. 'Betty? Betty!'

Betty mumbled, but didn't seem to awaken, even though she was in the bed nearer the door and lay between Patty and me as we spoke.

'Betty!' I said more insistently. 'Mrs Beddows wants you.'

'Tell Mrs Beddows to go and . . .' she murmured.

'Betty, sweetheart, you've got to wake up and—'

With a gasp, Betty sat bolt upright in bed. 'Oh my goodness!' she said, a look of near terror on her face. 'I've just had the most horrible nightmare. I dreamed Mrs Beddows was trying to awaken me, and I told her to . . . Oh.' She noticed Patty standing in the doorway.

'Sorry, miss,' said Patty. 'It's Mrs Beddows. She rang down, but when Lily went up to her, she sent her away with a flea in her ear and insisted we get you.'

In a state of near panic, Betty pulled on a dressing gown and hurried from the little bedroom, brushing past Patty with a muttered, 'Sorry, Patty, must dash.'

I flopped back on to my pillow.

'Can I bring you up a cup of tea, miss?' said Patience.

'No, dear, it's all right,' I said. 'I'll be down to the servants' hall in a minute. I'll get myself one then, before I take a tray up to Lady Hardcastle.'

'It's no bother, miss, really.'

'You're very kind,' I said. 'But I'll be fine. I don't suppose you could take one of these trays back down, though, could you?' I indicated the wreckage of our picnic on the rug. 'I can't manage them both.'

'Of course, miss,' she said, and set about stacking the empty plates. 'I reckon I can fit it all on one,' she said.

And in no time at all I was alone again. I contemplated trying to get back to sleep, but there really wasn't much point, so instead I set about getting up and ready for the day.

◆ ◆ ◆

After a hearty breakfast in the servants' hall, I took a tray up to Lady Hardcastle. I knocked and entered without waiting for a reply, which I didn't think would be forthcoming anyway. To my amazement, she was sitting up in bed, writing in her journal.

'Good morning,' she said. 'How was your evening?'

'Very enjoyable, thank you, my lady,' I said, putting the tray down on the writing desk by the window. 'And how about yours? You're rather more . . . upright than I had anticipated.'

'It wasn't that sort of do, sadly,' she said. 'Plenty of nibbles and a good quantity of rather nice champagne, but I rather felt I needed to keep my wits about me. Wouldn't want to give Fishy's new venture a bad name by having a drunken old biddy making a show of herself while the gentlemen of the press looked on.'

'How very thoughtful of you, my lady.'

'Well, quite. As it turns out the role of Lord Lushington was expertly played by Fishy's Uncle Algy, so I needn't have worried.'

'Did we know there was another Codrington in the house?' I asked.

'He's Fishy's uncle on his mother's side, a Garrigan rather than a Codrington. Apparently, he's part of the fixtures and fittings, and Fishy inherited him when his parents died. Lovely old chap, probably a bit of a lad in his day – he got blotto and tried to get some party games going before Fishy ushered him out.'

'Poor chap,' I said. 'Sounds like he would have been the life and soul.'

'On any other occasion, he might, but poor Fishy was trying to act the grown-up, so he had to go. What did you do?'

I told her about the picnic in the bedroom as I poured her tea and handed her a round of toast.

'Can't say I've seen anything of the fair Rosamund that would give the lie to Miss Buffrey's assessment of her as a nasty piece of work,' she said between mouthfuls. 'I say, you couldn't do me an enormous favour, could you? I think I left my reading glasses in the great hall.'

'Have you considered wearing them around your neck, my lady?' I suggested.

'I suppose I could,' she said absently. 'But it's much more fun to have you fetch them for me. You make such entertaining noises when you're huffy.'

I tutted, and set off in search of the missing optical aids.

Ignoring protocol, I used the main stairs and hang the con-sequences. In truth, it wasn't so much an act of rebellion as an acknowledgement that I had absolutely no idea where the great hall was, and I didn't believe I had any chance at all of finding it using the servants' secret passageways. The staircase was wide, and swept in a gentle curve to the entrance hall. I got the feeling it had been designed for grand entrances and exits by the earl and countess. What a shame there was no countess for Lord Riddlethorpe to sweep down it with.

Despite my initial uncertainty, it turned out that the great hall was very easy to find – I just followed the sounds of bottles and glassware being put into crates.

It really was a great hall. Thankfully, the hunting in this part of the country was limited to fox, so the walls were free of the usual racks of antlers, but Lord Riddlethorpe wasn't ashamed to show trophies of his own. In a delightful display of eccentricity, he had placed motor car badges, a radiator grille and even a wheel, complete with tyre, where his ancestors might have hung banners and trophies of war or the hunt.

I said a cheery good morning to the housemaids who were working their way through the wreckage wrought by last evening's party. They had their work cut out, and I assured them that I wouldn't be getting in the way, but wondered if any of them had spotted a stray lorgnette anywhere.

'Over there, miss,' said a plump little girl with mousey hair and a smudge of soot on her nose. She nodded towards a table by one of the huge windows.

Sure enough, the stray glasses were exactly where she had indi-cated, sitting atop a sheet of foolscap paper. I picked up the lorgnette and folded it, slipping it into my pocket. I was about to leave, but curiosity got the better of me and I had a quick look to see what was written on the paper. It was a list, written in Lady Hardcastle's neat hand.

Ladies' Race:
1. Lady Hardcastle
2. Mrs Beddows
3. Lady Lavinia
4. ~~Miss Titmus~~ Miss Armstrong

Gentlemen's Race:
1. Lord Riddlethorpe
2. Mr Featherstonhaugh
3. Mr Dawkins
4. Herr Kovacs

Mr Waterford shall act as Starter and Race Director. Miss Titmus shall be the Official Race Photographer.

I hurried back upstairs and burst into Lady Hardcastle's room without knocking.

'I say, steady on, dear,' she said. 'It's just a pair of reading glasses. No need to rush so.'

'What?' I said. 'Oh, the lorgnette. Yes, here you are, my lady.' I passed her the silver reading glasses.

She took the lorgnette, flicked it open and held it up while she re-read her journal entry. After a few moments, she slowly lowered the device and looked over at me.

'Is there something the matter? You look confubuscated. Bumsquabbled, even. Whatever's happened?'

'I saw a sheet of paper in the great hall, my lady,' I said.

'That can be quite a traumatic event, I agree.'

'What? No, there was something rather surprising written upon it.'

Realization slowly dawned. 'Ah,' she said. 'The races. Are you pleased?'

I all but squealed in my excitement. 'You did it! You managed to get me into the races. Thank you. Thank you.'

'I say, steady on,' she said, laughing. 'It was the least I could do. Although in truth, you have Helen Titmus to thank. Roz Beddows was badgering her to join in, saying that we couldn't have a proper ladies' race with just the three of us, but I could tell she didn't really want to. I caught her on her own a little while after all the plans had been laid, and let slip that you might be interested in racing. She was so relieved that she all but begged me to talk you into it. I said I'd see what I could do, and amended the race card accordingly.'

'You're the best employer a poor Welsh servant could ever wish for,' I said. 'What do the numbers mean?'

'They're the motor cars. We drew lots. It was all frightfully complicated, but the chaps insisted that Fishy shouldn't be allowed to choose his own motor because he knows them all so well, so we put the numbers in a bowl and drew them out to see who should drive what.'

'So that means I'm in Number 4?'

'I believe so, yes. It's Fishy's friend's racer – Herr Kovacs. He was quite pleased to have drawn his own motor for the gentlemen's race. They say it's quite a flyer.'

I just grinned idiotically.

◆ ◆ ◆

The plan was that we should meet at the starting line at noon, and we arrived a quarter of an hour early to find that three of the racing cars were already there. They were the three we had seen in the coach house the day before. Sleek, dark-green machines. Elegant and beautiful, but strangely aggressive and frightening. Warrior goddesses.

We could see Morgan driving up from the motor stable in the fourth, an unfamiliar vehicle whose bare metal bodywork glinted in the noonday sun like brushed silver.

Lord Riddlethorpe was inspecting his motor, making minute adjustments to various valves and tiny levers. He looked up from his tinkering as we approached.

'Hello, ladies,' he said in his cheerful, boyish way. 'I say, don't you two look just the ticket in your driving togs? Fanners said you drove, but I didn't think you took it quite this seriously. The other gels are going to have their work cut out for them.'

Lady Hardcastle laughed. 'I'm not sure we're up to your standard, dear,' she said.

'Perhaps, or perhaps not, but I'd wager you could give my sister a run for her money – she's a shocking driver. I've not seen Roz behind the wheel, but if she drives like she conducts the rest of her life, you'd both better watch out – I can't imagine she'll be giving any quarter.'

'Right you are, dear,' she said. 'You hear that, Flo? Watch out for Mrs Beddows.'

'Will do, my lady,' I said.

'Oh, you've got nothing to worry about, Armstrong,' said Lord Riddlethorpe with a chuckle. 'Fanners has been telling Roz a few choice tales, and I think she might be a little afraid of you.'

'Me, my lord?' I said.

'You, yes,' he said with a grin. 'Isn't that right, Monty?'

Mr Montague Waterford loomed up from behind another of the motor cars, where he had been lurking, unseen, apparently indulging in some tinkering of his own. He was a little older than Lord Riddlethorpe, perhaps around fifty years. His red hair was already white at the temples, and there were wrinkles around his eyes. It was hard to tell whether they were the result of squinting or smiling.

'What? Roz?' he said, wiping his hands on a rag. 'She looked positively terrified when Harry told her about you breaking that woman's wrist with a single kick. Or was she simply horrified that a visiting servant had been allowed to get that close to the lady of the house? I can't quite recall.' He winked. I began to suspect that the wrinkles were caused by a surfeit of mischievous smiling.

Lady Hardcastle let out a 'Pfft', but said nothing.

'The "lady of the house" was threatening to shoot a policeman,' I said. 'I just . . . sort of . . . stopped her. Anyone would have done the same.'

Both men laughed at this.

'Not me,' said Lord Riddlethorpe. 'I'd have been cowering under the table. Best place to be when there are guns about.'

'But I, for one, am looking forward to seeing you drive,' said Mr Waterford. 'There are a few ladies in the motor racing world, but not nearly enough. It'll be exciting to see how you all get on.'

I gave him a smile and a nod of thanks. He seemed about to say more when something else caught our attention. Harry, accompanied by Ellis Dawkins and a man I didn't recognize, was stomping across the grass towards us. Some way behind them, in a separate group, were Lady Lavinia and Mrs Beddows, who were stepping much more daintily, but with no less purpose. They had left Miss Titmus a little way behind as she fiddled with what appeared to be a rather natty little camera.

What had interrupted our conversation was not the sight of our fellow competitors, but rather the altercation that seemed to be taking place between two of them.

'*Nein, nein, es ist nicht das Gleiche,*' a wiry man with pince-nez spectacles was saying. 'Not the same thing at all.'

Harry rolled his eyes as the other two continued to glare at each other.

Lord Riddlethorpe chuckled. 'I say! Viktor! Steady on, old chap,' he called. 'Never met a man more determined to start an argument,' he added to Lady Hardcastle and me, *sotto voce.*

The bespectacled man stopped mid-rant and glared briefly at his host before raising a hand in surrender and smiling ruefully.

'My apologies, Edmond,' he said. 'I do not wish to sour the morning's activities, but this young fool . . .'

The young fool raised his hands in appeal, and Lord Riddlethorpe laughed again.

'Come on over here and meet our eighth competitor,' he said. 'You can save your rivalries for the track, what?'

The two combatants approached. Harry brought up the rear, a massive grin – so like his sister's – lighting up his face.

'Now then,' said Lord Riddlethorpe. 'Viktor, may I present Florence Armstrong of . . . I say, Miss Armstrong, where are you from?'

'Aberdare, my lord,' I said. 'South Wales.'

'I say, really? Well I never. This is Florence Armstrong of Aberdare, wherever the dickens that may be, but I'm sure it's enchanting. She is lady's maid to Lady Hardcastle, and all-round adventuress and good egg. Miss Armstrong, this is Viktor Kovacs of Vienna, racing driver, owner of *Die Kovacs Motorsport Mannschaft*, my bitterest rival, and dearest friend.'

Herr Kovacs clicked his heels and bowed slightly towards me. 'A pleasure to meet you, *Fräulein*,' he said. 'Actually, I am from Budapest, but I have lived for many years in Vienna. You are to be driving my motor car, yes? Do you race?'

'Not until today, sir,' I said. 'But I'm keen to have a go.'

He smiled. 'The ladies' race will be interesting, I think.'

'It will,' said Lord Riddlethorpe. 'And Dawkins you know already. He's from . . . er . . . somewhere or other. Bournemouth, or somewhere equally frightful, wasn't it?'

We nodded our greetings. Dawkins winked at me. I rolled my eyes and turned away.

'I'm Harry Featherstonhaugh, by the way,' said Harry from the back of the group. 'Just in case you were wondering.'

By this time, the ladies had reached us.

'What's this, Fishy?' said Lady Lavinia. 'Have we missed the introductions?'

'Lawks,' said Lord Riddlethorpe. 'Umm . . . Lavinia, Roz, Helen . . . This is Florence Armstrong.'

'A little perfunctory, dear,' said Lady Lavinia. 'But it shall have to do. Good morning, Miss Armstrong.' She smiled at me. 'We've heard so much about you.'

'I'll say,' said Helen Titmus quietly, with a smile and a wave. 'Super to meet you at last.'

The corners of Rosamund Beddows's mouth flicked briefly upwards in an approximation of a smile of greeting, but she resumed her studied, disdainful expression almost immediately and looked away.

'Well, that's that all done,' said Lord Riddlethorpe. 'Is everybody ready for some fun? What do you say we get on with the racing?'

There were cheers all round.

'Splendid,' he said, clapping his hands. 'Now who's got the race card?'

Harry held up the sheet of paper I'd seen in the great hall. 'Here, Fishy,' he said.

Lord Riddlethorpe took the proffered paper and glanced at it. 'Right, I'm in car number one,' he said, walking towards the motor. 'Fanners, you're in two, Dawkins is in three and Viktor, you're in your own silver machine, number four. Three laps of the circuit, and we'll forgo the foot race and start in the motors with the engines running . . .'

'Wait a moment,' said Lady Lavinia, stepping towards him and taking the sheet of paper. 'I think you'll find that the ladies' race is first.' She indicated the race card, where, sure enough, the ladies' race was listed first.

'Just politeness, Jake,' he said plaintively. 'It's my track; I say who gets to go first.'

She sighed. 'You're such a child, Edmond Codrington. We'll toss for it. Who has a coin?'

Harry rummaged in his trouser pocket and pulled out a florin.

'Two bob, Fanners?' said Lord Riddlethorpe. 'I had no idea you Foreign Office Johnnies were so well paid.'

'It's surprising how much money a chap can make if he's prepared to lift a finger and do an honest day's toil,' said Harry.

'Will the two of you just shut up and toss the blessed coin,' said Lady Lavinia impatiently.

With a grin, Harry dutifully shut up and tossed the coin.

'Heads,' called Lady Lavinia as it reached the top of its arc.

It landed with a ringing clink on the tarmacadam of the track, and we all bent to examine it.

'Tails it is, then,' said Lord Riddlethorpe. 'Gentlemen, to your motor cars.' He stuck out his tongue at his sister, who harrumphed and turned away.

'Just a moment,' said Miss Titmus in her timid voice. 'Would you mind awfully if I took a couple of photographs? I am the race photographer, after all.' She held up the camera, which she'd been carefully carrying all this time.

Mrs Beddows sighed. 'Oh, for heaven's sake, Titmouse,' she said. 'Must we?'

'Yes, dear, we must,' said Lady Lavinia. 'I think it's a splendid idea before we get all flyblown and oily, or whatever it is that happens during these things. Gentlemen, line up over there.' She pointed to a spot on the track where it would be possible to get both the men and the motor cars into the shot. 'How's that, Helen, dear?'

'Wonderful, thank you, Lavinia,' said Miss Titmus.

The men dutifully lined up, and Miss Titmus positioned herself for the photograph.

'Not yet,' said Lord Riddlethorpe. 'Fanners is still smiling.'

Harry, whose gaze seemed to be on Lady Lavinia, was indeed smiling, but he quickly composed himself, now blushing.

'I honestly don't know why we're not allowed to smile,' said Lady Hardcastle. 'Future generations will think us a frightfully po-faced, miserable lot.'

'Oh, just get on with it, Titmouse,' said Mrs Beddows. 'We haven't got all day to wait for you and your stupid camera.'

Miss Titmus took a few more seconds to compose her shot and then snapped the photograph.

'At last,' said Mrs Beddows, striding towards the motor cars for her own picture. 'Come on, Jake, let's get it over with.'

Lady Lavinia ushered Lady Hardcastle and me towards the designated spot. It looked for a moment as though Mrs Beddows might be about to object to my presence, but she held her tongue.

'Come on, girls,' said Lady Hardcastle brightly, once we were in position. 'What say we break with convention and show posterity that we really can have fun? Everybody smile.'

Lady Lavinia and I dutifully tried to smile, but Lady Hardcastle remained unimpressed. 'Hopeless,' she said. 'Harry? Tell us one of your jokes.'

'What?' said Harry. 'Well . . . I . . . er . . . This chap goes into a pub . . . and . . . er . . .'

'Hopeless,' she said again. 'Oh, I know what.' She gathered us into a huddle and whispered to us all. Propriety prevents me from repeating what she said to us, so it shall have to suffice to say that it left

Lady Lavinia and me guffawing, and even Mrs Beddows grudgingly sniggered.

We returned hurriedly to our places, genuine smiles on our lips, and Miss Titmus took her photograph.

'Splendid,' said Lord Riddlethorpe. 'And now let's race. Gentlemen, to your motors!'

◆ ◆ ◆

It took a few minutes for the men to pull overalls over their day clothes. There followed a small amount of fiddle-faddling once they were in their motors while Morgan went along the line cranking the engines to life.

Miss Titmus hadn't struck me as the sort of woman to become particularly animated under any circumstances, but as the drivers prepared to race, she scarcely stopped moving. Crouching here, leaning there, even standing on one leg, and all to get just one more photograph.

Harry gunned his engine as she pointed her camera at him. This elicited a monstrous roar from beneath the green bonnet of the motor car, which startled him. To our delight, this was the moment Miss Titmus's shutter clicked. He waved, grinning sheepishly as she moved on.

Lord Riddlethorpe didn't notice her, so intent was he on the dials and controls in his cockpit. She captured an image of rapt concentration, and moved on again.

Herr Kovacs didn't notice her, either. He was intent on the newer, experimental motor car beside him. I imagined a study of nonchalance as the shutter clicked, and Miss Titmus moved on once more.

Ellis Dawkins saw her and mugged at the camera. Even through his goggles we could see his cheeky wink.

Finally, she turned her camera on Mr Waterford and snapped a picture of him as he prepared to bring down his starter's flag.

Engines roared. Tyres squealed. They were off. Four of the most powerful racing machines in the land thundered away towards the first bend, with Miss Titmus managing to get one last photograph of them through the dust and exhaust smoke before they disappeared.

Over the past few months, I had grown accustomed to the pleasant, friendly clatter of the Rover's little engine as it pulled us along the lanes. I had heard the rumble of larger motor cars and even motor wagons in the city, but none of that had prepared me for the roar of those four monster machines. It was as though the motor cars we met in the streets of our towns and villages were the domesticated versions of some wild, ferocious beast. Somehow, Lord Riddlethorpe and his friends had captured a handful of the feral variety and were riding them around the track. They went from goddesses to tigresses in my imagination.

Even from the farthest point of the circuit, we could hear the roar of the engines, and I confess to feeling a twinge of excitement as the sound grew louder and the motor cars drew closer.

Suddenly, they were upon us. Lord Riddlethorpe was in the lead, but only just, with the silver car of Herr Kovacs almost level with his rear wheel. Dawkins, the other professional driver, was just a few yards behind the leaders as all three shot past what would soon become the finishing line.

Bringing up the rear, way off the pace, but still with an idiotic, boyish grin of glee on his face, was Harry. He gave us a wave as he passed the line and shouted something unintelligible. Miss Titmus had managed to get another couple of photographs, and I hoped that at least one of them came out.

Soon, Tail-End Harry had disappeared round the bend, and we were left waiting again for their thrilling return. The noise, the speed . . . It was intoxicating. Lady Hardcastle was standing to my left, chatting to

Miss Titmus about photography, while Lady Lavinia and Mrs Beddows were deep in conversation a little way off to the right. Mr Waterford was flicking at the grass with his flag.

I turned towards Lady Hardcastle as I heard her mention my name. I was about to ask her if she wouldn't mind repeating the question when we were all silenced by a terrible grinding screech, followed by a crash and thump. It was loud enough that we could imagine it was next to us, but we knew that it came from the woods about a quarter of a mile away, where the racing circuit snaked between the trees. We heard the other engines slow and stop, and then, almost as one, we began running towards the scene of the crash.

◆ ◆ ◆

Morgan Coleman, the chauffeur, was the first to arrive, closely followed by Mr Waterford. He held up his arms and tried to stop the rest of us from getting any closer.

'Oh, don't be such a silly ass,' said Lady Hardcastle, pushing past. 'They need help.'

I followed her to the wrecked motor car, but the other three ladies stayed back, gratefully obeying Mr Waterford's instructions not to look.

To our immense relief, we saw that the motor car was in reasonably good shape. The bodywork was dented and the number '3' painted on its side was a little scratched, but other than that it seemed barely damaged. Our relief was short-lived, though, when we realized, from the contorted angle of his broken body, that the motor car's driver, Ellis Dawkins, was dead.

Harry was next to arrive, with Lord Riddlethorpe and Herr Kovacs running up shortly afterwards from the opposite direction.

'Is he . . . ?' said Lord Riddlethorpe, trying to get closer.

'I'm afraid so, my lord,' said Morgan, standing up from where he had been examining the body. 'Seems he lost control on the bend and slewed off the track. I'd say he hit his head when the motor smashed into the tree. Died instantly, I'd reckon.'

'Why would he lose control like that?' asked Harry, all traces of his earlier excitement and enthusiasm gone. 'The man was a professional.'

'He'd have had to be going at a good old lick coming into the bend to spin this far off the track,' said Morgan thoughtfully.

'A fault with the car?' suggested Herr Kovacs. 'It was your proto-type, after all, Edmond. Perhaps your engineers have made mistakes.'

Lord Riddlethorpe was too shocked to speak.

'There's nothing we can do for Dawkins now,' said Lady Hardcastle in a calm, businesslike tone. 'Harry, take the ladies back to the house and call the police – they'll need to be notified of the death. Fishy, you'll need to contact Dawkins's family.'

'I'm not sure he had any family,' said Lord Riddlethorpe absently. 'I remember him telling me his parents were dead. I think there might be a sister in Bournemouth, but I've no idea how we'd reach her.'

'Herr Kovacs—' she began.

'Viktor, please,' he said with a bow.

'Thank you. Viktor, would you look after Fishy, please? I don't think he's coping well with the shock.'

'Of course,' he said, and gently led his friend away.

'Will you be all right, sis?' said Harry, hesitating slightly before setting off.

'Of course I shall, silly,' she said. 'Now go and be manly and master-ful – I think the others might need some reassurance.'

'Right you are,' he said, and went back to lead the rest of the party home.

'We're goin' to need to take a good look at this motor car,' said Morgan, walking round it, examining it carefully. 'I just can't see how someone like Dawkins could lose control like that. Now Mr Featherstonhaugh – no offence, my lady – him I could imagine overdoin' it a bit on the approach and skiddin' off, but even he'd not make this much of a mess of it. It's got to be somethin' wrong with the motor. He came in much too fast.'

'I'm not sure what the protocol is with motor accidents on private land,' said Lady Hardcastle, 'but I think we probably ought to leave everything as it is until the police and their surgeon have had a look. But then I think you should get the motor car back to your workshop and give it a thorough going over. One way or another, Lord Riddlethorpe will want to know how this happened – he's very shaken up.'

'Right you are, my lady,' Morgan said, and we stood to await the arrival of the authorities.

Chapter Six

'. . . a tragic accident. The coroner will have the final say, of course, and we'll have to take the body to the mortuary in Leicester until he releases it, but I don't think there's anything else for us to do here.'

The speaker was a rumpled police inspector from Leicester who had arrived to take over from the local constable when word reached HQ that a death had occurred at the home of the Earl of Riddlethorpe. He had introduced himself to Lord Riddlethorpe as Inspector Foister in a tone of obsequious respect that had evaporated the instant he spoke to any of the rest of the party. He had slightly increased the level of toadying when addressing Lady Lavinia – she was the earl's sister, after all – and Lady Hardcastle – a title's a title, even if one is only a knight's widow – but the rest of us were treated with an off-hand superciliousness that was beginning rather to get on my nerves by the time he was ready to leave.

He clearly thought that a gang of moneyed fools mucking about in high-powered motor cars was a recipe for disaster. We had got far less than we deserved, and I suspected it was only the fact that Lord Riddlethorpe was involved that stopped him from telling us all so. It wouldn't have been so bad, but it meant that Sergeant Tarpley, the local bobby, seemed to have taken the inspector's behaviour as leave to display the same dismissive attitude. He was still as polite and deferential to Lord Riddlethorpe as he had been when he arrived, but he seemed now to think that he was at liberty to dismiss the incident as yet further idiocy from the 'young' earl.

The earl himself was still in shock, and had said very little. When it became obvious that the inspector was wrapping things up and readying himself to leave, it was Lady Hardcastle who took over.

'Thank you for coming, Inspector,' she said, gesturing towards the library door. 'I'm sure you'll let his lordship know if there's anything else that needs to be done?'

'Of course, my lady,' he said, bristling slightly at the feeling he was being dismissed.

She led him across the room and opened the door to find the young footman lurking outside. 'Evan will see you out,' she said. She turned round to address Sergeant Tarpley. 'Perhaps the inspector will give you a lift into Riddlethorpe,' she said.

'No need, m'lady,' said the sergeant self-importantly. 'I come on me bike.'

'Of course you did,' she said with a smile. 'It really has been most generous of you both to give us your time and your professional reassurance.'

There was no doubt in either of their minds now that they had been given their marching orders. The inspector's eyes flicked towards Lord Riddlethorpe before saying a curt 'Good day to you', and marching off after Evan. In other company, I suspect we'd have got a 'Now look here' or an 'I shall decide when it's time for me to leave', but his snobbery got the better of him, and he decided that starting a row in the earl's house was bad form. Sergeant Tarpley trotted obediently in their wake, and we were left once more to ourselves.

The atmosphere was understandably subdued, and once again Lady Hardcastle took charge.

'Right,' she said briskly. 'At times like these, the proper English response is to have a nice cup of tea. Armstrong, dear, please pop down to the kitchens and see what you can scare up. Morgan, I think we need to retrieve the crashed motor car and bring it back to the coach house – it would put his lordship's mind at ease to know whether there was anything wrong with the machine. Press-gang any staff you need to assist you.'

'Who the devil put you in charge?' said Mrs Beddows coldly. 'Fishy should be ordering the servants about. Or Jake. Certainly not you.'

'Lady Lavinia?' said Lady Hardcastle.

'What?' said Lady Lavinia absently. 'Oh, yes. Yes, that will all be fine. Carry on, Morgan.'

Lady Hardcastle smiled, Mrs Beddows glowered, and Morgan and I beat a hasty retreat.

◆ ◆ ◆

News of the day's events had already reached the servants' hall and we were all but mobbed as we entered. Mr Spinney sternly called for order, and the hubbub died down, but it was clear that we weren't going to get out without sharing our side of the story.

As succinctly and as unsensationally as we could, we took turns to describe the events leading up to the crash. By the time we'd finished, the large, ordinarily cheerful room had fallen silent. One of the junior maids piped up. 'My ma always said nothin' good would come of them motor cars.'

There were murmurs of agreement.

'Dangerous contraptions,' said another. 'His lordship should be ashamed of himself, riskin' his friend's life like that.'

'That's quite enough of that,' said Mrs McLelland severely. 'We'll hear no more of that sort of talk, thank you very much, girls. Get back to your work now.'

'Quite right,' said Mr Spinney. 'Get back to work, all of you. His lordship still has guests, and we must be as quietly efficient as ever. More so, in fact.'

Muttering, the staff dispersed and went about their business.

While I organized a tea tray and one of the junior footmen to deliver it, Morgan had a quiet word with Mr Spinney. He left a few moments later, accompanied by the groom and the boot boy. I kept out of the way while Mrs Ruddle supervised the preparation of the tea and the provision of cake, and then I, too, left the staff to their labours and went back upstairs with the footman.

He set the tray down on a table in the library, and I poured cups for everyone. I joined Lady Hardcastle, who had separated herself from the ladies and was standing by one of the tall windows, looking out on to the grounds.

'Thank you,' she said as she took the proffered cuppa.

'My pleasure,' I said. 'How is everyone?'

'A little distressed by events, I feel, but they'll rally. One does, doesn't one?'

'I suppose so, my lady.'

'Fishy and Monty are taking it badly, of course. They've been over there, deep in muttered conversation, since you left. They're blaming themselves, but they would, wouldn't they? Herr Kovacs attempted to intervene, but they shooed him away. He tried talking to the girls, but they gave him short shrift, too – that's why he's sitting on his own over there.'

I looked around as she spoke, and saw Lord Riddlethorpe and Mr Waterford sitting in armchairs on either side of a low table. They had some papers spread out upon it and were leaning in, their heads almost touching, gesturing animatedly. Meanwhile, Lady Lavinia, Mrs Beddows, and Miss Titmus were sitting gloomily around another small table, while Harry tried gamely to keep the conversation flowing. It looked to be no easy task, with Lady Lavinia fidgeting, seemingly unable to settle comfortably, and Miss Titmus fiddling with her ever-present camera. Mrs Beddows was sipping her tea and looked thoroughly bored. Herr Kovacs sat in the corner of the room furthest from the other two groups. He didn't seem unduly put out at being pushed away. Indeed, he appeared to be enjoyably engrossed in an old book.

'Did Morgan get his assistants?' said Lady Hardcastle.

'Yes, my lady. He collared a couple of the younger lads and they set off to get the motor.'

'Splendid. I'd like you to take a stroll out to the stables, if you wouldn't mind. It shouldn't take young Morgan long to get the motor back to the workshop, and I'd really rather like to know what he finds out.'

'You suspect something, my lady?'

'Call it the healthy curiosity of an enquiring mind,' she said.

'"The nosiness of an interfering old busybody". Right you are, my lady.'

She raised her hand to aim a threatening flick at my ear, and I left before we were accused of a lack of decorum.

◆ ◆ ◆

I slipped quietly out of the library and back downstairs, where, by the ancient and reliable trick of appearing to be fearfully busy, I managed to pass through the servants' hall and out the side door without being waylaid. Patience was in the kitchen garden harvesting herbs for Mrs Ruddle, and we exchanged cheery greetings as I passed, but the old 'striding purposefully' trick worked its magic and she didn't detain me.

A few minutes later, I arrived in the yard, where I saw Morgan and his helpers wheeling the dented green motor car into the former coach house. He dismissed the two lads, and they ambled past me, as slowly as they thought they could get away with, on their way back to the servants' hall.

'It doesn't look too badly damaged,' I said by way of alerting him to my presence.

He turned sharply at the sound of my voice, but relaxed when he saw it was me.

'No,' he said, 'not too bad at all. She'm a bit banged up, but we can knock out them dents. Probably could have driven her back down here, to be honest.'

'Do you need any help?' I asked.

'I never say no to an offer of help,' he said, unclipping the bonnet latches. 'And even just some company would make a change. People mostly doesn't have time to loiter round the workshops. I don't mind bein' on me own, but a chat's always welcome. Can you hold this a minute?'

I reached across the bonnet of the car from the other side and held the half that he had just raised while he fiddled with the supporting brace.

'You can let go now,' he said. The bonnet stayed up on its own.

'Do you have any idea what you might be looking for?' I asked, rounding the front of the motor to peer into the mysterious mechanicals.

'Sommat as might have caused the accident, you mean?'

'Yes,' I said, continuing my journey round the motor.

'Could be anythin',' he said. 'Throttle cable might have jammed, brakes might have failed . . .'

'Does that sort of thing happen often?'

'More often than you might hope. Wonderful things, motor cars, but they ain't 'alf complicated. Hundreds of moving parts all workin' in harmony – it only takes one little blighter to start singin' out of tune and it all goes to pot.'

'I really ought to learn more about how these machines work if we're to properly enjoy our little Rover,' I said.

''Tain't all that difficult to understand, really,' he said, looking up from under the bonnet. 'Take the brakes, for instance. You press down on the pedal here.' He indicated the foot brake.

'That part I knew,' I said. 'And then the motor just sort of stops. By magic, presumably.'

He laughed. 'Not magic so much as mechanics. You push the pedal and it pulls this lever, and then that pulls these cables, and they pull these levers, and then they squeeze two metal shoes lined with grippy stuff against the inside of these drums . . .' His voice trailed away to nothing.

'What's the matter?' I asked, trying to follow his gaze.

'See this cable here?' He indicated the end of the wire where it emerged from its housing by the brake drum on the right-hand side of the vehicle. 'He's supposed to be connected to this lever here.' He reached over and tapped the connector for the threaded rod, from which a short length of wire protruded. 'Dawkins only had one brake goin' into that bend; no wonder he couldn't stop. Wouldn't have noticed at low speed, but if he was drivin' it 'ard like, he'd not have got anythin' like the brakin' he was expectin'. Would have been lopsided, too. Ain't no wonder he crashed, poor beggar.'

'It broke?' I suggested.

'No,' he said. 'See the way the ends of the wire are crushed? Someone cut it.'

◆ ◆ ◆

I stayed with Morgan while he checked the rest of the motor car. He found no other faults, and we returned to the house through the now-empty kitchen garden. After washing his hands in the gardeners' sink by the door, he gestured me to follow him, and we set off upstairs to the library.

He knocked on the door and entered. As he made his way briskly across to where Lord Riddlethorpe was sitting, I went to the window seat, where Lady Hardcastle had made herself comfortable with a book.

She put the book down as I approached, and I noticed that she was re-reading *The Woman in White*.

'What ho, Flo,' she said. 'What news from the workshop?'

'Not good, my lady,' I said, sitting down next to her. 'It looks awfully like sabotage.'

'Gracious,' she said. 'How certain are you?'

'Morgan gave the motor car a thorough going-over and everything was in full working order, except that one of the brake cables had been snipped through.'

'Well I never. "One of . . .", you say?'

'Yes, my lady, just one side. Left the other one intact.'

'Hmm,' she said. 'I suppose he's telling Fishy?'

'He is, my lady.'

'It won't make him feel any better, I don't suppose. He's been busy blaming himself, but blaming someone else won't necessarily help.'

As she spoke, Lord Riddlethorpe and Mr Waterford rose from their armchairs and followed Morgan out, presumably to inspect the damage for themselves. Harry took note of the comings and goings and excused himself from his losing conversational battle. He came over to join his sister and me.

'News?' he said.

'Someone sabotaged the brakes,' said Lady Hardcastle.

'Good lord,' he said. 'So someone killed poor old Dawkins. Why?'

'Why, indeed?' said Lady Hardcastle. 'Quite cunningly done, too.'

He looked at me quizzically.

'Whoever it was only disabled the brake on one side,' I said. 'The way Morgan explained it to me, it wouldn't have made much difference to anyone driving at normal speeds – bringing the motor car up to the track, for instance. But once a driver like Ellis Dawkins was at the wheel, taking the motor to its limits as he tried to see what it could do, only having half the brakes he thought he did could lead to disaster.'

'As it did,' said Harry thoughtfully. 'As it so very did.'

'Does he know when it happened?' said Lady Hardcastle.

'It could have been any time from yesterday afternoon, when he checked all three motor cars for the party, and this morning, when he took them all up to the starting line. They were in the coach house, but they weren't locked up, and the house was full of guests until one this morning.'

'So it could have been anyone,' she said.

'Anyone who knew enough about motor cars to know how to cut the brakes,' said Harry.

'Well, quite,' said Lady Hardcastle. 'That must narrow the field quite a bit.'

'You'd think so, my lady,' I said. 'But once you've taken a good look at the working parts of a motor car, it's not terribly difficult to work out how to cause them mischief.'

'Well, I certainly couldn't do it,' said Harry.

'You have trouble understanding how to fill a fountain pen, darling,' she said. 'But you're a special class of mechanical duffer. You always were.' She patted his arm affectionately. 'But apart from you, any number of people could have worked out how to sabotage the brakes. In my imagination, they're not wholly unlike the brakes on a bicycle, and anyone could do it. In fact, didn't I once do that to your bike, Harry?'

'You did,' he said with a smile. 'Crashed into the fish pond.'

'I remember it well,' she said. 'So we're back to everyone at the party, and everyone in the house.'

'Except Mr Featherston-huff,' I said.

'Yes,' she said, patting his arm again. 'Everyone except Harry.'

'I never thought I'd be so glad to be a bit of a duffer,' he said.

'You have other strengths, sir,' I said.

'Of course you do, dear,' said Lady Hardcastle.

He looked at us expectantly.

'Give us a moment,' she said. 'I'm sure we'll think of something.'

He harrumphed. 'I'm going to join the *real* ladies,' he said, and wandered back to his seat.

Lady Hardcastle hopped up from the window seat. 'Come, servant,' she said. 'We need to do some serious pondering, and I'd rather not be overheard.'

I followed her out of the library and up the stairs to her room.

❖ ❖ ❖

'Eyes and ears, Flo,' said Lady Hardcastle as I shut the bedroom door behind us. 'You need to be my eyes and ears.'

'Of course, my lady,' I said. 'Always ready for that sort of thing, you know me.'

'I do, I do. The thing is, though . . .' She paused. 'The thing is, I'm going to have to impose a little. I know we're treating this as a break, and under any other circumstances I'd hate to have to ask . . .'

'But you'd like me to get friendly with the servants and perhaps pitch in with a little work?'

'In a nutshell. Do you mind awfully? It would be an absolute boon to have another pair of ears hovering about at mealtimes, for instance. And there's always juicy gossip around the servants' hall in places like this.'

'I wouldn't mind at all, my lady. To tell the truth, I've had about as much of a break as I can stand – a mission would liven things up nicely.'

'Do you think you can swing it without arousing too much suspicion?'

'I'm sure people will be suspicious, my lady. Your reputation as a snooper precedes you, and for some reason I seem to have been tarred with the same brush. I'm not convinced that anyone in the household – family, staff, or guests – would expect you not to show at least some

95

curiosity in a case like this, but . . . Well, the thing is, we return to the reason you recruited me into your shady underworld in the first place: servants are invisible. There'll be a ripple of curiosity and suspicion at first, I don't doubt, but it won't take long before I'm just part of the furniture again.'

'You're never that, dear, but you do have an undeniable knack for blending in. How shall you approach the matter? Would you like me to have a discreet word with Fishy?'

'I don't think so, my lady. I think telling Mr Spinney part of the truth – that I'm more than a little bored and would welcome having something to do – would be more than enough to clinch the deal. Staff are always suspicious of strangers, but I've never known a brigade of servants who wouldn't welcome an extra pair of hands.'

'A "brigade",' she said with a slight chuckle. 'Is that really the collective word for servants?'

'Probably not,' I conceded. 'But one does have a "*brigade de cuisine*". It's probably "staff", or something mundane and downtrodden.'

'An obsequience of servants?' she suggested. 'A toadying?'

'It'll be a "revolution" of servants one day,' I said darkly.

'I don't doubt it for a moment,' she said. 'But in the meantime, you're comfortable with the idea of inveigling your way into their ranks and making sure you get to serve at High Table?'

'Leave it to me, my lady,' I said. 'I'm a mistress of inveigling when I'm pressed.'

'Indeed you are. Then off you trot. Inveigle away.'

'Right you are, my lady,' I said, turning for the door. 'Do you need anything?'

'I wouldn't say no to a cup of tea, if there's one going. And perhaps some cake?'

'I'll see what I can do.'

◆ ◆ ◆

Below stairs, the day's work had all but ceased as everyone gathered round poor Morgan and bombarded him with questions. He caught my eye as I entered the room, and looked pleadingly at me for rescue. One of the housemaids noticed his glance and turned towards me, nudging her friend. Within moments I, too, was besieged by chattering servants, clamouring not just for news of the crash, but for some indication of what his lordship and his guests were thinking, saying, and doing.

Under most circumstances, I'm not easily intimidated, but with so many people asking so many questions, and with me being so keen to stay on the right side of them so as to put myself into a better position to gain their trust and to work with them, I found myself a little overwhelmed. Almost all the staff were taller than me, and with nearly a dozen of them clustered around me, I felt as though I were at the bottom of a well.

I was struggling to answer them as best I could, and I'd almost regained control of the situation, but I confess to being rather relieved when Mr Spinney's loud, clear voice firmly said, 'That's quite enough now, ladies and gentlemen, thank you. Get back to your work and we can harangue Miss Armstrong again later.'

There were mutters and sighs from the assembled staff, and I shrugged and smiled as if to say, 'What can you do, eh? Tch. Bossy old Mr Spinney spoiling our fun,' but they quickly and obediently dispersed, despite their obvious reluctance.

When the room had cleared – even Morgan had taken the opportunity to escape – Mr Spinney turned to leave and bade me follow him. He led me along a short corridor I'd not taken before and through the door at the end into what turned out to be his own rooms. His office-cum-sitting room was cosily appointed. There were two overstuffed armchairs beside the small fireplace, and a modest bookcase in the corner. Against one wall there was a sturdy oaken desk, upon which sat a mechanical decanting cradle.

He invited me to sit in one of the armchairs.

'Please accept my apologies,' he said, settling into the other chair. 'You shouldn't have had to endure that.'

'Really, Mr Spinney, it was nothing. But thank you for your concern.'

'Thank you. I . . .' He paused, looking oddly uncomfortable, and not just because of the way he was sitting.

'Is something else the matter, Mr Spinney?' I said.

'It's really a little awkward,' he said.

'Come now,' I said. 'It can't be as bad as all that.'

'I'm reluctant to impose.'

'Is there something I can do?' I asked. 'I'm more than happy to help in whatever way I can.'

'You're most kind, Miss Armstrong, but we have strict standards at Codrington concerning the treatment of our guests and their servants. We endeavour to make everyone's stay as comfortable as possible, no matter their station in life. "Do unto others . . .", as the Good Lord said. One never knows when one might be a guest in someone else's home and be grateful of a warm and comfortable welcome.'

I nodded and smiled.

'And so, you see, we make it a rule never to ask anything unreasonable of those to whom we have extended our hospitality.'

'What would you like me to do?' I asked, trying to save the poor chap from having to dance around the subject any longer than he really needed to. 'I'm entirely at your disposal.'

'For his lordship's sake, we must find out who was responsible for the terrible death of poor Mr Dawkins. And for his lordship's sake, we must also avoid a scandal. I wonder . . .'

'If Lady Hardcastle and I would be willing to employ our snooping skills to get to the bottom of things without involving the local blue-bottles? We are nationally famous busybodies by now, after all.'

'Well, I . . . er . . .' he stammered.

'I'm so sorry, Mr Spinney, I mustn't tease. I should be glad to help, and I'm certain Lady Hardcastle shall be more than willing, too. Lord Riddlethorpe is one of her brother's oldest friends, after all.'

'Are you sure?' he asked, with obvious relief. 'You really don't mind?'

'Of course not,' I said kindly. 'It will be . . .' – I was about to say 'fun', but I stopped myself in time; it would never do to suggest that the investigation of murder was fun – '. . . satisfying . . . to bring the culprit to book.'

'To book?' he said with slight alarm. 'I was rather hoping we might deal with this without involving the courts. We must avoid a scandal at all costs.'

'I'm afraid I can't promise that,' I said. 'We might play fast and loose with the law on occasion, but we never break it.' This last was something of a white lie – we had broken the laws of many lands in the pursuit of our former employment as agents of the Crown, but he didn't need to know that. 'If we can resolve matters to everyone's satisfaction, however, while avoiding both scandal and the breaking of important laws, then we shall.'

'That's all I have a right to ask,' he said at length.

'Very well, then,' I said with a smile. 'Did you have anything specific in mind? Any ways in which you thought we might be better able to investigate things?'

'Well,' he said slowly. 'That's where we come to another rather presumptuous suggestion. I rather thought that if you were to spend more time below stairs, you might inveigle yourself into the confidence of the staff, and it would also grant you many opportunities to wander the house and observe the guests.'

It was all I could do not to laugh. 'What a thoroughly splendid idea,' I said. 'But why the staff? Do you have any suspects already?'

'One would hate to think that anyone on his lordship's staff would do anything so black-hearted as to kill Mr Dawkins,' he said gravely.

'But . . . well . . . for all my efforts, Evan Gudger shows no signs of mending his ways.'

'But he's just a headstrong young lad,' I said, 'testing how far he can push the rules.'

'I do hope so. And then there's Morgan Coleman. He's an ambitious young man.'

'Surely you don't think his ambition would push him to murder?' I said.

'Again, I do hope not. But that makes it all the more important that you be free to investigate, to observe, to question. You have the power to free these men from suspicion as soon as you catch the real culprit.'

'You make a good case,' I said. 'How shall we explain my sudden enthusiasm for work when I've spent the past couple of days conspicuously avoiding you all and idling in my room?'

He thought for a moment. 'Perhaps we might say that you have grown bored of indolence and would welcome some honest labour to keep your mind from dwelling on the tragedy?'

'You're a cunning and clever man, Mr Spinney. I shall leave it to you to introduce the idea to the others.'

Chapter Seven

Mr Spinney had worked his leadership magic upon the troops, and I had slipped into service with the staff without fuss or fanfare. I wasn't at all sure I was completely trusted, but as I had said to Lady Hardcastle earlier, no one ever turns down the offer of an extra pair of hands below stairs, so I wasn't going to be kicked out any time soon. I was also regarded as a potentially valuable source of gossip, which I think was the thing that really tipped the balance in my favour.

I had brought my best uniform 'just in case', and by the time dinner was served, I was shipshape and Bristol fashion and ready to play my part at dinner. I had helped the footmen with their preparations, and joined them in serving dinner. It most definitely wasn't the done thing for a lady's maid to be serving at table, but with guests for dinner and with Evan otherwise engaged – serving as valet to both Mr Waterford and Herr Kovacs – no one was going to refuse my offer of help.

Despite the shocking events of the afternoon, all the guests had assembled for pre-prandial drinks in the library, and the mood by the time they sat to eat was respectfully muted, but not sombre. Lord

Riddlethorpe was quietest of all, but even he was a great deal more buoyant than he had been earlier in the afternoon.

Mr Spinney's carefully thought-out seating plan had been completely ignored. The guests had simply seated themselves in the order in which they arrived in the dining room when dinner was announced, and this, to Mr Spinney's evident disapproval, meant that the ladies were all on one side of the long dining table and the gentlemen on the other. Lady Hardcastle sat at one end, with Helen Titmus, Lady Lavinia, and Rosamund Beddows to her left. On the opposite side were Lord Riddlethorpe, Viktor Kovacs, Harry, Montague Waterford, and an elderly gentleman whom I assumed to be Lord Riddlethorpe's Uncle Algy.

The table had been set with a selection of *hors d'oeuvres* on platters along the centre of the table, to which the diners helped themselves as they settled down. The sight of caviar and other delicate savouries seemed to be just what they all needed, and conversations sparked immediately up and down the table.

As the gigantic soup tureen arrived, spirits began to rise still further. I gathered from a whispered comment from one of the footmen that Mr Spinney was still a little grumpy as he coordinated the delivery of the dishes from the servants' hall, but up here in the dining room things were, if not actually jolly, at least pleasingly convivial. Mrs Ruddle had excelled herself. Everything looked and smelled delicious, and from the reactions of the diners, I assumed that the soup, at least, tasted as good as it looked.

With the soup course placed upon the table, we servants positioned ourselves around the edges of the room, ready to serve, but discreetly invisible. I could never work out whether people forgot we were there, or just didn't care enough to imagine that we mattered, but it happened in houses all over the country. Once we'd put the food in front of them and stepped away, it was as though we didn't exist. Some servants resented it (in private, at least) but I found it fascinating and sometimes extremely useful – when they felt as though there was no one there to hear them, the upper classes could often be wonderfully indiscreet.

I'm certain that one day some clever scientist will work out how we do it, but I find it's possible to focus on individual speakers in the hub-bub of dinner conversations. I was listening to Mrs Beddows complaining about the treatment she'd received at a dressmaker's in Kensington, when my attention was suddenly grabbed by an urgent, half-whispered comment from Herr Kovacs to Lord Riddlethorpe.

'All I am saying, my friend, is that the offer is there. In the light of . . . the recent events, I should be willing to discuss . . .'

I was unable to make out exactly what it was that Herr Kovacs was willing to discuss because his hushed voice was suddenly drowned out by Lady Lavinia.

'Really, Uncle Algy! You're incorrigible.'

I turned to look farther down the table and saw Uncle Algy giggling like a naughty schoolboy as he sipped his soup. Mrs Beddows was laughing heartily – the first time I had seen her express any emotion other than disdain, displeasure, or disapproval since her arrival – while Lady Hardcastle attempted to conceal her own laughter behind her wine glass.

'Not at the dinner table, you think?' said the old gentleman, still twinkling.

'Not even at the dinner table in a brothel, Uncle Algy,' said Lady Lavinia, which made Mrs Beddows laugh even more.

'I once had the most marvellous dinner in a brothel,' said Uncle Algy. 'I remember there was this one gal, Spanish I think she was, and she could—'

'Algy!' said Lady Lavinia sternly. 'No!'

He giggled again and scooped up another spoonful of soup. 'Don't worry, m'dear,' he said once the mouthful was safely swallowed. 'Young Rosamund here can look after herself. If I should chance to offend her,

I'm sure she'll give me what for. Told that Dawkins fella where to get off, eh?'

'What are you talking about, Uncle?' said Lady Lavinia.

'Last night. At the party,' persisted the old man. 'Damn near slapped the poor fella. That's when I tried to get a game of St Uguzo's Holy Cheese going. Lighten the atmosphere, what? Never saw what happened after that – young Edmond gave me my marching orders. No fun for Uncle Algy. No fun . . .' His voice trailed wistfully away, and he returned to the last few mouthfuls of his soup.

'You never said anything about any of this, Roz,' said Lady Lavinia.

'Didn't seem worth the bother,' said Mrs Beddows coldly. 'The oily tick said something vulgar, and I put him in his place.'

'Vulgar, dear?' asked Lady Lavinia.

'Suggestive,' said Mrs Beddows. 'Lewd. I told him I'm a married woman and he ought to mind his manners or . . .'

'Or what, dear?' said Lady Lavinia with growing concern.

'He never found out,' said Mrs Beddows. 'That was when Uncle Algy tried to organize his impromptu entertainment.'

'But Roz, darling, you—'

My attention was pulled sharply away from the conversation by a nudge from the young footman standing next to me as he alerted me to the signal from Lord Riddlethorpe that it was time to clear the soup course and prepare the way for the fish.

And then we prepared the way for the sorbet.

And the salad.

And the game pie.

And the puddings.

And finally, the coffee cups were cleared and the port decanter emerged, along with an enormous platter of cheeses. Lady Lavinia stood and said, 'Well now, ladies, there aren't very many traditions of which I approve, particularly since most of them seem to be aimed squarely at spoiling my fun, but I do rather think that there's one we ought to maintain. Let's withdraw to the library and leave the boys to . . . Actually, I've never been quite certain what it is we're leaving them to, but I'm convinced that we have more fun without them. Library. Cognac. Belgian *chocolat. Allons-y!*'

And with that, the other three ladies stood, dropped their napkins on the table, and trooped out. I caught Lady Hardcastle's eye, and with a slight tilt of her head, she indicated that I should follow.

I arrived in the library some minutes later, having taken the long way round via the kitchen. There I had prepared a fresh pot of coffee and had snaffled a selection of Mrs Ruddle's splendid-looking *petits-fours*, just in case the promised Belgian chocolate proved insufficient for their appetite for sweetmeats.

I placed the tray on the low table around which the four ladies sat in easy chairs. There was a small amount of fiddle-faddling while I rearranged the brandy decanter and glasses to accommodate the fresh coffee, but they dutifully ignored me, and their conversation continued uninterrupted. I withdrew, and divided my attention between the contents of the bookshelves and the chatter of the ladies as I waited patiently and invisibly in a shadowy corner of the large room.

Miss Titmus had been quite quiet for most of the evening. But she had already exuberantly sampled some of the finer vintages from Lord Riddlethorpe's cellar, and in this more intimate group of close friends, she was gaining in confidence and volubility. She had begun eagerly and earnestly questioning Lady Hardcastle about her life in China, Burma, India, and the palaces of Europe. Lady Hardcastle, never one to hide her light under a bushel when there was an attentive audience, was happy to oblige with tales of intrigue, espionage, and skulduggery, at least half of which were at least half true.

Miss Titmus hung on her every word, mouth agape, and actually shrieked at the end of a story that had seen the pair of us evading arrest by the secret police of an unfriendly European power while disguised as sailors.

'Oh my goodness!' she said, clutching her hand to her mouth. 'You didn't! No, really. Did you? You didn't. Goodness!'

Mrs Beddows broke off from leafing through a magazine to shoot a withering glance at her old friend.

'Really, Titmouse, do calm down. She's teasing you. Of course she didn't. Real people don't do such things. Honestly, you can be such a credulous chump sometimes.'

'Steady on, Roz,' said Lady Lavinia, putting a hand on Mrs Beddows's arm. 'I'd not be so quick to judge if I were you. Edmond has known Emily's brother for simply aeons, and he always hinted that there was more to his little sister than met the eye.' She paused and looked around the room. 'I say, Miss Armstrong. What are you doing lurking over there? Come and join us for a moment.'

I gave up my perusal of the pleasingly eclectic collection of books, and moved across the room to stand behind Lady Hardcastle's chair.

Lady Lavinia looked up at me from across the small table. 'Your mistress has been spinning quite a yarn over here. What's your version of events? Can you corroborate any of it?'

'Of course she can,' said Mrs Beddows dismissively. 'She's her maid. It's more than her job's worth to contradict her meal ticket.'

'Really, Roz,' said Lady Lavinia with increasing exasperation. 'Must you be so beastly *all* the time?'

As was so often the case in public, I found myself in something of an awkward position. While the essence of the tale was true, most of the details were not. But, of course, I didn't want to give Mrs Beddows the satisfaction of hearing me point this out. We *had* been abusing the hospitality of a foreign government by poking our noses into their affairs. However, their vaunted 'secret police' had been a corrupt shower of indolent duffers, more interested in feathering their own nests than in protecting state secrets. In fact, the danger had come from a gang of local smugglers who had decided that our snooping was a threat to their collective livelihoods. They had resolved to remove that threat by shuffling us, discreetly but permanently, from this mortal coil. We had escaped disguised not as sailors, but as policemen, which I always felt made for a much more exciting story. Lady Hardcastle steadfastly refused to remember this part, though, having honed her version of events over many retellings into a tale to make ladies shriek. In less belligerent company, I might have allowed myself some sport by correcting her many factual errors, but under the circumstances I felt disinclined to undermine her.

'The events unfolded much as Lady Hardcastle has explained them,' I said. 'If anything, she has understated both the danger we found ourselves in and the ingenuity of our escape.'

Put that in your pipe and smoke it, I thought. That should cover the 'she got everything wrong but it's true nonetheless' side of things without fibbing and, more crucially, without leaving an opening for Mrs Beddows to bully Miss Titmus any further.

'Ha!' said Lady Lavinia triumphantly. 'I told you not to be so hasty, Roz. I say, would it make you frightfully uncomfortable to pull up a chair and join us, Miss Armstrong? I'm sure you have a wealth of stories to tell, too.'

'Oh, do,' said Miss Titmus enthusiastically.

Mrs Beddows said nothing, and gave her attention to a minute examination of one of the seams of her glove.

'Looks like you're on, Flo,' said Lady Hardcastle. 'Pull up a pew and settle in.' She shuffled her own chair to one side to make room for me between herself and Miss Titmus.

'Splendid,' said Lady Lavinia. 'Would you care for a brandy?'

'Thank you, my lady, I should like that very much,' I said. I helped myself to a glass before hefting another comfortable chair into the circle.

And then the interrogation began. Lady Hardcastle and I faced an onslaught of questions from Lady Lavinia and Miss Titmus that might ordinarily have been uncomfortable. But it was accompanied by such enthusiasm, such glee, so many 'ooh's, 'ahh's, and 'oh, my goodness's, that it was impossible not to get swept along by it all. Nearly impossible. Mrs Beddows, though careful not to be rude, seemed to be working hard to maintain an air of unimpressed aloofness so that we might be certain that she was above such shenanigans.

Over the course of the next hour, we gave them the edited high-lights of our lives of public service, starting with Lady Hardcastle's recruitment while at Cambridge. We moved on through her espio-nage exploits while on foreign postings with her husband, Sir Roderick – while the authorities kept a close eye on the visiting diplomat, his socialite wife was free to snoop unobserved. I had travelled with them to Shanghai as her lady's maid, but I had been recruited as her assistant while they were there. We shared tales of a few of the more thrilling adventures we'd had before the horror of Sir Roderick's murder forced us to flee. We told them more of China, of Burma, of India, and of the backstreets of London, Paris, Vienna, and Berlin.

By the time we brought them to the present day, by way of murders, missing trophies, and haunted public houses, I thought Miss Titmus might burst. I'm not certain I've heard anyone say 'Golly!' quite so many times before or since.

'No wonder you two seem more like chums,' she said, once she had caught her breath. 'What lives you've led.'

'What lives, indeed,' said Mrs Beddows sardonically.

Lady Hardcastle was undaunted (or oblivious – it can be hard to tell after she's had a glass or two) and chose instead to redirect the con-versation towards the three friends. 'And now you know all about us,' she said, 'but we know so little of you. I mean, take you for instance, Lavinia. I'm ashamed to say that I didn't even know you existed until the other day.'

Lady Lavinia laughed. 'Surely not.'

'On my honour,' said Lady Hardcastle. 'Harry has known Fishy for twenty years or more – heavens, *I've* known Fishy for twenty years or more – but neither of them ever mentioned that he had a sister.'

'Brothers, eh?' said Lady Lavinia. 'Useless articles.'

'Quite so, dear. So tell all. How did you three meet?'

'We were at school together,' said Miss Titmus eagerly. 'Weren't we, girls?'

'We were,' said Lady Lavinia.

'I dreamed of being allowed to go to school,' said Lady Hardcastle. 'I was so jealous of Harry when he went away. You must have been among the first.'

'Pioneers,' said Lady Lavinia with a laugh. 'That was us. But I wouldn't be too envious if I were you. I suspect you and your governess had a much less . . . testing time of it.'

'I'm not sure my string of increasingly exasperated governesses would agree, dear. Was it awful? Tom Brown in petticoats?'

'All that and more besides,' said Lady Lavinia. 'But we survived. Got through it together, didn't we, girls?'

'Bonds were forged,' drawled Mrs Beddows.

'I, for one, am jolly glad they were,' said Miss Titmus. 'I don't know what I'd do without you two.'

'Were there midnight feasts and japes and pranks?' asked Lady Hardcastle.

'And beatings and cold baths and cross-country runs,' said Mrs Beddows.

'Oh, Roz, you old surly-boots,' chided Miss Titmus. 'We had plenty of fun.'

'Did we? I must have forgotten.'

'Take no notice of Roz,' said Lady Lavinia. 'She likes to portray herself as some manner of ice queen, immune from the petty pleasures of mere mortals, but she's a poppet really.'

Mrs Beddows gave an ironic smile.

'Oh, oh, Jake, do you have that photograph of us?' asked Miss Titmus excitedly.

'I really don't know,' said Lady Lavinia. 'If it's here at all, it will be on the piano in the drawing room.'

'Would you mind if we showed it to Emily?'

'If you can find it, we shall endure the embarrassment. I'm sure Emily likes a chuckle.'

Miss Titmus scampered off in search of the photograph.

◆　◆　◆

The next few minutes weren't exactly awkward, but neither were they the most comfortable of my life. Lady Lavinia tried gamely to keep the cheerful chatter going, and Lady Hardcastle joined in with her customary effortless charm, but Mrs Beddows just stared into her brandy glass, saying nothing and looking like she'd rather be in any other company but ours.

It was something of a relief when Miss Titmus clattered back into the room clutching a photograph in a silver frame. She was not alone.

'So this is where you've been hiding,' said Lord Riddlethorpe as he followed her in. 'Come on, chaps, they're in here.'

Harry, Mr Waterford, Herr Kovacs, and Uncle Algy meandered into the library and began moving chairs to join our group.

'Come on, girls,' said Lord Riddlethorpe, 'budge up. Make room there.'

We shuffled our chairs to accommodate the gentlemen, who had brought glasses with them and were helping themselves to brandy as they settled down.

'We thought you'd all gone off to bed,' said Lord Riddlethorpe. 'We were waiting for you in the drawing room.'

'You duffer,' said his sister. 'I told you we were coming in here.'

'You say that as though you imagine I might listen to anything you say.'

'That's scarcely my problem, is it? We were sitting in here all along, having a chinwag.'

'Us too,' he said. 'But in the drawing room. We could have wagged our chins together. I so seldom see you these days.'

'Poor Fishy,' she said. 'But you'd have been talking about business or motor cars or some such inconsequential drivel, and we had much more important things to discuss.'

Mrs Beddows snorted so forcefully that it might have been possible to imagine that a horse had strayed into the library.

'I bet I can guess what the "important things" were,' said Harry, looking at his own sister. 'I'd wager Emily has been yarning.'

'A little,' said Lady Hardcastle, poking out her tongue. 'But that was ages ago. We've moved on to talking about school. Well, the ladies have. I wasn't lucky enough to go to school, unlike other members of my family.'

'I've told you, Emily, you really didn't miss much,' said Lady Lavinia. 'Show her the photo, Helen. Let her see for herself what she was spared.'

Miss Titmus presented the framed photograph as though it were an object of worship, while Lady Hardcastle and I craned to get a better look. Around a dozen girls in dark skirts and white blouses were arranged around a large trophy. Those in the front were sitting cross-legged with cricket bats across their knees.

Lady Hardcastle laughed. 'You were in the school cricket team?' she asked delightedly.

'Evanshaw's School for Girls First XI, 1882,' said Miss Titmus proudly. 'Winners of the Japheth Fothersdyke Memorial Trophy.'

'Japheth Fothersdyke, eh?' said Lady Hardcastle. 'That well-known . . . ?'

'A deceased local mill owner,' said Mrs Beddows. 'It seems our parents all decided that London would be too decadently metropolitan, Geneva too exotic, Paris too frivolous . . . and so they packed us off to some godforsaken granite fortress on the Yorkshire Moors, home of dark satanic mills and their long-dead, dark satanic owners.'

'It was sandstone, dear,' said Lady Lavinia. 'And it was a former manor house, not a fortress. And Japheth Fothersdyke was a fair-haired church warden.'

'Bleak, forbidding, and bally awful,' said Mrs Beddows.

'Be that as it may,' continued Lady Lavinia, 'much emphasis was placed by Mr and Mrs Evanshaw upon the value of healthy outdoor pursuits, among which was cricket, at which, by lucky chance, we excelled.'

'Best days of my life,' said Miss Titmus wistfully.

'Doesn't say a great deal for the rest of your life,' said Mrs Beddows.

Lady Hardcastle produced her lorgnette and peered more closely at the photograph. 'Let me see, then,' she said. 'What do you reckon, Flo? Who's who?'

I leaned in and studied the faces. To me, they just looked like a crowd of anonymous posh schoolgirls, flushed faces padded with varying amounts of puppy fat. They wore their hair in the same style, and there seemed little to distinguish one from another, but Lady Hardcastle, as always, was able to see more than I.

'That's you, Lavinia,' she said, pointing to a fair-haired girl at the back. 'And Roz is next to you.' She pointed again. 'And . . . Oh, that one's Helen,' she said, triumphantly pointing at a third, plump, mousey-looking girl.

'Spot on,' said Miss Titmus with a smile. 'You have a good eye for faces.'

'It makes her quite the portrait artist,' said Harry. 'She has a wonderful way of seeing the essence of a chap. You should get her to sketch you before she goes.'

'Oh, would you, Emily?' said Miss Titmus. 'And I shall take photographs of you all. We can show them together.'

'Wonderful,' said Lady Hardcastle. 'Let's do that. And who's this girl between you and Lavinia? She looks a formidable sportswoman.'

We all looked more closely at the photograph. Sure enough, between Miss Titmus and Lady Lavinia stood a rather beautiful girl with dark hair and the most beguiling eyes. For an uncomfortable while, no answer came.

'That's Katy Burkinshaw,' offered Miss Titmus eventually. 'She—'

'That's a story for another time, dear,' interrupted Lady Lavinia. She took the photograph from Lady Hardcastle and passed it to Mr Waterford. 'What do you think, Monty? Weren't we just utterly utter?'

He laughed. 'A formidable-looking team. What say you, Viktor? Do you think we could have taken them on?'

Herr Kovacs took the photo and examined it closely. 'I'm not sure I could "take anyone on" at cricket, old chap. It's not a game quite so beloved by the mighty Austro-Hungarian Empire. To tell the truth, I'm a little surprised to find girls playing the game. I thought it was a sport for boys and men?'

'It's fallen out of favour with the ladies of late,' said Miss Titmus, 'but it was all the rage in the eighties. I wish we could bring it back. Did you play, Emily?'

'I'm afraid not, dear,' said Lady Hardcastle. 'A little tennis, perhaps, and I've been dragged into more than one game of croquet, but only socially.'

'Oh,' said Miss Titmus deflatedly. 'What about you, Miss Armstrong?'

'Not me,' I said. 'I was more of a rugby girl.'

'Good lord!' said Lord Riddlethorpe. 'Rugger? Really?'

'Really,' I said with a smile. 'Fastest wing three-quarter in the district, me.'

Lord Riddlethorpe laughed. 'Well I never. But you're so tiny.'

'Don't let that fool you,' said Harry. 'Swift and deadly, our Flo. I'd not want to try to take her on if she were coming at me at pace.'

'They played ladies rugby in . . . Where was it . . . Aberdare?' said Mr Waterford.

'No, I played on the boys' team until they banned me,' I said.

The men laughed.

'Too good for them, eh?' said Lord Riddlethorpe.

'They claimed it was because the laws didn't allow girls to play,' I said. 'But I consoled myself by choosing to believe your explanation.'

They all laughed again.

Herr Kovacs was still scrutinizing the photograph.

'Don't hog it, Viktor,' said Lord Riddlethorpe. 'Let everyone have a bat.'

Almost reluctantly, Herr Kovacs relinquished the photograph and let the other gentlemen have a look. Mr Waterford smiled as he flicked his gaze between the photograph and the grown-up versions of the girls sitting before him, but when it was Harry's turn, he lingered longer on the face of the present-day Lady Lavinia, and only reluctantly gave up the photograph and returned to the conversation.

'Now that we're all together, and now that we three have been thoroughly embarrassed by images of the gawky girls we once were,' said Lady Lavinia as she handed the photograph back to Miss Titmus, 'what say we play some games? It's been a wretched day, and our spirits are badly in need of lifting.'

'Exactly what I was saying, m'dear,' said Uncle Algy. 'St Uguzo's Holy Cheese, anyone?'

'No, Uncle Algy!' said Lady Lavinia firmly. 'Something much less bawdy, if you please.'

There followed a brief debate about which parlour game they should play. Between them, they knew a great many, and I decided that I shouldn't be missed if I were to leave them to it. It was one thing being invited to join in a conversation, but I felt I ought to spare everyone the embarrassment of having to try to accommodate me in one of their games. I whispered a quiet goodnight to Lady Hardcastle and slipped away unnoticed.

Chapter Eight

Next morning, Betty and I arose together and bimbled about, good-naturedly getting in each other's way as we washed and dressed.

'Did you see the body?' she asked as she brushed her hair. 'Poor Mr Dawkins, I mean?'

'Not closely,' I lied.

'I bet you've seen loads of bodies, though, haven't you? I mean, laid out all neat and tidy in a coffin is one thing, but out there in the world, all mangled and broken . . . It doesn't bear thinking about.'

For all that it didn't bear thinking about, she seemed to have given the matter considerable thought.

'I've seen my fair share,' I said. 'And it's never very pleasant.' I decided not to mention that a fair proportion of those whose bodies I had seen had died at my, or Lady Hardcastle's, hand.

She sighed. 'I've never done anything exciting,' she said sadly. 'Don't suppose I ever will, working for Mrs Beddows. She gets her fun from spreading gossip and being catty to her husband, which doesn't leave much for me to get involved in. You've been around the world.'

'If you hate it so much,' I said as kindly as I could, 'why not leave and find something else?'

'I probably should, shouldn't I? But it's always hard to take that first step, isn't it? Talking of which, I ought to take my first steps towards the kitchen. There'll be hell to pay if I'm not there with her tea a few seconds before she wakes up. You should have seen her yesterday morning.'

She sighed again, and with a final brush at her uniform to remove a stray thread, she set off to start her day.

I wasn't far behind, and we sat and chatted a little longer at the staff table, Betty hurriedly scoffing down a few mouthfuls of her own breakfast, while Patty prepared our trays.

'When you were little, what did you want to grow up to be?' I asked, sipping at some lukewarm tea.

'Rich,' she said.

'And how did you hope to achieve these riches?'

'I didn't want to *become* rich,' she said, spearing a sausage with her fork. 'I wanted to *be* rich. You see?'

'Not entirely, no.'

'I wasn't interested in getting money; I just wanted to have it. And I only wanted to have it so I didn't have to think about it no more. Money wasn't the important thing; it was never having to worry about it that I wanted. My ma and pa worked every hour, and we just about scraped by. They always quite liked what they did – she was a seamstress and he was a bricklayer – but they *had* to do it. They never had no time to call their own. They sold all their waking hours to someone else in return for a few bob to pay for a roof over our heads and food on the table. And they had to watch every farthing as it went out, 'less it run out on them. I dreamed of being able to do what I wanted with my time and never have to even think about where the next penny was coming from.'

'Isn't that what everyone wants?' I asked.

'Most folk, yeah,' she said. ''Cept the really rich ones. 'Less they inherited it, they must have spent all their days trying to work out how to get more money. They wasn't interested in *having* money; they was interested in *getting* money. See what I mean?'

'Almost,' I said. 'And what would you do with your time if you weren't selling it to someone else?'

'Not sure, really. That was always the problem. It's not that I don't want to work. It's not even that I don't want to work in service. I just . . . you know . . . sometimes . . .' She aggressively speared another sausage.

'Sometimes, yes,' I said.

'But you, you have a great life. You're busy; you've got an employer who respects you. You go places, do things. I heard you even took brandy with the guests last night.'

I laughed. 'News travels fast. Yes, the ladies invited me to sit with them while they idealized our exploits.'

'At least you have exploits to idealize. I'm not sure I've ever had an exploit. I got locked in a tool shed once by mistake, but the gardener let me out ten minutes later when he realized what he'd done. Not really the sort of story that gets you invited to sit down and take brandy with the ladies, is it?'

I laughed again. 'Come on, Nora-Never-Done-Nothing,' I said, standing up. 'Let's see what's keeping Patty with those trays, then we can get off and have some exploits.'

'Maybe you can . . .' she said glumly.

◆　◆　◆

To my immense surprise, Lady Hardcastle was once again already awake and sitting up in bed when I entered her room with the fully laden breakfast tray.

'Good heavens!' I said.

'What is it?' she asked in some alarm, looking up from her journal.

'You're awake, my lady.'

'Of course I'm awake, silly. It's . . . It's . . .'

'It's almost eight o'clock,' I said as I set the tray down on the writing desk.

'Oh,' she said, more surprised now than alarmed. 'Now I understand your consternation. It's not like me to be awake before eight at all. I wonder what it can be. The invigorating country air, perhaps?'

'We live in the country,' I said.

'Hmm, you have me there. In that case, I am at a loss,' she said, capping her pen and closing her journal. 'But wait. If you expected me to be still safely wrapped in the warm and loving arms of Morpheus, why are you here bearing such a substantial array of jentacular comestibles?'

'Ah . . . well . . . now . . . you see . . .' I began awkwardly. 'Wait a moment, my lady. "Jentacular comestibles"? Really? I despair sometimes.'

'Not bad, eh? But don't change the subject. What brings you here with breakfast nosh if I'm supposed to be asleep?'

'I wanted you to be awake. I thought we ought to confer before our day of investigation. If we were at home, we'd be sitting at the kitchen table together, planning and strategizing. I'm not sure the natives could cope with having me sitting at the breakfast table, so I brought its contents up to you.'

'Quite right – best not discomfit the natives,' she said. 'And we'll be wanting to talk about them anyway, so it's doubly important that they not be within earshot.' She indicated the tray. 'I take it some of that's for you?'

'That was the original plan, my lady,' I said, extending the tray's legs and placing it over her lap. 'But I know how you toffs like to gorge. It's all the rage nowadays. I'm beginning to wonder if I brought enough.'

'Hmm,' she said, tucking in. 'I'm sure we'll manage.'

I sat on the monstrosity of a bed, and did my bit to reduce the mountain of food.

'What are your thoughts, then, my lady?' I said after a while. 'Who do you fancy for the sabotage?'

She thought for a moment, then reached for her journal.

'In the absence of my beloved and much-derided crime board,' she said, 'I've been reduced to writing things in my journal like some sort of medieval peasant.'

She opened the book and leafed through it, trying to find the relevant page. Meanwhile, I tried not to point out how few medieval peasants would have had a leather-bound journal in which to record their musings. I had moved on to not reminding her how few medieval peasants would have been able to read and write in the first place, when she arrived at the notes she'd been seeking.

'Here we are,' she said. 'I've started from the assumption that it's someone among the household and their guests. If it should chance that none of them is involved, then we shall have to widen our search to the rest of the party guests. Although, actually, if we reach that point, then only a miracle would reveal the killer to us. There were dozens of people at the party, and by the time we've included coachmen, chauffeurs, and cabbies, there will be dozens more. If it's no one from the house, we're scuppered.'

'Sunk without trace,' I said.

'Quite. So I've made a list of everyone here. We begin with our host, Fishy.'

'I can't see it, my lady. It wouldn't make sense for Lord Riddlethorpe to sabotage one of his own motor cars. What would he gain from it?'

'That's what I thought, too,' she said. 'So we shall put a cross by Fishy's name for now. Then we have Jake. I can't see that she has any more motive than her brother.'

'Agreed,' I said.

'Roz? She's a startlingly unpleasant woman, but she strikes me as the sort who would have a great many imaginatively vicious ideas for settling scores before she resorted to something as crude as mechanical sabotage.'

'Possibly, my lady, but remember what Uncle Algy said: Mr Dawkins did say something "lewd" and "suggestive" to her at the party. If he offended her enough, she might have decided to take him down a peg or two by sabotaging his car.'

'Very well, we'll leave her as a possible. How about Helen?'

'"Titmouse"?' I said with a laugh. 'Hardly.'

'Sorry, dear, but if I can't drop Roz, you can't drop Helen. You know what they say about the quiet ones, and it strikes me she's probably got a lifetime's worth of bottled-up rage and resentment just waiting to burst out.'

'I'll grant you that. If I were her, I'd have bludgeoned Mrs Beddows to a gory death years ago, but why would that make her attack Mr Dawkins? Why would she sabotage his car?'

'Perhaps he rebuffed an advance from her just as Roz rebuffed him. Hell hath no fury, and all that. After a day of being belittled by her old "friend", perhaps he was the straw that passed through the eye of the camel's needle.'

'Perhaps, my lady,' I conceded. 'No cross for her, then. Next?'

'We move on to Fishy's friends now. Harry?'

'I think we can cross off your own brother.'

'It might have been a jape that went wrong,' she said. 'He's not a terribly practical fellow, after all. He might not have realized quite how dangerous his little trick was.'

'Possibly, but I should say that his ignorance of mechanical matters also makes it rather unlikely that he would have managed to work out how to sabotage the brakes in the first place.'

'Very well,' she said. 'To be truthful, I think he would have owned up by now if it were a joke that went wrong. Another cross for Harry, then. Monty?'

'Again, what would Mr Waterford have to gain from sabotaging one of his own racing team's motor cars and endangering the life of his main driver?'

'What if Number 3 were a prototype?' she said. 'What if it were one of Fishy's designs? Perhaps Monty wished to undermine it to promote his own design.'

'An intriguing possibility, my lady,' I said. 'Mr Waterford remains on the list, then.'

'And then there's Viktor Kovacs.'

'The evil Hungarian.'

'Well, quite,' she said. 'It does seem a trifle clichéd, doesn't it? Still, there's a reason that clichés become clichés.'

'He was talking to Lord Riddlethorpe at dinner last night, and it sounded as though he was offering to buy the racing team.'

'Really? I was down at the other end of the table listening to Jake trying to keep her Uncle Algy under control.'

'A losing battle, that one,' I said. 'I didn't hear the whole conversation, but Herr Kovacs mentioned an offer "in light of recent events", and that he'd be prepared to discuss something or other. I'm afraid that's the point at which Uncle Algy stepped over whatever line Lady Lavinia had drawn for him, and got a telling off. I couldn't hear the rest.'

'So you think Viktor might have sabotaged the motor car to destabilize his rival and make him ripe for a takeover? And if that didn't work, he'd eliminated the team's best driver.'

'Best driver?' I said. 'Wasn't Mr Dawkins in third place as they passed us?'

'My word, you're right. But everyone said he was an excellent driver. Perhaps there was something else wrong with the motor car after all.'

'Or perhaps it wasn't the new prototype?'

'Oh, lord, I don't know,' said Lady Hardcastle with no little exasperation. 'Cliché or not, I don't think we can take Viktor out of the running.'

'I take it we're not even going to consider Uncle Algy.'

'If the sabotage had been devised to make someone's trousers fall down or their skirts blow up, I would have that old rogue as my principal suspect,' she said with a chuckle. 'But I think he gets an automatic cross.'

I laughed. 'I agree,' I said. 'Though if I find out that any housemaids have been fondled, he should be top of the list. So that's everyone from above stairs?'

'I believe so, yes,' she said, putting her pen on to the tray. 'Below stairs . . . Well, I'm afraid that's rather within your purview. I'm embarrassed to say that I'm not at all certain who the runners and riders are within our host's household.'

'I can list the main ones for you, if you'd care to add them to your list.'

She picked up her pen once more. 'Say on, tiny one,' she said.

'There's Mr Spinney the butler. He's unusually affable and easygoing for a butler.'

'A little too perfect, you think? Something to hide?'

'No idea, my lady. Then there's the housekeeper, Mrs McLelland. I can't fathom her out at all. Polite and friendly, and yet at the same time oddly cold and distant. I'd like to know more about her.'

'Righto,' she said, making a note.

'The cook is the delightful Mrs Ruddle, and her maid is Patience, who prefers to be known as Patty. Lovely women. You'd think they were mother and daughter, the way they get along.'

'Perhaps they are,' suggested Lady Hardcastle.

'One never knows,' I said. 'Oh, Morgan the chauffeur – we can't forget him.'

'Well, no, we can't. But he was the one who pointed out the sabotage. Wouldn't he have tried to hide the deliberateness of it?'

'Perhaps, my lady. But it might be a cunning double-bluff.'

'Hmm,' she said, making more notes. 'We'll keep him in mind, but I have my doubts.'

'Very well,' I said. 'I've not met many of the others.'

'What about your pal Betty?'

'Oh, of course, yes. But she was in the room with me all night.'

'You're certain?'

'As certain as I can be, my lady,' I said. 'I'd been at the champagne and might have slept peacefully on if she'd got up in the night, but she'd been supping enthusiastically, too. I doubt she'd have been in a fit state to find her way to the stables, let alone track down a pair of wire cutters and find precisely the right place to employ them.'

'Good enough for me,' she said. 'Didn't they have a driver?'

'They did,' I said. 'Finlay. But he just dropped the ladies off and went back to London, so he wasn't even here.'

'Unless he sneaked back at dead of night and did the dirty deed. He'd know one end of a spanner from the other.'

'A weak point, badly made, my lady. Finlay Duggan shall remain unlisted.'

We sat a moment in thought.

'What was the name of that chap you said was a rum 'un?' said Lady Hardcastle after a while. 'You said he was "a handful", as I recall.'

'Oh, Evan Gudger,' I said. 'Footman of this parish, currently serving as guests' valet.'

'That's the chap. On the list?'

'Mischievous, rebellious, like as not a bit reckless. I'd say he was listworthy, yes, my lady.'

'Goodness,' she said as she wrote. 'It's quite a list, isn't it?'

'It is. And we've not covered half the staff.'

'Hmm,' she said, capping her pen and tapping it against her teeth. 'Well, we'll find out nothing more sitting here picking through the remnants of breakfast. Time to dress and start poking our noses into things, I think.'

'Righto, my lady,' I said, and stood to remove the tray from her lap.

◆ ◆ ◆

As we passed the open door of the library on our way to the front door, we saw Miss Titmus hunched over something at the large writing desk by one of the windows.

'What ho, Helen,' called Lady Hardcastle.

Miss Titmus looked round, slightly alarmed.

'Sorry, dear,' said Lady Hardcastle. 'Didn't mean to startle you. We're off for a stroll round the grounds. Care to join us?'

'Oh,' said Miss Titmus. 'Oh, yes. Thank you. That would be super. Just let me . . .'

She turned back to the desk, and I could see that she had been fiddling with her camera. She closed it with a snap, and brought the reassembled instrument with her as she joined us in the passage.

'You don't mind if I bring this?' she said, indicating the camera.

'Why on earth would we mind?' said Lady Hardcastle.

'To be honest, I'm not sure, but it does vex Roz so. She gets frightfully cross with me for carrying it about.'

'Well, neither of us is Roz, and I think it's a splendid little thing. I remember when cameras were great wooden boxes that arrived on the back of a cart with a team of six or seven men to operate them.'

Miss Titmus laughed. 'Oh, Emily, you do make me chuckle.'

'Glad to hear it, old thing,' said Lady Hardcastle. Taking Miss Titmus by the arm, she led us all out into the September sunshine.

We strolled around the formal garden that we'd seen from the terrace at the rear of the house. Despite having no practical gardening skills whatsoever, Lady Hardcastle's theoretical knowledge of flowers, herbs, shrubs, trees, bushes, mosses, weeds, lichens, and fungi seemed, to me at least, to be encyclopaedic. Such was her passion for matters botanical, she would occasionally break off mid-sentence to point out a plant, excitedly describing its origins, usually with plenty of references to the Latin names of its floral relatives. I was delighted to see that Miss Titmus was as nonplussed as I. Another town girl, clearly. But she made up for her lack of technical knowledge with an extraordinary enthusiasm for shape and colour. The pair of them made for very entertaining garden companions, even for someone like me who could barely tell a Passiflora from a park bench.

We stopped for a moment beside a bed of rose bushes, while Miss Titmus crouched before one particularly impressive specimen, apparently trying to capture its likeness with her camera.

'I know it's all the rage these days to photograph people,' she said as she stretched forwards to position herself more propitiously, 'but I do like to snap "things" when I can. You know, buildings, motor cars . . . flowers.' She finally stood. 'I just wish colour photography was more practical for the amateur. Wouldn't these look glorious in full colour?'

'It would be a treat, indeed,' said Lady Hardcastle. 'Is this new, all this photography lark?'

Miss Titmus looked at her curiously as we walked on. 'No, not really. I believe the first photographs were taken in the 1820s.'

Lady Hardcastle laughed. 'I'm so sorry, dear. It was a terribly badly worded question. I meant is it new to you? Have you been interested in photography for long?'

'Ohhh,' said Miss Titmus with a laugh. 'A couple of years. But I've been fascinated by the whole thing since . . . Well, since school, really. That photograph of the cricket team entranced me. I could scarcely believe that our images had been captured by that box – a moment frozen forever. It's quite magical, don't you think?'

'I rather think it is, when you put it like that,' said Lady Hardcastle. 'I dabble with moving pictures myself, you know.'

'Really?' said Miss Titmus. 'How marvellous.'

'You must come down and see us. I'm sure you'd enjoy the studio, even if our little village is a tad quiet.'

'I should absolutely love that. Do you process your own film? I'm about to turn the spare bedroom of my London flat into a darkroom, but it's a bit of a palaver. Until now, I've been imposing on a friendly professional photographer to do it for me. He's an old friend of my brother's.'

'I do it all at home,' said Lady Hardcastle. 'I've had a darkroom installed at one end of the studio. Do say you'll come.'

'I should be delighted. I sometimes think about taking it up professionally, you know? Portraiture and suchlike. I think it might be quite a hoot.'

'And why don't you?'

'Oh, don't be so silly. Whoever heard of a ninny like me doing something like that?'

'Hmm,' said Lady Hardcastle with a frown. As far as I'd been able to establish from all that I'd heard so far, the two ladies were very similar in age, but here on the freshly raked gravel of the garden path, Miss Titmus did indeed seem like a naive young girl when measured against my worldly-wise employer. 'If you want it, dear,' she continued, 'you should do it. I've never let the fear of people thinking me a ninny stop me from doing anything.'

'Good thing, too,' I said. 'Or you'd never have done anything at all.'

They both laughed. 'You're quite right, of course,' said Lady Hardcastle. 'I've come a cropper more times than I care to recall, but I carry on undaunted. I tell you what, I hereby commission you to come to Littleton Cotterell and photograph the house and the two ninnies who live there. Oh, and our beloved motor car. How about that? I shall pay your expenses and any fee you care to name. Then you shall be a professional and you'll have to go into business.'

Miss Titmus laughed again. 'We shall see,' she said. 'But perhaps you should take a look at some of my work before you make such an offer. I might be an absolute duffer, for all you know.'

'Hmm, I hadn't thought of that,' said Lady Hardcastle. 'I don't suppose . . .'

'As it happens, I always travel with an album of my favourites. I shall bring them down after lunch.'

Lady Hardcastle's eager agreement was cut short by a loud clattering some short distance away. We turned, and saw that a sizeable flock of doves had taken to the air.

'There's a dovecote as well,' said Lady Hardcastle. 'How lovely.'

'Wonderful birds,' said Miss Titmus. 'I've thought of getting some.'

Lady Hardcastle frowned. 'You have?'

'I have. Well, not doves, exactly. Homing pigeons.'

'Well I never. Would you race them?'

'Oh, no,' said Miss Titmus, becoming suddenly animated. 'I read an article in a photographic journal about a German chap who has designed a special harness and camera that he attaches to homing pigeons. They photograph whatever they fly over on the way home. Isn't that just utterly utter? I've got a copy of the magazine indoors. I'll show you later. That would set my photographic business apart, wouldn't it?'

Lady Hardcastle laughed. 'It would be a sin not to start a business like that. I say, you could photograph country houses from the air. I'm sure some of the more adventurous families would pay handsomely for the privilege.'

By now, we had left the formal garden and were walking around the edge of a rolling lawn, sticking close to the neatly trimmed hedge that formed the garden's outer border. From a little way ahead, we heard the sound of voices, then a woman's laugh. We came eventually to what might best be described as an 'alcove' cut into the hedge, where there sat a handsome Palladian stone bench. And upon the bench were Lady Lavinia and Harry, apparently deep in conversation.

'What ho, Harry,' said Lady Hardcastle breezily. 'And Jake, too. How are you both?'

'Passing well, sis, thank you. Anything we can do for you?'

'No dear, thank you,' she said.

'Well, don't let us detain you.'

'Righto, dear,' she said.

We carried on walking, holding our silence until we were out of earshot.

'About time, too,' said Lady Hardcastle when she was sure we couldn't be heard.

'What is?' asked Miss Titmus.

'Those two. You must have seen the way he's been looking at her these past couple of days.'

'No?' said both Miss Titmus and I together.

'Tch,' sighed Lady Hardcastle, and we strolled on.

Our walk eventually led us to the stable yard. The coach house doors were open, but we could see no sign of Morgan.

'Hello!' called Lady Hardcastle. 'Anyone about?'

There was no one about.

'Come on, ladies,' she said. 'Let's take a look at the scene of the crime.'

'The crime?' said Miss Titmus. 'Is this where it was done, do you think?'

'I can't think of a better place. The motor car was guaranteed to be here. It's out of the way. One can work in private. An ideal place for a spot of sabotage.'

'Gracious!' said Miss Titmus. 'Do you really think we ought? Shouldn't we leave things as they are? Isn't snoopery best left to the police?'

Lady Hardcastle laughed. 'Snoopery is our stock-in-trade, dear. As for the police, you heard what that frightful detective from Leicester said. It was a tragic accident and there's nothing else for him to do here.' She led the way through the open doors. 'I think it's our duty to have a bit of a poke about.'

We stood in the centre of the large coach house. The horse stalls had been removed to make way for workbenches. The three motor cars stood in line abreast, gleaming even in the dim light. The rightmost was horribly dented and scratched where it had struck the tree. Lady Hardcastle stood stock still for a few moments, looking keenly about.

'Is that a door over there in the gloom, Flo?' she said, pointing to the far corner of the stable. 'Be a dear and have a dekko for me, would you?'

Had we been alone, I might have invited her to look for herself if it were that important to her. We were in company, though, so I walked towards the indicated corner.

'It is a door,' said Miss Titmus just as I reached it. Again, I bit my tongue. Instead, I tried the handle. It was locked.

'It looks as though the lock is oiled and in regular use,' I said as I trudged back to the middle of the room.

'Do you know where it opens, Helen?' asked Lady Hardcastle.

'On the outside?' said Miss Titmus. 'Let me see . . . The kitchen garden, I think.'

'Easy to get to from the house, then. Someone who knew their way about could slip out here, snip the brake cable, and nip back indoors before anyone even knew they were gone.'

'Who knows their way about well enough to do that?' I asked.

'Everyone apart from us, I should think,' said Lady Hardcastle.

'Most of the party guests got lost on their way to the WC,' said Miss Titmus. 'But the staff would all know where the door is. And the family. Fishy's friends practically live down here, of course. I suppose I could have found my way down here. Roz, too.'

'Let's do your trick, Flo, of putting ourselves in the mind of the villain,' said Lady Hardcastle, walking purposefully towards the door.

Miss Titmus and I followed. Still I said nothing about my repeated walking of the length of the stable. I was thinking of nominating myself for a sainthood.

'She was absolutely marvellous, Helen dear,' she continued. 'We were trying to find a stolen emerald, you see. Flo had the simply cracking idea of standing in the room and imagining herself as the doer of the dastardly deed.'

We arrived back at the locked door and began looking around. Miss Titmus seemed excited, but clearly had no idea what was expected of her. Lady Hardcastle, as focused as ever, was concentrating on a minute examination of the workbench along the wall.

I, meanwhile, did as she had suggested. I was the dastardly saboteur. I had let myself into the stable through the side door. It was pitch black. I had a candle. I lit it. Good guess, Flo, I thought – there's some spilled wax on the workbench. I looked around. The motor cars were in a line. I wanted to cut the brakes. I went to the end of the . . .

'Why did the saboteur not disable the nearest motor car?' I said. 'He passed two perfectly nobbleable racers and snipped the brakes of the one farthest from the door.'

'He wanted to tamper with a particular vehicle?' suggested Lady Hardcastle.

'Seemingly,' I said. 'But why?'

'He knew who would be driving it?' said Miss Titmus tentatively.

'The race card!' said Lady Hardcastle and I together.

'Dawkins was going to be in Number 3,' I said.

'And Number 3 was at the end of the row,' said Lady Hardcastle.

I put myself back in the saboteur's shoes, and once more tried to imagine his actions. I could see the numbers painted on the sides of the motor cars. I found my target. Did I know exactly what I was going to do? Had I already decided on the brakes? I must have. I'd come down here with a key and a candle; it was unlikely that my plans stopped there.

So I needed a tool. I might have brought one with me, but I was on my way to a workshop. There were tools aplenty there. Why run the risk of being caught with something incriminating on my person when I could just lift something from the bench?

There was a row of hooks on the wall holding spanners, screwdrivers, and an assortment of other, well-kept tools. One hook was empty. So that was where I took my . . . my whatever-it-was. I imagined myself going to the motor car and getting down on my hands and knees. I couldn't see the cables. Flat on my belly. The brake cable. Cut. I stood. I'd forgotten where I'd taken the tool from. What to do? I dropped it and kicked it under the workbench. Better a lost tool than a tool out of place.

I got down on my hands and knees for real now. I felt about under the workbench. At first, nothing. Then my fingers brushed against something metallic. I managed to get hold of it. I got back to my feet.

'Pliers, my lady,' I said, holding up my treasure with my fingertips. 'I'd wager these are the murder weapon.'

'I say, Flo, well done,' said Lady Hardcastle.

'Yes, well done, you,' said Miss Titmus excitedly.

'Whoever it was would have been rather dusty,' I said. 'He'd have been flat on his belly to get to the brakes.'

'So we're looking for a grimy man who knows how to use a pair of pliers,' said Lady Hardcastle.

'One who had seen the race card you drew up at the party,' I said.

'And who wasn't afraid to kill someone to get what he wanted. We'd better get back to the house.'

Chapter Nine

We arrived back at the house in plenty of time to get Lady Hardcastle changed for lunch. It was a little early for the white, delicately embroidered tea gown we chose, but she declared that she wouldn't 'dashed well get changed again for tea so they'll have to lump it'.

I rushed to the attic to change into my indoor uniform so that I might report to the servants' hall for instructions. Lunches at Codrington Hall were informal, though, and so my services weren't required. Mr Spinney suggested I return later in the afternoon to help with tea, but gave me leave to disappear. There were a few things I needed to sort out for Lady Hardcastle, including a little mending, so I went up to her room.

Sitting alone at the window, expertly (if I do say so myself) repairing an unexplained (and, frankly, inexplicable) rip in one of Lady Hardcastle's evening gowns, I allowed my mind to wander. On Sunday, we had been packing our bags, anticipating a week of motor racing and jollity. Now it was Thursday, and we were up to our ankles in the unexpected. Again. A car had been sabotaged and a man was dead. We had no idea if his death was deliberate, or whether it was some sort of attempt to undermine Lord Riddlethorpe or his new motor racing team. Half the people in the house seemed to have a motive, almost everyone had an opportunity, and anyone who could find a pair of pliers in a darkened stable had the means.

A tiny, selfish part of me wished we could just pretend we didn't know that the crash was the result of malicious mischief and leave things alone. It would be wonderful to say our farewells and head for the seaside. We could take a proper break, eat winkles, walk by the sea, find a nice café for a cream tea, make up stories about the strange-looking locals . . .

Lady Hardcastle interrupted my reverie by bursting exuberantly through the door.

'What ho, Flo,' she said, somewhat surprised. 'I didn't expect to find you here. I thought you'd be downstairs, interrogating the lower orders.'

'I wasn't required for lunch service, so I was given leave to come and see to my regular duties.' I held up the gown. 'I fixed the rip,' I said. 'How on earth did you manage to do that?'

'What rip?' she said, looking at the gown. 'Ohhh, that rip. It was at the party on Tuesday. I was chatting to a lady from Leicester, wife of . . . Actually, I've no idea whose wife she was. She wasn't terribly impressed with her husband's behaviour, though. I remember that. A few glasses of wine had loosened her tongue, and she was unburdening herself to yours truly about his promiscuity and profligacy. I must have that sort of face. Do you think I have that sort of face?'

'What sort of face, my lady?'

'The sort of face that makes strangers take me into their confidence and throw caution and discretion to the wind by exposing me to the excruciatingly embarrassing details of their private affairs.'

'Oh, yes, you have that sort of face. I always thought that was what made you such a good spy. But what about the frock? Did you both rend your garments while lamenting the tragedy of her failing union?'

'If only it had been that dramatic. We were in the billiards room for some reason. I think I was looking for Harry and she was looking for her better half. Or her worse half, as I rapidly found him to be. Viktor Kovacs was playing at the table with Monty Waterford, chatting about . . . Oh.'

'Oh?' I said, having resigned myself by now to never learning the fate of the frock.

'They were talking about their motor racing teams. Something about how much money Monty and Fishy had tied up in their prototypes, and how any sort of setback would be disastrous. Viktor said something about being happy to talk about a merger if they wanted to, and Monty said they hadn't had any setbacks yet.'

'Yet,' I repeated. 'And so Kovacs sneaks out in dead of night and ensures that one of their motor cars does have a little setback, and if their senior driver gets hurt – or even killed – in the process, then so much the better.'

'It does all seem rather plausible now, doesn't it?' she said. 'We've not a shred of proof, mind you.'

'Then we get some, my lady. We search his room, scour the house and grounds for clues, watch the black-hearted devil day and night until he betrays himself somehow. We haven't been away from the spying game for so long that we've forgotten how to do it.'

She laughed. 'Very well. It's all we have to go on at the moment, after all. And the worst that can happen is that we'll prove him innocent and find that we've wasted our time.'

'Well,' I said slowly, 'the worst that can happen is that he'll catch us in the act and try to bludgeon us to death with a heavy wrench. I'm reasonably sure I could give him what for if he doesn't get the jump on us, but if he did . . .'

'You're right, of course, but I doubt it will come to that. It's a pity young whatshisname is serving as his valet – a more biddable servant might have been persuaded to keep an eye open on our behalf.'

'It could be worth sounding Evan out anyway, my lady,' I said. 'He might be eager to lend a hand if he perceives it as an opportunity for a spot of mischief. He can watch Mr Waterford while he's about it – two birds with one stone, and all that.'

'I shall leave it up to you. Perhaps you should disappear to the netherworld of infernal servitude and see what the lad has to say for himself. We shall formulate our plans and stratagems while we prepare for dinner.'

'I'll get down to the servants' hall at once. Do you want anything while I'm down there?'

'Not for me, dear, I'm stuffed.'

'One more thing . . .'

'Yes?'

'The rip.'

'Oh, yes, the rip. I caught it on the rack thing they store the billiard bats in.'

'Cues, my lady.'

'Really? I wonder why.'

◆ ◆ ◆

I found the servants' hall deserted but for the housekeeper, Mrs McLelland, who was sitting at the table with a pot of tea and the newspaper.

'Good afternoon, Mrs McLelland,' I said, pulling out a chair. 'Do you mind if I join you?'

She lowered the newspaper and regarded me across the top of the half-folded page. 'Ah, Miss Armstrong,' she said. 'Good afternoon. Please make yourself at home. There's at least one more tea in the pot, if you'd care for one.'

I turned, took a clean cup and saucer from the dresser, and sat down opposite her. As I poured, I said, 'How does everyone seem to be coping after the tragedy?'

'Coping?' she said, folding the newspaper and putting it to one side.

'Yes,' I said. 'Something like that can really shake people up. Even the best of us can suffer quite horribly after something dreadful like that has happened. I was just wondering if any of the staff were showing any signs of having been affected.'

She snorted. 'Want to pull themselves together if they have. I'll not have any malingering poltroons on my staff. If any of my girls feel the need to sit around feeling sorry for themselves every time something goes wrong, they can do it on their own time and well out of my earshot. We've all suffered tragedies, but where would we be if we sat around moping? Get up and make the best of it, I say.'

Heaven help anyone on the Codrington Hall staff who should suffer any manner of shock, I thought. The arrival of Evan Gudger saved me from telling her exactly what I thought of her attitude.

'Good afternoon, Evan,' I said cheerily.

'Eh?' he grunted.

'Good afternoon,' I said again. 'Are you well?'

'Well enough,' he mumbled.

'Jolly good,' I said to his retreating back as he disappeared down one of the many subterranean passageways.

'That young fellow needs to have some manners knocked into him,' said Mrs McLelland. 'I don't know what Mr Spinney is playing at letting him get away with that sort of discourteous behaviour. A spell in the army would do him good. Teach him some discipline.'

'I understood he'd had a troubled childhood,' I ventured. 'Lost his parents.'

She snorted again. 'People lose family members all the time. Doesn't turn them all into insolent jackanapes.'

I had clearly caught her on a bad day.

I drained my teacup in one last gulp. 'Well, I'd best be getting on,' I said, standing up. 'Is Mr Spinney in his room, do you know?'

'Yes, I believe so. Though I've one or two jobs that need doing if you find yourself with idle hands.'

'I shall be sure to seek you out if he doesn't need me,' I lied.

I set off in the direction of Mr Spinney's rooms, but turned off once I was out of sight. I made my way instead to the boot room, where I was sure I might find Evan, or at least someone who knew where he might be. As it turned out, he wasn't there, but one of the young lads was able to point me in the right direction. I found him loitering in the kitchen yard.

'Can I help you?' he asked truculently.

'As a matter of fact,' I said, in my cheeriest, friendliest voice, 'I rather think you might be able to.'

He looked at me quizzically for a moment. 'Has that old witch sent you to give me what for?' he asked.

I laughed. 'No,' I said. 'But she's not your most ardent admirer.'

'None of 'em is,' he said. 'Everyone's always on my back for something.'

'Have you ever wondered,' I asked, 'whether that might be because you go so very far out of your way to antagonize them?'

It was his turn to laugh. 'I reckon you might be right at that,' he said. 'But they're all such . . . such . . .'

'It can seem that way,' I said before he could find whatever insulting word it was that he was looking for. 'But you might give them the benefit of the doubt once in a while. You might find that they have your best interests at heart after all.'

'I doubt it. They just want to make sure everyone knows their place and stays in it. It gets so boring sometimes, I has to do something, you know, to stir 'em up a bit.'

'Perhaps I can help with that.'

His quizzical look returned. 'Oh?'

'I have a little mission that might amuse you,' I said, and outlined our plan for keeping an eye on Herr Kovacs.

◆ ◆ ◆

I left Evan to his loitering and returned to the servants' hall, where the unaccountably sour face of Mrs McLelland had been replaced by three faces I'd only previously seen to say hello to. If anyone was likely to be able to give the whisper on the goings-on both above and below stairs, it was going to be these three. Nellie Perrin was Lady Lavinia's lady's maid and Dan Chanley was Lord Riddlethorpe's valet, while Arnold Simkin had served as valet to Uncle Algy since both of them were young men.

'Aha,' said Mr Simkin as I approached. 'Here comes the woman herself. Sit yourself down, my lovely, and tell us your news. Miss Perrin, see if you can't scare another cup out of that pot.'

I raised an enquiring eyebrow as I sat in the indicated chair.

'Now then, Miss Armstrong,' continued Mr Simkin affably, 'what's this we've been hearing about you and your mistress investigating the accident?'

He was a small, dapper man with a neatly trimmed, snow-white moustache. He had a twinkle in his eye that suggested he might very well be just as much trouble as his employer.

'That rather depends,' I said, taking the cup of tea from Miss Perrin's waiting hand, 'upon what you've heard.'

'Aha,' he said, slapping the table. 'I told you she was a shrewd one. Not giving anything away, this one.'

I smiled, and raised my eyebrow once more in Miss Perrin's direction.

'Take no notice of him, my dear,' she said. 'He said nothing of the sort.'

'Thought it, though. Thought it,' said Mr Simkin. 'Knew she was cunning.'

Miss Perrin sighed. I judged she was closer to my own age, but something about her slightly motherly manner made her seem older.

'There's been a rumour going about the place,' she said, 'that the accident wasn't an accident. One of the footmen overheard his lordship telling Mr Waterford that Morgan had said the motor car had been interfered with.'

I smiled again. 'There's nothing quite so good as a first-hand account,' I said. 'But in this case, your Chinese whispers are correct. I was with Morgan in the stables when he found that the brakes had been tampered with.'

'Brakes, eh? So someone killed Mr Dawkins on purpose, like?'

'That's certainly a possibility.'

'You don't mess about with the brakes on a vehicle unless you intend someone harm,' said Mr Chanley, finally breaking his silence. 'Someone had it in for Mr Dawkins, make no mistake. His lordship is distraught. Hardly sleeping.'

'Back to my original question, m'dear,' said Mr Simkin. 'Are you and your mistress investigating?'

My mission below stairs had been to observe the servants while maintaining the illusion that I was some crazed work addict who couldn't sit still and relax while she was away from home. But I'd already decided that these three were the key to finding out what was going on, so it was worth letting them in on the act.

'You heard correctly, Mr Simkin. The police were satisfied that it was an accident – I got the feeling that the inspector rather felt it was by way of divine retribution upon the idle rich for their foolishness. But when it became clear that skulduggery was involved, Lady Hardcastle decided that we might serve our host by poking under a few rocks and seeing what scuttled out.'

'And that's why you're working down here all of a sudden?' said Miss Perrin. 'I did wonder.'

'Mr Spinney suggested it,' I said. 'He thought it might help. If I were working with the staff, I'd be free to come and go about the house, and no one would think anything of it.'

'That silly old fool?' she said. 'You should have just come straight to us. We'd have told you what's what. Wouldn't we?'

'Aye,' said Mr Chanley. 'It's a bad business, indeed. It needs sorting out.'

I looked round as one of the scullery maids scurried through bearing a basket of vegetables. It didn't seem to be a terribly private place to be having our conversation, but I could think of nowhere else that wouldn't cause even more gossip and speculation were we to be found out.

'What do you know of the motor racing team?' I asked. 'Is it just a fancy of Lord Riddlethorpe's?'

'We all thought it was at first, didn't we, Mr Simkin?' said Mr Chanley. 'I wouldn't have a word said against his lordship, and it's been my honour to serve him these past fifteen years, but he hasn't always been a man of purpose. He's never wanted for anything except something to do. He's taken to all manner of fads and novelties over the years. Painting, poetry, horse racing, horticulture – you name it, he tried it. He even packed himself off to Egypt at one point, with me trailing in his wake. Imagined himself an archaeologist, he did. Fancied he was going to discover lost tombs and treasures.'

'And did he?' I asked.

'He came down with dengue fever just as we arrived in Cairo. After spending two weeks in bed, he decided that archaeology wasn't for him and that what he really wanted was to be a potter. So we bought a couple of crates of local pottery as inspiration and shipped ourselves back home.'

I laughed in spite of myself. 'Something of a butterfly, then,' I said. 'But you seemed to be saying that you thought the motor racing was different? What changed?'

'His father died,' he said. 'He suddenly found himself the ninth Earl of Riddlethorpe. Grew up overnight. He threw himself into it like nothing he'd ever done before. It had been just another one of his fads until then, but it became an all-consuming passion once his father had passed. He bought motor cars, learned all about them, and then started building his own. He fell in with that Mr Waterford, and it went from being a gentleman's hobby to being a real business. He spent this past year building it all up; they even laid the test circuit in the grounds, and now here it is, all crumbling around him.'

'You said "that" Mr Waterford. Do you disapprove?'

'He's a bit of a fly one, if you ask me,' said Chanley.

'How so?' I asked.

'Can't say as I can put my finger on it precisely. You get a feeling, you know?'

'I do know,' I said. I turned my attention to Miss Perrin. 'And what does Lady Lavinia make of it all?'

'She was pleased as Punch when it finally looked like his lordship was settling down,' she said. 'Don't get me wrong, she loves her brother like billy-o, but it would be a lie to say she wasn't worried as to how he might never settle to anything.'

'Has she said anything about the accident?'

'She's as shook-up as everyone. She didn't really know Mr Dawkins, but she knows as how it could have been any of them who copped it. Any of "you", I should say – you were down to race, too.'

'Hmm, yes,' I said. 'I suppose I was. And what about "Uncle Algy", Mr Simkin? Has he said anything?'

Mr Simkin chuckled. 'Sir Algernon is an uncomplicated man, Miss Armstrong. As long as he has access to regular meals, a supply of decent claret, and young, amusing company, he is happy to let the world get about its business without his interference. He was saddened by the death of Mr Dawkins, with whom he had enjoyed several boozy evenings, but a gentleman of his age has known much death, and he isn't dwelling upon it. He did say that it was bound to happen sooner or later – he is unconvinced of the safety of motor cars in general.'

So much for that line of questioning, then.

'But what have you discovered, Miss Armstrong?' asked Miss Perrin. 'Where have your investigations taken you?'

I recounted my earlier conversation with Lady Hardcastle, during which we had run through all the people who had been in the house on the night of the sabotage. There were murmurs of agreement when I got to the part about Herr Kovacs.

'I never trusted him,' said Miss Perrin. 'You can't trust the Germans.'

'Actually,' I said, 'he's Hungarian.'

'They're all the same,' she said adamantly.

'Well, I've got young Evan Gudger doing some snooping for me. He's looking after both Herr Kovacs and Mr Waterford, I believe.'

'You've done what?' said Mr Chanley, almost choking on his tea. 'That little . . .'

'That young man is rude, ill-disciplined, ungrateful, lazy, and will almost certainly fall into a life of viciousness and petty crime if he doesn't mend his ways,' I said. 'But he'll be breaking the rules and thumbing his nose at authority by working for me, and I happen to think he'll be rather good at it.'

'I don't fancy your luck at all,' said Mr Chanley, but I saw a sly grin on Mr Simkin's face and a twinkle in his watery old eyes that gave me to believe that he, at least, agreed with me.

◆ ◆ ◆

Having dutifully played my part in the serving of afternoon tea, and having heard nothing of any consequence in any of the many conversations I overheard, I had returned to Lady Hardcastle's room. To be clear, it wasn't just that I had heard nothing that had any bearing on the mystery, I had heard nothing of any consequence whatsoever. Sometimes large groups of people can talk for hours without sharing any news, views, or information of any kind, and so it was with the houseguests that afternoon. Many words were spoken, many laughs were laughed, but very few thoughts seemed to pass across the minds of any of the participants.

I was laying out an evening gown for Lady Hardcastle when the lady herself returned.

'What ho, Flo,' she said, crossing the room to sit at the writing desk.

'Welcome back, my lady,' I said. 'Did you enjoy tea?'

'It was frightfully jolly, wasn't it? But I confess to feeling positively whale-like with all this eating.'

'We could arrange some calisthenics, if that would help. I'm sure the other guests would welcome the chance for some healthy exercise. I packed you some suitable clothes.'

'I'm sure you did. But no, I think I can best recover my poise by sitting quietly for a moment.'

'As you wish, my lady, but the offer's there.'

'You're very kind,' she said. 'What news from the netherworld?'

'Not much progress, I'm afraid. I tried to natter with Mrs McLelland, but she was a little out of sorts, so I tracked down Evan Gudger and recruited him to the cause.'

'Oh, I say, well done. Do you think we can trust him?'

'No.'

'Rely on him in any way?'

'Almost certainly not.'

'Can we do any better?'

'I'm not sure we can, my lady, but we can hope for the best. There's not much damage he can do, though. Even if he decides to turn the opportunity towards mischief, we're alert to the possibility that he's not playing with a straight bat after all.'

'I shall leave his management entirely in your capable hands, dear,' she said. 'Did you manage to beard anyone else?'

'I also spoke to the personal servants – Lady Lavinia's lady's maid, as well as Lord Riddlethorpe's and Sir Algernon's valets.'

'And what did they have to say for themselves?'

I briefly recounted our conversation while I hunted for a pair of evening shoes.

'Nothing much, then,' she said.

'Not a great deal, my lady, no. But at least they're on our side now.'

'Unless one of their employers is the guilty one. Now that you've tipped our hand, they'll be running back to their master or mistress to tell them how best to avoid our suspicions.'

'I take your point,' I said. 'But from the look of them, none of them is in much of a position to be running anywhere. I think even a brisk stroll would do for old Arnold Simkin.'

She laughed. 'I believe I've seen him wheezing about the place.'

'So there we are, my lady. Unless you've come across any clues, I rather fear we're stumped.'

'Clues, yes,' she mused. 'It's about now when we could do with coming across the distinctive prints of the culprit's shoe, set about with the ash of a brand of cigarette sold only in a single shop in Riddlethorpe, of which we alone are aware.'

'Perhaps there might be mud that we could identify as being unique to a particular area of that town.'

'And a torn thread from a coat worn only by members of a now-disbanded Indian regiment.'

'We've got a pair of pliers, my lady,' I said.

'That's pretty much it, though, isn't it,' she said with a sigh. 'Ah well, perhaps our snoop will come up with something after all.'

'Perhaps, my lady. Shall I draw you a bath?'

'Would you? That would be splendid. Are you serving at dinner this evening?'

'No, Mr Spinney has rearranged the roster, and I'm doing breakfast instead. I shall be dining in my room with Betty.'

'Oh, that'll be nice. I like her.'

'I do, too.'

'Well, if you give me a hand to get ready, you can toddle off to your garret.'

'Thank you,' I said, and began to draw her bath.

◆ ◆ ◆

By the time Lady Hardcastle was ready to set off for the library, I was more than ready for a break. She was never an especially demanding employer, and I treasured her company, but the four or five daily changes of clothes required during a country house stay became less and less fun as the visit went on. My final task for the day was to remind her where she had left her lorgnette (hanging by a long chain around her neck), and then I was free to trot up the back stairs to the attic room and flop on to my bed.

I had just picked up *The Time Machine* when there was a timid knock at the door. Betty's face peered round it as it opened.

'Betty, this is your room; you don't have to knock.'

'I know, dear, but I've never quite been able to work out the etiquette of sharing a room with a stranger.'

'Then let us declare ourselves no longer strangers so that you can bloomin' well relax and feel free to come and go as you normally would.'

'Righto,' she said. 'Are you going down to the servants' hall for dinner?'

'I feel as though I ought, but I'm really not certain I can face it this evening. I'm absolutely done.'

She sighed with relief. 'I can't tell you how glad I am to hear it,' she said. 'How would it suit you if I were to pay a visit to Mrs Ruddle and see if I can get a little supper to bring up? We can dine up here again away from all the hubbub.'

'That, Betty Buffrey, old chum, would suit me very well indeed.'

'I'll be back in two shakes,' she said, and scurried off.

By the time she returned with a modest cold collation on a tray, I had cleared a space on the rug and poured two glasses of water.

'Here we are,' she said as she put the tray down. 'Not quite up to the standards of the party night, but there are a couple of slices of pie and some nice ham. I managed to track down some chutney, too.'

She had indeed managed all those things. She had found some bread, a lump of cheese, and a few tomatoes as well. We tucked in with gusto – I, for one, hadn't eaten properly since breakfast.

'I heard you were working with the locals,' she said between mouthfuls of pie.

'I cannot tell a lie,' I said. 'I am indeed pitching in.'

'Oh, do say it's hugger-mugger. You're spying on them, aren't you?'

I laughed. 'You're a sharp one, missy,' I said. 'Yes, I'm using it as an opportunity to keep an eye on things. It gets me into meals upstairs, too.'

'Lawks, how exciting. Who are you spying on? I bet it's that Kovacs bloke. He's one of them Austro-Hungarian spies, isn't he? He's over here up to no good. You're still working for the King, aren't you?'

I regarded her quizzically for a moment. 'Do you really not know?' I said at length.

'Know what?'

'About the car crash.'

'Yes? We talked about it the other day. You said as how you'd seen the body.'

'And you know that it was sabotage?'

She turned sharply towards me, her eyes wide with surprise. 'No!' she said. 'Who would do such a thing?'

'That's precisely what we're trying to find out.'

'Does Mrs Beddows know?'

'That it was sabotage?' I said. 'I thought everyone knew by now.'

'Not me. And Mrs Beddows never said a word.'

'Does she tell you much?'

'To be truthful, no, she doesn't. Nothing important, anyway. I get to know about the Earl of Thingummy tupping Lady Whatnot, and how the Marchioness of Heaven-knows-where has tricked Sir No-one-you've-heard-of out of his fortune, but nothing I care about.'

I brought her up to date with the story so far. She sat goggle-eyed, with a slice of tomato wobbling on the fork that had stopped halfway to her mouth.

'That Mrs Beddows,' she said when I had finished my tale. 'She told me none of that.'

'It doesn't sound like it's the sort of thing she's especially interested in. Did she not mention the crash at all?'

'Not really. She was a bit off when she came back to her room that afternoon. When I asked her what was wrong, she just said, "Oh, that oaf Dawkins went and crashed his motor car, so we all had to come back inside." I didn't even find out the poor man had died until I heard someone talking about it in the servants' hall.'

'Did she not get on with Dawkins?' I asked.

'She was mad with him when I went to see to her on the morning after the party. "That upstart, flippin' gutter-blood driver," she said. Only she was a sight more ripe with her language. "He only went and made advances to me. To me, Buffrey!" she said. "Of all the . . ." And then she ranted on for a bit. Words I can't bring myself to say, most of 'em.'

'I had no idea she felt so strongly about it,' I said. 'I'd heard he'd tried it on with her, but she must get that all the time, a beautiful woman like that. Married or otherwise.'

'Oh, she does. And she loves it. But she makes a great show of not getting along with anyone. It's her special affectation. No one can get close to the fearsome Rosamund Beddows. She stands alone, and all shall tremble in her presence.'

'I say, Betty. That's not like you.'

She seemed to have surprised even herself. 'I don't suppose it is,' she said quietly. 'Sometimes, though . . . sometimes.' She paused again. 'You don't think it was her, do you?'

'Sabotaged the motor car? Anything's possible.'

'Was it difficult to do?' she asked.

'Not especially,' I said. 'Anyone who has ever ridden a bicycle could figure out how the brakes work.'

'She's definitely ridden a bicycle. Would it involve getting dirty?'

'Almost certainly. The saboteur would have to lie on their belly to reach under the motor car.'

'She'd never do that, then,' said Betty flatly. 'She has a phobia of being dirty. She bathes twice a day as it is. I can't imagine her lying on a coach house floor.'

'Even so,' I said. 'Would you be a dear and pay special attention to her clothes? She might have overcome her fear of dirt for the sake of teaching Dawkins a lesson. Even if she brushed the worst of it off, anything she was wearing would still show signs.'

Betty's half-smile was difficult to read. Was it anxious or gleeful? Was she horrified or delighted by the idea that her mistress might be a murderer?

Chapter Ten

'What ho, Florence,' said Lady Hardcastle sleepily the next morning.

'"Florence", my lady?' I said as I set down the breakfast tray. 'Have I done something wrong?'

'What? Oh, no. Did your mother do that, too? I was always "Emily Charlotte" if I'd been misbehaving. If I'd been especially beastly, she would add the "Ariadne", but she usually considered it too much effort. No, we were discussing names last evening at dinner, and it struck me what a wonderfully evocative name you have. Tuscany in the summertime, museums, the Ponte Vecchio. I vowed to use it more.'

'As you wish, my lady. Although I should point out that I was named after the Lady with the Lump.'

'I'm reasonably certain it was a "lamp".'

'That would be much more reassuring to wounded soldiers in the middle of the night, yes. Did my name come up in the conversation, or was this a private thought?'

'Your name comes up frequently,' she said. 'You always make an impression.'

'I hope that's a good thing.'

'Always, dear. But in truth, you remained in the conversational shadows. The boys became fixated on "The Fair Rosamund", who was, so she claims, named after that very lady.'

'Mistress of King Henry II?' I said.

'I say, well done, you. Fishy had to send one of the footmen to the library to fetch a volume of the encyclopaedia to settle that one. I guessed Henry I. Harry was absolutely insistent that it was Richard III—'

'The King with the Lump.'

'Quite so. He's a cabbage head.'

'Richard III?'

'No, silly, my brother. Anyway, you and your knowledge would have won me a fiver. There was a wager.'

'A fiver? I wish I'd been serving now – fools and their money are soon parted.'

'We should start a general knowledge game. You can be the ace up my sleeve.'

'As long as you split the winnings with me, my lady, I'm in.'

'Splendid. So much more reliable than cards. We shall introduce it to fashionable society and clean up.'

'Right you are. It's funny that you should mention Mrs Beddows, though, my lady. Her name came up in my conversation with Betty as well.'

'Did it? Gossip?'

'Perhaps,' I said. 'Do you mind if I pinch a slice of toast? I'm famished.'

'Help yourself, dear – I presumed you'd brought extra so we could share.'

'Thank you. Mrs Beddows, then. Betty reports that she was furious with Dawkins after his "improper" advances at the party.'

'Was she, indeed? You did say that it was possible that she was irked by it.'

'I did. Not merely irked, though. Actually hopping mad.'

'Mad enough to commit mischief?'

'Possibly, my lady.'

'Interesting,' she said, smashing open a boiled egg.

'The one thing that counts in her favour is that she has a phobia of dirt.'

Lady Hardcastle laughed. 'A phobia? Of dirt?'

'So Betty says. Even if it's no more than a fervent dislike, it still indicates strongly against her being inclined to get down on the floor and wriggle about in the dust.'

She was still laughing. 'To be truthful, I find it hard to imagine Roz wriggling under any circumstances. Wriggling is such a joyful activity. Roz and joy are not frequent companions, I feel.'

'That's the impression she likes to convey,' I said. 'Betty has the measure of her mistress, and that's very much her opinion, too.'

'We'd be foolish to discount her completely based on a dislike of grime, mind you. I've been giving some thought to the events of that night. Our examination of the stables yesterday morning was quite instructive, don't you think? We know – or at least we firmly believe – that someone let themselves out of the house in the dead of night in possession of a key and a candle. That person slipped into the stables by the side door, took up a pair of pliers and tampered with Number 3. He couldn't find the hook for the pliers in the dark, so he dropped them on the floor and kicked them under the workbench. Then he let himself out the way he came and went back to the house. I say "he", but it could as easily be Roz as anyone.'

'When did the party end?'

'At two. Sharp.'

'Could anyone have gone down there before then?'

'They could,' she said. 'It would have been a risk, though: the motor cars were on display as part of the celebrations. Anyone tampering with one of them could have been spotted at any moment. There'd be no especial need to come in through the side door, either: the main doors were all folded back. And no need for a candle: the place was lit up like a theatre stage.'

'So "dead of night" is right. If there were still guests here at two, and the junior servants started stirring at around four, our saboteur had less than two hours to get to work.'

'Indeed,' she said. 'The trouble is, I can't think of any suspect who would have been better placed to wander the grounds at three in the morning than any other.'

'No knowledge is entirely without value, though, my lady. You told me that.'

'Did I? How very pompous of me.'

'I cleave to your every pronouncement, my lady, however pompous. You know that. What plans for the day, though? Any special wardrobe requirements?'

'Sports togs, I think. Apparently, it's going to be sunny again, so there's talk of tennis. And blasted croquet of all things. I do so hate croquet. So petty and spiteful.'

'I shall make sure you're properly prepared,' I said.

'And you? More below-stairs snooping?'

'Below stairs, above stairs, in the grounds and gardens, my lady. No corner of the estate will escape my scrutiny.'

'That's the spirit,' she said. 'Would you care for some marmalade?'

◆ ◆ ◆

There was, as always, a massive pot of tea at the centre of the table in the servants' hall. Lined up in close attendance, like eager acolytes around their glazed china master, were fresh cups, a milk jug, and a sugar bowl.

153

It should have been a place of quiet relaxation and idle chatter. Of course, it wasn't.

There was quiet chatter, but the table was a hive of industry. Clothes were being mended, silverware polished, and one young maid was sorting candles into small bundles for delivery to bedrooms all over the house. There were two oases of calm: Mr Spinney was reading a newspaper, occasionally sharing titbits with Mrs McLelland, while Betty sat alone, staring into thin air. I squeezed in next to her.

'Good morning, Betty, *fach*,' I said. 'You were up early this morning.'

She smiled ruefully. 'I was summoned. Mrs Beddows needed to get ready.'

'I thought they were playing tennis,' I said. 'How much getting ready does that entail? I just laid out a tennis dress and a pair of plimsolls.'

'Ah, but Lady Hardcastle is calm and rational. And confident in herself. And not insanely competitive. There was hair to be set, make-up to be applied, muscles to be massaged. And that was before we got round to trying on six different hat-and-ribbon combinations. She brings two tennis rackets. Who owns two tennis rackets?'

I laughed. Mr Spinney caught my eye, clearly trying to decide whether to say something to a visiting servant about speaking so disparagingly about her employer. Unfortunately, Mrs McLelland's face showed no such indecision – she was obviously very annoyed – and I was unable to stop myself from laughing again. Mr Spinney returned quickly to his newspaper, having decided the battle was over before it had begun.

'That's handy,' I said. 'Lady Hardcastle's tennis racket was broken during our move to Littleton Cotterell. She never got round to replacing it. Her local friends aren't too keen on tennis.'

'Mrs Beddows would never lend her a racket. She's very particular about her tennis rackets.'

'She sounds like a keen player,' I said. 'Is she good?'

'She's rubbish. Absolutely hopeless.'

The maids and footmen were concentrating on their work, trying to pretend not to earwig, but their barely stifled laughter gave them away. Mr Spinney cleared his throat and rustled his newspaper, trying to regain control. Muted conversations were resumed.

'Still no news about Mr Dawkins in the newspaper, Mrs McLelland,' said Mr Spinney. 'I must say, I find that rather odd. A man dies in tragic circumstances at one of the country's most important houses, and no one bats an eyelid. Most odd.'

'Would you rather they made a fuss? Stoked a scandal?' said Mrs McLelland.

'Of course not. Perish the thought,' he said quickly.

'Well, then. Just be thankful they're leaving it be. It was a tragic accident, that's all. And no need for a fuss.'

The maid with the candles looked up from her work. ''Cept they says it wasn't an accident, Mrs McLelland,' she said.

'Who's "they", girl?'

'Morgan, for one. He says the brakes didn't work. Says someone fiddled with 'em.'

'You should all know better than to tittle-tattle,' said Mrs McLelland. 'The police are satisfied that it was an accident, and that should be good enough for us.'

'But—' said the maid.

'That's enough!' said Mrs McLelland sharply. 'Get on with your work. Those candles should have been taken up hours ago.'

She put down her teacup with a clatter and left the room. An awkward silence followed. Mr Spinney sighed.

I put my own teacup down a great deal more gently. 'Well, Betty, old chum,' I said. 'I ought to be getting on, I suppose. I have an important errand to run, but then I thought I might watch the tennis. Will you be free to join me?'

'I should think so,' she said. 'I'll see you later down by the tennis court.'

◆ ◆ ◆

My errand, of course, was to get a report from Evan Gudger. A good spy looks after her agents, makes them feel valued. Encourages them. I found him, as I'd expected, loafing in the kitchen yard.

'Good morning, Evan,' I said cheerily.

He mumbled a reply.

'Are you well?'

He mumbled again.

'Splendid,' I said. 'Did you manage to do as I asked?'

He looked at his shoes. 'As a matter of fact,' he said after a few moments' pause, 'I did. I had a good old poke around Herr Kovacs's room. And Mr Waterford's too. I didn't reckon he should be left out.'

I didn't reckon it was the first time he'd rummaged through their things, either, but I knew better than to say anything. Instead, I said, 'Well done. Did you find anything?'

He reached into the breast pocket of his jacket and produced a scruffy scrap of paper. 'I copied this off a letter on Herr Kovacs's writing desk.'

I took the paper. Evan's untidy handwriting was difficult to read in places, but if he had copied it correctly, it was a letter from Herr Kovacs offering to buy the racing team.

'This is very interesting, Evan, thank you. You're certain you copied it exactly?'

'You think I'm an idiot like everyone else?' he snapped. 'Just because I don't write so good.'

'I meant nothing of the sort. I shall be reporting this to my mistress, and I need to be certain of the source. We've put a lot of trust in you. Checking isn't a sign of mistrust.'

'Yeah, well, they all think I'm thick. But I ain't.'

'I don't give a tinker's cuss what "they all think", Evan,' I said. 'You're working for me now, and I'm just making certain.'

'I heard 'em talkin', too,' he said after another pause.

'Who?'

'Kovacs and Waterford. I was puttin' Mr Waterford's shirt studs on when Herr Kovacs comes in. "Ah, Monty," he says, all chummy, like. "Have you had time to think about my offer? With the bad publicity that will follow the accident, you know Lord Riddlethorpe stands no chance. I could be the one to save you from ruin." And Mr Waterford says, "We've only just announced the team, Viktor. We're not going to sell." It was somethin' like that, anyway.'

'I say, Evan, well done,' I said. I gave him a few coins from my purse. 'Keep your eyes and ears open, and I'll make sure there's more. I need you to do one important thing for me right away, though.'

'Yes?' he said, somewhat more enthusiastically than usual. 'What's that?'

'You can direct me to the tennis courts.'

'Ah, Flo, there you are. Be a love and pass me that towel. I'm all of a pother, as they say round our way.'

'You look . . .' I lowered my voice so as not to be overheard. 'To be honest, you look a horrific, sweaty mess, my lady. Are you sure you're all right?'

Lady Hardcastle laughed. 'It turns out that while one never forgets how to strike a good solid forehand smash, the heart and lungs do tend to grow more reluctant to keep the old body moving about at a sufficient pace to make proper use of it.'

'You poor old thing,' I said, handing her the towel. 'Imagine how bad it will get when you actually are old.'

'Well, quite,' she said, sitting on one of the benches beside the court, fanning herself with the towel.

I looked across the grass to where Mrs Beddows was talking animatedly to Miss Titmus. 'Is Mrs Beddows winning, then?' I asked.

'Is she, heck! I'm demolishing her!'

'Well done, you,' I said. 'Actually, that would explain her thunderous demeanour. I don't fancy Betty's chances when she turns up. It's odds-on where the wrath will be directed.'

'We shall have to keep her attention elsewhere, then. We'll be saving her from herself – it just doesn't do to bully the servants. In public, at least.'

'If they only knew, my lady.'

'Indeed. Is there any cordial left in that jug?'

I poured her a glass.

The gentlemen were playing doubles on the adjacent court, interrupted intermittently by Lord Riddlethorpe's exuberant Dalmatians. It seems they had been pressed into service as ball girls, but were having trouble understanding the limits of their duties. As well as retrieving balls that had gone out of play, they were also attempting to catch some of the slower-moving shots on the court itself.

Lady Lavinia was looking on with an indulgent fondness that wasn't always directed towards the dogs.

'I thought the ladies would be playing doubles, too,' I said. 'Why isn't Lady Lavinia playing?'

'It would have been much more fun, wouldn't it?' Lady Hardcastle said as she drank. 'We were ready to start – I was partnered with Helen – but when Harry pitched up in his flannels, Jake went weak at the knees and drifted off to watch the chaps. Helen didn't really want to play anyway, so it was left to me and Roz. Luckily, she couldn't hit an elephant's backside with a banjo, so my honour has been saved.'

'Not an entirely wasted morning, then.'

'Not in the least. What about your morning? What news from your agent?' she asked. 'Did he prove worthy of your faith in him?'

'I think I've already said that I had no faith in him whatsoever. As it transpires, though, I was wrong. He turned up trumps. Or it appears he did. He might have made it all up, of course.'

I handed her the crumpled copy of the letter, and recounted the brief conversation I'd had with Evan in the kitchen yard.

'Other than a couple of spelling mistakes, it certainly seems like a formal business letter,' she said. 'Do you think Evan is capable of composing such a thing on his own?'

'He might be surly and resentful, but he's also bright and self-confident,' I said. 'He's quick-thinking and cunning. He'd make a decent petty criminal – or spy, for that matter. But I think he lacks the education and experience to be able to come up with something like that on his own. He might have had help, of course, but I'm beggared if I know where from.'

'Well, then, let's take this letter at face value. It's nothing incriminating on its own, mind you, just an invitation to begin negotiations. What about Evan's report of the conversation?'

'He might have coloured it, but why would he bother? Even if he's embellished it a little, I think the general gist – Herr Kovacs wants to buy the team, Mr Waterford doesn't want to sell, and Kovacs expected the crash to help him – is probably dead-on. Again, unless someone else's hand is guiding him, I can't see what he has to gain from making it up.'

'Aside from the money you gave him,' she said.

'He'd have got that whatever he told me,' I said. 'He could have made up any old story, but the story he tells fits our own ponderings precisely.'

'True, true. And he had no idea what our ponderings were. I'd say this puts Herr Kovacs squarely in the frame.'

'It certainly does seem that way,' I said. 'I'll make sure Evan keeps an eye on him.'

'Thank you. Right, well, we've had our little breather. One more set for the match, then I can pass out in a flowerbed somewhere.'

'I thought there was croquet next.'

'Blasted croquet. Don't remind me.' She stood. 'Ready, Roz?' she called. 'One more set should do it, don't you think?'

Mrs Beddows thrust her spare racket into Miss Titmus's hands and stomped on to the court.

I felt a tap on my shoulder.

'What have I missed?' asked Betty.

'I've only just got here myself,' I said. 'I gather Mrs Beddows is being roundly thrashed, so there might have been some interesting tennis. On the other hand, Lady Hardcastle claims she's struggling a bit herself, so it might not have been so thrilling after all. Oh, I say!'

Lady Hardcastle's forehand passing shot had left Mrs Beddows looking helpless and bewildered in the middle of the court. Bewilderment rapidly gave way to her customary look of displeasure. She caught Betty's eye, and indicated with a flick of her head that Betty should be on the other side of the court with Miss Titmus. I walked with her.

'I'm for it now,' said Betty as we rounded the baseline. 'Somehow, that will definitely have been my fault.'

Miss Titmus was sitting on the bench, nursing the spare tennis racket in its press. Her own racket was leaning against the bench.

'Hello, you two,' she said as we approached. 'Come to watch the mighty gladiators at battle?'

'Something like that, madam,' I said. 'Though we seem to have missed the best of it.'

'It was the best of games, it was the worst of games,' she said distractedly as Lady Hardcastle sent a perfectly judged lob sailing over Mrs Beddows's head. 'Poor Mrs Beddows hasn't stood a chance.'

Mrs Beddows stalked back to the baseline to serve.

'Bad luck, Roz,' called Miss Titmus. 'Lovely shot, Emily.'

The game was a short one, with Mrs Beddows's service well and truly broken. She had managed to score no points at all, but there was no love in her eyes as she stalked back to her bench.

'It must be this racket,' she said. 'Give me the other one.'

Miss Titmus meekly handed her the racket. Mrs Beddows snorted frustratedly as she loosened the screws holding the press. I got the feeling she had expected her friend to do it for her.

'What are you doing here, Buffrey?' she said. 'I thought you were mending my dress.'

'All done, madam,' said Betty. 'I thought I'd come and cheer you on.'

Mrs Beddows snorted again. With a peremptory flick of her fingers, she indicated that she wanted the glass of cordial. Smiling, Miss Titmus passed it to her.

'I'd better get back,' said Mrs Beddows. 'Keep an eye on that Hardcastle woman. I'm sure she must be cheating somehow.' She glared at me.

'Oh, Roz, don't be so silly. She's a very good player, that's all,' said Miss Titmus.

Mrs Beddows stalked down to the other end of the court.

'She didn't mean it,' said Miss Titmus. 'That your mistress is cheating, I mean. One shouldn't speak ill of one's friends, but Mrs Beddows has never been a gracious loser.'

'Thank you, madam,' I said. 'But please don't worry. I'm surprised and delighted that Lady Hardcastle is doing so well. I'm certain she isn't cheating. Though I'm equally certain that if she were, we'd not be able to spot it. She's quite the dab at underhandedness and skulduggery when she puts her mind to it.'

Miss Titmus laughed. 'Surely not,' she said.

'You'd be surprised, madam,' I said. 'There's a Prussian colonel who lost his fortune, his mistress, and his political influence all on the same night thanks to Lady Hardcastle's skills with a pack of cards. All for king and country, of course.'

'King and country?' said Miss Titmus.

'A diplomatic incident was averted.'

'Gracious. What happened to his mistress?'

'He had to take back the diamond necklace he'd just given her. A gentleman must settle his debts. She didn't stay long after that. Who would have thought bridge could be such a dangerous game?'

She laughed again. 'I never know whether you and Lady Hardcastle are teasing me,' she said. 'Oh, I say, good shot, Emily!'

The set didn't last long. Mrs Beddows stomped over to us and all but threw her racket at Betty.

'I need to change for croquet. Hurry up, Buffrey.'

She marched away in the direction of the house. Betty gathered up the two tennis rackets and hurried after her.

Lady Hardcastle came over to join us.

'That poor girl,' said Miss Titmus. 'Roz runs her ragged. I'm sure she doesn't mean to. She seems to have a lot on her mind at the moment. She's been very distracted lately, you see. I think' – she looked around to make sure no one could overhear her – 'that her husband's affairs are becoming a bit more . . . blatant. I've tried to talk to her, you know, get her on her own, but I never seem to be able to.'

'Beard her in her lair one evening,' said Lady Hardcastle.

'I've tried that, but she never seems to be in her room. Do you remember the party? Oh, it seems so long ago now, after what's happened since. She was so distracted. I tried to speak to her after that, but I couldn't find her.'

'Not in her room?' asked Lady Hardcastle. 'When was this?'

'Oh, I don't know. It must have been about three o'clock. She was probably out walking the grounds, poor thing. But I do wish she wouldn't take it out on Buffrey. I don't know how she puts up with it.'

'Betty?' said Lady Hardcastle. 'I'd intended to divert some of the fire, but I seem to be too late. Ah well. I say, perhaps you should offer her a job, Helen. Lure her into a more unruffled life. Surely you could make use of a lady's maid?'

'Perhaps I should,' said Miss Titmus. 'It might be fun to have an ally against my housekeeper.'

Lady Hardcastle put her arm around Miss Titmus's shoulder, and we all started walking. 'You're a perfect match, you two,' she said. 'Where are they off to, anyway? I thought the croquet lawn was this way.'

'It is. Roz has gone to change.'

Lady Hardcastle laughed loudly enough to draw curious glances from the gentlemen. They were also packing up, ready for the main attraction: the great croquet match.

❖ ❖ ❖

'I suggest double-doubles,' said Lord Riddlethorpe, as the houseguests assembled on the croquet lawn.

'Really, Fishy,' said Lady Lavinia. 'You do talk such utter rot. What on earth is double-doubles?'

'We play doubles, but each partner is actually two people. Four a-side, d'you see? Each pair owns a ball. Sort it out between you who takes the shot. Any ball moved by the dogs has to be played from where they leave it, mind you. They're an additional hazard.'

'Girls against boys? Or draw lots for partners?' suggested Mr Waterford.

'You can draw lots if you like, dear,' said Lady Lavinia. 'But I'm playing with Harry.'

There followed a good deal of discussion, negotiation, and general horse-trading before the sides were finally agreed. I followed none of it, and instead sat with Betty on a stone bench beside the lawn.

Croquet, it has always seemed to me, is a thoroughly pointless activity. I've never seen anyone who was able to play with any degree of skill. I've never seen a game where anyone actually cared about the result. Mostly it seems to be an opportunity to lark about outdoors while chattering inanely. Nothing wrong with tomfoolery and inane chatter, of course; it's just that a croquet lawn always seems such a bland, featureless place to do it. What about a game of hide-and-seek in the woods? Or blind man's buff by the lake? There were one or two in the party I'd have happily seen get a dunking.

Lady Hardcastle wasn't keen on the game, either, but she seemed to have been partnered with Miss Titmus, so at least she would have amiable company.

Betty and I watched the proceedings with one eye each, in case we were called upon later to comment or commiserate. The play was as pedestrian and unskilled as predicted, although the Dalmatians did add a pleasing element of danger and unpredictability. I wondered if the Croquet Association might be persuaded to add 'mischievous large dogs' to its list of approved equipment. Most of our attention, though, was focused on earwigging their conversations as they passed us.

'. . . but, of course, without his spectacles he had no idea which platform he was on, so he ended up at Norwich, still clutching the package of tripe.'

'Oh, Emily, you are silly,' said Miss Titmus.

'To this day, no one knows what happened to the Polish attaché's new boots.'

I gave Lady Hardcastle a little salute as they passed by.

Next to come past our bench were Herr Kovacs and Mrs Beddows. They said nothing. Indeed, it didn't appear that they'd said anything at all to each other since they started playing. Their faces were impassive masks, either of intense concentration or complete distraction. I watched for a moment, and the poor quality of their play confirmed that it was the latter. They were both elsewhere.

Lady Lavinia and Harry were altogether more talkative, but no more interested in the game.

'Since we were at school, I think,' said Lady Lavinia. 'She was always the ringleader. I think it irks her that we're not still all in her thrall.'

'What about her husband?' asked Harry. 'She never talks about him.'

'No, she never does. Theirs is not a relationship filled with love and romance.'

'Which is why she didn't bring him?'

'Quite. She seldom allows him to accompany her. We always joke that she leaves him chained in the cellars when she's away. Sometimes I wonder how much of a joke it really is.'

Harry laughed.

Mr and Mrs Beddows did not seem to fit anyone's idea of a happy couple, I thought. If Miss Titmus's assessment was correct, they were only one small indiscretion away from a scandal. Unless she had misinterpreted things, and Mrs Beddows was just worried that she'd not left him enough food in the cellar.

I chuckled to myself. Betty looked questioningly at me, but I was unable to explain before Lord Riddlethorpe and Mr Waterford passed our way. They were similarly uninvolved in the game, but also deep in conversation.

'. . . well, I'm not bally well selling it to him,' said Lord Riddlethorpe. 'We've only just launched the company and he's already circling. I'm sure he means well. At least, I hope he does. But, I mean, really . . .'

'Just bear it in mind, Fishy, that's all,' said Mr Waterford. 'The newspapers don't seem to have made much of it so far, but if any of them decides to cause a stir, we're sunk. I'm not sure a new team could weather a scandal like that.'

'Like what, exactly?'

'Dilettante aristocrat playing at running a motor racing team; young driver killed in a racing game after a party. They could have a field day, if they chose to. And it's only a matter of time before someone in Fleet Street chooses to.'

'Is that how you see me, Monty? Just a dilettante aristocrat playing games?'

'No, Fishy, of course not.'

'Then stand beside me. We'll have no more truck with Kovacs and his cynical dealings. We'll just have to show him who's the best on the circuit. Shut him up for good.'

Chapter Eleven

The croquet match was abandoned when it finally descended into complete chaos. It hadn't been far from disarray since it began, but when Lord Riddlethorpe and Lady Lavinia began some serious sibling sniping over the legality of an attempted stun shot, Lady Hardcastle calmly suggested that they call it a day. Mrs Beddows and Herr Kovacs declared themselves the winners, and no one else had the will to argue.

The guests ate lunch on the terrace and the mood had lifted once competition was removed from the equation. Betty and I stayed to help serve once the household servants had brought everything out.

'The problem with you, Jake,' said Lord Riddlethorpe, 'is that you're too competitive.'

'It's your problem, too, brother dear,' said Lady Lavinia. 'You've never been able to cope with the fact that I'm so competitive. You never could stand being beaten by your little sister.'

The guests laughed.

'Not today, though, dear heart,' he said. 'Roz and Viktor won today.'

'Nonsense,' she said. 'We let Roz say she'd won because she's even more insufferable than you when she loses.'

Most of the guests laughed. Mrs Beddows glowered.

'We won fair and square,' said Mrs Beddows. 'Didn't we, Viktor?'

'Square *und* fair, *ja*,' said Herr Kovacs, eliciting more laughter.

'You can't say fairer than that,' said Lord Riddlethorpe.

'Or squarer,' said Mr Waterford.

The laughter continued. Things, as far as I could see, were back to normal.

'You three must have been a force to be reckoned with in your schooldays,' said Mr Waterford.

'Four, surely,' said Herr Kovacs.

'Four?'

'Was there not a fourth girl that was mentioned the other evening? The girl next to Lavinia in the photograph?'

'A story for another time, I think we said,' said Lady Lavinia quickly.

Lord Riddlethorpe steered the conversation in a fresh direction. 'While we're all here,' he said, 'I wonder if I might impose on you a little. It's to do with the, ah . . .'

'The elephant at the dining table?' suggested Mr Waterford.

'She's just big boned,' said Mrs Beddows, gesturing towards Miss Titmus.

Lord Riddlethorpe ignored her. 'Inspector Foister telephoned me this morning. There have been some . . . Let me see, what did he say? . . . Ah, yes, that's it, some "administrative delays" in the matter of poor Ellis Dawkins, and the inquest can't be held until late next week. We'll all be called as witnesses, of course. You're all welcome to stay, if you can. It would be a great help to me if you were able to – I should like to settle things as soon as we're able.'

There were murmurs of assent.

'We must get our stories straight,' said Herr Kovacs.

'Our stories?' said Lord Riddlethorpe. 'We don't need stories, Viktor. We simply tell the truth.'

'There will be a scandal if you don't watch out. You know how the newspapers . . . What is the word? . . . Misrepresent? Yes, misrepresent,

I think. You know how the newspapers misrepresent stories involving the aristocracy. You have your deference and your social rules, but you do not always have the respect of your newspapers. They will make much of this.'

'We have nothing to hide. The police are treating it as an accident, so they'll not ask about the crash,' said Lord Riddlethorpe. 'As far as Foister is concerned, Dawkins lost control on a bend and hit a tree.'

'But it wasn't an accident, Fishy, was it?' said Miss Titmus anxiously. 'Morgan said the brake cable had been cut. Emily's looking into it for you. Everyone in the house knows. We're all going to be in terrible trouble.'

'She's right,' said Mr Waterford. 'If we tell the truth, we'll have to mention the sabotage, and then the scandal would be unavoidable. Someone sabotaged that motor car.'

'No one will lie,' said Lord Riddlethorpe sternly. 'If they ask, we shall tell them what we know, and let the cards fall where they may.'

Herr Kovacs narrowed his eyes, but said nothing.

The lunch party broke up quickly after that. Everyone headed back to their rooms to change, but Lord Riddlethorpe hung back. He took Lady Hardcastle to one side, and she signalled for me to join them.

Lord Riddlethorpe was already speaking as I arrived. '. . . how you were getting on. You know, with your "investigations", as it were.'

'We're still getting the lie of the land, to be honest, Fishy, dear,' said Lady Hardcastle. 'It's still early days.'

'Early days?' said Lord Riddlethorpe, clearly trying to suppress his frustration.

'It's only forty-eight hours since the crash, dear,' she said equably. 'But a picture is beginning to form, wouldn't you agree, Armstrong?'

'Certainly, my lady,' I said.

'I'm sorry,' he said. 'I didn't mean to take out my frustrations on you. What sort of picture is forming?'

Lady Hardcastle outlined our suppositions about the chain of events leading to the sabotage. Lord Riddlethorpe pursed his lips as he listened.

'So the timing doesn't particularly rule anyone out,' he said when she had finished.

'Not really, no,' she said. 'But Armstrong has come upon some information that might rule at least one person in. Possibly two.'

He looked at me expectantly.

'How well do you know Herr Kovacs, my lord?' I said.

'I've been acquainted with him for a few years now. Decent enough chap. Surely you don't suspect him?'

Without mentioning Evan's involvement, I explained that we'd seen a copy of Herr Kovacs's draft letter offering to buy the racing team. I also recounted the conversation between Herr Kovacs and Mr Waterford, as though I had been the one who overheard it.

Lord Riddlethorpe thought for a moment. 'Just good business,' he said eventually. 'He knows the motors are top notch. He's seen a chance to acquire them at a knock-down price, that's all. Sound move. I'd do the same.' The words sounded sincere enough, but something in his manner suggested that he, too, had suspicions about Herr Kovacs.

◆ ◆ ◆

Mrs Ruddle, the cook, and Patty, her kitchen maid, were already hard at work on preparations for dinner when I brought in the last of the plates from the terrace.

'. . . but if you drizzle the melted butter, it doesn't split,' said Mrs Ruddle.

I put the tray of plates beside the sink.

'Hello, Miss Armstrong,' said Patty.

'Hello, Patty,' I said. 'How are things in the most important room in the house?'

The young kitchen maid laughed delightedly.

'It's always nice when the other staff appreciate us, my dear,' said Mrs Ruddle.

'Everyone always appreciates the cook, Mrs Ruddle,' I said. 'And if she's as accomplished as you . . . well . . .'

The older woman beamed.

'Have you worked here long?' I asked.

'Comin' on forty years,' she said proudly. 'I were younger than little Patty here when I started. I didn't know a Béarnaise from a brisket.'

'So you've known his lordship since he was born?'

'You could say as I built him into the man he is today,' she said. 'Feedin' him up, like. Course, they sent him away to school, so I didn't get a chance to look after him quite as I'd-a liked. Him and Lady Lavinia both. I never did understand that. Nothin' in the world more joyous than havin' little-uns about the place, and they send 'em away as soon as they can.'

'Lady Hardcastle would have given anything to go to school,' I said. 'She always says she was terribly jealous of her brother.'

'It's an adventure for them, I suppose,' she said grudgingly. 'But it still doesn't seem right. If there'd ever been a Mr Ruddle, I'd-a liked to think we'd-a made a home for our children as they'd not want to get away from so quick, like.'

'Was there ever a candidate?' I asked.

She laughed. 'For Mr Ruddle? I don't reckon as anyone would pay attention to an old lump like me.'

Patty looked up from her chopping. 'Rubbish, Mrs R, they'd be lucky to have you.'

'And look here, see?' said Mrs Ruddle. 'I've got a kid to be lookin' after as it is. My life's not worked out so bad. But now we've got to talkin' about school, I do wish I'd had a bit of schoolin'. I learned to read and write from Mr Selvester – he was the butler here when I was a scullery maid. He taught all us youngsters. Said it would "stand us in good stead". He was a martinet, mind you. Nasty, nasty man. I reckon he only taught us so we'd know which Bible verse we were disobeyin'. But he done us all a favour. I wouldn't be where I am if I couldn't read a recipe. How about you, my dear? Did you get any schoolin'?'

I paused for a moment. I usually didn't mind sharing my life story, but I had rather hoped to find out a little more about Lady Lavinia and her friends. Still, it looked as though that ship had sailed, so I decided to go along with it. Perhaps I could bring the subject back to her ladyship later. 'A little,' I said. 'I grew up in a circus—'

'You never!' said Patty. 'Ow!' In her astonishment, her knife had slipped and she had nicked the edge of her finger.

'Run it under the tap, girl. Quickly,' said Mrs Ruddle.

'I really did. One day the circus came to Merthyr Tydfil. My mother and her friends walked over the mountain to see it. The next thing Mamgu – that's what we called my grandma – the next thing Mamgu knew, my mother's friends were telling her my mother had run off with the knife thrower. They got married, and I'm the youngest of their seven children. Only youngest by twenty minutes, mind you.'

'And you lived in the circus?' said Patty. She was still bleeding, but no longer seemed to care.

'We did. We travelled all over the country. The lion tamer taught me to read. Whenever we were in a town big enough to have a library, I'd spend all day in there with the books. I didn't care what it was, just so long as I had my face in a book.'

Mrs Ruddle laughed. 'You ran away from a circus to read books,' she said. 'Now I've heard it all.'

'Shush, Mrs R,' said Patty. 'I think it's wonderful. Did you learn any tricks? I love the circus.'

'My father taught me knife throwing,' I said. 'I can do a little tumbling, too. And if there's ever an escaped circus lion on the estate, I know exactly what to do.'

'Oh my goodness,' said Patty. 'What?'

'Run like the clappers,' I said.

'You silly-billy,' said Mrs Ruddle.

Betty arrived at exactly that moment.

'What are we all laughing at?' she asked innocently.

That set the cook and her kitchen maid off again.

'Just sharing some of the secrets of the circus,' I said.

'The circus?' said Betty. 'That's nothing. Why not tell them about the espionage?'

'Espionage?' said Mrs Ruddle. 'Are you spinnin' us a yarn, Miss Armstrong?'

'No,' I said. 'The one follows the other. Mamgu was ill, so my mother went back to Aberdare, taking the three youngest children with her. My father and our four older brothers stayed with the circus, but Dai – he's just two years older than me – my twin sister, Gwenith, and I went back to live in the valleys. I was twelve by then, I think. We went to the local school for a year while we all tried to settle into life in a mining village. Dai ended up down the pit like his grandfather before him, Gwenith took over Mamgu's job in the grocer's shop, and I . . . I left home again.'

'To be a spy,' said Mrs Ruddle suspiciously.

'No, to be a scullery maid in Cardiff.'

'And that's where you met Lady Hardcastle?' asked Patty.

'No, I met her in London. I moved to a house in London after two years with the Williamses, and then two years after that, my new employers' friend, Lady Hardcastle, offered me a job as her lady's maid.'

'How wonderful,' said Patty.

'At seventeen?' said Mrs Ruddle. 'Now I know you're pitchin' a tale. Weren't never no seventeen-year-old ladies' maids. You take no notice, Patty.'

'No, Mrs Ruddle,' said Betty. 'That part's true. Mrs Beddows told me that part of it. She doesn't know anything about the circus, but Lady Hardcastle told them all about how she met Miss Armstrong. She told them about how she and Sir Roderick went to Shanghai and took Miss Armstrong with them. And about how Sir Roderick was murdered and they had to flee for their lives.'

'Well I never,' said Mrs Ruddle. 'I beg your pardon, Miss Armstrong, I'm sure. I've never heard the like. Well, well, well.'

She and Patty resumed their chopping and stirring, each apparently too dumbfounded to say any more.

Betty, too, simply stood there, lost in thought.

'Did you want me for anything, *fach*?' I asked. 'Or was it Mrs Ruddle?'

'What?' said Betty absently. 'Oh, no, nothing special. I just came to . . . to . . .'

'To get away from Mrs Beddows for a bit?' I suggested.

She sighed. 'You have no idea what it's like,' she said. 'I swear she's the most . . . the most . . .'

'Always was, my dear,' said Mrs Ruddle. 'She's always been the nasty one in their little gang. Lady Lavinia used to bring her little friends home in the school holidays. They was lovely girls, really. Always up to mischief, but usually nothin' nasty. If there was ever an undercurrent of nastiness, though, it was always little Rosamund Birchett, as she was then, who was the ring leader. She could be right spiteful.'

'What sort of things did she do?' I asked.

'It's hard to recall specific things,' she said. 'There was always summat goin' on. They loved to play little jokes and tricks on each other, and on the youngsters on the staff, too, sometimes. Good-natured things, for the most part. But if ever things turned ugly, it was always little Miss Birchett as was at the centre of it. They say something happened at their school once, too.'

'I'm surprised at you, Mrs Ruddle!' Mrs McLelland, the housekeeper, had appeared like the manifestation of an unquiet spirit. 'You should be setting Patience a better example than this. You know better than to speak disparagingly about our guests. That's not the way things are done at Codrington.'

Mrs Ruddle looked none too pleased at being told off in front of her kitchen maid, but, to her credit, she held her tongue.

'And as for you, Miss Buffrey, I should have thought you would be standing up for your mistress, rather than joining in with this tittle-tattle.'

Betty blushed crimson.

I decided I ought to try to rescue the situation somehow. Ignoring Mrs McLelland, I said, 'Are you expected back any time soon, Betty?'

'What? No, she's writing letters. I'll have to get her dressed for tea. And then again for dinner. But I've got an hour or so to myself.'

'Come on, then, *fach*,' I said. 'Let's go and see what mischief we two can get up to on our own.'

◆ ◆ ◆

As it turned out, Betty and I remained mischief-free. She was reluctant to give details about her most recent run-in with her employer, but it clearly had left her agitated and anxious. We walked in the kitchen garden for a short while, but conversation eluded us. I tried simply sitting on one of the low walls in companionable silence, but she couldn't settle. Eventually, she apologized for her mood and returned to work.

There was nothing for it: I would have to return to mine.

'Ah, there you are, Flo,' said Lady Hardcastle as I entered her room. 'I was about to ring down for you.'

'Is there something the matter?' I said.

'No, dear, there's rarely anything the matter. I was just thinking of having a bath.'

'I shall draw one for you at once.'

'You're very kind, but that's not why I was going to ring. I'll need you for hair-fettling duties, obviously, but I actually wanted to talk about Kovacs. He's very high on my list now.'

'I can see why,' I said as I went through to the bathroom to run her a bath. 'And Mrs Beddows, too.'

'Roz?' she called. 'Well, I—'

There was a knock at the door.

'Come in,' called Lady Hardcastle.

I stayed in the bathroom, kneeling beside the bath. The taps were already running, but I could still hear what was going on in the next room.

'Hello, Emily,' said Lady Lavinia. 'I do hope I'm not interrupting . . . Oh, you're running a bath. I'll come back.'

'Nonsense, Jake, dear. Do come in. Armstrong will take care of it.'

'She's here? I'd really rather we were alone.'

'It's up to you, of course. I can send her on her merry way, if you wish. If you prefer to come back, I shall be but moments – I'll be clean and scrubbed in no time. To tell the truth, though, I doubt she can hear us over all that running water.'

'Very well,' said Lady Lavinia. 'It's . . . Look, I'm not terribly good at this sort of thing. I'm not one of Nature's dalliers and I . . .'

There was a moment or two of silence.

'Do you think Harry could ever go for a girl like me?' she gabbled.

'Oh, Jake, you are silly,' said Lady Hardcastle. 'Of course he could. Haven't you seen the way he's been looking at you?'

'Well, I was hoping . . . but he could be a cad, for all I know. He might look like that at any available woman.'

'No, dear, he's smitten. It's true that we don't see each other as often as we ought, but I've never seen him behave the way he does around you. He's been engineering "chance" meetings all week. He hangs on your every word at the table. You must have noticed him showing off on the tennis court. He never puts that much effort into tennis. It's all for you.'

'Oh, I say. How splendid,' said Lady Lavinia. 'And you don't mind?'

'Mind? Why on earth should I mind?'

'Well, he's your big brother. I thought I ought to check. I feel terribly protective of Fishy. I'm sure I'd want a full account of any doxy making sheep's eyes at him.'

'Well, when you put it like that,' laughed Lady Hardcastle, 'I suppose I ought to be more concerned. Are you a doxy? And what are your intentions towards my brother?'

'Entirely dishonourable, darling, especially now you've confirmed that I might not be embarrassed if I made them known.'

'I should think you're on to what the gambling fraternity refer to as a "sure thing" there, dear. And, though I'm not certain it's my place to give it, you have my blessing.'

The bath was becoming alarmingly full, but I feared that if I were to switch off the taps, the conversation would end. I reached in to pull out the plug, keeping the taps running. It was stuck. Bath plugs never get stuck. I yanked fiercely at its chain, but it wouldn't budge. I stood to get better purchase on the recalcitrant plug.

I'm not entirely certain what happened next. I've pieced it together from the reports of others, but my own recollections are hazy. The tiles were wet. The soles of my boots were smooth. I leaned against the edge of the bath and bent forwards to grab the bath plug's chain. I gave one more mighty heave, and my feet slipped out from under me. I toppled forwards.

The next thing I knew I was lying on my back on the flooded bathroom floor. I was soaked through. My head was pounding. I didn't want to open my eyes. I felt hands on my face.

'Flo, dear?' said Lady Hardcastle. 'Can you hear me?'

I tried to nod my head.

'No, don't do that,' she said. 'Try to stay still.'

'I'll call for the doctor,' said Lady Lavinia. She sounded a long way off.

'Thank you, dear, but I don't think that will be necessary. It's a nasty bump, but she's had worse. Haven't you?'

Even without her injunction against nodding my head, the resulting bolts of pain from the past attempt would have dissuaded me from trying it again. I raised my hand instead, and she squeezed my fingers reassuringly.

'If you could help me to get her out of these wet things and into my bed,' said Lady Hardcastle, 'I'll keep an eye on her to make sure there's no lasting damage.'

'Of course, of course,' said Lady Lavinia.

Being capable, intelligent ladies – blessed as they were with the keenest minds, and having had the finest education available anywhere in the Empire – it took them almost half an hour to get me out of my wet clothes and into a warm, dry bed. By the time they were done, I was freezing cold and we were all exhausted.

Apparently, I smiled and said, 'Don't let that duck touch my books.'

'Do please let me call Dr Edling,' said Lady Lavinia when I was finally settled. 'It's really no trouble. He's a charming old stick. He'll be here in no time. It would reassure us all, I think.'

'I think so, too,' said Lady Hardcastle. 'Thank you.'

'I'll be back in two shakes.'

'There's no need, dear. You join your guests for tea. Give them my apologies.'

'Of course. Thank you. I'll get cook to send you both something. Armstrong needs hot, sweet tea, at the very least. And perhaps some sandwiches. And cake.'

'Brandy might help, too,' suggested Lady Hardcastle.

'Certainly. I'll make sure there's brandy, too.'

'Tea will be fine, your ladyship,' I said groggily.

'It's not for you, Flo, it's for me. I've had a terrible shock. Lie still and don't interfere.'

I could still hear Lady Lavinia laughing as she made her way down the passage to the stairs.

◆ ◆ ◆

The doctor came and went. I was feeling much better by the time he arrived, but I submitted to his prodding, stethoscoping, and tut-tutting. Despite my protestations of my own robust health, he insisted that I rest. Lady Hardcastle decided there and then that I should stay in her bed.

And so I lay there, alternately dozing and fidgeting impatiently. Later, I heard Betty come into the room to help Lady Hardcastle to dress for dinner. She said it had been Mrs Beddows's idea, but I suspected that the suggestion had actually come from Betty herself. Not only was Betty the kinder and more thoughtful of the two, she was also the one who would benefit more from spending a few minutes away from her usual place.

As they both left, Lady Hardcastle told me that Lady Lavinia had had another room made up for her so that she needn't disturb me again before morning.

Betty returned a little later, bringing tea, some cake, and my copy of *The Time Machine*. We chattered inconsequentially until it was time for her to return to Mrs Beddows's room to ready her for bed.

I read for a while once she'd gone, but, to my intense irritation, I found that everyone was right and that I really did need to rest. Betty had already switched off the light for me, so all I had to do was blow out my candle and snuggle down.

I slipped swiftly into a dream-filled sleep, in which Morlocks battled with an army of librarian ducks, and no one knew how to play croquet.

There was a loud click. I awoke instantly. It took me a moment to work out that it had been the sound of a bedroom door closing somewhere. I heard the creak of a floorboard outside the door as someone made their way carefully along the passage.

I tried to get up to investigate, but the pain in my head persuaded me not to be so stupid. There were all sorts of reasons for someone to be wandering about the passages of a country house in the middle of the night – few of them wicked, but some of them decidedly naughty. I had no idea of the time, but it was pitch dark. I decided that discretion was the better part of valour, and drifted back off to sleep.

I dreamed that it happened twice more.

When I woke again, there was sunlight streaming in through the curtains and a gentle knocking on the bedroom door.

'Enter,' I croaked imperiously.

The door opened to reveal Betty bearing a breakfast tray. 'Hark at you and your airs and graces,' she said. 'One night in the toffs' rooms, and suddenly you're the Queen of the May.'

'I was born to it,' I said as I sat upright.

'That's a lovely lump on your nut,' she said as she set the tray down. 'The story is that your mistress was trying to teach Lady Lavinia her tennis backhand and she caught you on the bonce.'

I laughed. 'As always, the story is better than the truth. Thank you for bringing this up, though. It's a rare treat.'

'It's my pleasure.'

'Shouldn't you be seeing to Mrs Beddows, though?'

'Ordinarily,' she said. 'But she sent me away with a flea in my ear this morning. She wanted a lie-in.'

She sat on the edge of the bed.

'Well, she did have a hectic day of being soundly thrashed at tennis,' I suggested.

'She barely broke a sweat. I reckon it was more likely her night manoeuvres.' She pinched a slice of toast from my plate.

'Mrs Beddows? Surely not. Who with?'

'I've said too much already,' she mumbled, her mouth still full of toast. 'I really shouldn't be gossiping.'

'Betty Buffrey, you're a wicked tease.'

Lady Hardcastle breezed in.

'Good morning, O bruisèd one,' she said. 'Oh, and good morning to you, Miss Buffrey. No, please don't get up. I just need to collect a few things. Do you know where my . . . actually, where anything is? I need suggestions for a morning outfit.'

I shooed Betty out of the way, and tried to clamber out of bed. I stumbled again as I became entangled in the voluminous nightgown I was wearing.

'What on earth?' I said.

'It's one of mine,' said Lady Hardcastle. 'We thought you ought to have something in case you needed to get up in the night. I must say I've always thought of myself as "statuesque" at worst. But seeing that on you, I rather feel like some manner of galumphing giantess. It looks like a marquee.'

'Nonsense, my lady,' I said as I untwined myself from the folds of cotton. 'It just needs taking in a bit round the . . . well, all over, really. But it was a kind thought.'

'You have things to do,' said Betty. 'I'd better be on my way. I'm sorry for intruding, my lady.'

'Nonsense, dear,' said Lady Hardcastle. 'Thank you for looking after Armstrong for me.'

Betty curtseyed and left the room.

There was nothing wrong with me apart from a slight headache that throbbed a little if I bent down, so I was able to help Lady Hardcastle get ready without too much trouble.

'What happened to my own clothes?' I said as I put the finishing touches to her hair. 'I dimly recall their being soaked.'

She looked around. 'Over there on the chair?' she suggested.

I looked and, sure enough, my clothes were folded over the back of the chair, clean, dry, and neatly pressed.

'How the Dickens?' I said.

'It's always baffled me,' she said. 'When I was a girl, I always believed elves did it.'

I raised my eyebrows, and instantly regretted it as the pain in my forehead intensified. 'More likely to be the girls in the laundry,' I said.

'Much more likely,' she said. 'Will you be fit to accompany me today? There's nothing planned, and the day has the potential to be frightfully dull without you.'

'With all your new friends to keep you entertained, my lady?' I said. 'Surely not.'

'I should love to go along with the jape and tease you a little, but the truth is that there's hardly anyone about. Fishy has gone off somewhere with Monty. Jake and Helen are giggling together, while Harry looks on like a lovesick puppy. Viktor and Roz haven't surfaced yet. I'm all on my own.'

'Herr Kovacs and Mrs Beddows aren't up yet?' I said. 'Betty mentioned that Mrs Beddows was having a lie-in. She suggested she was worn out from "night manoeuvres".'

'With Viktor? Oh, I say, that would be too, too funny.'

'And a trifle unlikely,' I said.

'Why? Oh, they're simply made for each other. Peas in a pod.'

The threat of renewed unpleasantness from the bruise on my forehead dissuaded me from raising my eyebrows disapprovingly. I 'hmm'-ed instead.

She laughed. 'Come on, then, lazy-bones,' she said. 'Get yourself dressed, and we can take the air.'

◆ ◆ ◆

'I take it you heard Jake talking about Harry,' said Lady Hardcastle as we took a turn around the grounds.

'That was what caused my tragic downfall,' I said. 'I was trying to get the plug out so that the bath wouldn't overflow.'

'Why not just turn off the taps?'

'You'd told her it was safe to talk because the sound of the water would cover your conversation. If the water stopped, then so would she.'

She laughed. 'Instead, you stopped her rather effectively in your own uniquely violent way.'

'And I have the lump to prove it. What do you think, though?'

'About the lump? It's very fetching.'

'No, my lady, about Lady Lavinia and Harry.'

'Ah, of course. Sorry. I think it's splendid. Poor Harry had a couple of ill-fated love affairs in his twenties, and then threw himself into his work. He's risen through the Foreign Office ranks, but he's lonely. And Jake's a sweetheart. It takes a genuine poppet to ask a chap's sister for permission.'

'Which you graciously gave.'

'Not strictly mine to give, old thing, but yes. After we'd left you to your slumbers, I told her it was actually a matter entirely between the two of them, and wished her the best of British.'

'So you won't tease him about it?'

'Heavens, Flo, what do you take me for? I shall tease him mercilessly. What manner of sister would I be if I didn't chaff him?'

We rounded a corner and found Lady Lavinia sitting on her favourite stone bench with Miss Titmus. Harry was approaching from the opposite direction at a fair rate of knots. Lady Hardcastle increased her own speed in an effort to reach the ladies before he did.

'What ho, you two,' she said jovially. 'What a glorious day.'

'We were just saying the same thing,' said Miss Titmus. 'How are you, Armstrong? Lady Lavinia was just telling me about your mishap.'

'I've had worse, madam,' I said.

'Gracious! You have? That looks bad enough as it is. You've really had worse?'

'Don't get her started, Helen, dear,' said Lady Hardcastle. 'You'll be stuck there all day listening to tales of danger, derring-do, and disaster. Meanwhile, I'll be left feeling terribly guilty because most of her wounds and injuries were sustained while protecting me when I'd foolishly overreached myself.'

Harry had caught us up by now and was hovering in the background, clearly eager to interrupt, but uncertain about doing so.

'Oh, do stop dithering, Harry, dear,' said Lady Hardcastle. 'Either come over or sling your hook.'

'Good morning, ladies,' said Harry as he joined the growing group. 'Good morning, Strong Arm.'

'Good morning, Mr Feather-Stone-Huff,' I said with a curtsey.

'That's quite a bump you've got there,' he said as he peered closely at my aching forehead. 'Rumour has it that our Emily clouted you with an ornamental doo-dah. Something to do with finally growing weary of your infernal cheek.'

'It was bound to happen sooner or later, sir,' I said. 'Usually, she doesn't leave marks.'

'Oh, Flo, you absolute beast,' said Lady Hardcastle. 'Take no notice, ladies. Harry, I blame you for encouraging her.'

I grinned unapologetically while the ladies laughed.

'Now, Helen,' said Lady Hardcastle. 'I wonder if I might have a word or two in private. Away from my brother's flapping lugholes.'

'Oh,' said Miss Titmus. 'Why, of course. Do excuse me, Jake, Harry. It seems my attention is required elsewhere.'

She stood, and the three of us strolled away, leaving Harry and Lady Lavinia on their own.

'Heavens, Emily,' said Miss Titmus. 'Whatever's the matter? Have I done something terrible?'

'No, you goose,' said Lady Hardcastle. 'I just wanted to leave the two lovebirds alone. Harry's a dear, sweet boy, and quite a whizz at the Foreign Office, but in matters of the heart he's as hesitant and useless as a . . . as a . . . Help me out, Flo. As hesitant and useless as . . . ?'

'You're on your own, my lady,' I said. 'If you're going to set off on these reckless similes without any idea of how to complete the journey, you've only yourself to blame.'

'Harrumph,' she said. 'You see what I have to put up with, Helen, dear? I think you're better off without a lady's maid. They're nothing but trouble.'

'I couldn't disagree more,' said Miss Titmus. 'I shall be placing an advertisement for a companion as soon as I get back to London.'

'Good for you. I should warn you, though, that Flo here is a unique treasure. You'll not find her like in even the finest agencies in London.'

'I very much get that feeling,' said Miss Titmus. 'Changing the subject: how are your investigations coming along?'

'Not so well, I'm afraid. We strongly suspect that Mr Kovacs might have had something to do with it, but it's just supposition – we've no proof. I'm beginning to think there might be a touch of xenophobia mixed in with it as well. We've had more than our fair share of run-ins with the fine folk of Austria-Hungary over the years, and I fear I might have taken against them as a nation.'

'I've never trusted the Belgians myself,' said Helen absently. 'Not quite French, not quite Dutch. They make delicious chocolate, mind you.'

'At least they'll be on our side if things cut up rough. Them and the French.'

'Are things likely to cut up rough, do you think?'

'It's only a matter of time, I feel. The German Empire seems to be spoiling for a fight.'

'I do feel like such a duffer sometimes,' said Miss Titmus sadly. 'I make no effort to keep up with international affairs.'

'I can't honestly say I feel like a better person for knowing,' said Lady Hardcastle. 'It's just a habit from a past life. There are more things in heaven and earth than are dreamed of in the philosophies of the politicians and diplomats. I'd as soon keep up to date with developments in science and the cinematic arts. Much more relevant, if you ask me.'

'I don't even do that. Well, I suppose I'm au fait with the world of photography.'

'Specialization is the modern way, dear,' said Lady Hardcastle. 'Expertise. That's the key . . . Oh, I say, how did we end up here?'

Our aimless wandering had led us into the kitchen garden. I waved to Patty who was, once again, carefully harvesting herbs for Mrs Ruddle.

'Let's cut through the stable yard and make our way to the front of the house,' said Lady Hardcastle. 'I've not really seen that side of the estate.'

We did as she suggested, using the arched doorway in the corner of the walled garden. Morgan Coleman, the mechanic, was already there. He was unlocking the large coach house doors.

'Good morning, Morgan,' said Lady Hardcastle brightly. 'Time to give the thoroughbreds a run out?'

He laughed indulgently. 'Something like that, m'lady,' he said. 'His lordship has an idea for some adjustments to the carburettor on the number two car. Thought I'd make a start before it becomes "urgent", like.'

'Good plan,' she said. 'He's lucky to have you on his staff.'

'Thank you, m'lady,' he grunted as he heaved the first of the enormous doors open. He walked back to do the same with the other door, but something caught his eye. 'What the devil?' he said. He made his way cautiously inside the coach house.

Intrigued, we stopped to watch.

'Lady Hardcastle!' he called. 'Could you come in here, please?'

Lady Hardcastle and I exchanged puzzled looks. She set off at once. Miss Titmus made to follow her, but something about Morgan's tone suggested that it might not be something she would want to see. I laid my hand on her arm.

'I think we should wait here, madam,' I said. 'Just in case.'

'In case what?' she said. 'Oh, I see. Very well.'

Lady Hardcastle re-emerged a few moments later.

'Helen, I need you to go into the house and find Fishy. Tell him I need him in the coach house. Tell him it's urgent.'

'But what . . . ?'

'Now, dear. Go.'

Miss Titmus looked bewildered, but Lady Hardcastle's tone brooked no disobedience. She left on her appointed mission.

'Come with me, Flo,' said Lady Hardcastle, once Miss Titmus had gone. 'This is a most unpleasant development.'

I followed her back into the coach house. Morgan was crouching at the far corner of one of the motor cars. He was examining something on the floor. As we approached, I was able to see the object of his scrutiny. Lying on the floor, a pool of dark, congealed blood around the remains of his skull, was the body of Viktor Kovacs.

Chapter Twelve

It wasn't long before we heard two pairs of footsteps in the yard. The door clattered as Lord Riddlethorpe pulled it further open. He was accompanied by Mr Waterford.

'What's all the fuss, Emily?' asked Lord Riddlethorpe. 'All Helen would say was that it was urgent but she . . .' He caught sight of the body. He swore.

Mr Waterford rushed towards the body, but Lord Riddlethorpe held him back. 'It's best not to touch anything.'

'He's right,' said Lady Hardcastle. 'We should leave everything exactly as it is for the police.'

Morgan indicated the hefty wrench lying on the floor. 'It looks like they used that to stove his head in, your lordship.'

'We'd worked that out for ourselves,' snapped Mr Waterford.

'Steady on, Monty,' said Lord Riddlethorpe. 'We're all a bit shocked, but there's no need for that.'

Mr Waterford turned to Lady Hardcastle. 'And if you were half the "detective" you make yourself out to be, Viktor wouldn't be lying there now.'

'That's enough, Monty!' said Lord Riddlethorpe. 'Emily – Monty and I will go back to the house. I need to call Inspector Foister. Please stay here and see what you can see before he gets here. Morgan – don't let anyone else inside.'

They both nodded their assent, and Lord Riddlethorpe led his friend away.

'What do you think, my lady?' I said as we looked at the scene.

'I'm sure the police surgeon will have a clear idea, but obviously we know that he was killed after midnight and before about half an hour ago. We were all in the library together after dinner, and he left for bed at midnight. If he'd been attacked less than half an hour ago, we'd have seen his attacker. Many of the smaller bloodstains are dry, so I should say it was a good few hours ago.'

'He was struck from the front,' I said. 'He saw his attacker.'

'Which would seem to suggest he knew him.'

'Or her,' I said.

'Or her,' she agreed. 'Again, the surgeon will have a better idea of the angle of the blow, so he'll be able to give us a better idea of the height of the assailant. It looks like just the one blow to the forehead, though, not just from the wound, but from the spray of blood on the floor. Do you see? As the murderer swung the wrench downwards after striking him, it left that spray of blood behind it. But it's neat. Just the one swing. And from this side of the room, I'd say.'

'So Herr Kovacs came down to the coach house,' I said. 'Why? To meet someone? Or was he here to sabotage another motor car?'

'Either is possible,' she said.

'He met someone. He was face-to-face with them when the blow fell. Were they talking? Arguing? Was someone trying to stop him? Did they suspect him of further sabotage and catch him in the act?'

'There are no other signs of a struggle,' she said. 'Nothing knocked over, nothing else damaged. It makes a meeting more likely. If he were surprised in the act of sabotage, he would be more likely to have tried to flee.'

'Or to brazen his way out,' I said. 'Stand up to his accuser and talk his way out of it.'

'Hmm,' she said. 'He might. Morgan, is the back door locked?'

Morgan made his way to the back of the workshop, carefully avoiding anything he thought might have been evidence.

'Locked,' he said when he reached the door.

'Interesting,' said Lady Hardcastle. 'And the main doors were locked when you arrived?'

'Yes, m'lady. You saw me unlockin' 'em.'

'So the attacker left and locked the door behind him. What's the most likely chain of events now, then?'

'It still doesn't point to either,' I said. 'If Herr Kovacs came down here with a key and let himself in, he could have been followed. His murderer would have come in through the open back door, confronted him, killed him, taken the key, and left the way he came. On the other hand, if it was arranged, it would be the murderer who had the key, let himself in, waited for Herr Kovacs, and then locked up after himself.'

'True. But the murderer had a heavy wrench in his hand. The tools are all stored on that back wall. If someone had followed Viktor down here to see what he was up to, they would both have come in through the back door. The murderer would have taken the wrench from the wall, and then come all the way round to the front of the coach house to approach Viktor from this side. Wouldn't he have grabbed his weapon and confronted him there and then? Why walk all the way round? Why put Viktor between himself and his only exit?'

'In that case, the murderer was here first,' I said. 'It was a prearranged meeting.' I looked more closely at the body on the floor. 'If Herr Kovacs had the key, he would have put it in his pocket, wouldn't he? And to get at it, the murderer would have had to search him. But look, his jacket is exactly as it would be if he fell on it. He's not been searched.'

'Good thinking,' she said. 'We really ought to leave all this to the police, you know. But my curiosity is piqued, and as long as we don't actually get in the way, we can't do any harm. Morgan, will you be all right here on your own? I want to take a look round in the house.'

'As you wish, m'lady,' he said. 'I'll wait here for the inspector.'

'Good man. Come along, Armstrong, we need to have a quick snoop before that awful Foister fellow gets here.'

◆ ◆ ◆

Lord Riddlethorpe was pacing the hall when we entered the front door. He ignored us as we hurried towards the stairs, but Mr Waterford glared at Lady Hardcastle.

At the landing, we turned left towards Lady Hardcastle's room, but we passed her room and continued down the passage to the next. Lady Hardcastle tried the door.

'This was Viktor's room. Let's have a quick rummage before anyone else realizes they ought to do the same,' she said.

'I didn't know this was his room,' I said. 'I think I heard him leaving.'

'Oh?'

'Yes. I've no idea what time it was, but I heard a door shut in the middle of the night. It woke me.'

'It would make sense. He certainly left his room in the middle of the night.'

'Mind you,' I said, 'it's hard to tell which door is which just by the sound.'

'Oh, it's quite easy with a bit of practice,' she said. 'They all have their own creaks and groans. One becomes quite adept at discerning who's sneaking about in the night.'

'I'm afraid I only heard the click as it shut. No distinctive creaks or groans for me. I thought I heard two more later, but I might have dreamed it.'

'Viktor leaving, and someone else leaving and returning,' she mused. 'Well, well, well.'

As she spoke, she was hunting around the room. Everything seemed to be in its proper place, though, so there wasn't very much to look at.

'You've got to give Evan some credit,' I said. 'He's clearly taking the role of valet very seriously. This place is immaculate. Look how neatly everything's been put away.'

'He'll go far, certainly. And we really need to speak to him.'

The cluttered writing desk by the window was the only real place of interest.

'What's this doing here?' she said as she picked up the photograph of the girls' school cricket team. 'He seemed fascinated by it at dinner the other night, and here it is in his room.'

She continued to rummage through the papers. Herr Kovacs seemed to have brought his work with him, and had clearly given Evan instructions that nothing on the desk was to be disturbed. 'Cluttered' was the first word that came to my mind, but it seemed scarcely adequate to describe the chaos on the small table.

'Hello,' she said. 'I think we can confirm the meeting hypothesis. Have a look at this.' She indicated a small piece of paper unfolded on the desk.

Without touching it, I inspected it carefully. It was a piece of Codrington Hall notepaper folded in two. It was of the sort that was placed in every room for the use of the guests. The crease was a little rumpled on one side, as though it had been pushed under the door and had caught on something on its way in. I looked back at the doorway and noticed that one of the floorboards sat a little proud of its fellows.

The paper bore a short message, written in a neat, rounded hand:

We need to talk. Meet me in the coach house at two o'clock. The back door will be unlocked. Come alone. R B.

'Blimey,' I said. 'You don't think . . .'

'The only "R B" I can think of is Rosamund Beddows.'

'That's easily solved,' I said. 'Lady Lavinia and Miss Titmus would know Mrs Beddows's handwriting in an instant. Should we take the note? We might be able to find out what it means before the police see it and jump to conclusions?'

'It's tempting, isn't it. But I think not. We can't interfere. We'll have to do as Fishy says and "let the cards fall where they may".'

I heard the sound of footsteps in the passage and touched Lady Hardcastle's arm to attract her attention. I put a finger to my lips and tiptoed to the door. I opened the door a crack and peeped out. I saw the retreating back of Mrs Beddows.

Lady Hardcastle raised an eyebrow in silent enquiry.

'Mrs Beddows, my lady,' I said quietly. 'On her way downstairs.'

'Gracious, she's late.'

'Betty said she was tired and wanted a lie-in.'

'So she did, so she did. A sleepless night, it seems.' She stood for a moment in silent contemplation. 'But we'd best not jump to conclusions ourselves. And we'd better slip away before anyone catches us in here.'

We stole cautiously out of the room. Once safely in the passage and away from Herr Kovacs's door, we strolled casually back towards the stairs – nothing says 'these two women are up to no good' quite so emphatically as seeing them skulking along a passageway.

The door to the servants' staircase opened ahead of us. Mrs McLelland emerged, followed by one of the housemaids.

The housekeeper was giving the girl strict instructions. '. . . but no one – no one – is to go into Herr Kovacs's room until Inspector Foister and his men have examined it. Do you understand?'

The girl nodded meekly.

'And take extra care with—' She stopped talking as she noticed us coming towards her. Lady Hardcastle swept imperiously past, and the two household servants bowed their heads in silence.

We were part way down the stairs before we heard Mrs McLelland's voice once more in the distance. The sound of it distracted me, so that I was looking the wrong way as Mrs Beddows came sprinting back up the stairs towards us, her head down. She almost bowled me over.

'I'm so sorry,' she said breathlessly. 'Oh, it's you. Good morning, Emily.'

'Good morning, Roz, dear,' said Lady Hardcastle. 'Someone after you?'

'What? Oh, I see. No, just need to get something from my room.'

'Don't let us detain you, dear. Shall we see you for lunch?'

'Doubt if we'll be getting any lunch,' said Mrs Beddows over her shoulder as she sprinted on. 'Haven't you heard? Another of Fishy's stupid friends has been found dead. The police will be here soon, and we'll never get any blessed food.'

She was out of sight before Lady Hardcastle could say another word.

◆ ◆ ◆

Inspector Foister was a great deal less supercilious and dismissive once he had a real murder to work with. He arrived within an hour of Lord Riddlethorpe's call, and set to work at once. During a thorough examination of the coach house, he left scraps of paper torn from his notebook, upon which he had written instructions for Sergeant Tarpley when he arrived: 'Take fingerprints', 'Sketch blood pattern', and the like. (I found them when I went for a snoop after he'd gone inside.)

Having diligently catalogued even the minutest details of the scene of the crime, he returned to the house, where Lord Riddlethorpe gave him the use of a small, informal room towards the rear of the ground floor. He called in guests and members of staff one by one, interviewing each of them for up to ten minutes.

I was waiting in Lady Hardcastle's room when she returned from her own meeting with the newly invigorated inspector.

'I say,' she said as she breezed in. 'He's a good deal more impressive when he's got something to get his teeth into.'

'He seems to be much more interested this time,' I said, and I told her about the notes I had just seen in the coach house.

'I'm not sure he's quite up to the standard of our own dear Inspector Sunderland, but he'd certainly give him a run for his money.'

'Do you feel suitably interrogated?' I asked.

'I've been more aggressively questioned – that chap in Bucharest with the rubber cosh and the buckets of iced water was more enthusiastic, for instance – but seldom more thoroughly or thoughtfully.'

'I shall look forward to taking my own turn,' I said.

'I'm glad you said that, dear – it's your turn now. He asked me to send you in next.'

'I shall get down there at once. Do I look presentable?'

'There's a smudge on your dress from when you were poking about in the coach house,' she said. 'But you'll do for an interview with a police inspector.'

I went downstairs.

The inspector was sitting in a comfortable armchair. Opposite him was a chair from the dining room. He invited me to sit. The room itself was uncharacteristically small for the grand house. Perhaps it had been a study in former times, but now it seemed to be a solitary sitting room. The comfortable chair and its companion table were the only other furniture. There was a family photograph on the table beside an ornate lamp. The walls were panelled in oak, giving more credence to the 'former study' idea. A sash window gave a view towards the formal gardens at the rear of the house.

'Miss Armstrong, isn't it?' said the inspector as I sat. I felt uncomfortably prim in the upright chair while he slouched in the armchair with his notebook.

'Yes, Inspector, that's right,' I said.

'And you work for Lady Hardcastle?'

'I do, yes.'

He made a note. 'For how long?'

'How long have I been working for her? Let me see . . . She first offered me a job as her lady's maid in ninety-four, so . . . fifteen years.'

'You can't have been very old,' he said as he made a note. 'What were you, fourteen, fifteen? No one employs a fifteen-year-old lady's maid.'

'I was seventeen.'

'Still far too young, mind you. Not the choice I should have expected someone in Lady Hardcastle's position to take.'

'People have incurred substantial losses betting on things they expected Lady Hardcastle to do.'

He didn't even look up. 'You arrived on Monday, I believe,' he said.

'That's right.'

'You were billeted in the servants' quarters with Miss Buffrey?'

'I was.'

'And yet last night you were sleeping in Lady Hardcastle's room.'

'I was. I slipped and bumped my head while I was drawing her a bath. She let me stay in her room rather than moving me. Lady Lavinia arranged for another room to be prepared for her.'

'So I gather. That means you were on the same corridor as Herr Kovacs. Did you see or hear anything last night?'

'I was awakened by the sound of a door closing,' I said. 'I thought I heard footsteps in the passage.'

'And what time would this have been?'

'I've no idea, I'm afraid. I don't own a watch, and I couldn't see the clock in the dark.'

'It was still dark, though?'

'Pitch black, as far as I could make out.'

'So it was certainly before five,' he said as he made another note. 'Possibly before four if it really was pitch black. Could you tell which door it was?'

'It was only once I was properly awake that I worked out it had been a door at all.'

'And what about the footsteps. A man, would you say?'

'Impossible to tell, Inspector. I heard the creak of a loose floorboard – nothing more telling than that.'

'And you went back to sleep? You didn't get up to investigate these strange noises?'

'I was still feeling a little groggy, I'm afraid, so I wouldn't have felt up to it, even if I did consider it worth the effort.'

'Not worth the effort?' he said. 'I'm given to understand that you and your mistress fancy yourselves as amateur sleuths.'

'In my fifteen years as a household servant, Inspector, I've learned a few things about the lives of our "betters". Comings and goings in the middle of the night are nothing out of the ordinary. The unspoken rule is that as long as everyone is back in their own room by daybreak, everyone else will pretend that nothing untoward has happened. To poke one's beak out of the door and catch someone in the act of slipping into someone else's room would be the height of bad manners.'

'I see,' he said disapprovingly. 'But if it were something of that nature, surely you would have heard another door once the sinner had reached his destination.'

He was right, of course. I already knew full well that I might easily have heard Herr Kovacs slipping out to his fatal rendezvous, but the inspector's observation made it more certain. If someone had left their room for what Betty referred to as 'night manoeuvres', I would probably have heard the click of the door at their destination. Unless . . .

'It's possible that his destination was in another part of the house,' I said. 'Perhaps he wasn't on his way to another guest's room.'

He turned back a few pages in his notebook. 'That would make it Mr Featherstonhaugh visiting Lady Lavinia in the family's part of the house,' he said, his tone reaching a level of puritanical disapproval I'd not heard outside the chapel in Aberdare.

'I can't rule it out, Inspector,' I said. 'But I've known Mr Featherstonhaugh for many years and honestly doubt it would be him. I rather think his intentions are more romantic than lust-filled.'

The inspector grunted. 'To be honest,' he said, 'I rather think you're right.'

'Which means I probably heard Herr Kovacs on his way to meet his unpleasant end,' I said.

'I'm afraid you probably did.'

'Unless I'm lying,' I said. 'I might have heard nothing. I might have been the one who lured him to the coach house and bludgeoned him to death.'

'It's true, miss, you might,' he said, smiling for the first time. 'It would have been a risky strategy to involve yourself in the discovery of the body, though. And your own concussion was real – several people have confirmed it. I don't believe you were capable of getting out of bed, much less wielding a wrench. Why do you say "lured", though? Is it not more likely that he was caught in the act of interfering with his lordship's motor cars?'

Had he not already searched Herr Kovacs's room? Had he not seen the note? I decided to say nothing about it. 'You're right, Inspector, of course. Just a maid's romantic fancy.'

He nodded, and made another note.

'Did you hear anything further?' he asked. 'Did anything else awaken you?'

'Nothing definite,' I said. 'I fancied I heard a door twice more, but I didn't wake properly, so I might have dreamed it.'

'I see,' he said. 'And you discovered the body this morning?'

'Not quite, Inspector,' I said. 'I was with Lady Hardcastle and Miss Titmus. We passed the coach house just as Morgan was opening it up. He discovered the body.'

'So he did, so he did. What happened then?'

I recounted the events as concisely as I could while he carried on writing. At length, he finished making his notes and looked up. 'Thank you for your help, Miss Armstrong,' he said. 'I think I have enough to be going on with now. Would you be good enough to send Miss Betty Buffrey to me, please?'

'Of course,' I said, and stood to leave.

◆ ◆ ◆

Back in Lady Hardcastle's room, I recounted my brief interview with the inspector.

'He doesn't waste any time on chit-chat, does he?' said Lady Hardcastle when I'd finished. 'I thought we'd be stuck in there for hours while he delved into every aspect of life here.'

'I was in and out before I'd had a chance to become uncomfortable in that dining chair,' I said.

'Nice touch, that: sit the victim in an awkward chair. Puts them at a disadvantage while he lounges in an armchair. Did you get the feeling he had any idea what's going on?'

'None at all,' I said. 'Although he might just be being cagey – he had no reason to let me in on the results of his deliberations.'

'No, you're right. Inspector Sunderland would have told us, mind you. Did he ask you anything about the crash?'

'Not as such,' I said. 'He suggested that Herr Kovacs might have been clubbed while he was interfering with the motor cars, that was all.'

'Ah, yes,' she said thoughtfully. 'And he made no mention of the note. Do you think he even saw it?'

'He wouldn't have pulled me up on my "lured" comment if he had. How could he have missed it?'

'He couldn't,' she said. 'Not a man who leaves notes all over the scene of the crime for his assistants to follow up.' She sat for a moment in thought. 'Keep cave for me for a moment, would you? I'm going to nip into Viktor's room again.'

I followed her out into the passage and loitered awkwardly while she slipped into the still-unlocked bedroom. She emerged scant moments later and waved me back into her own room.

'No sign of it,' she said once the door was closed behind her.

'So either the inspector has it and isn't letting on—'

'—or it was gone by the time he searched the room,' she said, finishing the thought for me. She sat down at the writing desk and waved me into the armchair.

'I wish we'd pinched it ourselves now,' I said. 'We could do clever things with the handwriting. Or something.'

'Or something,' she said with a laugh. 'Its absence tells us something, though, don't you think? I'd say that makes it odds-on it was sent by the murderer.'

'As opposed to . . . ?'

'Oh, I don't know,' she said airily. 'Some sort of red herring placed there by the Fates to throw us off the scent.'

'The Fates go in for that sort of thing, do they?' I said. 'Don't they have more important matters to concern themselves with?'

'Contumacious and capricious are the Fates. One never knows where they'll turn their mischievous attentions.'

'Right you are, my lady,' I said. 'It's still no real help, though. Anyone could have taken it.'

'Anyone?'

'We strolled nonchalantly in and out of the room without being noticed. We might have a little more experience at furtivity than everyone else in the house, but it didn't tax our skills even a tiny bit. Anyone who could find their way to Herr Kovacs's room could have filched the note, with no one else the wiser.'

'I'll concede that. But did anyone have an obvious opportunity?'

'Evan Gudger is supposed to be in and out of there all day if he's serving as valet. We met that housemaid in the passage, too.'

'With Mrs McLelland giving her stern instructions not to go in,' she said. 'And then, of course, there was . . .'

'Mrs Beddows?' I suggested.

'Roz Beddows, yes . . . R B.' She had been doodling on a page of her journal as we spoke. Now she stared pensively at the ceiling, tapping her mechanical pencil against her teeth.

'It might not be someone's initials,' I suggested. 'It could stand for anything. A coded instruction, maybe. Or some familiar signature between friends.'

'"Rule Britannia", perhaps?'

'Or "Rubber Bananas". Or "Reluctant Baboons". Or "Re-heated Beetroot"? The possibilities aren't limitless, but they're huge. So it doesn't have to be a person's initials.'

'It doesn't,' she said, 'but it's the most commonplace way of ending a letter, to sign it with one's name or initials. Would someone who was close enough to have a secret sign-off also be likely to bludgeon their friend to death?'

'I suppose not,' I said. 'What I've seen of Mrs Beddows over the past few days hasn't endeared her to me, and I've not heard much from Betty that would change my opinion. Nevertheless, I'm reluctant to believe that she's the sort to smash a man's head open with a big spanner.'

'Technically, I think it was a wrench. Adjustable, do you see? But I concur. The idea of her being a murderer doesn't sit well.'

'Someone else using her initials as a ruse, then?' I said. 'For all her character flaws, she's a strikingly attractive lady. An offer of a meeting with her might tempt any man.'

'And your pal Betty says she was on manoeuvres. Perhaps Viktor was the lucky recipient of her attentions. They were thick as thieves during the croquet match.'

'And if the murderer knew that, what easier way to lure Herr Kovacs to his doom.'

'It's all possible,' she said. 'I'm not sure I'd be overly thrilled by the offer of an assignation in a dusty, oil-stained coach house, mind you.'

'That would never have occurred to Herr Kovacs. He loved oil and machines. It would have been his own romantic paradise.'

'The question, then,' she said as she put down her pencil and stood up. 'Is who on earth had motive enough to lure him out there and do him in?'

There was a knock at the door.

'Yes?' called Lady Hardcastle.

The door opened and Miss Titmus poked her head in.

'Ah, Emily,' she said, 'there you are. Would you mind awfully if I came in?'

'Not at all, dear. Pull up a . . . Oh, there are no more chairs. That's a bit of an oversight.'

I rose from the armchair.

'Please, miss,' I said, 'take the armchair. It's surprisingly comfortable.'

'Oh,' she said. 'I don't want to push you out if you two are busy.'

'Nonsense,' said Lady Hardcastle. 'She can sit on the bed.'

'Actually, my lady,' I said, 'I was thinking of popping down to the kitchen to see if they were doing anything for your lunch. With the inspector doing inspectory things, and everyone all of a twitter, lunch seems to have been overlooked.'

'This is why you need a lady's maid, Helen, dear,' said Lady Hardcastle. 'I'm sure I'd starve to death without her.'

'I've said the same thing myself, my lady,' I said.

'Often,' she said. 'Off you trot, then, dear. To be honest, I'm not ravenous. See if you can scare up some sandwiches or something. Would you care to join me, Helen? We ought to take advantage of this wonderful weather and take them out on to the lawn for a picnic.'

I set off in search of food.

◆ ◆ ◆

The servants' hall was, as I'd suggested, all of a twitter. Beneath the usual chit-chat that accompanied the hustle and bustle of daily life, there was a tense, murmuring hubbub. Two deaths within a week, and the second was most definitely deliberate murder. The staff were rattled.

A couple of housemaids looked round guiltily as I came in, but quickly resumed their gossiping when they saw I was only one of the visiting servants.

Mrs Ruddle was busy supervising the production of sandwiches in the kitchen.

'Afternoon, Mrs Ruddle,' I said. 'Hello, Patty. Are those sandwiches intended for upstairs by any chance?'

'That's right, m'dear,' said Mrs Ruddle. 'His lordship said as how he didn't want no lunch. But I said, "You got to eat, my lord." Didn't I, Patty?'

'You did, Mrs R,' said Patty.

'So Lady Lavinia said we should send up a tray of sandwiches to the dining room and people could help themselves. I said, "That's no substitute for a proper lunch, my lady." Didn't I, Patty?'

'You did, Mrs R,' said Patty, with a little smile.

'But I suppose it'll have to do,' said Mrs Ruddle resignedly. 'If that's what they wants, that's what they gets.'

'They look scrumptious, Mrs Ruddle,' I said. 'Would you think me awfully cheeky if I were to divert some of them to Lady Hardcastle and Miss Titmus? They say they fancy a picnic on the lawn.'

'If you can carry it out yourself, m'dear,' she said, 'you can take whatever you think you need. I'll get Patty to make you up a tray. We're short of footmen with Evan gadding about goodness knows where, so the less we have to get to the dining room the better.'

'You're a marvel, Mrs Ruddle. Thank you.'

'Well, I don't know about that,' she said. 'I said the other day—'

'You did, Mrs R, you did,' said Patty, without looking up from her work.

Betty appeared in the kitchen doorway.

'Ah,' she said timidly. 'Hello everyone. I wonder . . .'

'What ho, Betty,' I said. 'Come to cadge some lunch for Mrs Beddows?'

'Why, yes, actually. How did you . . . ?'

'We're all at it,' I said. 'I'm trying to get something for Lady Hardcastle and Miss Titmus. They're having a picnic on the lawn. You should get Mrs Beddows to join them – it would save you a fair bit of mucking about. One lunch, and two of us to carry it.'

'I don't think she'd want that,' she said nervously. 'She's . . . ah . . . She's indisposed.'

'Righto,' I said. 'Can we leave it all in your hands, then, Patty? We'll be back in a few moments to gather our fancy fare and get out of your . . . hair. Come on, Betty, let's leave these good ladies to it.'

Without waiting for a response, I took Betty by the elbow and led her out into the servants' hall. It was busy, but that was all to the good. It meant that there was enough going on to cover a private conversation. I indicated that we should sit at one end of the long table, and poured us both a cup of tea from the ever-present pot.

'What's the matter, *fach*?' I said. 'You don't seem your usual happy-go-lucky self. Is it the murder? It can be unsettling, I know, but Inspector Foister will get to the bottom of it. We're in no danger.'

'Are you sure about that? You're not working for a murderer.'

I found myself unable to respond immediately. I stared at her for a moment with my mouth hanging gormlessly open. After a lengthy pause, I gathered myself together enough to say, 'Mrs Beddows?' Not my finest hour as an amateur sleuth.

Betty nodded.

'What makes you say that?' I asked as my wits returned.

'She killed Mr Kovacs,' she whispered. 'I'm sure of it.'

'Why are you sure?'

'She wasn't in her room all night, and now she's in a terrible state. It must be her.'

'Is that what you told the inspector?' I asked.

'No, I . . .'

'You're not as sure as all that, then,' I suggested.

'What else can it be, though? She did him in; she must have.'

'I thought you said she'd been "on manoeuvres" before. Perhaps she accidentally stayed too long. I confess I thought she might be seeing Herr Kovacs, but I take it I was wrong.'

It was her turn to look dumbfounded. 'Mr Kovacs?' she said, almost laughing. 'She's been carrying on with Mr Waterford. For months. I thought everyone knew.'

'Not me,' I said. 'Nor Lady Hardcastle. We're new to your set, remember. Does her husband know?'

'He ignores it for the sake of propriety. And so that he can conduct affairs of his own. Theirs is a "marriage of convenience", I think they call it. She wants his status, he wants her money. As long as neither of them causes a scandal, they just get on with their own lives. Their home is a miserable place for the most part, but she and I are seldom there, so it's not too bad.'

'How thoroughly awful. But how do you know she wasn't with Mr Waterford last night? Isn't that where she's been every night?'

'Maybe,' she said. 'Oh my goodness. What if they're in it together?'

'I still don't understand why you think she had anything to do with the murder of Herr Kovacs, though.'

'Was there a lot of blood?' she said.

I didn't want to get too deeply into the grisly details. Some people imagine themselves to be fascinated, but become surprisingly squeamish once you get down to blood-soaked brass tacks. 'A fair amount,' I said as blandly as I could.

'So the murderer would likely have got some on their clothes?'

'I should say that was inevitable,' I said.

'Mrs Beddows is fastidious about her wardrobe. Everything has to be just so. The right clothes for the right occasion. She has indoor clothes, outdoor clothes, sports clothes, evening clothes, lunchtime clothes—'

'They all do that,' I said.

'I know. She's very fond of a tweed skirt and jacket she bought this season for outdoors.'

'I've seen her in them. She looks very smart.'

'They're missing,' she said.

Chapter Thirteen

Betty helped me carry the impromptu picnic out on to the lawn, and then disappeared to sort out her own mistress's refection.

'You're a living marvel, Flo,' said Lady Hardcastle as I helped them both to sandwiches and wine.

'You really are,' said Miss Titmus.

'Thank you,' I said. 'One tries one's best. Will there be anything else, my lady?'

'No, I think you've met our every need and anticipated our every desire,' said Lady Hardcastle.

'Thank you. In that case, I shall leave you to your nattering.'

'Stay and eat with us, you goose,' she said.

'Yes,' said Miss Titmus. 'Please don't leave on my account. I know you two spend a lot of time in each other's company. I should hate to think you were having to behave any differently because of me. You're away from home in a gorgeous country house – you should be having fun. Both of you.'

'You're very kind, miss,' I said. I sat on the rug and helped myself to a sandwich.

'Helen and I were talking about photography again, I'm afraid,' said Lady Hardcastle. 'Did you know they've got a darkroom here? It was one of Fishy's Fancies so it's not used any more, except when Helen's here.'

'I had no idea. I've not really had many excuses to wander the main house.'

'The old snooping skills are fading,' she said. 'But it means we'll be able to see her photographs before we go.'

'How wonderful.'

'I was planning to get in there today,' said Miss Titmus. 'But what with all the ghastliness, it didn't seem right somehow. You know, to be doing normal things.'

'I know what you mean,' said Lady Hardcastle kindly.

'It's so upsettingly horrid. Who could have done such a thing?'

'I'm sure the police will catch him.'

'It must be someone from the town,' said Miss Titmus. 'It must be. Otherwise it's someone in the house, and that would be too, too, horrid. Too horrid for words.'

'I don't think we're in any danger, dear,' said Lady Hardcastle. 'It all seems to have something to do with Fishy's motor cars. And we have nothing to do with Fishy's motor cars.'

'I suppose not. You two didn't get to race, did you? Nor Roz and Jake. Let's hope that means the girls will be safe. Oh, but . . .'

'But what, dear?'

Miss Titmus looked around almost furtively. 'That thing I was telling you about earlier. You know . . . Roz.'

'Oh,' said Lady Hardcastle slowly as the penny dropped. 'Well, yes, I suppose that does rather . . .'

I smiled. 'I wouldn't ordinarily be quite this indiscreet,' I said, 'but I think I might be able to cut down on the number of unfinished sentences here if I reveal that I know about Mrs Beddows and Mr Waterford.'

They both laughed.

'We try to pretend that the servants never know what goes on,' said Miss Titmus. 'But we're only fooling ourselves.'

'You could have told me sooner,' said Lady Hardcastle. 'How long have you known?'

'I found out while I was fetching the picnic,' I said.

'Well, that makes things easier to discuss,' said Miss Titmus. 'What I was trying to say in my roundabout way was that Roz does have a connection with Fishy's blessed motor cars because of her and Monty.'

Lady Hardcastle and I exchanged glances, but neither of us commented. As far as we were aware, we were the only ones apart from its author who knew about the incriminating note in Herr Kovacs's room.

Talking of which . . . 'Do you remember showing us that picture from your schooldays, Miss Titmus?' I asked.

'The cricket team?' she said.

'Yes, that's the one. Have you any idea why Herr Kovacs might have taken it?'

She looked puzzled. 'No, none at all. How do you know he took it?'

'We had a quick poke about in his room before the rozzers arrived,' said Lady Hardcastle. 'It was on his writing desk.'

'Good heavens,' said Miss Titmus. 'How odd. He did seem rather taken with it, though, didn't he? Perhaps it was the cricket. Germans are baffled by cricket.'

'Austrians,' said Lady Hardcastle.

'Hungarians,' I corrected.

'Just so,' said Lady Hardcastle. 'But that must have been it. Cricket. Fascinating game. Roddy played, you know.'

'Roddy?' asked Miss Titmus.

'Oh, I'm sorry, dear. Roderick. My late husband.'

'Oh, yes. Jake did tell me. When did you lose him?'

'Ten years ago,' said Lady Hardcastle. 'In Shanghai.'

'An illness?'

'If only it were that mundane, dear. No, he was shot by a German agent. They thought Roddy was a spy, you see. Only he wasn't. It was me.'

'How do you know it was a German spy?' asked Miss Titmus, now clearly enthralled.

'Oh, we caught him, Flo and I.'

'You caught him? I say. What happened to him?'

'I shot him.'

'Gracious.'

'Quite. I'm sure he wouldn't have understood cricket, either.'

The mood of the conversation rose steadily as the level of wine remaining in the two bottles fell. By the time the sandwiches had gone and the bottles were empty, Miss Titmus was a great deal less concerned about the prospect of her own imminent murder. Her mental energies were, instead, entirely focused on trying to remember the words of a vulgar song she had learned at school.

I told Lady Hardcastle where Miss Titmus's room was and she steered her back there while I waited in Lady Hardcastle's room.

'I've taken her boots off and settled her on the bed,' said Lady Hardcastle when she returned. 'Remind me to pop back and wake her in time for dinner.'

'Right you are, my lady,' I said. 'First things first, though: how did you come to rip this?' I held up her tennis skirt. I'd been checking her clothes to make sure she had a dress clean for dinner when I noticed the damaged skirt.

'Heaven only knows,' she said. 'One moment it was whole, the next moment rent in twain. I never saw the doing of it.'

I sighed, then sat in the armchair and began to sew up the rip. 'Is Miss Titmus all right?' I asked.

'She was just a little unsettled, that's all. We gave her just what she needed.'

'By getting her sozzled and letting her sing filthy songs?'

'Just so. And she didn't actually sing the filthy song – she couldn't remember the filthy bit.'

'I suppose so,' I said. 'Did she tell you anything useful before I arrived?'

'Helen? She doesn't know anything about anything, bless her. Did you gather any useful titbits below stairs?'

'Not really. Betty told me that Mrs Beddows didn't make it back to her own room in time not to be noticed. Then she filled in some details about Mrs Beddows's marriage.'

'Not an entirely happy one, by all accounts.'

'Can you honestly imagine Mrs Beddows being happy with anyone?' I said. 'Actually, that's not fair – I've no idea what might make her happy. But I can't imagine her being able to bring herself to show that she's happy. It's against her religion.'

'To be perfectly truthful, I can't imagine anyone finding happiness in being with her, either. She's not the warmest of creatures.'

'All of which means that I wasn't at all surprised when I found that she and her husband didn't get along. But I was stunned to my boot buttons that someone else found her appealing in any way.'

'There's no accounting for taste,' she said. 'Although she is rather attractive in a cold sort of way. And for all we know, she might be a tigress in the boudoir.'

'A praying mantis, more like,' I said. 'Isn't that the one who eats their mate? I can imagine her doing away with her lovers.'

Lady Hardcastle laughed, but made no comment. She sat at the writing desk and opened her journal.

'We need to elevate ourselves above social gossip and make a proper effort at working out what's going on in this blessed house. We've been drifting about like a couple of . . . of . . .'

'I've told you before about recklessly setting off on these similes and just hoping for the best,' I said. 'But you're right. If we imagine ourselves worthy of the name "interfering busybodies", we need to be a sight better organized.'

'I prefer "amateur sleuth", dear, to be honest,' she said. 'But we do need a plan. What do we know?'

'We know that Ellis Dawkins died in a car crash on Wednesday,' I said, ticking the points off on my fingers. 'We know that the car was sabotaged. We know it was sabotaged in the coach house. And we know that happened in the early hours of Wednesday morning after the party.'

Lady Hardcastle began writing a list in her journal.

'We know that Herr Kovacs was clubbed to death in the coach house shortly after two on Saturday morning.'

'So those are our two mysteries,' she said. 'We shall assume that they're related.'

'That seems fair, my lady.'

'We don't know for certain that the sabotage was intended to kill anyone, but if it was, we know that Dawkins was the target.'

'Because the runners and riders were drawn at the party, and the race card was left in the great hall for all to see,' I said.

'Just so,' she confirmed. 'And we know that Viktor was lured to the coach house by a note, signed "R B".'

'Of which the police are unaware because it was pinched before Inspector Foister turned up.'

'Hmm,' she said as she wrote. 'We know that Viktor wanted to buy the motor racing team, and that Fishy wasn't interested.'

'We know that Mr Waterford wasn't interested, either – Evan heard him say so.'

'Yes, yes, he did, didn't he? And now we know that Roz is romantically entwined with Monty Waterford. It's looking black against Monty, as Inspector Sunderland might say. How about this? Viktor wasn't giving up on his takeover plans, and was becoming a nuisance. Monty wanted to have a stern word with him. Stern enough that there might be fisticuffs. He couldn't do it in the house, so he needed to get him alone somewhere. He got Roz to write a note to lure him out to the coach house in the dead of night.'

'And he was prepared for violence because he knew Herr Kovacs was a desperate man, who had already sabotaged one of the motor cars,' I said.

'It's not bad, but it's not terribly convincing, is it?' she said dejectedly.

'It's not. We still have no proof that Herr Kovacs really did sabotage Number 3. We have no real proof that Mr Waterford or Mrs Beddows were doing anything other than what one might expect them to be doing . . . Oh, oh.'

'What? What?' she said, smiling.

'I forgot to tell you. Mrs Beddows's outdoor tweeds are missing.'

'I'm sorry, dear, you've lost me.'

'Betty asked me about the body and about blood. Then she said that Mrs Beddows has a tweed skirt and jacket of which she is particularly fond. The clothes are missing.'

'And she has assumed the worst,' she said. 'They're in a bin somewhere waiting to be burned because they're covered in Viktor's blood.'

'That seemed to be her fear,' I admitted.

'It would be convenient, but there are still too many holes. We need more facts. More observations. It's a frightful cheek, but I think it might be worth telephoning Inspector Sunderland and asking him to get one of his minions to do some research for us. I want to know a little more about this motor racing business. And a great deal more about Viktor Kovacs.'

'And about the school, please, my lady.'

'The school?'

'The school that Lady Lavinia and the others went to.'

'I can't see what that has to do with anything, dear, but I'm sure they'll be able to dig something up for you.'

'Thank you, my lady.'

'And we both need a word with your agent, the boy Evan Gudger.'

'We do. I'll see if I can arrange a discreet meeting. In the meantime, do you fancy a cuppa?'

'I'm absolutely gasping. What was it that Gertie said the other day? "I could drink a muddy puddle through a farmer's sock."'

'A colourful lady,' I said. 'But they have a china tea service for guests here. I'll be back in two shakes.'

◆ ◆ ◆

I was in the bedroom passage, about to step through the door leading to the servants' staircase, when I heard a commotion downstairs. I closed the door, and made my way instead to the head of the main staircase.

'. . . your hands off me, you clodhopping oaf. My husband knows the Chief Constable. You've not heard the last of this.'

It was Mrs Beddows's voice.

Mr Waterford was more conciliatory.

'Calm down, Roz, darling,' he said. 'We'll get all this sorted out in a jiffy. You'll see.'

I took a few steps down the stairs, the better to see into the hall. I was in time to catch sight of Sergeant Tarpley leading Mrs Beddows and Waterford, both in handcuffs, out through the front door. Inspector Foister made to follow them, but he was hailed by Lord Riddlethorpe.

'I say, Inspector!' he called.

'Yes, my lord,' said the inspector.

'What's the meaning of this?' said Lord Riddlethorpe. 'Where are you taking my guests?'

'Mr Waterford and Mrs Beddows are under arrest for the murder of Mr Viktor Kovacs, my lord. They'll be held at the station in

Riddlethorpe until a motor car can be arranged to transport them to Leicester, where I can interrogate them properly. If charged, they'll appear before the magistrate on Monday.'

'Really, Inspector, I do think you've exceeded your authority in this matter. You can't possibly have grounds for holding them.'

'My authority has been clearly defined by Act of Parliament, my lord. And my duty in this matter is clear: I have grounds to suspect these two persons of involvement in a capital crime, and I must arrest them.'

He turned defiantly towards the door.

'But surely—' said Lord Riddlethorpe, but the inspector was already outside with the door closing behind him.

'Blast!' said Lord Riddlethorpe as he stamped back into the house.

Tea would have to wait – Lady Hardcastle would want to know about this. I returned to her room.

'Oh dear,' she said when I'd finished my report. 'That will never do. I know we reached the same conclusion only moments ago, but we dismissed it almost as quickly. I ought to go and talk to Fishy.'

'Would you like some help getting changed?'

'What? Oh, I see. No, hang it. Without Roz to look down her nose at us, we'll all be free to wear the same clothes all the way to dinnertime.'

'Right you are, my lady. Am I to come with you?'

'Ordinarily, yes, but I think we need to divide our efforts for maximum efficiency. I should like you to winkle Evan Gudger out of whatever hidey-hole he's secreted himself in. He must know something.'

'Meet you back here at five, my lady.'

Tracking Evan down proved to be no easy task. I started in the servants' hall, but only because it was where I hoped to find someone who might know of his whereabouts. I had no real expectation of finding him there.

Mrs McLelland was sitting at the table, cradling a cup of tea in both hands.

'Good afternoon, Mrs McLelland,' I said cheerfully.

She looked up. It seemed for a moment as though she couldn't quite fathom where she was, and I got the feeling I had dragged her back from some faraway place.

'Oh,' she said. 'Good afternoon, Miss Armstrong. Have you heard the news?'

'About Mrs Beddows and Mr Waterford?' I said.

'Yes. That such a thing should happen under his lordship's roof. And with his own so-called friends responsible.'

'We can't be certain yet that they are,' I said.

She frowned. 'What? Oh, "innocent until . . .", and all that. But we both know that the police never risk this kind of scandal without being certain of their case. She'll swing. And a good thing, too. Nasty, evil woman, that one.'

I might have asked her what had happened to the 'no gossiping about the guests' rule, but I said nothing – I wasn't in the mood for confrontation. I didn't share her confidence in the police's concern for avoiding scandals, but I decided to say nothing about that, either. And for all that I didn't much care for Mrs Beddows, nor did I share Mrs McLelland's desire to see her hang. Overeager policemen had been making mistakes ever since there had been policemen, and this particular policeman had an axe to grind. I'd seen the look in his eyes when he talked about what the 'sinners' had been getting up to. He strongly disapproved of Mrs Beddows and Mr Waterford.

'I know I can rely on someone as experienced as you to keep the below-stairs gossip under control,' she said, clearly back to her normal self. 'It doesn't do to let the younger ones get too far above themselves.'

'Of course,' I said.

'That good-for-nothing Evan Gudger is the one most likely to stir up trouble. You seem to have quite a rapport with him – perhaps you could set him straight. Spinney won't say anything.'

'I could have a word with him now, if you know where he is,' I said, trying not to sound too much as though this was exactly what I had been after all along.

She frowned. 'He's a bad lot, that boy. He disappears for hours on end, and Spinney won't do a thing about it. They both think we have no idea where he gets to, but when he's not in the boot room larking about with the younger lads, or loafing in the kitchen yard, he'll be hiding out in the wine cellar.'

'It might be a good idea to mark his card for him,' I said. 'You're quite right – he's definitely the sort to stir up gossip just to make mischief.'

'I dare say he is. If the wine cellar key isn't on the board, it'll be in his pocket. And his pocket will be sitting on a barrel in the far corner of the cellar reading a penny dreadful by candlelight.'

I left her to return to her musing. She still hadn't set the cup back in its saucer.

There was no sign of the wine cellar key on the huge board outside Mr Spinney's room. This was good news – it meant I had a fair idea where Evan might be. It was also bad news – I had no idea whatsoever where the wine cellar might be.

It took a fair few minutes of trekking through the labyrinthine corridors to track it down. I went back to the servants' hall to ask Mrs McLelland for directions at one point, but she had gone, and I was wary of asking anyone else. I had no business being in the wine cellar, and I would have had to concoct some sort of story to explain my interest. I tried a few doors and discovered a store cupboard, a passageway of some sort, and two laundry maids gossiping while folding a pile of bed linen.

Eventually, I worked out which door I needed – it was the one with a wooden sign screwed to it that read: WINE CELLAR.

I tried the door, but it was locked. I muttered an oath in Welsh. If only I had some discreet means of breaking in . . . But then I remembered. For my birthday in March, Lady Hardcastle had bought me the gown I wore to dinner with the Farley-Strouds. But she had bought me another special gift as well, an ornate silver brooch. I wore it all the time and had quite forgotten its little secret: concealed within was a pair of picklocks. I pulled on the edge of the brooch and the tiny burglary tools fell into my hand.

The simple lock succumbed in seconds.

I opened the door as quietly as I could, and slipped inside. With the door closed behind me, there was precious little light to help me find my way – just the faint glow from the gap at the bottom of the door. This wasn't the first time I'd explored a darkened cellar, though. My eyes became quickly accustomed to the gloom, and I was able to feel my way around the racks of wine bottles without too much difficulty. As I moved deeper into the room, I became aware of another source of light off to my right. Flickering candlelight.

'Evan?' I said quietly. I didn't fancy a struggle if I startled him. It's not that I couldn't best him, but we were surrounded by many very breakable bottles of extremely expensive wine.

I heard the rustle of a book closing. 'Miss Armstrong? Is that you?' said Evan.

'It is,' I said. 'I thought I'd come down for a chat.'

I rounded the final rack and found him, as Mrs McLelland had said, perched on a small barrel in the corner of the cellar. He'd made himself quite a pleasant little nest, with a larger barrel as a table to hold his candle and his books. He'd even brought himself a cup of tea.

'Don't go givin' me away now, will you,' he said as he put his book down on his makeshift table.

'I'll not say anything,' I said. 'But I think that ship may already have sailed. It was Mrs McLelland who told me where to find you.'

'That interferin' old trout,' he said. 'I might have known she'd have stuck her beak in.'

I wasn't at all convinced that trout had beaks, but I didn't want to antagonize him. 'Have you been down here long?' I asked instead.

'Since the lunch that never was,' he said as he stretched extravagantly. 'Lovely little break.'

'But you spoke to the inspector?'

'I did. But don't worry, I never tell coppers nothin'. We've reached an understandin', see, me and the local law. They don't like me, and I don't like them. It keeps things nice and simple.'

'Right you are,' I said. 'So you've not heard what's happened?'

'No? Has someone else been done in?'

I laughed. 'Nothing like that,' I said. 'But almost as interesting. Inspector Foister has arrested Mrs Beddows and Mr Waterford on suspicion of murdering Herr Kovacs.'

He gaped at me. 'He's never,' he said eventually. 'Well, I'll be blowed. What did he do that for?'

I outlined the case that Lady Hardcastle and I had built up against them.

'What a load of rubbish,' he said. 'She was in his room last night. I walked in on 'em this mornin', just as she was getting out of bed. He gave me a sovereign to keep me mouth shut.'

'You probably ought to give it back,' I said.

'Ha-ha, very funny. I reckon he'd think it was worth it if I saved 'em from the noose.'

'He would, I'm sure. But you can't be certain they were in there all night, can you? They would have been able to get down to the coach house and still be back in time for you to catch them. Maybe you didn't "catch" them. Maybe that was part of the plan. Maybe you were their alibi.'

He frowned. 'Look, Miss Armstrong, I didn't pay no attention at school. Truth is, I hopped the wag more often than I showed up. It's only Old Man Spinney's naggin' that's got me readin' at all, so I ain't no scholar like you or Lady H. But I ain't stupid, neither. And if anyone in this house knows about alibis, it's me. They weren't up to no good. Well, unless you count . . . you know . . . what they were up to.' He blushed and turned away slightly.

I had one more card to play. 'Miss Buffrey says that her mistress's tweeds are missing. She has convinced herself that they're hidden away, covered in blood from the murder.'

He laughed. 'She's almost right,' he said. 'They are hidden away, and they are covered in something, but it's mud, not blood. It was the other day – Thursday, I reckon – and they'd been off together in the afternoon. When I went to see if he needed any help gettin' dressed for dinner in the evening, he gave me some clothes. "There's ten bob in it for you if you can get these cleaned and no one the wiser," he says. It was a tweed skirt and jacket. Caked in mud, they was.'

'You're doing quite well for yourself keeping Mr Waterford's confidences,' I said. 'But it does give the lie to Miss Buffrey's suspicions.'

'Like I says, it weren't them.'

'No,' I said. 'Lady Hardcastle and I didn't think it was, either. How about Herr Kovacs? Was there anything noteworthy there?'

'He was an odd fish,' he said. 'Odder than odd. I'd go in there and find him mutterin' gibberish to himself. Mad as a hatter.'

'To be fair, he was probably muttering in Hungarian or German. Have you been in his room since he was killed?'

'No,' he said bluntly. 'No need. A dead bloke don't need no valet.'

I smiled. 'No, I suppose not. Just one more thing: did you ever notice that he had a photograph?'

He looked suddenly defensive. 'I never pinched it. He asked me to get it for him.'

'The photo of the school cricket team?'

'Yes, that's the one. He asked me to get it from the library. I don't know what he wanted it for. Can't say as I ever saw him even lookin' at it.'

'Interesting,' I said. 'We might need to have a look at that ourselves.'

'I can get it for you, if you like. It wouldn't be no trouble.'

'That's all right,' I said. 'I think we can manage. Are you staying down here?'

'What, now? No, I s'pose I'd better show my face and look like I'm workin'.'

'I shall leave you to tidy up,' I said. 'And thank you for all your efforts. You've been most helpful.'

◆ ◆ ◆

It was almost a quarter past five by the time Lady Hardcastle returned to her room.

'Gracious me,' she said as she burst in. 'Sorry I took so long.'

'That's all right, my lady,' I said. 'It's not as though I have any urgent appointments.'

'No, but when a lady says she'll meet at five, she should jolly well be there at five.'

I laughed. 'You've never been on time for anything in your life.'

'Not for frivolous things like parties or dinners, but when was I ever late when we were working?'

'Actually, you're right. I apologize. How did you get on?'

'Not wonderfully well. Fishy's all of a twitter, as you can imagine, but he doesn't seem to know anything useful. Kovacs was a good egg; Monty's a good egg. He struggled to find something good to say about Roz, but he doesn't believe her capable of murder.'

'Everyone struggles to find something good to say about her.'

'Well, quite. I learned a little more about Inspector Foister's reasons for arresting them both, though. It seems that when he'd been asking about the race the other day, Kovacs had told him that Monty had been fiddling with Dawkins's motor car just before the start. His chain of events goes: Monty sabotaged the motor car, Kovacs saw him, Kovacs was blackmailing him to get him to sell the company, Monty and his adulterous lover kill Kovacs.'

'It's not illogical,' I said. 'Mr Waterford was fiddling with a motor car when we arrived, and Herr Kovacs wasn't far behind us. But he doesn't have a motive for the initial sabotage. Why would Mr Waterford sabotage one of his own motor cars?'

'I'm sure he'll come up with something. What news from your man, Evan?'

'None at all,' I said. 'It took me longer to track him down than to find out that he doesn't really know very much, either. He does know what happened to Mrs Beddows's missing tweeds, though – they're being discreetly cleaned. Evidently they were covered in mud as a result of some *al fresco* shenanigans. He also said that he was the one who fetched the cricket team photograph from the library on Herr Kovacs's orders, although he has no idea why Kovacs wanted it.'

'Did he? Did he, indeed? Talking of photographs, I popped in to see Helen on my way back here. She wittered on about how awful everything was, and I thought I ought to try to give her something to do to take her mind off it all. I suggested she develop her photographs. It'll keep her busy.'

'It keeps you busy,' I said.

'Hence my suggestion. And Inspector Sunderland sends his regards.'

'You spoke to him as well? No wonder you were late getting back.'

'Yes, Fishy let me use his telephone. The inspector will call me or wire me when he knows anything further about Kovacs and the world of motor racing.'

'And the school?'

'And the school. I didn't forget.'

'Thank you, my lady.'

'And now, I think there's time for a bath before drinkies. Fishy is determined that his remaining guests should be well looked after, so he's summoned us all to the library for a pre-prandial bracer. Or two. I made Helen promise to come down. And Harry will be there, of course, even if only to moon over Jake. Do you think you might be able to persuade Spinney to let you serve this evening? It would be nice to have you there.'

'I shall see what I can do, my lady. Would you like me to draw you a bath?'

'Are you sure you're up to it, dear?' she said as I stood. 'Treacherous blighters, baths.'

'I'll manage,' I said.

Chapter Fourteen

There was no real need for me to serve at dinner that evening, but Mr Spinney agreed anyway. The last time I had been in the dining room at dinner time had been on Wednesday, after the fatal crash. The mood then had been subdued, and I was expecting the same this time, but, to my surprise, I found everyone except Lord Riddlethorpe to be in good spirits.

Without Mrs Beddows's continual sniping, Miss Titmus came out of her shell. She and Lady Lavinia kept Lady Hardcastle amused with tales of their schooldays, when many of their exploits bordered on the recklessly criminal. Meanwhile, Uncle Algy – with Harry as his straight man – was doing his best to entertain Lord Riddlethorpe. In the end, even his lordship succumbed to the cheerful mood around the table, and was laughing with them all when Uncle Algy did his (apparently famous) impression of the king trying to explain the laws of cricket to his nephew Kaiser Wilhelm.

Just as before, the ladies retired to the library once dinner was over, and once again I was invited to accompany them. I served the brandy, but this time there was no delay in my being asked to sit with them.

The reminiscences had stopped and conversation had finally turned to the events of the past twenty-four hours. Lady Lavinia and Miss

Titmus were keen to find out if we knew anything they hadn't heard already. It turned out that we didn't.

'Surely you must have some clever theories, though,' said Lady Lavinia. 'You two are quite the utterest utter, as far as I'm concerned. I've never known anyone quite as brainy as you.'

Lady Hardcastle laughed. 'I think you must be moving in the wrong circles, dear. We're not nearly as clever as you think.'

'You speak for yourself, my lady,' I said.

'Actually, she's right. Flo here is as brainy as they come. Despite that, though, we have more questions than answers at the moment.'

'But at least you have questions,' said Lady Lavinia eagerly. 'We don't even have those, do we, Hels?'

'No, Jake,' said Miss Titmus. 'Well, I have a few, but they make me feel such a duffer.'

'So what are your questions, then, Emily?' said Lady Lavinia. 'What's your clever-clogs brain asking?'

'Let's see,' said Lady Hardcastle. She took a sip of her brandy while she pondered her response. 'Who really sabotaged Dawkins's motor car? It could have been Monty, but why would he do it on the track in full view of everyone? It would be much easier to snip the cable in the coach house under cover of darkness – we even found a pair of pliers kicked under the work bench. Why would they kill Viktor? Surely if he were blackmailing them, someone as resourceful as Roz could dig up some dirt on him in retaliation. It would be stalemate. Gossip is her speciality. She could scandalmonger for England if there were a World Championship.'

'Quite aside from anything else,' said Lady Lavinia, 'I just can't see either of them as villains.'

'I'm not sure that will convince a jury,' said Lady Hardcastle, 'but I know what you mean.'

'What about you, Armstrong?' said Miss Titmus. 'What questions are you asking?'

'I'm afraid Lady Hardcastle thinks my question rather foolish and red herringy,' I said.

'What was it Miss Blenkinsop always used to say in History lessons, Hels?' said Lady Lavinia. '"There's no such creature as a stupid question, only stupid answers." What are you asking, Armstrong?'

'I've been asking why Herr Kovacs was so obsessed with your old school photograph,' I said. 'What's so fascinating about a cricket team?'

'He was what?' said Lady Lavinia.

'He had your team photograph in his room.'

'He spent ages hogging it after dinner on Wednesday, didn't he, Jake?' said Miss Titmus. 'I thought it was a bit off, to be honest. I wanted everyone to have a look.'

'Well, we've added it to the growing list of questions,' said Lady Hardcastle. 'Do you know anything about the rivalry between Fishy and Viktor, Jake?'

'I thought it was all very schoolboyish and friendly,' said Lady Lavinia. 'You know what chaps are like. Edmond is just like that, only more so. He's an overeager little boy wearing his father's suit and pretending to be a grown-up. Their "rivalry" was more like two boys arguing over a game of conkers.'

Lady Hardcastle smiled. 'You see? Always questions, never answers.'

The conversation had drifted on to the subject of Lady Hardcastle's latest moving picture project by the time the men joined us. Once Lord Riddlethorpe learned what we were talking about, he began to bombard her with increasingly technical questions. We were all saved from a detailed description of the workings of the latest camera by Uncle Algy loudly insisting that we join him in a game of Jean-Pierre's Magical Vineyard.

We made it to bed by one in the morning.

◆ ◆ ◆

Sunday passed, as Sundays do, in a dreary blur of indolence and inactivity. After leading the entire household through the pouring rain to church and back in the morning, Lord Riddlethorpe retired to his rooms. Lady Lavinia also disappeared, though I had no idea where. Miss Titmus locked herself away in the darkroom for the day, and so Lady Hardcastle borrowed her camera to take some photographs of her own.

I spent most of the day in the room I shared with Betty, alternately reading and gossiping. Betty was torn: should she do the noble thing and stay loyal to her unpleasant (and allegedly felonious) employer, or should she look to her own best interests and cut herself loose from the scandal? By bedtime, we had still reached no conclusion. Despite having seemingly done nothing all day, I was exhausted when we finally said our goodnights and snuffed out the candles.

Monday was brighter, and so was the atmosphere in the house. Breakfast was served in the dining room, and everyone managed to attend at roughly the same time. I stood in the corner as though I were serving, but I fooled no one. It was obvious that I was just hanging around, but no one seemed to object.

Lord Riddlethorpe and Lady Lavinia both announced that they had business in Leicester and would be out for the day. Harry said he would accompany Lady Lavinia 'if that's all right with you . . . I mean, I wouldn't want to . . .'

His mumbly stumbling evoked laughter from his sister, and he glared at her. When Lady Lavinia patted his hand affectionately and said that it would be delightful to have his company, his embarrassment increased tenfold, and I was certain we could have toasted crumpets on his reddened cheeks.

Miss Titmus still had a little work to do in the darkroom, leaving Lady Hardcastle at something of a loose end.

'Don't worry,' said Miss Titmus. 'I'll only be an hour or two, then we can have lunch and plan some games for the afternoon. Do you play golf?'

'No,' said Lady Hardcastle. 'It's not something I've ever got round to trying.'

'I can teach you,' said Miss Titmus. 'It's really jolly simple. Do you have any clubs that Emily can borrow, Jake?'

Lady Lavinia wrenched herself away from her close scrutiny of Harry's eyes. 'I'll get Perrin to dig them out for you, dear,' she said. 'They're not in terribly good shape, mind you.'

'Not to worry,' said Miss Titmus enthusiastically. 'We'll just be hacking about around the racing track. That's all right, isn't it, Fishy?'

'What? Oh, yes. The dogs'll help. They love to fetch golf balls.'

'That's settled, then,' said Miss Titmus. 'See you at noon for lunch and golf, Emily. Bring comfortable boots and the dogs.'

She plonked her napkin on the table and bounced out of the room. Mrs Beddows's absence clearly agreed with her.

With her employer still in the chokey, Betty was also at a loose end, so I persuaded her to join Lady Hardcastle and me as we took a turn around the grounds after breakfast. The intention had been to loosen our limbs and build up an appetite for lunch, but we took things at far too leisurely a pace for that. We did, though, walk for miles.

The estate was vast, and we hadn't explored half of it before Lady Hardcastle consulted her watch and declared that we ought to be making our way back to the house for lunch.

It was almost half-past twelve by the time we arrived at the terrace. Miss Titmus was sitting at the table, reading a magazine. There were two bags of golf clubs leaning against the low wall.

'I'm so sorry we're late, dear,' said Lady Hardcastle. 'I hadn't realized quite how extensive Fishy's place is. It must cover half of Rutland.'

Miss Titmus laughed. 'Don't worry,' she said. 'I've been keeping myself busy.' She waved the magazine. 'I couldn't face a big meal, so I asked them to send up some sandwiches. I hope you don't mind. I got Mrs R to make up some ham and piccalilli for me – it's my absolute favourite – but I got a selection for you chaps, just in case.'

'That's perfect,' said Lady Hardcastle as she sat down. 'I'm not particularly fond of piccalilli, so I think your sandwiches are safe. I say, you don't mind if Buffrey joins us, do you, dear? She's been keeping us company.'

'Not at all,' said Miss Titmus. 'Buffrey and I have known each other for simply ever, haven't we? I'm sure Roz would have apoplexy at the very thought of you sitting down to lunch with us. But she's not here, is she?' She seemed positively gleeful at the thought. 'Pull up a pew and dig in. I think Mrs R has been overgenerous as usual. There's enough for everyone.'

Lady Hardcastle noticed Lord Riddlethorpe's two Dalmatians lying to either side of Miss Titmus's chair.

'You are a poppet. And you even had to fetch the dogs yourself. I was supposed to find them,' she said.

'They found me,' said Miss Titmus as she patted the dogs on their heads. 'Didn't you, girls? Have you met Asterope and Electra, Emily?'

'I can't say we've been formally introduced. Pleased to make your acquaintance, ladies.'

'They're sisters. There were seven in the litter – all girls – so they were named after the Seven Sisters. Fishy kept these two. Their mother died last year. He was heartbroken, poor love.'

While she was talking, she took her plate from the table and sat back, ready to eat her sandwich. The dogs were suddenly sitting up and drooling slightly. Miss Titmus turned to her right and patted one dog's head. While she was distracted, the other quickly leaned in from the left and took the sandwich from her plate.

'Oh, Electra, you bad girl,' said Miss Titmus. 'That was my special lunch.'

To add insult to injury, the dog took one bite and spat the rest out. She barked.

'Serves you right,' said Miss Titmus with a chuckle. 'Don't like piccalilli, eh? That'll teach you to pinch a girl's sandwich.'

She reached down to retrieve the stolen food, but quickly thought better of it.

'So much for my special sandwich,' she said. 'Good thing Mrs R made plenty after all.'

'Try the cheese and tomato, dear,' said Lady Hardcastle. 'There must be something about the soil out here. Or the sunshine. I've never tasted such sweet tomatoes.'

We tucked in. There was wine, as usual, and the mood became quite convivial. Betty had seemed a little uncomfortable at first, but by the time we finished the last of the food, she and Miss Titmus were getting along famously.

Feeling full and rather jolly, we gathered the golf clubs, summoned the dogs, and set off towards the middle of the racing track.

◆ ◆ ◆

There was a small patch of smooth, level grass just inside the racing track. We stopped there and dropped the two golf bags. The Dalmatians bounced around us excitedly.

Lady Hardcastle allowed Miss Titmus to demonstrate the correct technique for holding the club and addressing the ball, and then took a few inept practice swings of her own. Miss Titmus corrected her stance and guided her once more through the mechanics of the perfect golf swing.

'Let me have a go with a ball, dear,' said Lady Hardcastle, after a few more attempts. 'Let's see if I've got it.'

Miss Titmus produced a small rubber mat and a scuffed old ball from her golf bag. She carefully placed the ball on the raised tube in the centre of the mat and stood back.

'It's all yours,' she said. 'Nice big swing, and remember to keep going after you've hit it. "Follow through", as they say.'

'Right you are, dear.'

If Lady Hardcastle were a man, she would have been labelled a bounder and a cad. Sadly, there were no equivalent terms for a lady. Her oh-so-innocent claim of inexperience on the golf course – 'It's not something I've ever got round to trying' – was an outright lie. She had been playing for at least twenty years, and if Harry hadn't been so distracted by Lady Lavinia, he would have set the record straight at breakfast.

She addressed the ball, took her swing, and struck the ball cleanly on the centre of the club face. She launched the ball on a long, looping trajectory, which took it sailing over the crest of the small hill ahead of us.

'Something like that, dear?' said Lady Hardcastle with an impish grin.

'Why, you absolute beast,' said Miss Titmus, laughing. 'You've been having me on all this time. You rotter.'

'It's all down to your instruction, I promise.'

'Pfft. I've half a mind to send you off to fetch it yourself,' said Miss Titmus. 'But that would just be denying the girls their chance of a run.' She ruffled the ears of the two eager Dalmatians. 'Go on, girls, fetch the ball,' she said in that eager voice everyone reserves for speaking to dogs and small children. 'Fetch it.'

The dogs didn't need to be told twice and were already on their way.

'Do you fancy a go, Buffrey?' asked Lady Hardcastle. 'It's awfully good fun.'

'Well, I . . .' mumbled Betty.

'Oh, go on. Give it a try,' said Miss Titmus. 'While the evil old cat's away, what?'

'Yes,' said Betty, with sudden resolution. 'Yes, all right.'

She took the proffered club and did her best to imitate the swing that Lady Hardcastle had just demonstrated. Her first effort dug up a large divot in front of the tee and tipped the ball off the mat. Her second swooped high over the ball, and the momentum of her swing spun her round on her smooth-soled boots.

When we had all stopped laughing, she made herself ready to give it another try. There was a brief pause while we waited for the Dalmatians to return. Eventually one of them hove into view and trotted over to drop Lady Hardcastle's now-slobbery ball at our feet. And then Betty took her third swing. This time she made contact with the ball and lobbed it about thirty yards in the direction of the hillock.

'Nicely done,' said Miss Titmus. 'You're a natural. And what about you, Armstrong? I bet you play with your mistress. Or are you going to try to kid on that you've never so much as seen a golf club in all your days?'

'It would be amusing to try to pretend, miss,' I said. 'But Lady Hardcastle taught me to play years ago.'

'I knew it,' she said. 'Well, let's see what you've got, then.'

I played my stroke. I could tell from the moment the club hit the ball that it was going to be a good one. It flew straight and true. To my eye, it gained a good deal more height than Lady Hardcastle's had, and I was disappointed that her ball had already been retrieved. It would have been fun to see how much further I'd hit it.

'You two simply must come down to my local golf club on ladies' day,' said Miss Titmus gleefully. 'I dare say you'd give some of the chaps a run for their money.'

She took her own shot, which disappeared over the hill along the same line. Grinning, she dispatched the eager dog to fetch the balls. I didn't share her confidence that the Dalmatian was capable of understanding the need to retrieve three balls, but we had nothing better to do, so we stood around discussing our golfing exploits while we waited.

Five minutes had passed before we decided that the dog almost certainly wasn't going to come back, and that we should probably move our game to the other side of the grassy hillock. We gathered up the golf bags and Miss Titmus's tee, and set off in the direction of our shots.

We all looked about as we crested the small hill, trying to see what had happened to the dogs and the golf balls. We saw the Dalmatians about fifty yards down the hill. One seemed to be resting, as though the effort of trotting over the hill had exhausted her. It was when we heard the other one whining that we knew something was wrong.

'Oh, good lord,' said Miss Titmus. 'Electra! I think we must have hit the poor girl with one of the golf balls. She's unconscious.'

She quickened her pace towards the stricken dog, and we followed. As she reached it, she bent down and examined it.

'There's no sign of anything,' she said. 'We'd better get her back to the house, though. Do you think we could carry her?'

'We might be able to,' said Lady Hardcastle. 'But if she's injured, we should probably be a little gentler. Flo, dear, pop back to the house and see if you can find a handcart or something.'

'I'll come with you,' said Betty. 'I think I know where they keep one.'

'And a blanket,' called Lady Hardcastle as we set off back towards the house.

◆ ◆ ◆

I left Betty to find and deliver the handcart while I went into the house to see if Lord Riddlethorpe had returned. I'd never owned a dog, but I was certain that if I had, I should have liked someone to let me know when it had been floored by an errant golf ball.

I found him in his study.

'Why, Miss Armstrong,' he said as I peered round the door. 'What can I do for you?'

'Sorry to interrupt, my lord,' I said, 'but Electra has been in an accident.'

His face whitened. 'Oh, good lord,' he said quietly. 'Can this dreadful week bring any more tragedy? What's happened?'

'We're not sure,' I said, 'but it looks as though she was hit by a stray golf ball. She's out cold.'

He relaxed. 'Is that all?' he said with a faint smile. 'Stupid creatures get into all sorts of scrapes. I'm sure she'll be fine.'

'Miss Buffrey is taking a handcart out to fetch her back. Lady Hardcastle and Miss Titmus are looking after her.'

'Thank you,' he said. 'I'm sure she's in good hands. I'll telephone the vet, just in case. He lives just this side of the town. He can have a look at her.'

'Right you are, my lord. If you don't mind, I'd better be getting back to them.'

'Of course. Thank you for letting me know.'

By the time I'd made my way back through the house and out towards the racing track, the stretcher party was already heading in. Miss Titmus was pushing the handcart, with Betty comforting the stricken dog, and Lady Hardcastle walking behind with a morose-looking Asterope.

I waited for them and helped manhandle Electra into the hall, where we gave her into the care of her master.

'Thank you, ladies,' said Lord Riddlethorpe. 'The vet's on his way.'

'I'm so sorry, Fishy,' said Miss Titmus. She was in some distress. 'It's all my fault. She was still fetching a ball when we sent a couple more over the hill. I should have waited. I do hope she's all right.'

'Don't worry about it, Helen. There's nothing you could have done. She's had worse, haven't you, old girl?' He crouched down and gently stroked the dog, who had come round and was now wrapped in a blanket. She looked dreadful. She spasmed and then lay still. 'Don't worry, old thing. We'll have you back to your old self in no time.'

Lady Hardcastle caught my eye and signalled that she wished to speak to me in private. We slipped away and went back through the house to the terrace.

She examined the area around the table.

'The dog wasn't biffed on the head by a golf ball, was she?' I said.

'No,' she said, still searching. 'You saw the state of her. She was poisoned. Something like strychnine, if I remember my poisons correctly.' She picked up a small piece of half-chewed sandwich that had been missed by the household servants when they tidied up. 'Luckily, she barely ate any of it. Saved by piccalilli.'

'You think so?' I said. 'It was deliberate? That means someone was after Miss Titmus.'

'It really does look that way, doesn't it,' she said. 'I'll pop in and give Fishy the bad news. Perhaps the vet will be able to do something for her if he knows what's wrong. I rather suspect that country vets might have to deal with accidental poisonings rather more often than one would hope.'

'Right you are, my lady,' I said. 'Is it worth my while asking around in the kitchens, or do you have a master plan?'

'That sounds like the best we can do for the moment. But keep it to Mrs Ruddle and her kitchen maid. I can't see that a cook would be so foolish as to poison her own food – she'd be the first to fall under suspicion – but I wouldn't like anyone else down there to know that we're on to them.'

❖ ❖ ❖

Finding Mrs Ruddle was never a problem – I'd never known her not be in the kitchen. Unfortunately, being confined to the kitchen meant that neither she nor Patty had seen anything.

'I put 'em out on the table in the servants' hall,' said Patty. 'Then I come straight back in here.'

'Who ordered them?' I asked.

'Alfie come down from Miss Titmus.'

'He's one of the footmen?'

'That's right,' she said. 'I called out that they was ready and just left them.'

'So everyone knew they were there?'

'That's right.'

'And who knew about the ham and piccalilli? Who knew they were for Miss Titmus?'

Patty and Mrs Ruddle both laughed. 'Everyone did, dear,' said Mrs Ruddle. 'Every time she comes down here with her ladyship, we has to make sure we gets piccalilli in special. No one else likes it. If there's piccalilli in a sandwich, it's bound for our Miss Titmouse.'

This was no help at all. Almost every member of the household would have had reason or excuse to be in the servants' hall before lunch, and if all of them knew whose sandwich was whose, there was no way to narrow things down.

'Thank you, ladies,' I said, and made to leave.

'Was there something wrong with the sandwiches, then?' asked Mrs Ruddle. 'Something wrong with the piccalilli? It was fine when it left my kitchen.'

'Nothing at all, Mrs Ruddle,' I said cheerfully. 'Just something Lady Hardcastle was wondering. You know what "them upstairs" are like.'

She nodded sagely, and I took my leave.

I found Lady Hardcastle strolling along a path in the formal garden at the rear of the house, kicking at the gravel as she walked.

'You'll ruin those boots,' I said as I caught up with her.

'Sorry, Mother,' she said without looking up.

'How's Electra?'

'She should be all right. The vet said he sees a few accidental poisonings every year, so he knows just what to do. It's a good thing Fishy called him.'

'How did he take the news that it came from a poisoned sandwich?'
I asked.

'I decided not to tell him that part. He's hopping mad that someone
left rat poison out where the dogs could get at it, but he didn't question
me too closely on the details. Good thing, too – I had no credible story
to explain how she came to eat it.'

'He'll have to know.'

'He will, but I'd rather take him an explanation than just another
mystery. And I'm not sure Helen would cope particularly well with the
news that someone tried to bump her off.'

'No,' I said. 'I don't suppose she would.'

'Harry and Jake arrived while the vet was loading Electra into his
four-wheeler. To be honest, I didn't really relish the thought of all four
of them getting in a flap.' She kicked morosely at the gravel again.

'I can understand that,' I said. 'We shall just have to redouble our
efforts.'

'We shall,' she said.

We walked on.

Before long, we had left the formal garden, and we found ourselves wandering aimlessly across the estate in the vague direction of
the long, tree-lined drive. Through the trees, I caught a glimpse of
what looked like Lady Lavinia and Harry wandering towards us with
a similar aimlessness. I nudged Lady Hardcastle and nodded towards
them.

'Looks like I'll need to go shopping for a new hat,' she said when
she saw them.

'They've only just met,' I said. 'Surely you can't be marrying them
off already.'

'Care to make a wager? Ten bob says he pops the question before
we go home.'

'You're on,' I said. 'It'll take him months to pluck up the— What
on earth?'

There was a crunch of gears as Lord Riddlethorpe's Rolls-Royce Silver Ghost lurched along the drive in the direction of the main road. It was gaining speed.

'I say,' said Lady Hardcastle. 'Who the Dickens do you suppose that could be?'

'Lord Riddlethorpe?' I suggested.

'No, he's a much better driver than that. So's Morgan. I wonder— Harry!' she yelled suddenly as Lady Lavinia and Harry stepped on to the drive. They were directly in the path of the now-speeding motor car.

Hearing his name, Harry looked up to see his sister waving frantically at him. Then he turned and noticed the motor car. He shoved Lady Lavinia in the small of her back, sending her sprawling across the drive and safely on to the grass. He leapt backwards himself, but he wasn't quick enough. The mudguard clipped his hip as he jumped, and he fell awkwardly. The Rolls didn't stop, and was quickly out of sight.

We ran towards them.

By the time we reached the drive, Lady Lavinia was crouching over Harry. There was blood on her hands where she had scratched them as she fell, and her dress was torn, but she didn't seem to care. Harry was dazed.

'Harry?' she said. 'Harry?' she repeated, slightly louder this time.

'What?' he said irritably. 'Oh, Lavinia, I'm so sorry, I didn't . . . I say, my leg doesn't half hurt.'

'Being knocked down by a speeding motor car will do that, brother, dear,' said Lady Hardcastle. 'No, you oaf, don't try to stand. What's the matter with you?'

Harry slumped back down.

'Man's an idiot,' she said.

'He is,' said Lady Lavinia, stroking his head. 'But he's my idiot.'

'Flo,' said Lady Hardcastle. 'Be a poppet and trot back to the house for that handcart. We ought to get the idiot off the road. Bring some muscle as well – I'm not certain we can lift him by ourselves.'

'Tell Fishy to telephone the doctor as well, please, Armstrong,' said Lady Lavinia. 'I think this might need plaster.'

'I shall ask his lordship to do that,' I said.

Lady Lavinia laughed. 'No, dash it, *tell* him. He's just as much of an idiot as Harry. They need telling, these idiots.'

Chapter Fifteen

Harry's leg was badly bruised. Although there was nothing broken and there seemed to be no lasting damage, he was kept at the local cottage hospital overnight as a precaution. Lady Lavinia remained by his bedside, and I began to suspect I'd lose my ten shillings. It wasn't a wager I'd mind losing.

They arrived back at the house together just as Lady Hardcastle and Miss Titmus were sitting down to breakfast. There was no one else about, and so they invited me to join them. I declined – it was possible that I would still need to be in with the household servants, and I didn't want to turn them against me by hobnobbing. I compromised by hovering nearby with a sandwich I'd made with a brace of bangers and a couple of slices of buttered toast.

The sound of clumping footsteps came from the hall. The door opened.

'What ho, sis,' said Harry as he hobbled into the dining room on Lady Lavinia's arm. 'Saved any bacon for us? Or have you yaffled the lot?'

'I've already saved your bacon, dear. Many times. You're better, I take it?'

'Fit as a flea, old thing. Morning, Helen. And Strong Arm! What are you doing lurking there?'

'He's not fit at all,' said Lady Lavinia. 'He's under strict instructions to rest, and I intend to see that he obeys those instructions.' She patted his hand.

'Help a chap to the table, then, old girl, and I'll rest there. With the bacon.'

They both sat down.

'I see they found the Rolls,' said Lady Lavinia as she helped herself to toast. I was a little surprised by her matter-of-factness. 'We assumed it was gone for good, so we took a taxi from the hospital. I would have telephoned for Morgan if I'd known.'

'Yes,' said Lady Hardcastle. 'It had been abandoned in the lane. I'm not certain of the name. Church Lane? Borders the estate to the east. Morgan and some of the lads found it and brought it back last night.'

'It's awful,' said Miss Titmus. 'After everything else. Why would someone want to hurt you, Harry?'

'Who knows why these people do anything?' he said. 'Some ne'er-do-well coming down to the house on some pretext or other, happens upon the Rolls, nicks it, clobbers me, then dumps the motor when he realizes how deep he's got himself. We'll never understand it.'

Lady Hardcastle and I exchanged glances. It was quite the most absurdly unlikely explanation I could imagine for the previous evening's events, but a tiny shake of her head let me know that we weren't going to gainsay him. Then I caught Harry's eye, and a similar look told me that he didn't believe it any more than I did.

'Thank goodness that's all it was,' said Miss Titmus.

'I shouldn't think there's anything else to worry about,' said Harry. 'I say, do you think Mrs R might be persuaded to fry me a couple of eggs? I'm partial to a fried egg, but she seems keener on boiling the blighters.'

'I'll pop down to the kitchens and have a word, sir,' I said.

'Thank you, Strong Arm, you're a marvel. She's a bally marvel that one, sis. You hang on to her.'

'Yes, Harry, I shall,' said Lady Hardcastle. 'Jake, dear, what did they give him?'

'Something for the pain,' said Lady Lavinia, 'but I don't know precisely what. He's been babbling like this all the way here.'

◆ ◆ ◆

Miss Titmus had agreed to meet us in the library after breakfast to show us her photographs from the previous week. We clustered around the desk by the window, which provided a good natural light.

'Look, Emily, here's one of you and Armstrong,' said Miss Titmus.

'Gracious,' said Lady Hardcastle. 'I had no idea you'd taken this one. I think you might be on to something with these, you know, dear. Photographs always look so stilted and formal – everyone in their Sunday best, staring at the camera. In these . . . Well, you seem to have caught us just being us. Flo never looks like that in photographs – that's how she looks in real life. You have a gift, dear, a true talent. You really should try to do something with it.'

'I've been thinking about it a lot, lately,' said Miss Titmus. 'I really think I shall.'

'Good for you.' Lady Hardcastle continued leafing through the small pile of photographs. 'I say,' she said suddenly as one caught her eye. 'Look here. What do you see?'

Miss Titmus and I craned a little closer. It was a photograph taken on the day of the crash. The motor cars were lined up on the starting line. Lady Hardcastle and I had turned towards the camera as we heard Miss Titmus and the others approaching. Lord Riddlethorpe was leaning over Number 1, adjusting something under the bonnet. Morgan Coleman was sitting in Number 4, grinning, and clearly very aware of how dashing he looked in the sleek racing car. Mr Waterford was standing with a spanner in his hand.

'What are we looking at, my lady?' I said.

'Poor Dawkins was killed in Number 3,' said Lady Hardcastle. 'Inspector Foister's story is that Monty tampered with the brakes when the motor car was on the starting line. He had any number of witnesses, myself included, saying that we'd seen Monty working on one of the motors.'

'And you were right,' said Miss Titmus. 'There he is in his overalls with a tool in his hand.'

'Oh,' I said, when I realized. 'He's behind Number 2. He's nowhere near Number 3.'

Miss Titmus looked again. 'So he couldn't have tampered with Number 3,' she said.

'Well, let's not get carried away,' said Lady Hardcastle. 'All this shows is that the inspector's version of events is incorrect. It doesn't prove that Monty didn't tamper with the brakes in the coach house. Which is where we believe it actually happened.'

'Well, no,' said Miss Titmus. 'But still. I'm going to tell Fishy to telephone the inspector at once. We'll have them out in no time.' She picked up the photograph and hurried out.

'It's hardly conclusive proof of his innocence,' said Lady Hardcastle when Miss Titmus had gone.

'No,' I said. 'But the inspector had no conclusive proof of his guilt, either, other than some statements from witnesses. And the photograph makes it very clear that the witnesses didn't see Mr Waterford working on Number 3.'

'True,' she said. 'I suppose if we stick around long enough, everyone will be killed, or removed from suspicion by some random piece of evidence, and the only one left standing will be the killer.'

'Detection by attrition,' I said.

'Well, quite. And that's all very well, but the trouble is that the people who'll be killed will be our friends. The killer has already taken a swing at Helen and Harry. Who's next?'

Helen returned a few minutes later, flushed with excitement.

'I told Fishy what you found, and he's thrilled. He telephoned Inspector Foister straight away. He was being terribly firm with him when I left. I think Roz and Monty will be home before lunch. Should we send the motor car for them? We should, shouldn't we? They'll need a lift, won't they? Or will the police bring them?'

Before Lady Hardcastle could answer, Lord Riddlethorpe appeared at the door.

'Well done, ladies,' he said. 'Thanks to your eagle eyes, I persuaded Foister to let them out on bail. I need to drive over at once to make the arrangements and bring them back. I owe you a bottle of something splendid. Each.'

'Think nothing of it, Fishy, dear,' said Lady Hardcastle. 'All part of the service.'

He waved a cheery goodbye and closed the door behind him.

It opened again almost immediately.

'Clean forgot,' said Lord Riddlethorpe, poking his head round the door. 'Chap on the telephone for you, Emily. Inspector Middlesbrough, or something. Toodle pip.'

'Sunderland!' called Lady Hardcastle, but he was gone. 'Best not keep the poor chap waiting any longer,' she said. 'I'll go and see what he wants. Could you be a poppet and get us some coffee, Flo? You'd like some, wouldn't you, Helen?'

'We could just ring for it,' said Miss Titmus.

'We could, but we can also send Flo. Six of one and the square root of thirty-six of the other.'

'Don't worry, Miss Titmus,' I said. 'I'll nip down to the kitchens. I've a couple of things I need to do down in the Netherworld anyway.'

◆ ◆ ◆

'Might I trouble you for a pot of coffee for the library, please, Mrs Ruddle?'

The cook looked up from her mixing. 'Of course, dear. Patty will see to that for you. You could have just rung down for that, you know.'

'I know,' I said. 'But I like coming down here and seeing everyone.'

'You're a sweetheart for saying so, dear, but most of us would stay upstairs if we could. Patty! Make up a tray of coffee for the library.'

'Thank you, Mrs Ruddle. You know, I—'

I was pulled up short by the sound of a kerfuffle in the servants' hall. Mrs McLelland was giving someone what-for, and she wasn't concerned about being overheard.

'. . . ungrateful, evil, lying, deceitful, THIEF!' This last word was shouted with such force that it seemed to overcome her and render her momentarily incapable of further speech.

Mrs Ruddle slammed her mixing bowl down on to the work bench with unaccustomed passion. 'She's gone too far this time,' she said as she wiped her hands on her apron. 'I don't care what's gone on, but that ain't no way to deal with it.' She started towards the hall, but I gently held her arm and stopped her.

'Leave it to me, Mrs Ruddle,' I said. 'We'll be gone soon, and it doesn't matter what she thinks of me. I'd hate to see you burn any bridges.'

She was still fuming, but she allowed me to ease her back towards her work. I went through to the servants' hall, where I found a *tableau vivant* worthy of a theatre show: 'The Astonishment of the Servants'. There were two parlour maids, a footman, a boot boy, and a laundry maid standing in mute horror at the outburst. The only movement was the retreating back of Evan Gudger as he stomped out of the room. Mrs McLelland looked around sharply.

'Get on with your work, all of you,' she barked. 'And what do you think you're looking at?' she said when she saw me. 'What do you want?'

'I want you never to address me like that again, for starters,' I said.

'Oh, just get out of my servants' hall, you jumped-up housemaid,' she said, and she stalked off in the direction of her room.

I shrugged, and went back to the kitchen to fetch the coffee.

◆ ◆ ◆

I delivered the coffee tray to the library, where Lady Hardcastle and Miss Titmus had made themselves comfortable in two of the armchairs. They had arranged three of them around a low table, upon which I placed the tray.

'Sit down and join us,' said Lady Hardcastle. 'You don't mind, Helen?'

'I never mind, Emily; I've told you that. You're always welcome to sit with us, Armstrong.'

'Thank you,' I said, and sat down.

'The reason I double checked,' said Lady Hardcastle, 'is that I've had some news from our inspector friend in Bristol, and I rather need to ask you some questions. About your schooldays.'

'Oh,' said Miss Titmus. 'I see. Well . . . No, go ahead. You probably *should* know.'

I raised an eyebrow enquiringly, but Lady Hardcastle signalled that now was not the time.

'You see, dear,' she said, 'we've been working on the assumption that all the dreadful things that have happened this past week were somehow connected to Fishy's motor racing team. The sabotage of one of his motor cars, the attack on his rival, Viktor.'

Miss Titmus nodded. Her customary shy smile had vanished to be replaced by a look of . . . sadness? Regret?

'That is to say,' continued Lady Hardcastle, 'that *I* assumed that. Florence, on the other hand, was inclined to look in another direction. Where I was insistent that all the clues we needed were to be found in newspaper stories about motor racing and in the minutes of board meetings, Flo kept on asking about your schooldays.'

Miss Titmus nodded again.

'And so when I said I was going to ask Inspector Sunderland to look into the affairs of the motor racing team, Flo pleaded that I also ask about Evanshaw's School for Girls. It seems her instincts were better than mine, as usual. Obviously, I can't rule out business intrigue, but I think the events of the past week are probably part of a much more human story.'

Miss Titmus simply sat, her hands folded in her lap, staring at the floor.

'The inspector found a newspaper report from June 1883.'

'Emily, don't,' said Miss Titmus. 'I can't bear it. I've never been able to bear it. Please don't.'

'I'm sorry, dear, but I believe that somehow the events of that summer are tied up with the events of this summer, and I really do need to hear your side of the story.'

'The newspaper story was broadly correct,' said Miss Titmus.

I didn't want to break the spell by galumphing in with idiotic questions, but this obliqueness was beginning to become a little wearing. I raised an enquiring eyebrow once more.

'Forgive me, dear,' said Lady Hardcastle. 'This must be terribly frustrating. You remember when we first saw the photograph of the cricket team? There was a rather beautiful girl with dark hair. We asked who she was.'

'Katy Something-or-other,' I said.

'Burkinshaw. We asked for details, and Lavinia said it was a story for another day. It's another day now, I'm afraid. You see, the newspaper story that Inspector Sunderland found was a report of a tragedy at Evanshaw's School for Girls. A young lady, just sixteen years old and soon to leave for Switzerland to complete her education, was found hanged in the folly in the grounds of the school one evening. It was Katy Burkinshaw.'

A tear ran down Miss Titmus's cheek.

'Poor Katy,' she said quietly. 'It was my fault. I should have stopped her. I should have seen what was going to happen.'

'You can't stop someone when they've made their mind up, dear,' said Lady Hardcastle kindly. 'Once someone has reached that level of despair . . .'

'Not Katy,' said Miss Titmus, with some surprise. 'I meant Roz. I should have stopped Roz.'

Lady Hardcastle and I both goggled. 'Roz killed her?' we said together.

It was Miss Titmus's turn to goggle. 'What? No! No, good heavens. Well, not like that. In a way, though. You know Roz. She's a . . . She's—'

'She's a bully,' I said.

'She is,' she said. 'Always has been. She's reduced me to tears more times than I can count.'

'Why on earth do you still knock about with her?' asked Lady Hardcastle.

'She's my friend,' said Miss Titmus. 'I love her like a sister. She's as fragile and insecure as the next girl, deep down. That's why she's so spiky. Her wretched marriage is no help. She needs her friends.'

'What happened at school?' said Lady Hardcastle.

'You saw that photograph. Katy was a beauty. Roz was always pretty, but Katy had a radiance about her. Something inside shone out. Roz was horribly jealous. She did everything she could to undermine and belittle Katy. All the time, ragging her, getting her into trouble. Katy pretended not to care. But it got worse when she fell for a boy from the village. We weren't allowed to go to the village on our own, but we often sneaked over the wall. Katy met a boy. She made the mistake of telling us she'd kissed him. That did it for Roz. Her attacks increased, getting nastier and more spiteful. Still Katy seemed unfazed, but when Roz threatened to tell Mrs Evanshaw that Katy and the boy had been seen in . . . amorous congress, she couldn't cope any longer. She begged, she pleaded. But then Roz knew she had her. She kept up the taunting until . . . Until . . .'

'Until Katy hanged herself in the old folly at sunset,' said Lady Hardcastle quietly. 'I think we might have been a bit reckless in telling Inspector Foister to release Roz Beddows.'

◆ ◆ ◆

After all that, I thought my news from below stairs would be a little anticlimactic – so much so that I very nearly didn't bother to say anything. A light lunch was laid out in the dining room, to which the two ladies helped themselves before returning to the library to look at more of Miss Titmus's collection of extraordinary photographs.

The conversation drifted amiably on for quite some time before Lady Hardcastle casually asked if all was well in the dungeons. It was only then that I thought it worth my while telling the story of Evan's dressing down. I was somewhat taken aback when she insisted that I should track Evan down without delay and get his side of the story.

My first thought was to try the wine cellar. I ruled it out immediately – it was Mrs McLelland who had told me about it, so why would he hide from her in the one place she knew he might be? After fifteen minutes' fruitless searching, I ruled it back in again – she was so furious with him that she wasn't going to be looking for him anyway, so why not hide there? While I was still on my way, I ruled it out again – if she wanted to make trouble for him, she would complain to Mr Spinney, so there was no point in hiding where Mr Spinney would be sure to find him. Once Evan had been found, Mr Spinney would have no choice but to reprimand him, no matter how reluctant he might be to do so. And then . . . And then I just went to the wine cellar. It was the only place I hadn't yet looked.

I found Evan in his corner, sitting on his barrel and staring at the vaulted ceiling. Even in the flickering candlelight, I could see that he had been crying.

'What do you want?' he asked. I imagine that he had intended to sound belligerent, but the fight had gone out of him, and instead he sounded weary and defeated.

'I came to see if you were all right,' I said. 'That was a disgraceful display from Mrs McLelland. She has no business treating anyone that way, but you're not even her responsibility. You're one of Mr Spinney's footmen.'

'Not for long, I don't reckon,' he said forlornly. 'I was only doin' what you asked, an' all.'

'What I asked?' I said.

'I was only doin' it for you,' he said. From beneath the pile of books on his barrel table he produced the cricket team photograph and two pieces of foolscap, each folded neatly in half. He handed them to me.

'They was in Kovacs's room,' he said. 'I thought you said they was important, so I took 'em before they got tidied away.'

'Tidied away?'

'Soon as the police is done, they'll clear everythin' out, won't they? Only the old witch caught me comin' out of the room.'

The photograph was quite familiar by now, but I was curious to find out why Evan had attached such significance to the papers. I unfolded the first. It was a familiar list, written in an even more familiar hand – the race order for the fateful motor race. The second was somethin' new, somethin' I knew would interest Lady Hardcastle very much.

'Thank you, Evan,' I said. 'I have a feeling that Lady Hardcastle will want these. I think she's on to something.'

'Something worth losin' my job over, I hope.'

'It won't come to that. I have them now, so Mrs McLelland has no proof that you've done anything. And I'll make sure Mr Spinney knows you were working on our behalf, even if she complains. There's nothing she can do to you.'

''Cept make my life a misery,' he said.

'She does her best to make everyone's life a misery. We'll soon settle her hash.'

'His lordship won't do nothin'. He reckons she's the best house-keeper anyone ever had.'

'We'll see,' I said. I refolded the paper and placed it with the photograph. 'Don't do anything rash, like skedaddling out of here. We might still need your help.'

He huffed dispiritedly, and I left him to pull himself together.

◆ ◆ ◆

I closed the wine cellar door behind me and made my way to the servants' stairs, still clutching the purloined items. A few junior members of the household staff bustled past me as they went about their own business. I didn't see anyone I knew until I rounded the last corner and was all but bowled over by Betty Buffrey, who was heading in the opposite direction. She was crying. It was clearly the day for that sort of thing.

'Oh,' she said. 'Flo. I'm so sorry.'

'Whatever's the matter, Betty, *fach*?' I said.

She sniffed loudly and wiped her eyes on the sleeve of her dress.

'Oh, Flo,' she said, and threw her arms about me as she began weeping again.

As gently as I could, I manoeuvred her to the foot of the stairs and helped her to sit down.

'Tell me what happened,' I said.

'The old cow got back from gaol,' she said between sobs. 'I told her I'd given it careful consideration, but given everything that's happened, I have my own reputation to think of. I told her I'd stay with her until she found somebody else, but that I'd be looking for a new position.'

'But that's good, isn't it?' I said. 'Well done, you.'

'It would be good, except she said, "Well if that's the way you feel, you disloyal little trollop" – she had the bloomin' cheek to call me a trollop, after everything she's done – "if that's the way you feel, you can go straight away. I don't want you. You can make your own way back to London. If you haven't picked up your traps by month's end, I'll sell anything valuable and give the rest to the church jumble sale." I'm out on my ear, Flo. I've got no job, no home . . .' She resumed her snotty sobbing.

There was an obvious solution. Obvious to me, at least, and to anyone who wasn't currently sitting on a stone staircase crying their eyes out and wiping their nose on the sleeve of their dress.

'I'm not intending to sound overly harsh, Betty,' I said, 'but how quickly do you think you can stop crying and pull yourself together?'

'What?' she said through a renewed bubbly sob.

'We can almost certainly get you re-employed in five minutes flat. There's actually no rush, and the job will probably be yours even if you don't apply until next month, but, you know, strike while the iron's hot, and all that.'

'What?' she said again.

I gave her my handkerchief. 'Dry your eyes, blow your nose, and follow me,' I said. 'There's a new position waiting for you upstairs. Chop-chop. No, it's all right, you keep it. I've got another.'

◆ ◆ ◆

By the time we reached the library, Betty had calmed down a little, though she was still very puffy around the eyes. We found Lady Hardcastle and Miss Titmus still in the armchairs.

'Ah, there you are,' said Lady Hardcastle. 'We were beginning to fear you might have been abducted.'

'Sadly no, my lady,' I said. 'I'm still here. No escape for me. I brought you a present.' I gave her the photograph and the two sheets of folded foolscap.

'You shouldn't have,' she said. 'Oh, I've already seen these.'

'Only two of them,' I said. 'The third is rather interesting.'

'So these are what Evan pinched from Herr Kovacs's room?'

'And earned him his wigging,' I said.

'Ah,' she said. 'We must have missed this other sheet in all the clutter on that writing desk. Good old Evan. It's a shame his light-fingeredness sent Mrs McLelland into a rage. We might have to do some work there to sort things out for him.'

'I'm sure we can talk her round. She's a bit of a martinet at times, but she's an intelligent and rational woman.'

'Just so,' she said. 'But well done, Evan. And well done, you, for getting him on our side. This gives us plenty more to ponder. Now then, you seem to have brought a colleague. Welcome back, Miss Buffrey. Your mistress has returned, I hear. We've not actually seen her – she went straight up to her room – but his lordship did pop in to tell us that all was well.'

Betty merely nodded.

'Yes, my lady,' I said. 'That's actually why I brought Betty up here. There's been a bit of a falling out.'

'Oh no, how awful. She's been through a lot, though. Perhaps we should make allowances?'

'That would be the proper thing,' I said. 'But it's gone a little further than harsh words that can be taken back in calmer times. Mrs Beddows has sacked her.'

'I say,' said Lady Hardcastle. 'That will never do.'

'Well, quite. The thing is, you see, I was wondering . . .'

Miss Titmus had been silent through all this, but was now suddenly alert.

'Actually,' she said, 'I think it will do rather nicely. Miss Buffrey, would you like a job? You see, I've recently been persuaded that I'm very much in need of a lady's maid. And, well, there's a rumour going round that you might be in need of a new position.'

'Oh,' I said, 'that was easy. Betty?'

'I . . . er . . . I don't know what to say,' said Betty.

'You say, "Thank you, Miss Titmus, that would be wonderful,"' I said. 'Then you shake hands and agree to work out the details later.'

'Thank you,' said Betty. 'That would be rather wonderful.'

'Well, that's all splendid,' said Lady Hardcastle.

'And so much easier than I imagined,' I said. 'I thought it would take much longer than that to get them both to realize what a good idea it was.'

'Your ideas are always marvellous, dear,' said Lady Hardcastle. 'They were always bound to get there in the end.'

'Do you know anything about photography?' said Miss Titmus.

'Only what I see in the magazines,' said Betty. 'And the pictures you show Mrs Beddows. But it's fascinating.'

'Even splendider,' said Miss Titmus. 'I shall have a lady's maid and an assistant in my new business venture. You can be Titmus Photographic Services Limited's very first employee.'

'And your first commission will be to photograph our house,' said Lady Hardcastle. 'Or the motor car. Or The Grange, where my dear friends the Farley-Strouds live. Or anything at all we can find in the village. You must capture the village in all its glory. And change the name, dear; it's a bit cumbersome.'

'You're on,' said Miss Titmus. 'I was a little down in the dumps earlier, but this has rather cheered me. In celebration, Buffrey, I give you the afternoon off. Take your ease, do as you will. I shall see you after breakfast tomorrow, and we can discuss terms and duties.'

'That's very kind, miss,' said Betty, whose sniffles had finally ceased.

'And if you bump into Roz, you have my permission to thumb your nose at her.'

'Oh my,' said Betty. 'I don't think I could do that.'

'No,' said Miss Titmus, 'nor me. Frightens the life out of me, that woman. Always has. But take comfort in daydreaming it, and then we shall start afresh tomorrow.'

'Thank you, miss,' said Betty, and she left the library a much cheerier woman than she had arrived.

Lady Hardcastle was examining the photograph again.

'She doesn't look at all troubled here,' she said.

'Who, dear?' asked Miss Titmus.

'Young Katy Burkinshaw. She's so pretty, too.'

'May I?' I said. She handed me the photograph and turned her attention instead to the folded papers.

The door handle rattled as Mr Waterford opened it and poked his head round the door.

'Good afternoon, ladies,' he said. 'I don't suppose you've seen Roz?'

'I'm afraid not,' said Miss Titmus. 'We thought she'd gone straight up to her room. Have you tried there?'

'Yes, no sign of her. Can't find her anywhere. And Buffrey's absent, too. Ah, well. If you see her, please tell her I'm looking for her.'

'Right you are, dear,' said Miss Titmus.

He left.

I looked back down at the framed photograph in my hand. There was the now-familiar group of young sportswomen. Unstoppable champions, with nothing to block their path to success and happiness. Lady Lavinia with her bat. Mrs Beddows with a ribbon tying back her hair, leaning on her friend's shoulder, with one leg crossed in front of the other. Miss Titmus with her chubby face and her eyes slightly downcast. Katy Burkinshaw with her warm smile, a little brooch pinned to her chest relieving the starkness of the uniform. I looked more closely at the brooch as a thought struck me.

'Miss Titmus,' I said. 'Did Katy Burkinshaw have a sister?'

'What? Oh, yes. A couple of years below us. Worshipped her big sister. What was her name? Oh, it'll come to me in a moment . . . Rebecca. That was it. Rebecca.'

I tried to pass the photograph back to Lady Hardcastle, who was still poring over the race order.

'My lady,' I said. 'Have another look at Katy Burkinshaw. I think I know why she looks familiar.'

She did as I asked, then looked back at the race order.

'Did Monty just say Roz was missing?' she said.

'Yes,' said Miss Titmus. 'He said he's looked everywhere.'

Lady Hardcastle stood abruptly. 'I rather fear she's in terrible danger. We need to find her at once.'

Chapter Sixteen

'Helen, I need you to go and find Fishy and Monty. Bring them here, please. Don't tell them Roz is missing, or they'll go haring off on their own and we'll never find her.'

Miss Titmus looked slightly taken aback. Lady Hardcastle tended to affect an air of slightly dizzy affability among new acquaintances. This confident, decisive, commanding Emily Hardcastle seemed to have come as a bit of a shock.

'Righto, Emily,' she said. 'What about Harry and Jake?'

'Harry's on the sick list – he'll be no use to us – and Jake will be better employed keeping him out of our way. Best leave them out of it. No, wait, you're right. Fetch them. They can set up camp in here, coordinate the intelligence. Battalion HQ, and all that.'

Miss Titmus hurried off.

'Armstrong, go down and find Spinney, and ask him to come up. I'd ring down, but there's no telling who will turn up, and I need Spinney to coordinate the servants, so it will be quicker to fetch him directly.' Lady Hardcastle was in charge.

'On my way, my lady,' I said, following Miss Titmus.

◆   ◆   ◆

Rumours of Betty's 'sacking' had already begun to take hold below stairs, and I was delayed for a few moments while I set a few people straight.

'You pal around with that Miss Buffrey, don't you?' said one of the cheekier young housemaids. 'What did she do to get herself sacked? Did she pinch something?'

'She wasn't sacked,' I said. 'She resigned. And if I hear any more accusations of pinching, I'll box your ears.'

'Have to catch me first,' she said, and she skipped off.

I eventually found Mr Spinney in his parlour.

'Come in, my dear,' he said. He was sitting at his table, using the decanting cradle to decant a bottle of port. He looked up from the delicate work as he greeted me. 'What can I do for you this fine afternoon? I hear young Miss Buffrey has been dismissed. I do hope it wasn't anything too terrible. Poor Mrs Beddows doesn't need any further ugliness in her life.'

'I'm afraid you're the recipient of inaccurate gossip, Mr Spinney,' I said.

'Oh? How so?'

We really didn't have time for all this, but I needed him on our side, and I decided that brusquely dismissing his question would do us more harm than good in the long run.

As briefly as I could, I told him the full story, of Mrs Beddows's bullying, and of Betty's dismay at the scandal that would follow news of the affair and the arrest. 'And in the strictest confidence,' I continued, 'I can tell you that she was immediately engaged by Miss Titmus. I think they'll get along splendidly, but we should probably wait until it's all been properly agreed before we say anything.'

'I apologize,' said Mr Spinney. 'One should never listen to servants' gossip. The problem is that we always have quite the best gossip, so it's hard to ignore it. But I've diverted you from your purpose. You wished to see me?'

'I did,' I said. 'Would you be kind enough to come up to the library, please? Lady Hardcastle wishes your help with an urgent matter.'

'Of course, of course,' he said as he stood. 'She should have rung down.'

'It was quicker this way. And there's a need to be discreet at the moment.'

'Oh dear. I do hope it's nothing too terrible. You should have said so straight away.'

'Not to worry,' I said. 'I'm glad I had the opportunity to clarify Miss Buffrey's situation. But I think we should hurry.'

◆ ◆ ◆

By the time Mr Spinney and I returned to the library, Miss Titmus was already there with Lord Riddlethorpe and Mr Waterford. Harry and Lady Lavinia arrived soon after.

'Quite the gathering,' said Harry as he hobbled to one of the armchairs and flopped into it. 'An impromptu party, sis? Where's Roz?'

'As always, Harry, dear, you've hit upon the nub of it all quite by accident,' said Lady Hardcastle. '"Where's Roz?" is the question we need most urgently to answer.'

'I get the feeling it's not a game, though,' said Harry.

'I'm afraid not. This time, it's deadly serious. And I'm not being melodramatic. Well, I am, I suppose, but I really do fear that Roz is in danger.'

Six people in various states of agitation started talking at once.

'Quiet, please!' called Lord Riddlethorpe. 'Let Emily speak.'

'Thank you, Fishy,' said Lady Hardcastle. 'I believe I know who our murderer and mischief-maker is, and I think they have Roz. I think they mean to do her harm.'

Another clamour erupted.

Once again, Lord Riddlethorpe's voice cut through the hubbub. 'Quiet! Who has her, and what do they intend to do?'

'I think Rebecca Burkinshaw has her. And I think she means to hang her.'

'Rebecca who?' asked three male voices at once. Miss Titmus and Lady Lavinia simply gaped.

'I'll tell you the complete tale later,' said Lady Hardcastle. 'But for now, action is more urgent than understanding. Fishy, I need you, Monty, and Helen to search the house. Guest rooms and family rooms, upstairs and down. Every nook and cranny.'

Lord Riddlethorpe seemed happy to allow her to take charge, and nodded his agreement.

'Spinney, please gather some reliable servants and search every inch of your domain. Attic rooms, cellars, private rooms, and offices. Leave no door unopened.'

The butler, too, nodded in acknowledgement.

'Harry, you and Jake stay here. If anyone finds anything, deal with it as you see fit, but report to Harry and Jake, so that we know what's going on. And remember that "we've not found her" is important information, too.'

'And you, sis?' asked Harry.

'Armstrong and I will search the outbuildings. Are we clear?'

There were murmurs of assent.

'Fishy,' said Lady Hardcastle, 'do you have a pistol?'

'No,' said Lord Riddlethorpe. 'We just keep shotguns.'

'No good,' she said. 'Too imprecise. No matter. Off you go, then. And hurry. If I'm right, we have until twenty to seven at the absolute latest.'

'Twenty to seven?' said Mr Waterford.

'Sunset.'

◆ ◆ ◆

Lady Hardcastle and I left by the front door and hurried around the outside of the house.

'This whole ghastly business began in the coach house,' said Lady Hardcastle as she strode towards the stable yard. 'It would be gruesome, but fitting, if it were to end there, don't you think?'

'I'm not at all sure what to think any more, my lady,' I said. 'I'm still trying to come to terms with what's been going on. The answer's been right under our noses all along, but it still boggles my mind; I don't know about yours.'

'My poor old mind is in a perpetual state of bogglement, dear; you know that well enough by now. Ah, look, the doors are shut. I'm not certain whether that's a good sign or bad.'

'There's no way to tell from out here,' I said. 'Shall I nip round the other side to cover the back door?'

'Good thinking. Give the old signal when you're in place, and we'll go in together.'

'Right you are, my lady. I might have to force my way in, but at least no one will get out while I'm kicking the door down.'

I trotted softly across the flagstones of the old stable yard, past the Rolls-Royce, and then worked my way round to the back of the building. The rear door was closed, but I couldn't tell if it was locked.

One of my less-celebrated skills is the ability to imitate the call of the jackdaw. It's not the sort of thing one might do as a party piece, but it had served us well as a secret call over the years – no one thinks anything of the sound of such a common bird. Even China has a type of jackdaw, whose call could only be distinguished by an experienced ornithologist.

I readied myself for action, and let loose the high-pitched 'jack-jack' signal. Almost at once, I heard the sound of the coach house doors opening. I turned the handle of the rear door, but found it locked.

This was no time to worry about damaging Lord Riddlethorpe's property, though, so I took a step back and kicked at the door near the lock.

Old wood is the burglar's friend, and the soft, damp wood of the frame around the lock was no match even for my tiny Welsh foot. The door burst open, and I rushed inside to find . . . three motor cars and a disappointed widow.

'She's not bally well here,' said Lady Hardcastle.

'So I see,' I said. 'Where now?'

'There's nothing for it – we'll have to search all the sheds and other outbuildings. This is going to take longer than I thought. I was so certain it would be the coach house.'

And so we searched. We turned the potting sheds, the tool sheds, even the greenhouses, upside down, but there was no sign of Mrs Beddows.

After three quarters of an hour, Lady Hardcastle was certain we had looked everywhere.

'We'd better get back to the library, and hope that the others have had more luck,' she said. 'It's already nearly six o'clock, and I fear we're running out of time.'

◆ ◆ ◆

The others were already in the library, waiting anxiously for our return.

'Well?' said Mr Waterford impatiently as we entered. 'Have you found her?'

'No,' said Lady Hardcastle, 'I'm afraid we haven't. I take it you haven't, either.'

'Not a trace,' said Lord Riddlethorpe. 'We've searched the house from top to bottom. Spinney has done the same in the servants' rooms. She's not in the house.'

'She's not in the coach house or any of the sheds or outbuildings, either,' said Lady Hardcastle.

'We must have missed her,' said Mr Waterford. 'She can't simply have vanished.'

'Was the Rolls still in the yard?' asked Harry.

'It was,' I said.

'Then she's still on the estate somewhere. There's no other transport.'

'Is there anywhere we haven't looked, Fishy?' said Lady Hardcastle. 'Any other outbuildings?'

'Or barns?' said Miss Titmus. 'Didn't you used to have hay barns out on the other side of the estate?'

'We did,' said Lord Riddlethorpe, 'but we had them torn down when we sold the last of the horses. No need to store food for the beasts any longer, so we got rid of them.'

'Then she's somewhere else on the estate,' said Lady Lavinia. 'Acres and acres of parkland with your blessed racing track running through the middle of it. We'll never find her.'

The middle of it, I thought. There's something in the middle of it. 'The rotunda,' I said suddenly. 'On that first day, my lord, when you were showing Lady Hardcastle the racing track. We had lunch by the lake. In the rotunda.'

'By George, you're right,' said Lady Hardcastle. 'Fishy?'

'It's the only place we haven't looked,' said Lord Riddlethorpe. 'The Rolls would be the quickest way to get us all there.'

Leaving a bewildered Mr Spinney, a frustrated Harry, and an anxious Lady Lavinia to hold the fort, the rest of us raced back towards the stable yard and the waiting Rolls-Royce. There was a bowl of fruit on the sideboard beside the door, and I paused to grab the small fruit knife that sat beside it. You never know when such a thing might come in handy if things cut up rough.

Mr Waterford all but barged Lord Riddlethorpe out of the way so that he could drive.

'She's my . . . She's . . . I . . . I'll drive,' he said as he jumped into the driving seat.

Lord Riddlethorpe cranked the engine, while Lady Hardcastle and Miss Titmus clambered into the back.

With the engine now purring smoothly, Lord Riddlethorpe jumped in beside Mr Waterford.

Betty came haring into the yard.

'Don't leave me behind,' she panted. 'She might be a hateful old harpy, but if I can help stop her from being a dead old harpy, I will.'

The Silver Ghost comfortably seated four. There were now six of us. Somehow, we managed to squeeze Betty into the back seat between Lady Hardcastle and Miss Titmus.

I wasn't going to be left behind for want of somewhere to sit, so I jumped on the running board on the left-hand side and clung on for dear life.

Mr Waterford was an experienced racing driver, but the Rolls-Royce Silver Ghost was not built for speed. Nevertheless, he managed an impressive pace as he shot out of the stable yard and turned on to the road that ran towards his racing track.

As we neared the circuit, I imagined he would head out across the parkland towards the lake. Instead, he turned sharply to the right and on to the racing track itself.

'We need to get to the middle, Monty!' yelled Lady Hardcastle from the back of the motor car.

Lord Riddlethorpe turned in his seat. 'No, he's right,' he called. 'This is quicker. Rotunda's on the other side of the lake. Quicker on the track than on the grass.'

We sped on.

On the racing track he had helped to design, Mr Waterford showed great confidence. He knew every twist and turn, every bump,

Death Around the Bend

every rise, every dip, and although the Rolls-Royce was nothing like the sleek racing cars he usually coaxed around the circuit, he knew exactly how to get the greatest possible speed from it.

I was beginning to wish he didn't.

The first turn wasn't too bad – it was to the left and threw me into the motor car. The turn that followed was to the right, though, and pushed me outwards. It was only Lady Hardcastle's quick thinking and strong grip that prevented me from flying off into the grass beside the track. She held on to me from then onwards.

Abruptly, Mr Waterford turned left, off the track and on to the grass. I'd thought that speeding along the track was hairy, but this new, rough, uneven route across the park was an altogether new form of horrible. The Silver Ghost's suspension was designed for comfort, to smooth out the imperfections of the road. But out here on the undulating grassland, it seemed to amplify the bumps and, once again, it was only Lady Hardcastle's strength and our combined determination that kept me from ending up lying in a bruised and undignified heap while they sped off without me.

At last, the rotunda came into view. Mr Waterford's own desperation seemed to communicate itself to the Rolls-Royce, which managed to find an extra burst of speed to serve its anguished driver.

The brakes squealed. The wheels locked. The motor car slid to a stop beside the rotunda, and we all piled out.

◆ ◆ ◆

There was a ragtag shambles of uncoordinated scrambling to get to the entrance to the rotunda. The wide, double doors were thrown open, as they had been on that first day, but the sight that met us was very different.

Where we had first seen a table set for a magnificent lunch, there was now a tall, wooden stool.

Standing on the stool, a rope around her neck, her hands tied behind her back, was Mrs Beddows.

Beside her, a shotgun in her hands, stood Mrs McLelland. She raised the gun to her hip and pointed it towards the doors.

'That'll do,' she said. 'You can see perfectly well from there.'

'Rebecca,' said Lady Hardcastle. 'You don't need to do this. Let her down.'

'Rebecca?' said Mr Waterford. 'Who's Rebecca? I thought Mrs McLelland was called Muriel. She's Muriel, Fishy, isn't she? You hired the blessed woman.'

'It is Rebecca, though, isn't it?' interrupted Lady Hardcastle. 'Rebecca Burkinshaw.'

'The amazing Lady Hardcastle and her famous detective skills. Brava. Took you long enough to work it out, though, didn't it, *Emily*.' She stressed Lady Hardcastle's Christian name, pouring on as much discourtesy and disdain as she could muster.

'What's she talking about?' said Mr Waterford angrily. 'What's going on?'

'Oh no,' said Mrs McLelland. 'Poor Monty. Poor, confused, stupid Monty. Is your popsy in peril? Tell him, Helen. Or are you still too timid to stand up for yourself?'

Mr Waterford turned to Miss Titmus.

'What on earth is going on?' he said.

'I think Emily's right,' said Miss Titmus. 'I think this is Rebecca Burkinshaw.'

'So everyone keeps saying,' said Mr Waterford. 'But who—?'

'Her big sister Katy was at school with us,' she said. 'She wasn't a happy girl.'

'She was a perfectly happy, wonderful girl until you evil shrews made her life a misery,' said Mrs McLelland.

Miss Titmus pressed on. 'She took her own life one evening at school,' she said.

'At sunset,' said Mrs McLelland. 'Not long to wait now.' She gestured with the shotgun.

We all turned to see that the sun had almost reached the horizon.

I tugged on Lady Hardcastle's sleeve, and she bent slightly towards me.

'Keep everyone moving around a little,' I murmured. 'There are too many of us for her to keep track of everyone if we don't stand still.'

'Righto,' she said. 'Watch for your signal?'

'You'll know when to go,' I said.

She nodded.

I stepped slowly to my right as Lady Hardcastle turned to mutter something to Lord Riddlethorpe. As I took another step, I could just about hear him whispering to Mr Waterford. They both had the aggrieved look of men-of-action who have been asked to wait for someone else to take the lead, but they seemed to be complying for now. They shifted about, calmly, naturally.

Another step took me to the very edge of the stone steps leading to the doorway as Betty crossed in front of Miss Titmus. I could see that Lady Hardcastle had already reached the opposite side of the steps, so that the six of us were now spread out across Mrs McLelland's entire field of view. She could still see us all, but she couldn't focus on all of us at once.

As instructed, the other four continued to shuffle about while Lady Hardcastle began to speak again.

'We know you blame Katy's friends for what happened, Rebecca. But this isn't the way to settle things.'

'It isn't?' said Mrs McLelland. 'And how do you propose we "settle" it? How do you propose we "settle" the vile bullies who hounded my sister to death? They destroyed my father, too. Drink. Gambling. He lost everything. Why do you think I came to be working as a governess? How did I end up here, cleaning up after this undeserving shower of titled nonentities?'

'How *did* you end up here, Rebecca?' persisted Lady Hardcastle.
'That oaf Kovacs suggested it.'

'You knew him, didn't you? He had a letter from Lord Riddlethorpe's father, the previous earl. They met in Vienna, along with your father. The earl was the one who introduced Viktor to his lordship. You must have met him when you were a little girl on trips with your father. Did he become a family friend? Did he look out for you when things went wrong?'

Mrs McLelland laughed. 'Only as far as it suited his own ambitions. He was sweet on my mother, mostly, but she wouldn't give him the time of day. Once he got over that, he "looked out" for me. Didn't want to actually help. No money. He wanted me "to stand on my own feet". And then when he told me that "Fishy" was looking for a new housekeeper, he said I should come and work here. "It would be more money for you. Better prospects. A promotion. A grand family, too. And while you're there you could perhaps keep me informed of his lordship's progress with his motor cars." The old fool.'

'He didn't know about Lavinia, Helen, and Roz, did he?'

'He was an old fool who knew nothing. I came here. I did his sordid spying for him. But I had plans of my own.'

'And they started to unravel when he saw a picture of the girls,' said Lady Hardcastle. 'He knew Katy at once. He realized what you were up to. He tried to stop you. That's why you met in the coach house. Did you mean to kill him?'

'I had to stop him. He was going to ruin everything.'

'But it's over now, Rebecca. We can help you. There's no need to make things worse than they already are,' she said. 'Another death isn't going to make things any better.'

'It's not going to make things any worse, though, is it? Two useless articles already dead; a third won't make them hang me any less. Might as well be hung for a—' She noticed for the first time that everyone was moving slowly about in front of the doors. 'What do you all think you're doing? Stand still!'

'But it won't bring—'

'It won't bring Katy back? Please tell me you weren't going to say that. The great Emily Hardcastle and her Big Girl's Book of Clichés? Do please shut up, dear. Just a few more moments and the sun will go down. Then this useless, evil article can suffer the same way as my dear Katy. They say hanging is quite a horrible way to go without the hangman's drop. And I do so want to make sure it's as horrible as it can possibly be.' Her maniacal grin was proof, as though any were needed, that she had passed beyond the point where appeals to reason might have any effect.

Out of the corner of my eye, I saw Mr Waterford tense as he began to charge up the steps. Some people just won't do as they're told.

Mrs McLelland saw him, too, and was swinging her shotgun round towards him.

I had the fruit knife concealed in my hand. I had hoped to get into position for a better throw, but needs must . . .

'Get down!' I yelled. I flicked my wrist and sent the tiny knife flying towards her. It embedded itself in her left forearm an instant before she pulled the trigger.

It was a risky stratagem. From where I stood, there was no way I could stop her from shooting. I couldn't rush her, and with such a tiny knife, there was no way I could incapacitate her. My best bet was to disrupt her aim and hope that everyone had the good sense to obey my shout and follow me to the ground.

A shotgun blast is terrifying when the gun is discharged indoors. The sound of shattering glass is always startling, too. The sight and sound of an ornamental stone pineapple falling from a door lintel ought to be comical, but when it crashes into the back of a heroically foolish man – even one who has ignored explicit instructions to wait for the signal to attack – that, too, is disturbing.

Mrs McLelland had flinched as the knife struck her, and her shot had gone high, blasting the window above the door and dislodging the aforementioned ornamental pineapple. She was a game girl, though, and was already steadying herself for her second shot as I leapt up and charged towards her.

She didn't manage to level the gun before I cannoned into her, but she did manage to kick the rickety stool to one side. As I attempted to wrest the shotgun from Mrs McLelland's grasp, Mrs Beddows screamed, fell, and then silently kicked as the rope tightened around her neck.

I decided that I'd rather the heavy shotgun were only useful as a club, so as soon as I was sure it was pointed safely away from any of Mrs Beddows's would-be rescuers, I squeezed Mrs McLelland's trigger finger and forced her to fire it harmlessly against the wall. Harmlessly for us, at least. It proved to be Mrs McLelland's undoing.

Unbalanced by the recoil from the gun, she was easy to topple. An elbow here, a knee there, and a well-placed boot just so, and she was lying on the floor, disarmed and choking.

I was finally able to turn my attention to saving Mrs Beddows, but that urgent matter was already well in hand.

First to the scene had been, of all people, Betty Buffrey. Somehow, she had managed to get underneath her erstwhile employer and was supporting her on her shoulders. While Betty held her aloft like some victorious sportswoman, Lady Hardcastle and Miss Titmus worked to untie the rope, which had been thrown over a roof beam and secured to a sturdy sconce embedded in the stone wall.

Lord Riddlethorpe was doing his best to steady Mrs Beddows as she swayed on Betty's shoulders.

Mr Waterford was out cold on the steps, but seemed to be breathing.

At last, Miss Titmus managed to loosen the knot, and between them they laid Mrs Beddows on the stone floor, where they untied her wrists and comforted her as she began to weep uncontrollably.

Lady Hardcastle brought me the rope, and we secured Mrs McLelland. I left the knife in her arm. It's dangerous to remove a knife without medical supervision. And it would hurt like blazes if we left it there.

Chapter Seventeen

It took two trips to get the wounded and the prisoner back to the house. Betty and Miss Titmus had accompanied Mrs Beddows (shaken and wheezing) and Mr Waterford (conscious but woozy). Lady Hardcastle and I had waited with Mrs McLelland (alternately angry and snivelling).

Dr Edling arrived from Riddlethorpe shortly after we had unloaded the still-bound Mrs McLelland from the back of the Rolls-Royce. Lord Riddlethorpe directed him to take care of Mrs Beddows first.

'French military doctors have a word, my lord: *triage*. It's the name for the way we assess and prioritize the wounded for treatment. Your housekeeper's wound is more urgently in need of attention than your guests'.'

'The French have a great many wonderful words, Doctor,' said Lord Riddlethorpe. 'Do they have one to describe the lack of concern a householder might have for the woman who has just tried to murder one of his sister's oldest friends? It's a rather specific situation, I grant you, so perhaps they do not. Treat Mrs Beddows first, then Mr Waterford. When they're both settled, you may see to the moaning wretch in the corner.'

'At least let me make her comfortable, my lord. You wouldn't treat a dog this way.'

'If a dog had tried to kill one of my friends, Dr Edling, I would have shot it. Suffering is good for the immortal soul, and hers needs as much help as it can get. Treat my friends.'

With an almost theatrical display of reluctance, the doctor did as he was told.

Mrs Beddows was pronounced free of any lasting damage. Her throat was badly bruised and there were abrasions on her wrists from the cord that had bound them, but 'it could have been worse, old thing, what?', as Uncle Algy said later. She was prescribed a sedative and told to rest, but she insisted on staying downstairs so as not to miss anything.

The falling stone pineapple had only struck Mr Waterford a glancing blow, but it had bruised his back rather badly. The stone step that rose rapidly to meet him as he fell had raised a lump on his forehead to rival the bump on my own. It had also knocked him out cold for a while, but he, too, was pronounced fit for active duty.

'You'll have a sore head for a few days,' said Dr Edling. 'If you feel confused or giddy, or if you feel at all queasy, call me at once. But you should be as right as rain in no time.'

He moved on to Mrs McLelland.

'What manner of knife is this?' he asked as he examined her forearm.

'A fruit knife,' I said. 'Drop point blade, about two inches long. Not well balanced, but not really designed for throwing, anyway. Looks like it passed straight between the radius and the ulna. Good shot, if I do say so myself.'

'You threw this?' he said. 'It's buried to the handle.'

'My father taught me,' I said.

'You could have severed an artery. This was most reckless. Very reckless indeed.'

'It was that, or let her shoot one of us,' I said. 'Sometimes, one weighs up the risks and a madwoman gets a knife in the arm. Looks like I missed all the arteries, though – she'd have bled to death by now.'

He glared at me, but he was forced to concede that I was right. He gave her a shot of morphia, and patiently eased the knife from her arm. As he was dressing the wound, the doorbell rang.

It was Inspector Foister and Sergeant Tarpley.

I could see we were in for a long night.

In fact, though, it took little more than an hour for the inspector to take our statements. His expression flitted, seemingly at random, between anger, irritation, astonishment, disapproval, and admiration at such a pace it was as though he were performing some newfangled facial calisthenics.

'I dare say I ought to be thanking you, my lord,' he said as he was leaving. 'You've wrapped up a most unpleasant case. But I do wish you'd call the professional force if you ever find yourself in similar difficulties.'

'There was no time, Inspector,' said Lord Riddlethorpe. 'And it's Lady Hardcastle who you should be thanking. It was she who puzzled it all out. Without her, this Burkinshaw creature would be on trial for three murders instead of two, and we'd be short one more dear friend.'

'Then I dare say I should be thanking you, too, my lady,' said the inspector. 'Your friend Inspector Sunderland speaks very highly of you. I'm not sure I'd be quite so indulgent of you as he seems to be, but you've saved a life this night, and I can't begrudge you credit for that.'

Lady Hardcastle inclined her head in acknowledgement.

'As for you, miss,' he said as he turned to me. 'You might want to consider a life in the circus with a knife-throwing talent like that.'

'As a matter of fact—' I began, but Lady Hardcastle cut me off.

'A story for another time, Inspector,' she said.

He frowned, but clearly knew better than to pursue it. With a polite goodbye to Lord Riddlethorpe, he and the sergeant led their prisoner out into the night.

◆ ◆ ◆

Mrs Ruddle had 'thrown together' what she called a 'cold collation', but which by anyone else's standards would have been a sumptuous feast, lovingly prepared by an expert cook.

It was served in the dining room, and Lord Riddlethorpe invited me to join them at table.

'I don't care what you do to make your living,' he said. 'Tonight, you saved more than one life with your knife trick, and I'd be honoured if you would dine with us.'

'Thank you, my lord,' I said. 'You're most gracious.'

'I'll never get you to call me Fishy, will I?' he said with a laugh.

'May I be frank, my lord?' I asked.

'You've earned it tenfold,' he said with a smile.

'I can't honestly fathom why you'd wish even your closest friends to call you "Fishy", let alone a visiting lady's maid.'

He laughed again. 'It's astonishing what a chap learns to put up with over the years,' he said. 'Come and sit with us. I think you and your mistress might have to explain to us all exactly how you came to suspect Muriel. Rebecca, I should say. I thought she was quite the best housekeeper we'd ever had at Codrington. How wrong I was.'

Lady Hardcastle waited until the clattering and chattering that accompanied everyone helping themselves to dinner had subsided before she began to speak.

'You know, Fishy,' she said, 'for the longest time I was convinced all this had something to do with your racing team. When poor Dawkins died and we discovered that the motor car had been tampered with, it seemed so obvious.'

'What on earth did you think was happening?' asked Mr Waterford. 'Why did you say nothing?'

'Because, Monty, dear, you were a suspect.'

'Me?' he said. His astonishment and outrage were muted by the need to avoid aggravating the pounding in his head.

'Of course,' she said. 'If it had anything to do with commercial intrigue, you and Viktor were the obvious suspects. And then Viktor copped it . . .'

'I still can't quite work out why she killed Viktor,' said Harry, who had been highly miffed at missing out on all the excitement, and was keener than ever to be involved now. 'Or Dawkins for the matter of that. Or poisoned the poor dog. Or why she had a go at me – I presume it was she who ran me over in the Rolls.'

'It was Rebecca Burkinshaw driving the Rolls, Harry, yes,' she said. 'But it wasn't you she was aiming for; it was Jake.'

'As soon as I learned who she was,' said Lady Lavinia, 'I began to think it might have been me she was after.'

'I'm still lost, old thing,' said Harry.

'Let's start from the beginning, shall we?' said Lady Hardcastle. 'It began about a year ago. Actually, no, let's go back to the very, very beginning.'

'Dinosaurs and whatnot?' said Harry.

'Shut up, dear,' said Lady Lavinia. 'Let her speak.'

'This other document,' said Lady Hardcastle, holding up one of the sheets of foolscap that Evan had taken from Kovacs's room, 'is an old letter from your father, Fishy. He tells Viktor all about your new racing venture, and asks him if he might be persuaded to offer you some advice and guidance. He reminds him of how they met when he accompanied Mr Burkinshaw on a trip to Vienna. He flatters him about his engineering expertise.'

'Good heavens,' said Lord Riddlethorpe. 'I remember Viktor suddenly getting in touch out of the blue. He wanted to hire me to work for his racing team. I told him I was flattered, but I wanted to make a go of it on my own. He seemed to accept it. But then his team started floundering a bit, and he got a little more persistent. Once I decided to launch the team with Monty, he offered to buy us out before we'd even started.'

'So he was here as a last throw of the dice?' suggested Mr Waterford. 'One last attempt to get you to join him?'

'I suppose so,' said Lord Riddlethorpe. 'Though why he was fixated on me, I'll never fathom. Plenty of other chaps out there who know far more than I do.'

'But he'd already established a rapport with you. Of sorts,' said Lady Hardcastle. 'He must have found it very difficult, as a foreigner, to make any headway with English motor racing folk.'

'I suppose so,' said Lord Riddlethorpe.

'But we're getting ahead of ourselves,' said Lady Hardcastle. 'We know from the letter that he knew the Burkinshaws before the tragedy. He knew the girls. Perhaps he had a youthful infatuation with Mrs Burkinshaw. If we assume that her daughters inherited her looks, she must have been quite the head-turner. Whatever it was, he stayed in touch with the family, and stepped in to help where he could. Rebecca was none too impressed with his efforts, but I doubt she would be impressed by anything very much. He kept a watchful, avuncular eye on Rebecca when the family fell on hard times. There was little he could do from Vienna, but he kept up to date, at least. When he found out that you were looking for a new housekeeper, Fishy, it was the answer to all his problems. He could have a spy in your household, and his friend's daughter could have a better job. That was about a year ago, I think you said, Fishy? Isn't that when you engaged Mrs McLelland?'

'About that,' said Lord Riddlethorpe. 'Answered an advertisement when our old housekeeper retired. She'd been working as a governess, but she had excellent references. Spinney spoke to her and recommended her to me. When I met her, I couldn't fault her. She seemed so competent and organized. It didn't hurt that she was younger than most housekeepers, and a damn sight more attractive. Just the sort of woman to shake the place up and bring us into the twentieth century.'

'But she had other motives for being here. Although, I suppose, shaking things up was part of the plan. Working here in your household, she knew that sooner or later she'd get an opportunity to take her revenge.'

'But if she wanted revenge on the girls,' persisted Harry. 'Why did she kill Dawkins?'

'She didn't intend to at all,' said Lady Hardcastle. 'We all started from entirely the wrong place. We all thought the motor car had been sabotaged as a way of getting at Dawkins, or at least Fishy. We assumed that the killer knew about the race order and had deliberately targeted Dawkins's motor car. It wasn't until Armstrong brought me the original slip of paper that I saw our error.'

She showed them all the other sheet of foolscap that Evan had found among Herr Kovacs's things.

It read:

Ladies' Race:
1. *Lady Hardcastle*
2. *Mrs Beddows*
3. *Lady Lavinia*
4. ~~*Miss Titmus*~~ *Miss Armstrong*

Gentlemen's Race:
1. *Lord Riddlethorpe*
2. *Mr Featherstonhaugh*
3. *Mr Dawkins*
4. *Herr Kovacs*

Mr Waterford shall act as Starter and Race Director. Miss Titmus shall be the Official Race Photographer.

'Do you see?' she said. 'I wrote the list in the order we made the draw: ladies first. Anyone who saw the list would reasonably have assumed that we intended to race in precisely that order. Indeed, that actually was our intention. And that means they would have assumed that Jake was going to be in Number 3 for the first race. It was only once we got to the starting line that we had to toss a coin to see which race would be held first.'

'So Jake was the target all along,' said Harry.

'Just so, dear,' she said. 'We left the race card in the great hall, and Burkinshaw must have seen it there. It was a simple matter for her to let herself into the coach house by the back door and clip the brake cable. She had access to all the household keys, and who among the servants would dare to question the formidable housekeeper if they happened upon her as she wandered about by night?'

'Even if she were covered in dust and muck?' asked Harry. 'Messy beasts, motor cars.'

'Never underestimate the power that senior servants hold, sir,' I said. 'Butlers and housekeepers are like ships' captains. Never disobeyed, never questioned. She could dance a *pas de deux* through the servants' hall with a bewigged badger and they would bow their heads and get out of her way. A bit of dust and grime would attract no attention.'

Harry frowned, but said nothing.

'I think she intended to kill all three women, but had no real plan beyond Roz's sunset execution. But she was clever, an improviser. When she caught sight of the race card she immediately saw an opportunity to kill the first of her sister's tormenters. She might not have succeeded, actually. If Jake had been driving it's possible that she wouldn't have been travelling fast enough to kill herself, but poor Dawkins was much quicker, and so the poor chap met his end on a fast bend.'

'Well, that explains Dawkins,' Harry said. 'What about Viktor? He had nothing to do with Katy's death.'

'No, Viktor was killed to protect Burkinshaw's secret. I don't suppose you remember that night after the race when we ladies went off to the library, do you? You joined us after quite a while, claiming you'd been looking for us everywhere.'

'I remember it well enough.'

'You finally learned where we were when Helen came into the drawing room looking for an old school photograph. Jake and the girls, all lithe-limbed and fresh-faced. Athletes flushed with victory.'

'I remember some gawky girls in cricket togs,' said Harry.

'Your lack of a poetic soul notwithstanding,' she said, 'we are talking about the same photograph. Viktor saw something in it that none of us could see. Well, none of us except Armstrong. It was she who insisted that the whole thing might have something to do with the photograph. But Viktor most definitely recognized the girl standing between Roz and Helen. He had known the Burkinshaw girls when they were young. He knew the story of Katy's suicide, and he knew exactly who her sister was. He thought he'd sent Rebecca here to spy for him, but he had no idea that she might have plans of her own until he realized that Jake, Helen, and Roz were Katy's school friends.'

She passed Harry the photograph, and he examined it closely.

'As soon as he saw the photograph, Viktor knew there was something up,' said Lady Hardcastle. 'I suspect he confronted Rebecca and told her not to ruin his plans. All he wanted was a way to buy Fishy's racing expertise – he had no idea what else he might have unleashed. We might never know exactly what passed between them, but she knew she had to silence him, or she would be undone before her plan was complete.'

She reached once more under her chair and produced the folded sheet of Codrington Hall notepaper.

'I'm afraid I've been thoroughly naughty,' she said. 'I searched her room before the inspector got here. We can give him this later, but I thought you should all see it first.'

She showed them the note we had originally found in Herr Kovacs's room, the one inviting him to his fateful meeting. The one signed 'R B'.

'I'm embarrassed to have to confess that we thought it might have been from you, Roz, dear,' she said. 'We knew of no other "R B"s at the time. We couldn't say anything to anyone, because no sooner had we found the note than someone pinched it. Burkinshaw, as it turns out. It was shoved down inside the pocket of one of her dresses – she must have forgotten to destroy it.'

The note was passed round the table.

'She invited him to the coach house – she knew by now that she could do whatever she wished in the coach house by dead of night, and no one would be any the wiser. He went down expecting to be able to take control of the situation, to get his own plans back on track. But she caved his skull in with a wrench instead.'

'That's Dawkins and Viktor, then,' said Miss Titmus. 'But what about poor Electra? Surely she can't have worked anything out. The Dalmatians are clever girls, but . . .'

'It was the sandwich,' said Lady Hardcastle. 'It was piccalilli – your favourite. It was meant for you. She put rat poison in the ham and piccalilli sandwich before it was brought out for lunch. It was a slight gamble, but since you're one of the only living people who actually likes piccalilli, it was a gamble worth taking.'

'Oh,' she said. She put down the slice of pie she had been about to eat. 'Oh,' she said again.

'I'm afraid this whole thing was about you three,' said Lady Hardcastle. 'Rebecca Burkinshaw blamed you for her sister's suicide and wanted her revenge.'

Mrs Beddows looked up from her plate for the first time since Lady Hardcastle had begun speaking. 'She was right, though,' she croaked. 'It was my fault. I was a beast to Katy Burkinshaw. An absolute beast. I've been a beast ever since.' There were tears in her eyes. 'I'm so sorry. I'm so very sorry.' She stood abruptly and left the room.

'Go after her, Monty,' said Lady Lavinia. 'Don't let her be on her own. Make her take the sedative Dr Edling left for her. She needs to sleep. She'll feel better in the morning.'

Mr Waterford stood, too. 'Thank you,' he said, and he left by the same door.

'What a bally awful mess,' said Lord Riddlethorpe. 'I'm grateful to you for explaining it all, Emily. I just wish it had never got this far. Perhaps we should retire. What do you say? Put this horror behind us, and start afresh in the morning. I'll get Spinney to make us a round of nightcaps, and we'll call it a day.'

◆ ◆ ◆

Betty was still awake when I finally crawled up to bed.

'I thought you'd never get here,' she blurted as I opened the door. 'You've got to tell me everything. Did the old trout say anything? Oh, I shouldn't speak ill of her behind her back. Especially not after everything she's been through. But she is a dreadful old trout. What happened? Did Lady Hardcastle explain everything? Do you know what really went on? Is that brandy? Might I have some?'

'I think you might need it,' I laughed.

I poured her a small measure in one of the tumblers I'd brought with me, and she sipped at it gratefully.

'Mmm, that's better,' she said. 'His lordship has better brandy than the trout. But don't you be distracting me with gifts from the master's cellars. Tell all.'

And so I did. As clearly and succinctly as I could, I recounted the events of dinner, including Lady Hardcastle's explanations and finishing with Mrs Beddows's tearful departure.

'Oh,' said Betty. 'I feel awful now. Should I go back to her, do you think?'

'I think you'll both be better off if you don't,' I said. 'This might have softened her a little, but that bit in the Bible about leopards and their spots isn't just there to add a bit of exotic decoration. Deep down, she's a spiky sort, and she needs a spiky maid to stand up to her. You and Miss Titmus couldn't be more suited as employer and servant if you'd been handmade for her by Edna Fitzwilliam's Bespoke Servant Manufacturers of Bolton.'

'You do talk tosh, Flo,' she said.

'I do. It's part of my charm. Now get to sleep, or we'll be no use to anyone tomorrow.'

◆　◆　◆

After we had woken and dressed our respective charges, Betty and I persuaded Mr Spinney to let us serve at breakfast. With the housekeeper arrested and the staff in uproar, he was keen to get everything back to normal as quickly as possible, and tried, at first, to object to having two visiting lady's maids serving in the dining room.

'I had no issue with it when you needed to be part of your mistress's investigation,' he said. 'Indeed, it was my own idea, as I recall. But in the end, it's not right, not right at all. Lady's maids don't serve at table. You must see how we're fixed now. With that woman gone, it's left to me to take charge of the maids. With the mood they're all in, it's going to be hard enough to get them to do a hand's turn today as it is, without you two doing their work for them. I can't countenance it.'

'Might I make a suggestion, Mr Spinney?' I said.

'I'm all ears, Miss Armstrong. All ears.'

'Why don't you ask Mrs Ruddle to take charge of the maids until you can engage a new housekeeper? Patty is more than capable of running the kitchen, as long as her mentor is nearby to lend a hand.'

'Well,' he said slowly. 'That would certainly seem to be a possible solution, provided everyone agrees . . .'

'Strong leadership, Mr Spinney, that's all it takes. You tell them how wonderful they are, what a magnificent opportunity it is, how much his lordship needs them at this difficult time – all that old guff. They'll fall into line quickly enough.'

'You're right, of course,' he said.

'Splendid. And now that crisis is averted, what say Miss Buffrey and I take breakfast up one last time? And then, sort of loiter within earshot so we don't miss out on anything.'

He sighed. 'Very well,' he said. 'At least you'll be out of the way while I try to get everyone organized.'

We hurried to the kitchen to fetch the first trays before he thought better of it.

Miss Titmus and Lady Hardcastle were already in the dining room when we arrived, and had helped themselves to coffee from the great silver pot on the sideboard.

'Ah, there you are,' said Lady Hardcastle. 'Why are you carrying food? Have all the staff done a bunk?'

'We wanted to lurk in the company of our betters,' I said. 'Such that we might try to lift ourselves above our humble origins by taking wisdom from their learned discourse.'

'And earwig on the gossip.'

'That, too, my lady,' I said. 'Sausage?'

'No one's called me "Sausage" for years,' she said, almost wistfully. 'Oh, I see what you mean. Yes, please. Shove them down over there, and I'll help myself in a moment.'

Mrs Beddows came into the room, wearing a high-collared blouse to hide the marks on her neck. She saw the four of us, and it seemed, for a moment at least, as though she might turn round and head straight back out again.

'Roz, darling,' said Lady Hardcastle. 'How are you, my dear? Come and sit down. Let me get something for you.'

Mrs Beddows smiled weakly and sat at the dining table.

'Here you are, dear,' said Lady Hardcastle as she and Miss Titmus sat with her. 'Get that down you.'

'Thank you,' croaked Mrs Beddows. She looked up and saw Betty and me. 'Ah, Buffrey,' she said. 'Mr Waterford has persuaded me that I owe you an apology. I've treated you badly. I shall pay your wages until you find a new position, of course.'

'Thank you, madam,' said Betty. 'You're very kind.'

'I can't see you out on your ear. I shall do all I can to help. You'll have a glowing reference, of course.'

'Actually, Roz,' said Miss Titmus, 'she already has a new position. She's going to be working for me as lady's maid and photographer's assistant.'

'Is she?' said Mrs Beddows. 'Is she, indeed? Well, good for you. The both of you.'

Mr Waterford breezed in. 'Good morning, darling,' he said when he saw Mrs Beddows. Belatedly, he noticed the other two ladies at the table. 'And good morning to you as well, ladies. How is everyone today?'

'Passing well, Monty,' said Lady Hardcastle. 'Mustn't grumble.'

'One must not,' he said. 'I, er, I wonder if I could . . .'

'Yes, dear?' she said.

'Well, I was going to ask if Roz and I might have a moment's privacy.' Looking round, he noticed Betty and me for the first time. 'But . . . well . . . I didn't know the room was so . . . Oh, hang it all. There'll be a scandal no matter what, once all this comes out. Roz, darling, I want you to leave James and come and live with me.'

'He'll never give me a divorce,' she croaked. 'He needs my money.'

'I'll settle his hash, don't you worry. I simply couldn't bear it yesterday when I thought I might lose you forever.'

I, for one, was beginning to wish that he had sent us out after all, but we were saved further embarrassment by the arrival of Harry and Lady Lavinia.

'What ho, you chaps,' said Harry as he limped in with Lady Lavinia on his arm. 'I say, everyone's here.'

'Except Fishy, dear,' said Lady Lavinia.

'Except Fishy what?' said Lord Riddlethorpe from behind her.

'Ah, splendid,' said Harry. 'Lavinia and I have a bit of news. An announcement, as it were.' He stood and grinned foolishly for a moment. 'We are engaged to be married. And you're all invited.'

There were delighted cheers, kisses, and hugs all round as their friends congratulated them.

'That's ten bob you owe me, Flo, dear,' said Lady Hardcastle when the hubbub had died down.

'Were my romantic entanglements the subject of vulgar wagering, sis?' said Harry.

'Of course, dear. I'm always on the lookout for something to make you seem more interesting. You're such a tragically dull fellow.'

'Well, of all the . . .' he said.

'At least I bet on you popping the question,' she said. 'It was Flo here who doubted your resolve.'

'Strong Arm!' he said. 'How could you? I thought we were friends.'

'We are, sir,' I said. 'I just thought Lady Lavinia would have seen you off long before you got the chance to propose.'

I ducked the slice of toast that came sailing my way.

◆ ◆ ◆

Packing to go home is always a great deal simpler than packing to go away. There are no decisions to be made, nor is there any great need to pack with the same thoughtfulness and care. As long as it all fitted in the cases and trunks, that was fine – we were going to need to unpack it all and get it cleaned as soon as we got home anyway.

And so the packing proceeded with pleasing swiftness.

Lady Hardcastle was sitting at the desk by the window, writing in her journal as I folded a dinner dress.

'Oh, for . . .' I said.

'Yes, dear? I discern that you might have a problem of some sort. Is it something I can help you with?'

'This frock, my lady,' I said, holding it up.

'Ah, yes. I love that one. Any darker and it would be black by candlelight. Any paler and it would look brash and tawdry. It's from that dressmaker in Clifton. We should go back there. She does wonderful work.'

'It's very fetching,' I said. 'But I doubt the sincerity of your protestations of love.'

'You do?'

'Yes, my lady. If you loved it, I'm certain you wouldn't have ripped it.'

'Ah, yes. I thought you might scold me for that.'

'How on earth . . . ?'

'You remember I was wearing it the other evening when Uncle Algy insisted we join him in his game?'

'Jean-Pierre's Magical Vineyard,' I said.

'Just so. There was that moment when Harry and Jake had finished "grafting the rootstock" – quite illegally, I might add; it was Jake's turn, and Harry had no business helping her with her *débuttage* like that – well, I got it caught on something. The chair, I think.'

I sighed.

'Oh, don't be like that, dear. You'd get so very bored if you didn't have things to mend.'

With the packing done, I went below stairs to say goodbye to the household staff. Mr Spinney was nowhere to be seen, but I found Mrs Ruddle in the housekeeper's room.

'Look at me, dear,' she said with a cheery smile. 'A housekeeper. I shouldn't be doing this sort of work. They need me in the kitchen. Poor Patty, she'll be all at sixes and sevens.'

'It suits you, Mrs R,' I said. 'Gives you an air of authority.'

'I have plenty of authority in my kitchen,' she said. 'Skilled work it is, too. You wouldn't put an engineer to work in an office, would you?'

'Well . . .' I began. But I thought better of it. 'No, Mrs R, you're right. But it's just a temporary measure, I'm sure. You'll have a new housekeeper in no time, and then you'll all be back to normal.'

'I dare say,' she dared to say. 'But enough of my belly-aching, my dear. What can I do for you?'

'I just came to say my farewells and offer my thanks to you all for your warm hospitality.'

'It's been a pleasure having you, my dear. And it's we who should be thanking you. Without you and your mistress, we might have lost poor Mrs Beddows as well as Dawkins and Mr Kovacs.'

There was a tentative knock at the door.

'You wanted to see me, Mrs R?' It was Evan Gudger.

'Ah, Evan, yes. Mr Spinney has had to go into town. He asked me to tell you to see to the wine for tonight's dinner.'

'But that's the head footman's duties,' he said.

'That it is,' said Mrs Ruddle. 'And what do you suppose that means?'

'Blimey.'

'Blimey, indeed, young man. You'd best make sure your livery's brushed and pressed, and your shoes and buttons polished, hadn't you.'

'Congratulations, Evan,' I said. 'A well-deserved promotion.'

'Thank you, miss,' he said. 'Thank you, Mrs R.'

'Off you go, lad. You've a lot to do.'

He hurried out of the room, wearing quite the most enormous smile.

'He'll be all right, that boy,' said Mrs Ruddle. 'He's been a different lad since you've been here. I don't know what you said to him, but he's quite the new man.'

'I just trusted him and gave him something interesting to do,' I said.

'Well, it's done the trick. Are you sure you wouldn't like to stay?' She winked at me.

'No, Mrs R, I must go where my lady leads.'

'You stick with her, my dear,' she said. 'She's a good 'un.'

'Quite the very best.'

◆　◆　◆

Unknown hands brought our cases, bags, and trunks down to the hall. All I had to do was mention our imminent departure to the new head footman, and they appeared, as if by magic.

I waited by the luggage while Lady Hardcastle said her goodbyes. As Morgan and one of the other footmen loaded everything into the Rolls-Royce, a succession of new friends came to wish us well.

While Lady Hardcastle was forcing Miss Titmus to promise to come to Gloucestershire as soon as she was able, Betty sidled over to me and gave me an unexpected hug.

'I'm so glad to have met you,' she said. 'It looks like we'll be seeing more of each other, too.'

'I do hope so,' I said.

'I don't know the first thing about photography,' she said. 'I don't know how much use I'm going to be to her.'

'You'll soon pick it up. Or not. It doesn't matter. Lady Hardcastle has been dabbling for a few years now, and I just smile and nod. As long as you hold whatever it is they want you to hold when they want you to hold it, I find it all goes smoothly enough.'

'Oh, but I want to learn,' she said earnestly. 'It's tremendously exciting.'

'Good for you, Betty Buffrey. I hope you have a wonderful time.'

'Thank you for saving the old trout,' she said. 'I still think she's quite the vilest woman ever to wear bloomers, but I'd not wish her dead.'

I laughed. 'It's entirely my pleasure,' I said. 'I've not stuck anyone with a blade for simply ages. I was beginning to miss it.'

It was her turn to laugh.

'Come along, Buffrey,' said Miss Titmus. 'I think we should leave Lady Hardcastle to her goodbyes. And I want to show you the darkroom.'

Mrs Beddows and Mr Waterford appeared next. Mr Waterford offered Lady Hardcastle his hand, which she shook warmly.

'Thank you, Emily,' he said. 'And thank you, too, Miss Armstrong. You got us out of gaol, and you saved my Roz. I'll never be able to repay you, but if you ever need anything at all . . .'

'We still haven't had a go in your wonderful racing cars,' said Lady Hardcastle. 'But I think we'll leave that for another time. I'll not forget, mind you.'

'Any time you like,' he said.

Mrs Beddows said nothing. Instead, she took a step towards Lady Hardcastle and hugged her. This was not at all the same woman we had met a week before. But if that was surprising, it was as nothing compared with what followed. Having released Lady Hardcastle, she came over to me and offered me her hand. As we shook hands, she leaned in close so that no one else might hear as she murmured, 'I owe you my life, Armstrong. Thank you.'

I had no idea how to respond, so I simply smiled and said nothing.

She and Mr Montague left hand in hand.

'What did she say?' asked Lady Hardcastle.

'Discretion forbids me from revealing details of a private remark, my lady,' I said. 'Something nice, though.'

'Well I never,' said Lady Hardcastle. 'All it took was a madwoman with a noose to turn her into a decent human being. If only we'd known, I could have fashioned a noose at the beginning of our visit.'

Lord Riddlethorpe came out of the drawing room with his sister and Harry.

'Ah, Emily,' he said. 'We thought we could hear you out here. You're off?'

'We are, Fishy,' said Lady Hardcastle. 'Thank you so much for your hospitality.'

'I'm not sure having half one's guests murdered by one's house-keeper features in any etiquette guide I've ever read,' he said, 'but it's gracious of you to pretend you had a good time.'

'No pretence required, Fishy, dear. The company of new friends is all I need. I'm glad to have met you all.'

He smiled. 'I've had a word with the coroner, and he's happy with your written statement, so you'll not be called upon at the inquest. And the local magistrate is a pal of mine. He's agreed not to call you for the committal. You'll be needed for the County Court trial, of course, but the assizes aren't for a while yet. You must stay here when they call you.'

'Thank you, dear. I shall look forward to your company, if not the trial.'

'Cheerio then, sis,' said Harry. 'Safe travels, and all that.'

'Goodbye, Harry, darling. Do promise to come and visit. You too, Jake, dear.'

'We'd love to,' said Lady Lavinia. She was already a 'we'.

'And you, too, Fishy. All of you. You must all come down. We might have to put you up in our neighbours' house if you all come together, but it would be such fun to have you.'

We were saved from having to try to work out exactly how this might be arranged by the sound of a throat being quietly cleared at the front door.

'Aha,' said Lord Riddlethorpe. 'I believe Morgan's trying to tell us that the motor car is packed.'

'It is, my lord,' said Morgan. 'With the Water Board digging up the main road to Riddlethorpe, we'll have to take the long way round to the station.'

'Then you ought to leave at once,' said Lord Riddlethorpe. 'Goodbye, Emily. Goodbye, Miss Armstrong. Until we meet again.'

Chapter Eighteen

There was a slight delay at Birmingham. A signalman slipped on some wet leaves on his way to the signal box and spilled tea on himself. He was scalded quite badly, leaving the main line to Bristol without proper signals for an hour, until his assistant could be roused and sent to work in his place. It gave us the opportunity to eat lunch in town, though, and we resolved to visit the city more often.

Back in Littleton Cotterell, not much had changed. The same dog cart that had first brought us to the house the previous year was waiting for fares at Chipping Bevington station. The same driver was as helpfully obliging and as quietly uncommunicative as he had been the first time we saw him.

He carried the bags into the hall, and was rewarded with Lady Hardcastle's usual generous tip.

'I do like going away,' said Lady Hardcastle as we closed the front door and took off our hats. 'But I think I like coming home slightly more. Did you warn Edna and Miss Jones that we would be back today?'

'I wired them from the station at Leicester,' I said. 'While you were chatting to that lady about her dachshund.'

'He was an adorable little fellow,' she said. 'And so well behaved.'

'So I gather. More importantly, it gave me an opportunity to let Edna know our plans.'

'I don't know what I'd do without you.'

I checked in the kitchen, where I found the range lit, a pie ready to be re-heated, and a box of vegetables ready to be cooked.

'Miss Jones has left everything we need for dinner,' I called.

'Splendid,' said Lady Hardcastle from the hall. 'Did she leave any tea?'

'I'll put the kettle on.'

I brought out a tray a few minutes later bearing tea and some of the biscuits Miss Jones had baked for us. Lady Hardcastle was still checking through the post.

'I'm not sure I fancy unpacking tonight,' she said, indicating the jumble of trunks and cases. 'Do I have something to sleep in?'

'I should think we can find you a nightdress in the wardrobe among the many dozens of nightdresses you seem to own,' I said.

'Then we shall leave the unpacking for tomorrow. Get the pie on and we'll have an early supper, a glass or two of wine, and a bit of piano before an early night.'

◆ ◆ ◆

Edna helped me to drag the luggage upstairs the next morning.

'If I'd thought about it, I could have told our Dan to come and help with these,' she said as we hauled the largest trunk up to the main bedroom. 'He don't mind helpin' me out, if you ever needs any fetchin' and carryin' done.'

'Not to worry,' I said. 'We seem to be managing. Just about.'

'True,' she said. 'But it never hurts to keep him busy. Did you have a nice time?'

'Not bad. One or two minor mishaps, but it was an interesting break.'

We set off back downstairs for the last bags.

'How did you like the racin' cars?' she said.

'Sadly, that was one of the mishaps – we didn't get to drive them in the end.'

'Oh, I'm sorry to hear that,' she said. 'P'raps his lordship will invite you some other time.'

'I do hope so. I— Oh, blast.'

The telephone had begun to ring.

'You answer the telephone, my lover,' said Edna. 'I'll take these last 'uns up.'

I picked up the earpiece from its cradle.

'Hello,' I said loudly and clearly. 'Chipping Bevington two-three.'

'Hello?' said a strident, female voice. 'Hello? Is that you, Emily? Hello?'

'Good morning, Lady Farley-Stroud,' I said. 'Hold on one moment and I'll fetch Lady Hardcastle for you.'

'Ah, Armstrong,' she said. 'It's you. Would you get Lady Hardcastle for me, please?'

'Of course, my lady,' I said, and I put the earpiece down on the table.

I found Lady Hardcastle in the study.

'I heard,' she said. 'I'm on my way.'

I went upstairs and began unpacking.

An hour later, I'd put away everything that could be put away, and had presented Edna with a large pile of laundry.

'I'm not sayin' as I minds, dear,' she said. 'But you'd-a thought a big house like that would offer to do some laundry for their guests, wouldn't you? They've got the staff for it, a'n't they?'

'They have, and they did,' I said. 'This is just the stuff that we couldn't get done before we left. It's only a couple of days' worth.'

She shook her head disbelievingly. 'She don't wear this many clothes at home,' she said. 'How many times a day was she changin'?'

'At least three outfits a day,' I said. 'Usually four or five. It's a tough life among the toffs.'

She laughed. 'We don't know the half of it, do we? The worst we has to think about is workin' our fingers to the bone from dawn till dusk. We should think ourselves lucky we only has one dress each to worry about.'

I decided it would sour the mood to mention that she only worked half-days, and that I'd often seen her out in a variety of rather nice dresses. Instead, I chuckled politely and went to see if Lady Hardcastle needed anything.

'Ah, Flo, there you are,' she said when I finally tracked her down in her studio in the orangery. 'I was thinking of coming to find you. Do you have any plans for this evening?'

'I was thinking of collapsing in the drawing room with some of your best brandy and an improving book,' I said.

'Then you shall have to send your apologies to the decanter and the bookshelves,' she said. 'Tonight, we dine with the Farley-Strouds.'

'Both of us again?'

'Both of us. Gertrude has learned of our return and is keen to hear our tales.'

'News travels as fast as ever.'

'I suspect it was your telegram to Edna that alerted the entire village. As for our having tales to tell, it seems we made the newspapers.'

'It was only a matter of time,' I said. 'I know Lord Riddlethorpe was keen to minimize the scandal, but he was never going to keep the press away from a story like that.'

'Well, quite. And in return for supper and a raid on their wine cellar, Gertrude expects a first-hand account.'

'Will Sir Hector also want a solution to his go-cart mystery? What are you going to tell him?'

'Oh, that,' she said. 'I've had the solution to that since Thursday. Simple, really, and yet ingenious and fascinating at the same time.'

'You're not going to tell me, are you?'

'Of course not, dear. You heard the answer as clearly as I did. You'll just have to wait until dinner.'

'They'll never find your body,' I said. 'You'll just disappear one day. "Where's Lady Hardcastle?" they'll say. "I've no idea," I'll say. "She didn't even leave a note. But she always was a little peculiar." "Yes," they'll say. "A very odd fish. Still, good luck. Let us know if she contacts you, won't you." And that will be that.'

'You're quite frightening sometimes, dear. Is there any coffee?'

There was something comforting about the unfashionable shabbiness of the Farley-Strouds' home after the classic elegance of Codrington Hall. Where Lord Riddlethorpe's furniture had been in the family for generations, Sir Hector and Lady Farley-Stroud had had to furnish their home from scratch when they returned unexpectedly from India. They had a few family pieces, but most had been purchased brand new thirty years ago. Where Lord Riddlethorpe's furniture was old, the Farley-Strouds' was merely old-fashioned. Some items would be rare and valuable antiques in a hundred years, but for now they were just out of date. And I liked it like that. Theirs was a home, not a museum with bedrooms.

'Bring your drinks through to the dining room,' said Sir Hector when Jenkins announced that dinner was served. 'Pretty certain it would make a sommelier faint, but I always find that gin goes with everything, what?'

We entered the dining room. Mrs Brown had done herself proud again, and the meal was wonderful. Jenkins had done well with his wine choices, too, and my gin and tonic was forgotten as I indulged my palate with the clever combinations of food and wine through five delicious courses.

With less than her customary level of embellishment, Lady Hardcastle recounted the events of the past week. With less than their customary level of interruption, Sir Hector and Lady Farley-Stroud hung upon her every word.

'I say!' said Lady Farley-Stroud when the tale was done. 'Emily, you do live a far more exciting life than we. And how lucky your friends are that you were there. It doesn't do to think of what that dreadful woman might have done if you hadn't been there to stop her. That's why we never have attractive young women working at The Grange, dear. They'd never be able to resist Hector. Trouble waiting to happen.'

I declined to mention Dora, the extremely attractive young house-maid. Sir Hector's look of bewildered pride that anyone might find him a temptation was a treat.

'Very wise,' said Lady Hardcastle. 'And how has everything been here while we've been away? How's your cart coming along, Hector?'

'Slow goin', m'dear,' said Sir Hector. 'Tryin' my damnedest to keep it secret from Jimmy. Makes it hard to get anything done. Poor Bert is tryin' to work in secret, but without knowin' how Jimmy's cheatin', we can't take too many chances.'

'I think I can help you there,' said Lady Hardcastle.

'You can? I thought you'd have been far too busy tryin' to catch murderers to give any thought to my little problems.'

'I can, indeed. I think you said that Jimmy races pigeons.'

'He does, yes. Got a few little beauties. Champions. Races 'em all over the country.'

'And what exactly does a pigeon race entail?'

'You take all the birds off to a spot miles from home, and the first bird to get back to its owner is the winner. Simple enough. Damn clever birds, pigeons.'

'They are,' said Lady Hardcastle. 'They have an uncanny knack for flying home. No one knows how they do it.'

'Quite so, quite so,' he said.

'Now, my new friend Helen Titmus – charming woman, by the way – takes the most exquisite photographs. She's setting up a business. You should get her to photograph the house. And the family. How is dear Clarissa? And her new husband . . . ? Adam, that's it. How are they? Are you feeling better about it all now?'

'It was a bit sudden, wasn't it?' said Lady Farley-Stroud. 'Especially after the business with the Seddon boy. But they do seem happy. And she's expecting their first child in February. Telephoned the other day.'

'I say,' said Lady Hardcastle. 'What wonderful news. Congratulations, Grandmama.'

Lady Farley-Stroud beamed proudly. Sir Hector's pleasure was slightly dimmed by his frustration at having his explanation interrupted.

'Knows a lot about pigeons, then, this Helen Titmouse of yours?' he said.

'Oh, Hector, I'm sorry. I do get distracted. But it's wonderful news, don't you think? Your first grandchild?'

'Spiffin',' he said. 'As long as it doesn't inherit its father's looks, it'll be fine. Or its father's brains. Or its mother's brains, for that matter.'

'Hector!' said Lady Farley-Stroud in her sternest voice.

'Well,' he said. 'Couple of buffleheads, the pair of them. I'll bet your Helen Titmouse isn't a bufflehead.'

'Titmus, dear,' said Lady Hardcastle. 'And no, she's as sharp as a hedgehog's overcoat, that one.'

'And she solved my riddle?' he persisted. He really was a patient old chap. I was on the verge of snocking her one.

'Not quite, dear,' she said, and he almost sighed. 'But she did tell me about a gadget invented by some German fellow. She was quite excited about it. She showed me an article in a magazine.'

Sir Hector raised his bushy eyebrows expectantly.

'I rather think that your pal Jimmy has made himself a pigeon camera.'

'A what?'

'This German chap, I forget his name. Neubronner, or some such. He was using pigeons to deliver medicine, and he thought, "I know what. If I put a camera on the pigeon instead of the medicine, it will photograph whatever it flies over. Wouldn't that be splendid?" So he did.'

'And you think Jimmy has done somethin' like that?' said Sir Hector.

'It all fits. It's impractical, it's convoluted, it's extremely silly, and it suits your pal Jimmy down to the ground.'

He laughed. 'I'll say. So what does he do?'

'Well, the pigeons always fly straight home. He just has to take the camera-bird to some spot out in the country, a place where your house is on the route home, and let it go. Flap-flap goes friend pigeon, fluttering homeward. As it flies over your stable yard, snap-snap goes the camera, and Jimmy has photographs of what you've been up to.'

'Preposterous,' said Lady Farley-Stroud.

'Marvellous,' said Sir Hector. 'I'll get Bert to put up a tarpaulin or somethin', so the blighter can't see into the yard. We'll beat him, by George. We'll beat him yet.'

The race took place a couple of weeks later, on the last Sunday in September. As promised, Sir Hector had invited a number of friends, and quite a few villagers had also turned out to join in the fun.

'Why didn't we know about this?' asked Lady Hardcastle as we walked past the onlookers. 'It seems as though most of Littleton Cotterell and more than half of Woodworthy are here. It's quite the local festival.'

'You were indisposed this time last year,' I said. 'Bullet in the belly.'

'Ah,' she said. 'Yes, that would account for our absence.'

The course ran from the gates of The Grange, down the hill and into Littleton, with the finishing line just beside the village green. There was a festival atmosphere on the green. Holman the baker and Spratt the butcher had set up stalls to supply the crowd with food, while Old Joe from the Dog and Duck was selling beer and cider from a table outside the pub.

The crowds thinned out as we climbed the hill, with little knots of onlookers on the more dangerous-looking bends. The Farley-Strouds' friends were gathering on the lawn in front of The Grange.

'What ho, Emily, old girl,' said Sir Hector as we walked through the gates.

'Don't call her that, dear,' said Lady Farley-Stroud. 'She's easily half your age.'

'Hardly,' said Lady Hardcastle.

'Term of affection, what?' said Sir Hector, as unfazed as ever by his wife's remonstrations. Lady Farley-Stroud left to welcome some newcomers.

'How go the plans?' asked Lady Hardcastle. 'Is your wingèd chariot fully fettled and poised for victory?'

'As ready as we'll ever be,' said Sir Hector. 'Not seen Jimmy's go-cart yet, mind you. It's over there on that wagon. Covered up.'

He pointed down the drive to where a delivery cart stood, its horse munching contentedly in a nosebag. A tarpaulin covered its cargo.

'Must say, though,' he said, 'he doesn't seem his usual cocksure self. Might be in with a chance this time.'

Dora the housemaid was circulating with a tray of drinks. She offered one to Lady Hardcastle, and made to walk off. Lady Farley-Stroud strode over and called her back.

'I think Miss Armstrong needs one of those, Dora,' she said.

'Thank you, my lady,' I said. 'But there's really no need.'

'Nonsense, m'girl. Don't remember my history lessons too well, but I'm sure the gladiators got a tot of something before going into battle.'

'I beg your pardon, my lady?'

'What? Has Hector not asked you yet? He's a buffer, he really is. Hector!'

'What, dear?' said Sir Hector.

'I thought you were going to ask Miss Armstrong something.'

'I was, dear. Just getting round to it. Give a chap a chance.'

'Ask me what, sir?' I said.

'Well, you see, m'dear, the thing is, Jimmy and I aren't nearly so young as we once were, so we've had to change the rules a bit this year. We used to race the go-carts ourselves, but at our age . . . You know how it is. Reactions not what they used to be. Joints not what they used to be, either. Eyesight's a bit shabby, too, to tell the truth. So this year, we decided we ought to nominate someone to drive for us. A champion, d'you see?'

'I see,' I said. 'And . . . ?'

'Quite right,' he said. 'And I chose you. Spoke to Emily about it. She said you were disappointed you couldn't drive the racin' car at her pal's place. So we thought this would be the next best thing.'

'Oh, Sir Hector, that's wonderful,' I said. 'But I'm not dressed for it.' I indicated my uniform.

'We thought of that,' he said. 'See the memsahib and she'll kit you out in some overalls. Might be a bit big for you, but I'm sure everything will roll up. Will you do it?'

'I'd be honoured, Sir Hector,' I said.

◆ ◆ ◆

Jimmy Amersham had picked a young lad from Woodworthy as his champion. They both smirked when they saw me in my ill-fitting overalls, battered leather helmet, and goggles. Their smirks faded when Bert and Sir Hector wheeled the go-cart out of the old stable yard and onto the drive beside Jimmy's horse-drawn wagon.

I didn't know much about the mechanics of wheeled vehicles, but I could tell that there was something clever about Sir Hector's go-cart. The shell was of beaten tin, and looked sleek and modern, of course. But there was something going on with the wheels. They weren't the wobbly wheels that kids pinched from abandoned prams; they were sturdy, with thick tyres. And the chassis looked like something Mr Waterford would have designed for one of Lord Riddlethorpe's racing cars.

'What do you think, Jimmy, old chap?' said Sir Hector. 'D'you think I've got a chance this year?'

'Never give up hope, m'boy,' said Jimmy, with a great deal more cheer than his expression might have predicted.

'Let's see whatcha got, then,' said Sir Hector, who was clearly enjoying his friend's discomfort.

Reluctantly, Jimmy and the village lad manoeuvred a couple of planks to serve as a ramp at the back of the wagon. They lifted the tarpaulin to reveal their go-cart. Superficially, it appeared very similar. The hammered tin shell was suitably modern, and just different enough from Sir Hector's so as not to be a direct copy. It was obvious where its inspiration had come from, though. The real differences were in the wheels and the chassis. Jimmy had used much thinner wheels mounted on a much flimsier frame.

'We tried somethin' like that a month or so ago,' said Sir Hector with a grin. 'Had to abandon it. Wheels kept comin' off.'

Jimmy was not best pleased.

'What's the matter, Jimmy, old chap?' said Sir Hector. 'Did my pigeon-proofin' spoil your spyin'?'

'Put the kibosh on it good and proper,' said Jimmy ruefully.

'Put up a tarpaulin to stop your camera pigeons seein' into the yard.'

Jimmy laughed delightedly. 'You cunning old buffer. How on earth did you fathom that? I thought we'd definitely got you on that one. Pal of mine put me on to it. You remember Tug Wilson?

Commanded the HMS Whatchamacallit. Lives in Cheltenham now. He read about it in some journal or other and thought it would be just the job for beating you.' He chuckled. 'Ah well,' he said at length. 'Cheats never whatnot, and all that. Can't be helped. You tumbled me, then?'

'Knew somethin' was up when you kept beatin' me. M'friend Emily suggested camera pigeons, so we put up the tarpaulin.'

'She's a wee bit too clever, your pal,' said Jimmy. 'Cleverer than Tug and me, at any rate. Come on, then, old boy, shall we race?'

'We can't let our public down, old chap. Are you ready, drivers?'

We nodded.

The rules were simple. We started on opposite sides of the road. We were to be given a shove to get us going. If we came off the road, we were allowed to enjoin such spectators as were willing to help get us going again.

I sat in the cart and waited for the starter's signal. The steering seemed simple enough, as did the brakes. I thought of poor Ellis Dawkins, and double-checked that everything was properly connected. The starter raised his flag. We were off.

A heavy cart is a fast cart in gravity racing, and the substantial farm lad in Jimmy's go-cart should have had the advantage. Fortunately, my own diminutive size was offset by the bulk of the chassis that Sir Hector and Bert had built. We were neck and neck as we arrived at the first bend, but that was where Sir Hector's new design really came into its own. My opponent forced me to the outside of the turn, but even so, I managed to keep pace with him. His wheels looked a little shaky, but mine were firmly planted, guiding me exactly where I pointed them.

I gained a little ground on the straight, but it was the next bend that saw his undoing. I was on the inside as we approached, and had confidence enough in my little machine that I decided not to brake. John had begun to slow on the approach, but when he saw that I wasn't bothering, he laid off the brakes, and we both hit the bend at full pelt.

I took it easily, holding my line as the little go-cart shot round the curve. John wasn't so lucky. Despite his brave efforts, he couldn't control the cart, and biffed sideways into the hedge. A barrage of colourful curses was followed by urgent entreaties to the assembled crowd to give him a push. And what a mighty push they gave him.

I could hear him thundering up behind me as we neared the home straight. One last little bend and we'd be home. But he was gaining. The push had really given him an extra burst of speed, and as I glanced over my shoulder, I could see his front wheel drawing level with my back wheel.

As we came to the last bend, he had one last trick to try. He was on the inside again, and as I turned in, he kept going straight ahead. I clipped his wheel, but he carried on. He was trying to push me off the road.

But then I learned why Lord Riddlethorpe needed Mr Waterford. Engineering was everything in motor racing, and it turned out to be rather important in go-cart racing, too. Jimmy Amersham's flimsy front wheel design was no match for Sir Hector's machine, and John's attempt to push me aside was thwarted when the mounting gave way and the wheel bounced off down the road on its own.

I pulled ahead again as John tried to nurse the three-wheeled go-cart on towards the finishing line.

The cheers as I crossed the line were equal to anything I might have heard at Brooklands. And certainly more than I'd have got at Codrington Hall.

I'd won a race at last.

◆ ◆ ◆

I was still in my overalls as I stood on the village green with Lady Hardcastle. We were sipping cider from Old Joe's makeshift stall, while I accepted congratulations from the villagers. No one had told us that there was as much rivalry between Littleton and Woodworthy in the event as there was between Sir Hector and Jimmy. The pride of the village had been resting on my shoulders, it seemed.

'Well done, Armstrong,' said Lady Farley-Stroud heartily. 'Knew you could do it.'

'Thank you, my lady.'

'Means a lot to Sir Hector. Done him proud.'

'I'm glad I could help,' I said. 'Any time you need a racing driver, I'm at your service.'

'Might hold you to that, m'girl,' she said. 'But not till next year. Poor old Bert needs a rest from all the work Hector's been making him do on that blessed go-cart.'

'They both did a marvellous job,' said Lady Hardcastle. 'Perhaps it's time for you to indulge one of your own interests now, though, eh?'

'Already in hand, m'dear,' said Lady Farley-Stroud. 'And you're an essential part of it.'

'I am? How splendid.'

'You are,' said the older lady. 'I've managed to get one of those travelling picture shows to come to the village in a few weeks. We'd like to see some of your work. You can show off your moving pictures to a real promoter. It could be your big break.'

'Gosh,' said Lady Hardcastle. 'I'll have to see if I can get anything finished in time.'

'That's the spirit,' said Lady Farley-Stroud. 'Now come along, you two, I think there's some sort of prize ceremony over by the church.'

Sir Hector beamed with pride as Reverend Bland handed me the tiny trophy that the two old friends competed for every year.

'You earned that, m'dear,' he said as he shook me by the hand. 'Think we might have to retire that little trophy and let you keep it. Couldn't have won it without you.'

'Thank you, Sir Hector,' I said. 'But this doesn't mean the end of the go-kart racing, I hope.'

'The end, m'dear? I should say not. Already workin' on designs for next year. You'll drive for me again?'

'Of course,' I said. 'I've got a taste for it now.'

About the Author

 T E Kinsey grew up in London and read history at Bristol University. He worked for a number of years as a magazine features writer before falling into the glamorous world of the Internet, where he edited content for a very famous entertainment website for quite a few years more. After helping to raise three children, learning to scuba dive and to play the drums and the mandolin (though never, disappointingly, all at the same time), he decided the time was right to get back to writing. *Death Around the Bend* is the third in a series of mysteries starring Lady Hardcastle.

You can follow him on Twitter – @tekinsey – and also find him on Facebook: www.facebook.com/tekinsey.